THE FREY SAGA

BOOKS 1-3

MELISSA WRIGHT

THE FREY SAGA

BOOK I: FREY

THE
FREY SAGA
BOOK
1
FREY
MELISSA WRIGHT

PROLOGUE

I stood in the center of a council chamber I had never seen before. A vast library lined the walls, interspersed with decorated frames and ornate mirrors. A great vaulted ceiling rose overhead, embellished with intricate carvings and painted in exquisite detail. Across the empty space before me was an elaborate table that seated six leaders of High Council, my executioners.

No, not executioners. I was being absurd, surely. *How bad can the punishment be for what I've done?*

Guards stood behind me, within arm's reach on either side. To the left of them were council members, and as I glanced right, in walked the dark stranger who'd come into my life only days before I had managed to destroy it.

Chevelle stood at attention, facing the council table. He did not acknowledge me.

I could hear others enter behind us, presumably witnesses, and I wondered if my tutor—my only possible ally in this ordeal—was among them.

Even she might not be able to save me from this fate. *It's over*, the voice in my head kept telling me. *This is it*. But I was getting ahead of myself.

1

(DAYS EARLIER)

That morning, I was out of the house early. I'd wanted to avoid my aunt, who was determined not to let me forget what a burden it had been to take me in, even if it used every spare ounce of her energy to do it.

The thought annoyed me as I rushed up the path and through the village gate, keeping my head down. No one generally went out of their way to speak to me, but I wasn't one for taking chances. The other elves didn't have much use for one who wasn't able to contribute, and my lack of magic and skill usually put me far from their minds, except for Evelyn of Rothegarr, with whom I'd nearly tussled the day before. She'd gone into a bit of a coughing fit right before it had descended too far into unpleasantness, and I'd been saved from my own dark thoughts about how to deal with her.

When she'd gotten to the village, though, she'd progressed from coughing to choking and, according to my aunt, had blamed the whole thing on me, as if I could work magic.

I slipped around the village and through the tangle of brush behind Junnie's house, darting past a trellis and toward the door. As I ducked under the hanging ivy, my foot caught on a vine and I stumbled forward, cursing as I nearly ran into a boulder—a boulder wearing a shirt.

Gradually, I tilted my head back and blew my too-long bangs aside to peer up first at a strong chin, a stern mouth, and then the darkest sapphire-colored eyes I'd ever seen. A lot of elves had blue eyes, but always bright and shimmery. These were of the deepest blue. *They must appear black in the shadows.*

The thought made me flush.

He turned from me without a word and disappeared in a few long strides. I watched him go. With his short dark hair, dark eyes, and a large, strong build, he certainly wasn't from this clan.

Behind me, Junnie cleared her throat. "Freya?"

I hadn't realized she was watching me from the open door. "Who...?" I trailed off.

"You needn't bother yourself with him." She could see that I would. "Chevelle Vattier. He's from a northern clan. He'll be here only a short while. Council business."

That brought me back to my mission. "Fannie said there was some trouble with Evelyn?"

"Yes." There was something in her tone I didn't recognize. "She's fine now."

"Yesterday, I saw her."

"Yes." She half-smiled. "Don't worry yourself, Freya. Come, now. Let's study."

I hesitated. Evelyn had mentioned me, but not accusingly, and surely, there was more Junnie could have said. But she only placed a gentle hand on my shoulder and led me inside.

Junnie was older than I but remained striking with the blond hair, blue eyes, and thin features that seemed to be standard-issue among the village elves. The Council had assigned her as my tutor, citing my advanced age as the reason I couldn't learn with the others, but I suspected it was my stunning lack of ability that had landed me there.

"So," I said, forcing a smile, "what's on the agenda for today?"

She avoided my gaze, straightening the deep-blue sash that tied her tunic. "How do you feel about studying the lineages?" She knew I hated trying to memorize endless pages of names and dates, and she didn't seem surprised by my groan of complaint. "Well, let's get to it, then," she said, leading me toward the back room through the tiny living area.

She didn't have or need a great deal of space. Much as I was, Junnie was practically alone. Her family had all received the calling to serve elfkind. I didn't know exactly what that meant, only that the elf usually left with fanfare and seldom returned in fewer than a hundred years. It was apparently a very honorable thing, though she never seemed proud.

Just off the living area was the study, which was larger than the front room, stuffed full of documents, and lit by a pair of dim oil lanterns. Dust covered the decrepit scrolls and books lining the walls, but aside from a well-used worktable, the room was clean. Settling onto my usual stool, I leaned forward, elbows on the carved edge of the table to prop my head up for the monotonous hours to come.

I went back over our conversation, trying to find some meaning in the lack of information from my tutor. I recalled the dark-headed stranger and became distracted.

Junnie's books of lineages distracted me too. I would have time to worry about Evelyn later. In the meantime, I had my chance to find out about Chevelle Vattier.

After leafing through a dozen or so volumes, my determination began to falter. There were many lineages, but I needed something on the northern clans, something on Vattier, and Junnie didn't have that. I would need a library, maybe even the council library. I shivered —I definitely wasn't sure about that. Even if I worked up the nerve to sneak in, I didn't have the magic to search documents quickly enough to find what I was after, as the council members did. I would have to stick to the village library.

I explained to Junnie that I wanted to leave early to collect various plants so I could easier identify the species the way she'd always urged me to. I expected at least a speculative gaze, but Junnie was distracted, scratching away at a scroll with quill and ink. I knew better than to go directly to the library. The village was small, and word wouldn't take long to get back to her, so I took a rambling, rarely used path out of the village and found myself wandering idly through the trees. Eventually, I came into an abandoned, overgrown garden, where I did not attempt anything useful like identifying the species but instead tried again to grow with magic.

Evelyn, daughter of a council elder, had caught me trying with a thistle the day before and had quite plainly informed me I was to be punished. But I was tired of being the only one who couldn't do it. Of course, I'd been warned not to practice without supervision, but I didn't see what harm could come if I wasn't able to do anything more than light a lantern. Her disagreement with that assessment was what had started the argument, and though I felt alone in the field, I couldn't help but glance around for her presence.

I concentrated first on one weed then on each of the others, attempting the same tingle that came when I sparked a small flame. I had no luck for hours, but soon, a small thorn tree and a couple of noxious strains began to mature in response to the magic. Not much, but there was enough of a change to prove it was working.

I stared at the plants in awe.

All that time, I'd thought something was broken in me, that something had happened when I'd lost my mother, but maybe Junnie was right. Maybe I just needed to get my focus and to work until the magic came through.

Then I thought of Evelyn accusing me of practicing magic, and my panic rose anew. I stood, kicking dirt over the offending plants.

I ran back toward the village, brushing the evidence of my foray off the legs of my trousers. My heart raced as I straightened my hair and cut through the trees toward the village center. I would go to the library. It was safe there.

But then I remembered why I was going and hesitated. It felt wrong. I had no good reason for researching Chevelle Vattier, except I was curious. *There's nothing wrong with being interested, is there?*

Heat crept into my face for no good reason, and I picked up my pace to the old tree that housed the library. I knew my shoulders were drawn in, and I was glancing around too often, but I couldn't seem to help it. It felt illicit. I felt guilty.

Twice, I imagined a set of dark eyes on me, and a pricking sensation ran over my spine. I was going to have to pull myself together. I was being ridiculous. At that rate, I would have been fawning at him and flipping my hair like Evelyn by sundown.

When I finally walked into the library, I remembered why I didn't go there to study lineages. There must have been a thousand volumes and tenfold more scrolls on the main level alone, and I had no magic to lead me in the right direction.

I sat for hours, exploring the early texts, stories of the river clans and their battles with the Imps of Long Forgotten, firsthand accounts of the Trials of Istanna, and the long lineages of the eldest families. In all those records, there was nothing about a Vattier and nothing on the north.

A whisper roused me from my studies, and I realized it was late, so I decided to give up until the following day. Rising unsteadily, I heard the whisper again, but it was only the wind.

I glanced backward. Papers scattered on the floor. I surveyed the library, but it was practically empty. Someone on a higher level must have caused the pages to fall. I bent over and read the closest document. It was an account from the northern clans—I was stunned. I managed to stash the papers in my shirt then attempted a casual exit, convinced I should read them at home to avoid getting caught.

I'd made it out of the library and almost to the gate when I noticed a dark figure half hidden by a wide tree. It was Chevelle speaking with a councilman. He turned his head, glancing toward me, and I was caught by his eyes.

I was ashamed to admit I was staring. Worse still, I'd stopped walking to look at him. Color rose in my cheeks as I turned away. I couldn't understand what was wrong with me. The pages stuffed in my shirt felt like fire against my skin. It felt the way it did when I tried to lie.

I quickened my pace, stumbled on a root, and glanced back to see if he had noticed. But he was gone. I didn't know whether I was relieved or not.

My mind went over the encounter again as I made my way home. He'd had such a stern expression and such an intense gaze, but I thought I knew why: because I wouldn't stop staring at him.

It seemed that my aunt Francine always knew when I didn't want to be bothered and went out of her way to ensure that I was. I quietly entered the house, hoping to slip off to my room, but there she was, smack in the center of the sitting area, drunk as a two-day jamboree. She had the same dull blond hair and muddy-brown eyes as I did, though mine were specked with green. She stopped me on my way through and forced me to sit and be her audience. I watched her as she rambled. She never mentioned Evelyn again, so neither did I. All I could think of were the papers I'd hidden away.

After a long evening of ducking her verbal jabs and listening to her theories on the Council's secret conspiracies, I finally made it to my room. With a flick of my fingers, light flooded the tiny space. I took a quick inventory: the seal on my wardrobe was intact, my drawings were still scattered across the floor, and the stash of walnuts remained on the table beside my bed. My mother's pendant hung from a woven-leather chain above my pillow, shooting refracted beams across the bed, and I smiled as I sat beneath it.

Scanning the pages I'd brought home from the library, I tried to find some order. I sorted them as best I could onto the worn comforter and sat rigidly while reading, unable to fathom why the document had me so anxious. For days, I'd been on edge.

The first pages contained the usual detailed description of the record-keeper, including his lineages and how he'd come upon the information. He was apparently a scribe for Grand Council and was responsible for copying scrolls and adding new information from their various local libraries for each of the northern clans.

Some of the information was suspect, such as gossip from the neighboring fey guild about strange activities and reports from travelers about deserted villages—or maybe they weren't deserted. One description seemed to imply the village was empty not only of elves, but absent of all evidence that it had ever been inhabited. There were maps of mountains and forests I'd never seen, showing each village and town. Curved lines of azure representing rivers and streams cut through the page, and I had a pang of regret for not studying maps with Junnie.

The next pages were a copy of the record-keeper's report to Grand Council about his findings, including his conclusion. There were missing pages, but something dreadful had happened, for certain. His official report should have been factual and serious, but the description was loaded with fear. Even his script became shaky as it reached the final word, *extinction*. All of the northern clans were gone, according to his account. Something had wiped out an entire region.

I wondered why that wasn't something I'd learned in my studies or been told in stories.

The last pages were lists of clan members, in order of family names. There must have been thousands, but pages were missing there too. F, G, L, N, and V were just gone.

As I reached the end, I took a deep breath. I had gotten so involved in the terrified man's story and page after page of family names that I had forgotten why I was reading in the first place. I sighed. Of course, the pages with the V names were missing.

I felt a small stab of guilt for the selfishness of the thought while looking over such loss and tucked the pages under my mattress.

Lying back on the bed as I looked up at my mother's pendant, I closed my eyes, trying to remember her. I could see her face, her straight nose, her gentle smile. Her long hair waved around her shoulders, stray locks caught by the wind. She wore an embroidered white gown with bell sleeves and a low-cut neck. Her pendant hung there. It started to refract light, but there was only darkness around my vision of her. The wind picked up, and her dark hair began to whip back and away from her face. She was smiling gloriously, her arms outstretched. The pendant started to glow, and the darkness cracked. The wind was howling. I could barely see, or maybe something was covering my face. When I screamed, the sound was lost. I tried again, but suddenly I was blind, mute, and still. And yet I knew everyone was dying, running and screaming and dying.

I jerked upright in bed, gasping, my ears ringing. My face was damp, and as I wiped it away, I was surprised to find it was not tears but blood. My nose was bleeding.

It took another moment to get my bearings. My bed sheets were a tangle, and my clothes were disheveled. It had only been a dream. I had fallen asleep looking at my mother's pendant, trying to remember her, and somehow combined it with the disaster I had read about the northern clans. *Just a dream*, I reminded myself.

Shaken, I sat up, struggling to collect myself. I reached up to remove the pendant from the hook and squeezed it tightly in my fist. It felt good, like a connection, and I slid the leather chain over my head, pulling the pendant down to rest on my chest. It felt right there, and I knew I should have been wearing it all along.

As I let go, I realized I'd gotten blood on my hands, so I headed to the hall and poured water from the pitcher into a ceramic basin. Staring into the mirror was not my favorite pastime—it mostly made my head hurt. But I had to clean the blood from my face and straighten the nest of hair on my head.

When I leaned forward, a flash caught my eye. For a moment, I thought the pendant was reflecting light from somewhere in the dark hallway, but my brain must still have been muddled from sleep. I examined the stone more closely and saw blood smudged there as well, so I rinsed it clean.

I lingered there, clutching it tightly—it was a comfort to hold. It seemed to warm something deep within me. I vowed to keep it on as I shook a thought from the dream away and headed for the door.

It was a gloomy day, and I didn't miss having to squint against the bright sunlight. Early as it was, I decided to take the long way to town, meandering through the fields and thinking of all that had passed in the last days until I reached a patch of weeds that reminded me of Evelyn's taunting. I felt a momentary spasm at the thought of her choking in the pit of my stomach. Then I remembered growing the weeds in the garden, and I was suddenly in a rush to get to Junnie's.

I rapped our special knock, and in a heartbeat, Junnie was opening the door. "Morning, Frey. Early start today?"

I was determined. "Yes. I want to practice growing."

She glanced at the pendant against my chest. She was silent for a moment as she looked into my eyes, almost searching, probably worried I was sad or missing my mother. "Not today. It seems I have business with Council this morning." Her mouth turned down in a grimace.

"Oh." It wasn't like I didn't have plenty to do—I would just head to the library and try to find the missing pages to the northern clan documents. "Well, I'll see you then." I smiled at her and headed around to cut through the village.

I took my time to allow her to make her way to the council building. As my feet scuffed along the path, I heard angry whispers and glanced up to find their source. A Council member was leaning toward a dark figure, wearing a harsh expression and pointing out fingers on his other hand. *Counting reasons for his argument?*

He turned his head as if scanning for an audience. He found one —me. As his eyes hit mine, I had the feeling I was intruding and that I should look away, but something kept me staring.

It was him again: Chevelle Vattier. I swallowed hard and forced myself to continue walking, determined not to trip. As the path wound closer to them, I became excruciatingly aware that it was going to split, heading either to the gate or to the library. I still hadn't decided how to make my escape when Chevelle turned back toward the councilman and spoke something low, cutting the conversation off. The councilman shot me a quick look before storming off.

Chevelle remained standing where he was, his back to me. I had to make a decision. I could walk within feet of him to continue to the library to research him, or I could run home and hide, coward that I was. My stomach tightened. It was ridiculous. I kept walking.

He turned to me, scarcely a few feet away. "Good morning." He nodded as he spoke, his voice as smooth as velvet.

My body seemed to angle itself toward him of its own accord. I mentally cursed, but I could recover—I would just keep going in the same direction, as if I was on my way to the village center, because I *was* on my way to the village center. There was no need for him to know it was to research someone associated with the Council, someone like him.

I tried to respond to his greeting but felt choked and instead only nodded, my jaw clenched. I kept on the path, not daring to look back in case he was behind me. I was convinced he was. He wouldn't have been taking the back way to Junnie's, and he wouldn't have been leaving the village without a pack—he was likely going to a council meeting. He was certainly right behind me, following me into town.

Somehow, I made it to the library without tripping or looking back, though I was nearly overcome with the temptation to turn at the door so I could see him one more time. I didn't know what was happening, only that it was far past time to pull myself together.

The library steps curled around the interior of the tree, shelves cut into every space above and below, and tables, racks, and patrons were scattered about the remaining areas. I found a dark, empty corner on the third level and relaxed onto a seat, leaning against the inside wall of the old tree and taking in the scent of ancient paper and binding materials.

After a momentary pause to blot out my latest incidence of poor self-control, I decided to attempt to locate the missing pages by magic. I had, after all, succeeded in growing only days ago. I concentrated as hard as I could, and though nothing flitted out of the shelves and onto my desk, I had a strong feeling I knew where the documents were, mostly because I knew the approximate area from where they had fallen the day before. I made my way over then took a few volumes and scrolls back to my secluded table. I was able to find several documents on the northern clans and even one of the missing pages of names—L.

I had spread them out on the table and was studiously examining them when a shadow crossed my desk. I realized someone was standing there and distractedly glanced up to see who.

My instinct to breathe deserted me.

It was Chevelle Vattier.

2

Chevelle stood there, staring down at me as I leaned halfway across the table of documents concerning the northern clans to conceal that I was researching him. I tried not to betray myself by glancing at the papers, but the only other place to look was at him.

He didn't look away. I had no way of knowing if he'd seen the documents before I realized he was there, and I stared at him, frozen for what seemed like an eternity. I was unable to decipher his expression or guess how I should explain having the documents. Words abandoned me when I opened my mouth to speak.

He finally broke the silence. "Freya."

He'd used one of Junnie's pet names for me. I couldn't believe how much I liked that.

He reached out his hand. "I am Chevelle Vattier."

I nodded a slow, stuttering nod.

He wasn't smiling. His face was unreadable. "I am an old friend of Junnie. I saw her at Council this morning. She was disappointed that she has been too occupied by clan business of late to guide you. I offered to help her—to help you."

The stranger I had been obsessed with was going to help me with my studies. I melted, sliding down into my chair. He was still holding his hand out to me. My back pressed against the wall, and as he took a step forward, I became wholly aware of how small and isolated the library space I had chosen was.

He turned his outstretched hand palm up, indicating the stool beside me, as if that had been his intention all along. "May I?"

I nodded once, and he slid onto the stool, facing me, not the table spread with documents.

I still had not spoken.

His dark eyes moved to the pendant against my chest then quickly back to my face, as if he had committed an indiscretion.

We sat there for a few more moments, but my words would not return, not with the imposing stranger inches before me.

When he finally spoke again, I realized his offer of help wasn't a request. "Let's begin with histories." He flicked the middle finger of his left hand, and a thick ivory tome flew from a shelf, opened, and floated steadily between us, as if on a table. There was something so wrong about it, but I couldn't say why.

I pushed away the urge to question an associate of Council, instead asking, "Chevelle?"

He smiled. It was only one word, but he understood. I was asking if I could address him in the common parlance, not the official titles and formalities of Council that he might have been used to. He tilted his head in a nod.

We sat tucked in the narrow space behind a small library table for hours. He pulled books between us and returned them to the shelves, never once glancing at the papers referencing the northern clans, spread out beside us. Nothing we studied touched on the histories of those clans—there was nothing of his histories, nothing of mine. But conversation had become easy as soon as I had spoken that first word, as soon as I had said his name and he'd smiled in return.

I found myself leaning toward him as he spoke, actually paying attention at times, for he had a pleasant voice and an unusual dialect. He wove histories as if they were stories of his childhood friends instead of useless facts, and I became enthralled. It felt as if we were alone there in the quiet corner of the third level, the occasional murmur below and whisper of flipping pages the only other sound in the dim setting. A small knothole made a window in the wall across from me, and some light from the cloudy day occasionally came through, putting Chevelle's face in shade. I had been right—his eyes appeared nearly black in the shadows.

I leaned forward, listening to him as a small gray bird landed on the lip of the knothole and chirped once. Not many animals feared the elves. It seemed curious about what we were doing.

It chirped twice, and I winced at the annoying cheeping, working to focus on Chevelle's story.

Then it chirped three more times. I gritted my teeth, but I could not block out the irritating sound. It broke into a melody that pierced my ears, and I barely restrained a growl of frustration as I cursed the devilish thing. That was when I heard the hollow thud of its body smacking the floor.

I jerked upright. My ears were still ringing from the harsh song, but the bird lay dead on the wooden planks below the window. Chevelle started to turn to find the source of the muffled thump, and before I realized what I was doing, I flicked my right hand, and the bird's body flopped behind a shelf and out of sight. When Chevelle turned back to me, I stared right into his eyes, as if I had not seen or heard a thing, wondering why he wasn't still explaining the histories of Grah. He glanced past me... or maybe at the crown of my head, as if he was avoiding my eyes. *My lying eyes.*

I was too worried about being caught to feel guilty about the bird, to think about its soft gray feathers or the wing that was bent awkwardly beneath it. I didn't know about where Chevelle was from, but in the village, one didn't just kill birds, especially not for singing.

After a moment, my tutor continued the lesson, but his demeanor had changed. He watched the book, and occasionally his gaze wandered from my face, back up and out of focus just above me. But he did not look directly into my eyes as he had before. It bothered me, and I didn't think it was because of my conscience.

When he reached the end of the book, it returned to its home on the shelf, and he stood, placing a hand briefly on the top of my head. It was only a momentary touch, but electricity surged though me. A flash of confusion or frustration passed over his features too quickly to identify. He looked into my eyes one last time as I sat stunned and speechless, my skin still tingling from the contact.

"Enough for today," he said, nodding as he turned, his long strides taking him from my view.

I sat motionless as I watched him go and remained so for some time. I hadn't realized how exhausted I'd been.

When I finally rose to leave, I stashed a few more of the northern-clan documents under my shirt. My head was swirling with all that had happened—not simply my new tutor, but the magic. On my way out, I walked past the shelf that hid the body of the dead bird. I'd never been able to move objects, but it seemed that I had done it without thinking. It wasn't just that, but the weeds and thorns in the old garden bothered me too. I needed to see Junnie.

The door was partially open when I reached her house, so I peeked my head in and called for her. When she didn't answer, I slipped in to check the back room.

As I walked through the sparsely decorated living area, I passed a carved mirror on the wall and noticed something off in my reflection. I knew I was flushed—I could feel the frustration and worry—so I stopped to get a closer look. There *was* something not right with my complexion, but what was really off was just above my face. I squinted, leaning toward the mirror as my hands reached up seemingly of their own accord.

The first quarter inch of my hair was blackened. I parted my hair in a different area and then again, but the roots of my hair were dark over my entire scalp. My fingers began to tremble against my skin. I could come up with no plausible explanation for the change. "Junnie," I called again.

She didn't answer. The study was empty. I let out a shaky breath and glanced around. Nothing was out of place except for a thistle on the table. It was thriving but unplanted. I examined it closer. It was rather large, and though the blooms looked healthy, the exposed roots were black, seemingly rotted. I didn't understand how a plant could survive without soil and with such decay. I scanned the table, but it was the only plant there, aside from Junnie's potted ivies and flowers, which hung as they always had.

At my touch, the thistle leaves crumbled, my skin tingling with the unfamiliar feel of my own magic. I watched its ashes fall, landing on scattered seeds and bulbs, and realized in horror what it meant. It was the thistle I had grown. *The garden.*

I rushed out, leaving the door open as I had found it. I hurried from the village, almost running under the cloudy skies, trying to remember where the abandoned garden was located. It wasn't hard to find because of its new size, but if I hadn't been half expecting and half fearing the excessive growth, I might not have recognized it. Each of the strains I had attempted to grow was flourishing. Noxious weeds were taking over the meadow.

I stood there, overwhelmed, frozen before the changed garden. I had to press my eyes closed to *not* see. Light rain began to fall as I raised my head to the sky, drawing in a deep breath. The cool water trickled down my face, calming the heat of my pulse, but it didn't clear my head. I still couldn't understand.

A painful fear shot through me at the thought of the destroyed thistle on Junnie's worktable, and I tilted my head forward to run through the growth. Vines, thorns, and leaves turned to muddy ash as they touched my outstretched arms, wet with rain. When I reached the edge of the garden, I stopped to kneel, digging my fingers deeply into the soil to form a trench. When I saw the bare roots, black and rotted, I was suddenly exhausted. It was too much.

It took me to a familiar, mindless place, and I turned to walk home, void of any sensation save the slow rain on my skin.

When I entered the house, Francine was there, but I trudged past her on the way to my room. I barely took notice of her expression and the suspicion in her eyes as she took in my mud-streaked clothes and dripping hair. I didn't speak—I was spent, and I just couldn't make myself care. In the darkness of my room, I collapsed onto the bed. I didn't bother lighting a flame. I wanted to be alone, and in the dark, I felt more so. I closed my eyes, dropping asleep to the thrum of falling rain.

I AWOKE gasping from another dream of my mother and destruction. The rain had stopped, and the sun was rising, so I wiped the sweat from my brow and went to the hall pitcher to splash my face. The dark roots of my hair were stark in the mirror's reflection, and I recalled the dream. The memories of my mother were fuzzy, but I'd always thought she'd had light hair, beautiful and golden like Junnie's. In the dream, though, it was as black as the roots of my hair had become.

I stood there for a long moment, staring at the darkness, then spun as I made another stupid, rash decision. Slinking past Fannie's room, I headed for her makeshift vault. She kept all the things I wasn't allowed to touch in that room, which was supposed to be off-limits, not that I'd bothered to explore it before. There was a large flat stone, covering where it hid in the floor, which I'd never been able to move. But that was before.

I wasn't sure how the magic had worked with the bird, but I knew it had, so I dropped to my knees, held my hands above the stone, and closed my eyes, concentrating with everything I had. Nothing happened right away, and my mind wandered a bit with thoughts of what might be inside and how I wanted to see and needed to touch my family heirlooms, the things that had belonged to my mother.

The stone lid scraped across the floor as it shifted. It didn't go far, but I didn't need it to move much. I reached down and drew out a small leather pouch, its bronzed decorations weathered and worn. I laid it aside, reaching back in. My fingers closed around a tube, prob-ably a scroll case. I started to take it out when I heard a wheezing growl behind me. I froze.

The stream of profanities that followed was long and harsh, and part of it sounded as though it was in another tongue. I released the tube and turned slowly toward Fannie, who was red-faced and shaking. She stepped toward me, and I slid the pouch that lay against my leg behind my sash. She didn't seem to notice.

The blow was quick, and I hadn't seen it coming. My head turned with the contact, whipping back toward her before I had a chance to rein in my shock and anger. Fannie's eyes lit with anticipation, as if she wanted me to fight back.

I had never even talked back to Fannie. I didn't have the size to fight her, let alone the magic, and she was conniving. When I'd first come to live with her, she had sent me to Council repeatedly, complaining of my behavior. I had undergone hours of evaluations under the scrutiny of council members, exams and trials, endless questions, and black blots on parchment that made abstract shapes. "What do you see, Elfreda?"

I'd known what they'd wanted to hear, something about butterfly and flower species. But I was so resentful to Fannie for putting me there that I usually saw a black blob of death consuming her. "A Monarch," I would say instead.

She looked beyond me at the few inches of open floor, and I took the opportunity to bolt past her and down the hall, straight out the door at full speed. I ran from the house, ignoring the paths—other elves would be no help to me. I kept running until I was certain she wasn't coming, and then I collapsed at the edge of a meadow, breathless. I dropped my face into my hands and might have wept if I hadn't been so fueled by fear and adrenaline.

"Freya?" a soft voice asked.

I looked up, startled.

Chevelle stood just in front of me. He dropped to his knees and reached out to touch the mark across my cheek left from the slap. Shame flooded me, and I turned my head to hide the evidence, but he cradled the side of my face.

"Freya," he repeated in a softer voice as he lifted my chin. He appeared concerned as he glanced from the welt to my eyes, and I struggled to keep the tears that were welling from falling. I'd not had a caring touch from anyone for so long that I didn't know how to react. And I was ashamed. Fannie had authority over me, but I wasn't a child. It was only that I had nowhere else to go. I couldn't leave.

"You'll need to learn protection spells."

"I-I can't..."

"We won't tell Francine or the Council," he promised, and I didn't miss the way he said her name. "We won't even tell Junnie," he added softly.

I didn't understand. Cold moisture from the ground seeped through the material covering my legs, and I shifted, fidgeting as I looked up at him. "I mean I can't do magic. Just useless stuff like lighting candles—"

"Then we'll start with fire." Chevelle lowered his hand to mine and stood, pulling me up and toward the center of the clearing.

Once we'd distanced ourselves from the tree line, he stopped and turned back to me, still holding my right hand. My eyes followed his as he looked down at our clasped hands. A cool blue flame lit on my right sleeve.

Immediately, I jerked my free hand up to extinguish it, but Chevelle took it and stopped me from smacking at the flame, which had already disappeared. "No," he said. "Use the magic. Feel it."

I nodded, and he returned his gaze to our hands. He couldn't have been much older than I, but his hands dwarfed mine, and it made me feel suddenly and fleetingly like a child again.

A spark lit at the hem of my left sleeve and slowly worked its way up my arm. I wanted it off of me, needed to put it out. When I concentrated on that, the flame flickered. It flared again, and Chevelle squeezed my hands. *I have to be able to do this.* I focused hard on the base of the flame as it wavered then fell back toward the hem, where it finally choked off. I glanced up at Chevelle. He looked pleased.

"Again," he said as he stepped back and released my hands.

The meadow seemed to open as a circle of fire grew in front of me. I tried to see past it, through the flames to Chevelle, and then it was gone. He moved farther back, raising his right hand so a stream of fire followed it, arcing in my direction. I was afraid I wouldn't be able to extinguish it before it hit me. My feet were frozen in place. I could only think of one thing: *fight fire with fire.* I flung my arm toward the incoming stream of flames, and a tongue of fire akin to a dragon's shot out and collided with it.

I was shocked. I'd only used my power to light candles and lanterns. I'd had no idea I could produce such a vicious plume of flames. I looked at Chevelle.

"Yes," he said, exalted. He raised his arms above his head to construct a massive circle of blazing heat. When his eyes returned to mine, he smiled. He liked playing with fire. Then he shoved the fireball toward me with frightening speed.

I threw both hands in front of me, palms forward, and forced out the largest mass I could in response. Chevelle flicked his wrist, and the flame dodged up and angled back toward me. I shook my hands frantically, spitting sharp bullets of heat at it, hoping to break it up. But he pulled his hands apart, and the thing split, each side curving toward me. There were suddenly two, and they were closing in fast.

I leapt forward just as they collided where I'd been standing, and I lost my footing while I watched the fireworks behind me. Spinning into a tumble to keep from landing flat on my face, I rolled to my feet, thrilled from the fire play and from the magic. I let out a breathless laugh, and Chevelle joined in, though in all fairness, he might merely have been amused by my fall.

We spent the next several hours there in the meadow, sculpting my craft. The exercises grew increasingly more difficult, but it seemed Chevelle was only toying with me. He must have had experience with fire magic, because the flames he produced behaved like an obedient dog. Mine, on the other hand, were about as compliant as a wet cat.

Exhausted by the day's work, I began to sway a bit. Chevelle led me to the base of an old willow tree, and I slumped against the trunk, sliding down to lie on my back. Chevelle reclined against the tree, his legs coming to rest just above my head in the soft grass.

I gazed through the immense mass of leaves and branches overhead and breathed deeply. I felt the need to explain the welt, and my eyes rose toward him as I lightly touched my cheek. "I was searching for my mother's things…"

He stared straight out into the meadow, not responding, so I returned to watching the canopy of leaves.

"I can't remember her," I said. I hadn't discussed it with anyone before, but once I started talking, I couldn't seem to stop. Without his response, I kept on, explaining my dreams—purposefully leaving out the part I had read about the northern clans—and closed my eyes in an attempt to see them more clearly. I was recalling the details of her dark hair blowing in the wind and the feeling of being trapped when my thoughts faded into the blackness of sleep.

I AWOKE in my own bed, the room dimly lit by a single flame suspended above my table. A flash of embarrassment hit as it dawned on me that Chevelle must have placed me there—he must have seen where I lived, my room. And then I smiled because he had left me a flame.

I stretched my entire body, rejuvenated from the rest. I was unsure how long I'd slept, but it looked like the sun was rising again, and I wanted to be out of the house before I ran into Fannie.

It was probably too early to hope to see Chevelle. I'd spent the last two days with him, but he hadn't revealed anything of himself, and that only made me more curious. I retrieved the documents I'd hidden after my day with him at the library to find out whether they added anything to the report from the council scribe. There wasn't much new there, mostly more names, but I did notice a watermark on one of the pages. I held it up to the light to see better. There was a council marking and something else.

I dug out the first pages from under my mattress and examined them. The pages directly from the record-keeper's report all included the same council mark plus a string of characters. I tried to decode them and realized that one of the symbols was likely a page number, and the others were probably locators. I felt like a fool. They were just like the codes used in the library, only more elaborate. No one really used the ciphers—they weren't needed with magic, but they had been added to many of the pages when the fey had started tracking clan histories.

I was holding in my hand the information I needed to find the northern clans in the council's library. My stomach tightened, but I found myself getting up and heading toward the village, regardless of the consequences.

I argued with the impulsive part of myself the entire way to town. *I shouldn't do it. I couldn't. But I am. I am going to do it. And if I get caught, I can claim ignorance. The entire clan thinks I'm an imbecile, in any case. Maybe I'll just see how close I can get. Maybe I'll just try...*

And then I was there, standing in front of the council building then walking in. My attempt at stealth was poorly executed, but no one ever seemed to pay much attention to me, anyway. I casually leaned around a doorway to see into the next room, where a small group of villagers stood, blocking my way. They spoke in low voices, and as I tried to figure a way past, something seized my attention.

"Evelyn has been a model citizen... doesn't seem right..."

My nerves twitched as the worry caused by her supposed accusation returned. I remembered the risk I'd put myself in to go there. I strained to listen but could only pick out parts of the conversation.

"Well on her way to becoming a council member... if anyone should leave..."

"Yes, but who can trust him..."

"Why can't we simply banish... who knows if the spells will even hold... dark magic can't be trusted..."

I struggled to hear them, irritated that they were talking so quietly, and the harder I listened, the more I perceived a dull, buzzing hum. My ears popped. And then, at once, the group began to scratch at themselves feverishly, clawing at forearms, abdomens, and necks. Each wore an uncomfortable, even frightened expression as they hurried out of the room and into an inner council chamber.

It was more than a little strange, and I glanced after them as I made my way through the newly vacant room, but I was distracted by the sight of the library door.

I had no way of knowing if there was a protection spell on the entry. When I walked through, there were no obvious repercussions, and I assumed that, with so many council members around, they must have thought it unnecessary.

The council library was overwhelming. It housed copies of all the books in the village library as well as hundreds more that were too delicate or important for public use. And according to my aunt Francine's theories, they held secret documents containing things they didn't want commonly known there as well.

The walls were stark white like carved marble, and the room felt cold and empty despite the abundance inside. I found a shelf to hide behind and placed my pilfered documents on the floor. I examined the shelves in front of me, looking for a match to the symbols, and found the sections to be arranged by groups, with each shelf divided into categories. I walked the library in search of the section for either of the characters listed in my documents and was about to give up when I noticed some encased racks in the center of the room. I checked the small section. The symbols fit.

I smiled, thinking it had been easy as I slid my fingertips across the volumes on that shelf. My fingers tingled as they crossed a thin section of pages bound together. I slid them out just as I became aware of some sort of commotion that sounded like it was getting closer.

The tingle hadn't indicated that I'd found what I was looking for. It was a protection spell. I ran.

As I shot through the rooms, all I could think of was not getting caught. I shoved the pages under my shirt before I made it through the last door. The village was crowded with elves oblivious to my horror. The protection spell must have alerted only Council. I ran from town and pushed through the brush at the edge of the village, taking the shortest direction out of the boundaries. I kept running until I became winded then hastily searched for some kind of shelter. Burrowing deep in a briar patch, struggling to catch my breath, I wrenched the wad of papers from under my shirt, buried them in the soil beside me, then waited for my punishment to come.

But no one was coming. I was naïve to think they would chase me like hounds on a fox. They had magic—they were High Council.

I stayed in the patch of briars for most of the day, cowering despite myself, but as the sun lowered in the sky, I crawled out on my belly to start the long walk home.

It was late by the time I reached the tree, and I was tired enough that I didn't care as much about being caught. I didn't even know if they knew who broke the seal, if they knew I was the guilty party. But I was still quiet as I entered the house then my room and slid into bed.

THE NEXT MORNING, I slipped out early to call on Junnie. When I reached her door, it was cracked open again. I pushed it aside and scanned the front room, to no avail. I walked through to check the back, but still found nothing. Junnie was exceedingly clean and organized, so I couldn't tell if she'd even been home. I wandered to the front door and was surprised by a tall figure there. The elaborate robe and tassels of a decorated council member blocked my way, and the fear returned.

"Elfreda."

I cautiously dipped my head in respect.

"Juniper Fountain has received the calling."

I stared at him in disbelief. "What?" But then I shook off the question, because I had heard clearly enough. The more important question was, "When?"

He grimaced at my disrespectful manner. "Not long."

Not long? Not long ago? Not long from now? I felt sick. I knew I was testing his patience, but I had to keep pushing. "Where?"

His mouth tightened. "That is council business, Elfreda. That is Juniper Fountain's path, not your own." He stepped aside and rolled his hand to encourage me out. "Make your way."

I pushed past him feverishly, starting for town. But I quickly recalled the incident at the library and turned, heading home. I remembered my run-in with Fannie over the vault and realized I had nowhere to go. A pain throbbed deep in my chest. My instinct pushed me, and I ran for the clearing where I'd learned magic with Chevelle.

He was there, waiting for me. The pain in my chest dulled a little, or maybe it was overwhelmed by a new pressure. I crossed to him slowly. Junnie was all I'd had since I'd arrived, and she was gone. For a hundred years, she would be gone. I wanted nothing more of Fannie, nothing more of any of it. I didn't know what I would do, but by the time I reached Chevelle, I knew that I wanted to retrieve my mother's things from the vault and leave that wretched place behind.

I made my stance more formal to match his. "I want to learn transfer magic."

His mouth tightened, and he turned his head in a half shake.

"You taught me fire," I argued.

"For protection, Freya."

"Please," I begged.

He hesitated.

I didn't know how to convince him. *Is it too soon for me to learn? There's an order to the spells, and you must earn the knowledge. If you go too fast or out of sequence, you could endanger yourself.*

"There is no hurry," he said, clearly trying to persuade me.

"There is," I insisted. "I am running." I didn't know why I chose that word. I wasn't bound to the place. "Leaving" would have sufficed, but it felt like running, like escape. I knew I was trapped. Someone would stop me. *Yes, I'm running.*

My head swung to locate a noise at the edge of the clearing behind me and I saw long robes... two council members. My throat went dry, and Chevelle grabbed my shoulders as he said in a low voice, "Home, Freya. Run."

I didn't hesitate. I sprinted straight home without looking back.

The house seemed empty, but I didn't check. With my heart pounding, I went directly to my room and closed the door behind me. The single flame still flickered above my bedside table, and as I walked closer, I noticed a package on my bed. I spun my hand and lit the room to better see. It was a wide ivory box tied with tweed. There was a small note under the knot.

Dearest Elfreda,

I must away without saying goodbye. I am sure you cannot understand, but please trust in me. Don this immediately. —J.

I tugged at the tie, and the string fell away. I sucked in air as I opened the lid. It seemed that I couldn't quite catch my breath anymore. Reaching inside to draw out the long white gown, I could not fathom Junnie's reasoning—she must have gone through much to get me the package. Numbly, I stared at her words while I unfastened my shirt and sash. The pouch I had rescued from the vault fell to the bed. *How had I forgotten that?* I kicked off my shoes and pulled my top and pants off before sliding the gown over my head, straightening the length with my hands. The corset laced tightly at my waist, and the plunging neckline was lower than anything I would ever wear.

I retrieved the leather pouch from the bed to examine the contents, but before I loosened the binding, I heard a crash behind me. Three council guards had busted open my door. I tucked the pouch under the long bell sleeve of the dress as they crossed the room to seize me by the arms.

4

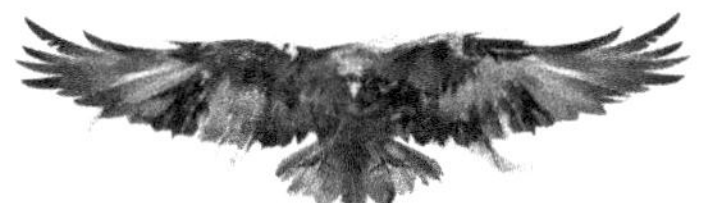

In the center of the Council chamber, I waited for my trail, listening as they called my full name. I had always hated it—to be named for the ancient word for "elf" was bad enough, but the flowery string of words that followed just made me cringe. I had never known my father, but given that they were traditionally responsible for choosing the names of their firstborn, I blamed him for it.

"Elfreda Georgiana Suzetta Glaforia stands before High Council..." The formal tone of the speaker severed my rambling thoughts, dragging me back to a frightening reality. *What will they do to me? How bad could the punishment be for sneaking into a library and stealing a book?* Maybe it wasn't even about that. Maybe Fannie had told them I broke into the vault. But they were my family's things too, so it couldn't be that bad.

She could lie.

I swallowed hard. Maybe it was about something else entirely. Maybe a dead bird.

A guard approached me. I had been drifting again, lost in thought. *What had they said?* The council leaders were focused on the pendant at my chest, where it lay exposed against my skin in the V of the low-cut gown. They had ordered the guard to remove it. I didn't understand why they would want my mother's pendant, but I knew better than to ask. I knew what would happen if I spoke before being instructed.

The guard stood facing me, both hands poised to take the leather chain over my head as I stared on insensibly. His touch lingered, and I glanced down, surprised to see that he had a firm grip on the necklace but wasn't lifting it—*couldn't* lift it. I looked to the council leaders as the guard turned toward the table and decisively stepped away from me.

"The crystal will not be removed," he said. Though he spoke only to the elders, it set into motion a wave of murmurs that filled the room, reverberating up the high ceiling.

A council elder silenced the witnesses then trained his gaze on me. "Who instructed you in fusion?"

I didn't have an answer. I'd never heard of fusion. I wasn't sure what to do, and I looked out of desperation toward the only person in the room who'd ever helped me. Chevelle was watching me, surprise clear on his face. Whatever I'd been accused of, he hadn't expected it.

The council elders mistook the exchange as an answer. "Chevelle Vattier, you have led this fusion?"

His head whipped back toward the council table, and he shot out a forceful "no."

They focused once more on me. "I ask again, Elfreda. Who taught you the magic to seal yourself to the crystal?"

I was at a loss. I stood helplessly as Chevelle spoke up. "Elfreda." He'd used my given name, I hoped simply because we were in a formal setting and not because of whatever horrible thing I had been accused of. "Where did you learn how to fuse the pendant with your blood?" he pleaded.

Fuse the pendant with my blood? What is he talking about? I heard someone behind me: "How did she know to keep it from being removed?" And someone else: "Who even left it with her?"

It came together then, the feeling I'd had when I'd awakened and placed it around my neck, the part of the dream I'd shaken off as I stood before the basin washing up, cleaning the blood from my hands and from the pendant. I wanted to explain, to tell them what I'd seen in the dream, but it was foggy and half-remembered. I was too slow to pull it into thought.

I was too late. They had already passed judgment—harsh judgment—on me. The deep voice boomed with finality: "… convicted of practicing dark magic…"

The elder's staff slammed against its wooden base, echoing into the tumult of discord rising behind me. I reached out my hand to plead for mercy, to beg to be given a chance to explain, and he began to list my lineage for the records. I was flooded with fury at the injustice as I heard my mother's name. My outstretched hand became a fist.

The speaker's voice cut off. He grabbed his throat as the other council leaders rushed to him. His choking face stared directly at me, unquestionably an accusation, and I realized with a start that he was right. I was cutting off his windpipe as if it were there in my outstretched fist. I released my grip.

He was surrounded, and the room was filled with a roar of commotion and terror. My ears rang sharply. I had to look away from it all. When I turned, I caught my reflection in one of the larger mirrors, but it wasn't me. *No, it must be me, but I'm unrecognizable.*

Not unrecognizable, another voice inside me whispered. My hair was dark and windblown. The bell sleeve of the long white gown hung from my outstretched arm. It was the dream in the flesh. The pendant against my chest seemed to glow at my revelation.

I ran.

As I RACED from the chamber, I couldn't tell if anyone had even noticed. They all appeared to be staring at the speaker, but regardless, I concentrated furiously on not being followed. *Do not catch me. Do not find me. Let me go,* I was almost chanting in my thoughts. As I raced out the building and out of the village, running as fast as I could, I kept thinking it over and over and over. I didn't know where I would go. I just wanted away.

I found myself heading in the same direction I had the day before, but hiding in a briar patch wasn't going to work again—they would come for me. As I frantically tried to decide where to go, my previous conclusion snaked through my mind. They would find me if they wanted to. There was no stopping them. I had no magic, no tracking skills, and no clue.

I stopped running. My heart pounded, and the wind cut against the damp sweat on my skin. I wanted to understand what had just happened, but I couldn't process it. It was too painful. I was confused, drained to the point of exhaustion. I had no way out. When they found me, I would have to surrender. I could see no other option.

But no one came.

I wasn't foolish enough to go back voluntarily, but for some reason, they hadn't followed. I didn't know what to do with myself. I had nothing outside of home, outside of the village. I didn't know where I was or where to go. It was just another clearing outside of the only town I'd ever known, or at least the only town I remembered knowing.

I wandered toward the briar patch, finding it easily. It wasn't far, and despite my exhaustion, I crawled through the narrow path I'd made the previous time. It hadn't seemed such a tight fit in only pants. I settled in, jerking a length of skirt free from the thorns with a spray of colorless beads.

Brushing the loose dirt off the papers I had buried, I lay the soiled documents across my lap and untied the laces binding them together. I stared at the words on the ancient parchment, unable to believe that what I was reading was true. It had to be—it was signed with the official seal. The documents stared back at me from the smudged white fabric of my skirt, the letters on the page as real and words as patent as they could be.

They held the details of the trial and the punishment of Francine Katteryn Glaforia, who had been found guilty of practicing dark magic.

Her sentence included some sort of service to Council and a spell binding her from using any magic except practical magic. I was dumbfounded. It had never crossed my mind before, but as I considered it, searching for proof the documents were wrong, I realized my aunt had never used magic for anything but service. It hadn't seemed unusual to me because it was just the way it had always been. And besides, I could barely do anything aside from lighting candles.

Was this why Council was so quick to accuse me of practicing dark magic? It was rarely discussed and never tolerated. *What had Fannie done?*

I flipped through more pages, realizing something was out of place. It didn't make sense that official documents about Fannie would be among those relating to the apparent extinction of the northern clans, and I couldn't figure out why all the documents I'd found about the tragedy were separated, mixed up, and missing pages. I tried to sort it out but found there were other council documents there too.

I kept reading, quickly scanning for something of interest. My eyes caught on his name a second before my mind recognized it: Chevelle Vattier. As I backed up to read, my shock turned to fury before I could even finish the page.

Chevelle Vattier had been a volunteer watcher, a Council spy. He had volunteered to watch *me*.

Swift, white-hot anger flooded through me, and the pages I held burst into flames. The brush around me caught next, burning away as I stood to push free of the blazing patch of briars. *They had set a watcher on me. Why? Because Fannie had practiced dark magic? Were they afraid she'd teach me? I'll show them dark magic. I'll learn and go back... But how? How can I learn without a teacher?*

Chevelle.

The fire died as I thought of the concern he'd shown me in the clearing and the tender moment we'd shared. With one word, the flames caught again, burning with a vengeance through the field.

None of it had been real. He was a watcher. He'd volunteered to monitor me and to keep me in line.

So I decided to teach myself, to take the risk and learn the magic without guidance. I had nothing else to lose. I formed a plan: I would practice until I was strong enough to return to the village. There was nothing holding me back, nothing to do but that one thing.

I spotted a small toad as it leapt across the clearing in a desperate attempt to escape the inferno. I concentrated on it, willing it to change. Its wide body started to swell, its sides bubbling out and puffing it into a tiny green balloon. It did not transform into that monarch butterfly I had imagined. It burst, spewing entrails across the hem of my dress.

My head fell into my hands as I groaned.

It took a while, but the anger eventually faded to a point where I realized I would need a new plan. I couldn't help but regret that the flames had consumed the documents that had caused everything in the first place. I should have fully read them first.

My heart tripped at the sound of cracking timber beneath boots across the clearing. The fire had burned out, but the ashes were plenty evidence that I'd been there. I ducked under the cover of a large spruce and watched. Chevelle walked through the tree line, and my jaw clenched tightly against a silent curse.

He was alone, carrying nothing but a small pack and wearing the same dark clothes and tall boots he'd had on during the trial. He kept walking as he looked in my direction, surveying the damage from the fire. I was convinced he would know it had been me, but he didn't stop or even slow. It made no sense why he hadn't investigated further. *Is he not here looking for me?*

He was my watcher, and I was missing. *So where else would he be going?*

Before I had torched the documents, I had seen Junnie noted as his contact. My pulse sped at the idea that he might be going to her, to get her help in finding me. If he was my watcher, I was his responsibility, and she was the only one who knew me at all, aside from Fannie.

He had gone a good fifty yards farther as I considered.

My feet were moving before I actually decided to follow him. My determination faltered. *How far should I go? What if he isn't even going to find Junnie?* And then I thought, *What else do you have to do, sit here and blow up frogs?* It was all the convincing I needed. Slinking out from the branches of the spruce, I crept along the trees and brush as I followed my watcher north.

5

Chevelle kept a quick pace, and I found myself struggling to keep up. Unlike me, he wasn't dodging between rocks and trees, bending out of sight, and watching the ground to keep from breaking twigs while he tried to keep from being spotted. I cursed the formal dress I'd been dragging as it snagged on a low-lying thicket, flinging another string of beads into the soft dirt. I considered dumping it, but didn't think it was the best idea to be sneaking around the forest unclothed. After crossing a few soggy patches of moss, the hem was damp and darkened. I might have ripped some of the excess material off, but Chevelle's quick movement wasn't leaving me time for that.

Finally, just before nightfall, he approached a small village, which didn't look like more than half a dozen structures scattered against the base of a large hill. He dropped his simple pack beside a tree and hunched down as he slowed his pace. The stance mirrored mine and gave me pause. He was sneaking into the village.

I watched as he crept around the back of a small hut, knowing that if he was hiding, I definitely didn't want to get caught. He leapt into a rear window, and I followed as slowly and low to the ground as I could. When I reached the last tree I could use for cover, I darted up against the hut and peered through a gap in the twigs that patched it together. There was whispering.

"... mustn't let them find you... shouldn't have come..."

It was dim inside, but I caught a glimpse of a figure through the wall. *Junnie.*

Chevelle was whispering his reply to her, and though I couldn't quite hear, he must have given her a short account of the morning's events. I moved closer to the window, finding a larger gap there.

"Were you able to track her?" Junnie asked in a low voice.

"Not exactly. She's following me."

Heat flooded my face. I couldn't believe he'd fooled me again. I'd been trekking over rocks and through bramble half the day, he'd known all along, and Junnie knew everything.

I didn't care what else they had to say. I stood and marched away, fuming at the idea that both of them were in on it. They might have been council members, but it didn't stop the feeling of betrayal. They'd lied to me, acting as if they'd cared. I was done with them and with everyone. I wanted to get as far as possible from all of it.

But I didn't make it very far. Exhaustion caught up with me a few miles later, and I found an old oak tree then slid down its massive trunk to rest my aching legs. I'd never run so far in my life, and my head throbbed. I was seething with anger and frustration and the feeling of being ensnared. I didn't sleep. I just sat against the tree like a petulant child. I held a hand up and flipped a flame, tossing it up and down, rolling it above my palm. I was hungry, but I didn't eat. I was too stubborn and angry to go find food, too resentful I didn't have the magic to bring it to me. Yes, I was acting like a foolish, sulky child.

BRIGHT SUN and chirping birds tore into my still senses. I opened my eyes then squinted, resisting the urge to stop the birds. It was the first time I'd slept away from my bed, and disoriented, I glanced around. It didn't help. I'd never been far from home, and the new landscape was unsettling. When I looked away, I noticed a neatly stacked pile of fabric and a loaf of bread positioned beside me. I silently cursed the watchers who had apparently found me during the night.

I didn't see them anywhere, so I assumed they'd left me out there as punishment. Some part of me wanted to burn the pile for spite, but my stomach overruled the thought. Reaching out to grab the bread and then, since I had already defied my would-be belligerence, the stack of clothes, I stood to find a creek to clean up in, happy that I could finally get out of the ridiculous dress.

It took a moment to locate the trickle of water, but there was a creek only a short distance away. I walked down the softened earth to where the water had pooled then knelt, leaning over to splash my face.

Panic shot through me as someone stared back at me. I nearly bolted upright, planning to flee, but caught myself. The woman in the reflection was me. That was my dark hair and flushed skin. Cautiously leaning over the pool once more, I convinced myself it was only the dark water, a trick of light and shadow. My eyes were not that green, my hair not that dark. I straightened and held a lock of it forward to examine. It shimmered glossy black in the bright sunlight. My hand fell away.

Maybe I could just wash it out. Nauseous, I stepped into the pool, sinking beneath its surface. A thought that was darker than the rest said that maybe I should stay under, but the pressure to draw air stung my lungs. I could not drown the desire to breathe.

I pushed through the water, gasping and cold, struggling to climb from the muck as I stood and walked out. I was drenched, the material of the long gown soaked and heavy and more uncomfortable than ever. I loosened the wet corset ties and dropped the dress into a pile at my feet, shivering as I stepped free of it and onto a rock. I grabbed a shirt from the pile then the slim pants, aware of how nice the fabric felt and how good the cut was. A leather vest laced over the top. It seemed they were tailored for me. I'd never had such luck making my own clothes, but the new outfit was trim, made for traveling, not that I knew where I was going.

My desire to trail Chevelle had been smashed, but there was no way I could return to the village. I glanced around, still finding no sign of the watchers as I slid my shoes on. I should have kept running during the night, but I'd been too exhausted.

There was a pack in the pile as well, but I didn't have anything aside from a soaking wet dress. I stretched it over a low branch to dry, and the pouch I had hidden before the trial fell free.

I sat on the rock, picking up the small, weathered bag. I'd carried it for days now and still didn't know what was inside. I pulled the binding loose to dump the contents into my hand: a dark ruby, a silver medallion, and a tiny scroll. I held the stone up to the light. Aside from the depth of color, it didn't seem extraordinary. I also examined the medallion but didn't recognize the emblems. I dropped them back into the pouch then opened the scroll, reading aloud the first line of the tiny script: *"Fellon Strago Dreg."*

Electricity shot through my hands and I dropped the scroll. My palms felt as if they had been scorched. The unmistakable stench of charred flesh turned my stomach, and I twisted my hands to inspect the damage. There were curving lines and symbols burned into the skin of my palms. I gasped. I'd been around fire magic for as long as I could remember, and it had never burnt me or any other elf, as far as I knew—it would only burn what it was meant to burn.

I glanced back down at the scroll, realizing the fire magic *had* been meant to burn. I should never have read the words aloud. I carefully picked it up and rolled it back into place, certain I would never read from it again. Binding the pouch as I had found it, I tucked it into the pack. When I checked my hands to decipher the lines, I realized I was seeing a map like the ones I'd found in the council documents burned into my palms. I couldn't fathom why anyone would have cast a ridiculous spell like that, but it struck me that it had come from the vault, from my own family's things.

I bit down hard on my lip, fighting the impulsive urge that always got me into trouble. But I didn't want to go back to the village, not ever. And I only had one chance, one small moment before they came to retrieve me.

I grabbed the dress, the last evidence of me being there, off the tree branch and threw it into the pack. Swinging it around onto my back, I started to run. I didn't know where I was or where the map would take me, but I finally had a purpose. There were mountains burned into my palms, and there was only one place to find mountains: in the north.

I COULDN'T REMEMBER MUCH of my life before going to live with my aunt Fannie. The village and surrounding meadows and forests were the only home I'd had, the only place I'd known. It wasn't exactly a comforting place, but there was something to be said for knowing where you were and where to find food, shelter, and water.

I'd been filled with determination when I started running, concentrating on north and nothing else. But as I made my way, I became aware of the sheltered life I'd been living.

The land started to roll, the trees a deeper green than what I was used to, their trunks too narrow. It didn't seem as if I'd gone that far, as it had only been half a day following Chevelle and then the time on my own. The changes in the landscape made me anxious to see the North.

I glanced at my palm once more. I thought I'd figured out most of the lines—creeks curving through the landscape, mountains a jagged ridge across the top—but there were still a lot of unanswered questions. I squeezed my hand into a nervous fist but kept moving.

I tried not to think about all that had happened—not Fannie or the trial, not Junnie, and especially not Chevelle. I just kept putting one foot in front of the other. I couldn't even imagine what lay in the mountains where I was heading, but there was no going back.

I wasn't tired anymore, at least not as I had been every day since I'd been using magic. I forced those thoughts away, counting steps as I ran. I was miles from a home I might never return to.

I pushed myself forward through the day, only stopping when I found a patch of sweet berries and a small, babbling creek. The berries were wild, small, and much less palatable without the guiding hand of an elf, but the water I gathered from the stream was cool and refreshing. As evening approached, so grew my underlying discomfort with the idea of the coming darkness. I'd spent my share of time alone at home, just not alone in the middle of a strange forest outside. I might have run through the night and slept during the day, but it made little sense to struggle out of fear.

It didn't stop me from seeking out a decent shelter before nightfall, though. Slowing my pace, I gave my surroundings more attention.

The strangeness of the sparse brush was a little shocking, and I had to surrender the idea of finding a proper tree. But a half mile or so later, I came upon a suitable hollow in a low embankment guarded by the curling roots of a sycamore. It wasn't bad, but I still gathered some shrubbery to cover the entryway, the bitter stench of its sharp green leaves giving me a little more security, or at least the feeling of it. The sun hadn't set when I'd finished lining the floor with vines, but I went ahead and settled in, sitting so I could see through an opening in the frond-covered entry.

It was quiet, harder to fight the thoughts that were trying to creep in. I began to run songs through my head for distraction, mangling the lyrics and humming through the parts I couldn't remember at all. My fingers tapped soundlessly into the dirt until a flicker of movement just outside stopped me. I held my breath for what I was sure was impending, painful death and saw it again.

I released the breath, which was not, in fact, my last. A soft white rabbit loped in front of the bushes I'd made into a doorway. My stomach was interested, but I'd never prepared meat. I'd only ever gathered berries and vegetables that someone else had grown. I didn't have the first idea how to make a bow, let alone shoot one, and I'd never killed anything except plants and a bird. I had no idea if an animal killed by magic was edible. I thought of the thistle, its black roots, and how it had turned to ash. The rabbit sniffed the air in my direction and continued on its way, answering the matter for me.

I was sitting in a hole, utterly alone, and it was beginning to get dark. Night bugs chittered, their high-pitched keens rising with the loss of light. I lit a thin flame to practice fire magic, leaning forward as I danced it back and forth above the ground. My control had progressed a good deal since my training had begun, and it seemed almost easy to navigate the small flame. I smoothed it out into a line and traced arcs then more intricate designs. The designs started to resemble portraits, and I had to concentrate hard to keep from seeing the faces of council members and the people I'd left behind, so I focused on landscapes, but those grew from tiny village houses and trees to rolling hills and curving creeks. Before long, the hills rose to mountains that melted into unidentifiable monsters. I snuffed the flame with a wave, and the den was black with night.

Eventually, the clouds broke, and the soft glow of moonlight filtered through the opening. I leaned onto an elbow to examine the glistening patches of light on the skin of my outstretched hand, twisting it from day to night, pale to dark. Weary and as if I was in a trance, I lowered my head, tucked my arm back as a pillow, and fell into a deep sleep.

6

———

The early morning sun streaked through every break in the makeshift door, lighting the entirety of the hollow. I considered covering my head with that damp dress and sleeping for the rest of the day, but my stomach ached for food, and Chevelle might not be far behind. I crawled out, rubbing my eyes and squinting, and was able to locate a few roots and greens that would have to be enough to tide me over until I could figure out a way to hunt.

After knocking the brush away from my shelter, I slung the pack over my shoulder and trudged north once more. There was an abundance of streams running through the hills and a few patches of fat, amethyst berries along the way, so I couldn't complain. The route was undemanding. The ground was smooth with nothing too overgrown to make passage difficult, and there were none of those nasty snarls that could form from a maze of thorn trees or the network of vines that could tangle around legs and cause falls. The grass was tall but soft, so it rolled over, hiding no more than the occasional field mouse or vole. Sporadic wildflowers dotted the hills in small sprays of pinks or spiky yellowbird. The sky was cloudless and blue, the sun a constant companion as I carried on through the days and hills.

Each new day was something unexpected, and the trip became

less daunting than it might have otherwise been. I was moving every moment of light, so exhaustion pulled me into sleep for every moment of darkness. I concentrated on each step, breathing in the new scents, counting trees, and doing anything I could to keep myself on task and the past out of my mind.

I was counting fallen catclaw seeds when I crested another hill and spotted a bridge in the valley. I hesitated before slowly making my way down. *A bridge might mean a village was nearby, and a village meant elves.* I didn't want to get caught, not after everything, so I was fully prepared to run by the time I reached the crossing. Its stacked gray stones were bulkier than those that had been appearing more frequently on my path. Water flowed beneath, smoothing the stones at the base. They were so worn that they must have been in place for centuries.

The leather soles of my shoes skimmed over ancient stone, the bridge curving gently before flattening out into a worn dirt path on the other side. It was more traveled than I would have liked, so I swung wide and moved through the trees instead. The wind shifted, and the scent of roasting meat assaulted me, dragging my attention and my feet its way. Despite my concerns about other elves, my stomach tightened, my mouth watering as I followed the smell through the trees.

They broke into a small clearing, and there in the center stood a cloaked figure, kneeling as he turned a meat-covered spit. Pressed tightly behind an oak tree, I shuffled sideways to get a better view. I was sure from his size he was a male elf. The smell of real food consumed me, and I was watching the cooked meat roll over the flame as I moved again. A dry leaf crushed beneath my foot.

"Come, then. There's plenty for both of us," he called.

I cursed then walked cautiously out of the trees. He turned, tossing the cloak aside as he propped one leg on a rock as if posing. He scrutinized me, and I resisted the urge to straighten my hair and brush the dirt from my clothes.

"Don't be shy." The stranger beckoned, gesturing to an upturned log beside the fire. The meat sizzled and popped as I crossed to him and sat obediently. *It's too late to hide, so I might as well at least have something decent to eat.*

The smell was unfamiliar, but I didn't care. It smelled like food. He reached down, tore a hunk from the spit, and tossed it to me with a wink. When I blushed, he smiled a wicked smile. My mouth went dry. He was tall and broad with dark hair and eyes, like Chevelle. Handsome too, I supposed, though I could tell even from a few gestures that he was a bit cocky. He reminded me of Evelyn, always so proud of herself for finding me out.

The stranger watched me as I ate. After I devoured the first piece, he laughed and threw me another. I hoped I looked appropriately abashed. As I finished the second serving, he stepped closer to sit on the misshapen rock that rose through the earth beside me. He held his hand wide, and a canteen flew up from a pile of things on the other side of the fire. He passed it to me, and I tilted it back, expecting cool water. I almost choked when warm wine hit my throat. He leaned forward to get a better look at me as I lowered the container.

He looked as if he thought I might spook—otherwise, I guessed he had plenty to say hidden beneath that smirk. It didn't stop him from moving uncomfortably close, though, or eyeing me with what I was certain was the same look I'd just given my meal. I cleared my throat, thinking I'd made my sense of discomfort clear when he started to move, but he only stood, which brought him even closer. Well, parts of him.

I turned toward the fire, tugging the pack tightly against my shoulder as I prepared for a graceful exit, for departure from food and warmth.

I jumped a little when a tree uprooted across the clearing. It was only a sapling, but a second and third tree followed.

"You look like you'll need shelter, sunshine," he explained.

I stared in disbelief as the trees split to form a low lean-to. He shot me another wink, but I couldn't be sure he was kidding. The tearing and popping noises ceased, and I examined his creation, which was quite impressive, really. He didn't even seem to be watching, let alone concentrating, and he put no blessings on it, nor did he pause to show his gratitude. It seemed he was just enjoying himself, not being responsible to the magic.

It was magic that I needed and wanted. He was good enough—there was no question of that. *He would definitely be able to teach me.* I started to ask but fell short. I had no idea who he was, and I probably shouldn't let on who *I* was.

He noticed my expression and sat again, eyeing me questioningly, all humor gone.

"You seem to be very good at magic," I offered.

He chuckled. "Is that so?"

"Yes, and... Well, I need to learn."

"Learn?" The humor was gone again. "What do you mean learn?"

"I've never, well, except for fire, and I need someone to teach me... and you're..." I waved a hand in his direction to indicate his skill.

His brow rose. "I don't understand," he said, clearly concerned about my mental state. Maybe I was a few nuts short of a bushel.

"I've lost my mentor. Can you teach me magic? Help me, so I don't do something out of order, hurt myself?"

He knitted his brow, and as he began his reply, a fallen branch cracked at the edge of the clearing. His head snapped toward it. I sucked in a harsh breath as Chevelle strode our way. The elf who had been sitting with me moved into a fiercely protective stance in front of me. I leaned around him to see, placing my hand on his leg as I angled my head past it. That broke his stare, and he glanced down at me.

Chevelle still walked casually toward us as if there weren't two angry panthers preparing to pounce on him. I must have appeared about as threatening as a kitten, because the leg I was gripping shook with laughter. My angry gaze turned on my new acquaintance, and he raised his hands in surrender, still chuckling. "I take it you know him?" he asked.

"He's following me," I announced too loudly.

He gave me a concerned look, so I let down my guard, moving to stand behind him. Chevelle approached us, staring directly at me as if the tall form of the stranger wasn't between us. He let me see his irritation for one long moment before his features melted back into their standard sternness. For some reason, it infuriated me, and I nearly berated him right there. Then I remembered that I was on the run and that there was a strange elf in front of me. I decided to keep my mouth shut before I dug a deeper hole.

An arm wrapped around my shoulder and drew me forward. "Introduce us, buttercup."

I grimaced. My companion was certainly enjoying himself.

Chevelle held his hand out in a formal greeting, his entire posture making it clear he was not one to be trifled with. "Chevelle Vattier."

"Vattier, eh?" I thought I heard the stranger mutter under his breath, "Well, you can call me Bonnie Bell."

Chevelle seemed unmoved.

They stared at each other for one long moment, both tall and broad-shouldered, with dark hair and dark eyes. Their clothes were plain and well-fitted but trail-worn, but where the stranger wore brown, Chevelle donned black. There was something vaguely hostile about their silent exchange, but I could not pin down exactly what it was. The other elf finally held his hand out in return. "Steed. Steed Summit."

They shot me a glare as my giggle slipped out.

Steed stared down at me, not seeming to think it was funny. "Our lineage is long, and we breed the best stallions in the land."

Chevelle spoke up, clearly trying to draw back the man's attention. "Yes, I have heard much regarding the lines of Free Runner and Grand Spirit. Tell me, is that what brings you out this far?"

They carried on with the discussion, and Chevelle explained that we needed horses. I sat, defeated, knowing he was there to drag me back to the village to serve my sentence. I listened as plans were made for a trade. Steed agreed to bring in the herd so Chevelle would be able to choose, and they kept talking, settling into conversation. Steed offered Chevelle what was left of the roast, and they sat, Chevelle beside me and Steed across from us.

I picked up the canteen and choked down more wine.

The evening carried on, and though the conversation still held a formal tone, neither man talking of anything personal. In spite of their glaring lack of easy humor, they seemed to be getting along. I faded in and out of the various discussions, listening occasionally but never talking. There wasn't anything for me to say.

Steed seemed markedly aware of me, watching me in a way no one ever had. It must have been obvious, because when he excused himself to check the herd, Chevelle studied me, sliding a strand of my black hair through his fingers. "It suits you better."

It was a familiar gesture and it should have made me flinch. Maybe it was the wine, but as I looked at him, my anger faded. The way he'd reacted when Fannie had struck me and the caress against my cheek were not the actions of a council elder. As we sat so near, it was hard to believe the concern wasn't real. His eyes burned with intensity, even darker than before. *Dark... like mine.*

I looked away.

Steed broke through the trees, gesturing in the direction from which he'd come. "They aren't far. Ready and able for a morning adventure." As he approached, he glanced at me then Chevelle, who still sat close beside me. "We can get an early start." He lifted a pack from beside the fire. "Bluebell?"

I stood, following the stranger without question, not missing the irritation on Chevelle's face. Steed unclasped the pack to roll the blankets out with a flip, a twinkle in his dark-brown eyes as he nodded good evening before stepping away from my hastily constructed hut. I unlaced my vest and threw it down, kicked off my shoes, and fell into the blankets, stretching happily in something like an actual bed. The conversation outside quieted, and I slipped off to sleep, trying not to think about my capture and coming return to the village.

∽

"Freya."

A low voice broke into my dreams of gently rolling hills and soft gray stone. I peered through slitted eyes to see Chevelle standing outside the entrance, his back to me as he watched the dull-red horizon. I sat up, laced the vest over the thin material of my blouse, and slid on my shoes to join him.

"It's dawn," I complained.

"And good morning, sunshine," Steed called from atop a large, black stallion. The beast's nostrils flared, its breath steaming in the cool morning air. Two more of the animals pawed in the distance behind him. Steed chirped a whistle, and they walked forward, the slim, muscular one moving to stand beside Chevelle as a mammoth crossed in front of me and knelt. I drew in a startled breath at the sheer size and nearness of it.

Steed shot me a mischievous wink. "Well?"

I was speechless, my mouth agape. Up close, the thing seemed as large and black as a starless night. Steed was clearly pleased with my reaction, but Chevelle's eyes rolled heavenward. He didn't comment, though. He simply held out a hand to help me mount before swinging onto his own horse.

"I will ride with you as far north as Naraguah then make my way east to trade with the imps at Bray," Steed told Chevelle.

I swung a shocked look at my watcher, who simply nodded. Steed saw my confusion and gave a disapproving glance in Chevelle's direction. He sat straighter, leaving me alone with Chevelle as rider and horse shot past us, a long black tail whipping in their wake.

I stared at Chevelle. "North?"

He looked back at me, his calm a contradiction to the thundering beat of my heart.

"You aren't taking me back? You are going—*we* are going north?"

"I'm sorry, Freya," he said. "I let my guard down at the creek." His gaze fell to my hands, which closed instinctively into fists, protecting my newly-scarred palms. "I was distracted. I should have been paying closer attention. I should have prevented this." Regret was thick in his voice.

I could only stare at him, mystified.

"It's too late now. You'll never rest until you've followed the map."

He was wrong. I'd forgotten my plans and surrendered to my captor. I had thought it was over.

"Yes," I answered boldly, the word echoing with the thrum of my pulse. It made no sense, but I didn't take the time to think it through, didn't give him a chance to change his mind. I smiled, kicking my heels hard into the horse's sides.

The animal jolted forward, and I gripped the saddle with all my might as its hooves cut into the earth. I'd never ridden a horse. There weren't any near the village, and I'd only ever seen one from the occasional visitor. The beast was huge, and I could feel his power as the ground rushed beneath us. We were gaining on Steed. I glanced over my shoulder to find Chevelle's horse running too, but not with the same determination as mine. Wind whipped my hair as we caught up to Steed, who gave me a wide smile and edged beside us.

"Enjoying the beast?" he shouted over the thunder of hooves and the rush of wind.

I smiled in return, but as the horse kept up speed, we started to pass him, and I realized I didn't know how to slow down. I didn't know how to stop. For nuts' sake, I didn't know how to *ride*. My head jerked back to find Steed, my exhilaration replaced by fear.

Recognizing my panic, he let out a short, sharp whistle, and the horse slowed at once, falling in beside his. Our legs almost touched as the animals loped in tandem. "Never ridden?"

"No." My voice was shaky, along with my hands and legs.

"We only train them with commands for the imps. Just use your magic."

I tamped down an image of the horse bursting into flames. "I haven't learned animal magic."

His lip pursed, one brow dropping low, the same strange look he'd given the first time I'd mentioned learning magic. "Just feel it, Elfreda." I ignored the slight annoyance that Chevelle must have told him my full name.

"I don't understand."

"You don't *learn* magic," Steed said. "It's a part of you. Feel it. Think about what you want the horse to do."

My confusion must still have been evident.

He shook his head. "It's like a muscle. You didn't think about lifting your leg to get on the horse, you just knew you wanted to climb on, and your leg lifted."

Chevelle caught us then, riding up and cutting off Steed's explanation. "This isn't the time for a magic lesson," he said in a clipped tone.

All three horses slowed to a walk as Chevelle shot Steed a glance. I could only think of our lessons, of the fire in the clearing. It had been so obvious once Chevelle had urged me to control a stronger flame, I guessed because I had been using the power in small doses for so long. "What about your hands?" I asked.

"What do you mean?" Steed said, ignoring Chevelle's warning glance.

"Why do you use your hands, if you just think it, I mean?"

He laughed. "A quirk, I guess. Habit. Like when you're playing flip ball and you want your piece to go in so badly that you lean hard to help it."

I remembered the game from when I'd first come to the village. The children would be bound from magic and have to throw an odd-shaped piece into the corresponding hole on a game board across from them. They would lean forward after they threw, sometimes bouncing and chanting, "Come on, come on," twisting as if wishing would somehow make the ball respond. The game had held no interest for me. I didn't have to be bound to not have magic. It wasn't a novelty. It was everyday life.

"We should stop for breakfast," Chevelle said.

We hadn't been riding long, but it wasn't a suggestion. I didn't mind because I'd eaten mostly berries for days and I wasn't quite sure about riding yet.

"I suppose you're right. Might as well enjoy the journey," Steed said, throwing me a private grin.

We stopped under the canopy of a red oak, and Steed grabbed me as I slid awkwardly from the horse. "You may ask him to kneel, Elfreda." He didn't appear to mind handling me about the waist to help me down.

Looking up at him, I pushed the hair away from my face. "Yes, well, I guess I should start practicing."

Heat brushed my skin as the fire Chevelle was building flared. It returned to its proper size, and Chevelle commanded, "Sit, Elfreda."

Steed followed as I walked to a fallen limb by the fire and settled atop the widest part, drawing my legs up from the ground. He sat as well, apparently not concerned about who was finding us breakfast.

Irritation rolled off Chevelle as he ran into the thick line of trees that bordered the clearing. In only a moment he was back, carrying three large, white birds.

"Where is your bow?" I asked.

Steed's laugh was loud. "She's a hoot!"

Chevelle looked as though he could be in danger of losing his temper. I didn't get the joke.

"You're serious?" Steed said, his humor vanishing as he gaped at Chevelle. "What, she's a bright lighter?"

Chevelle was across the gap and in his face almost before Steed could stand. I jerked back in response, but a screeching siren pierced my ears, and I doubled over, covering them. It was inside, a screaming, terrible howl coming from my ears.

I tried to force my eyes open, hoping someone would help me, but they were just standing there, chest to chest, arguing. *Do they not see me?* I ached to scream for help but couldn't get a sound out and couldn't breathe. They leaned toward each other, oblivious to anything else. My eyes closed as I curled into a ball. The seconds dragged on, and I began to wonder if I would die.

Then it stopped. I sucked in a ragged breath, then another. I seemed fine, maybe a little dizzy, but otherwise, it was gone. Unclenching my body, I looked around, expecting someone to be leaning over me, attempting to help. But nothing appeared out of place. I pushed up on shaky limbs. Chevelle was by the fire, preparing to roast the birds. Steed stood beside his horse, adjusting the saddle's straps. Both had their backs turned to me as if they hadn't even noticed.

A wave of vertigo hit when I tried to speak, and I fell back against the tree limb to steady myself. It seemed only a moment, but when my eyes opened again, the scene had changed.

Steed reclined beside me, an elbow resting on a bent knee as he lazily wound a feather in his hand. Chevelle was across the fire. He looked up at me through his lashes, past his furrowed brow, and then brought me a piece of meat. It was cold.

I sat stunned. *Have they nothing to say? Do they actually not know?* I wanted to scream, but the words wouldn't come. I was too drained. And I was scared. I didn't know what had happened or what was wrong with me, but I was certain that whatever it was, Chevelle would take me straight back to the village, where I would be punished.

We stayed there for some time, a fact for which I was grateful. Even though whatever had happened seemed to have passed, neither man gave the impression he was in a hurry to go. Chevelle glanced at me occasionally but kept himself busy around the fire. Time seemed to be moving strangely.

Steed still played with his feather, entertaining me with it. It spun toward me and turned down, tickling my arm and then my nose as his magic made it dance. I giggled despite my wariness and reached up to rub my nose where the plume had brushed it. I noticed the map on my palms. "What about spells?"

He eyed my hands. "Been working spells?"

"Not on purpose."

His grin was automatic, and I had the feeling delight came easy to him. Steed was charming and warm, and there was a strange sort of magic to the way he looked at me—as if he truly saw me. And yet, I couldn't quite forget someone else's eyes were on me as well. "Yes, spells can be dangerous."

"Yes," I agreed, "but why do you need words for spells and not magic?"

"A spell can be left, set with a trigger, or larger than your magic.

They are complicated and wicked things. And the ancient language is... tricky. Definitely something you should stay away from. Years of learning and practice, and you can still wreck a spell pretty good."

I thought about that for a moment.

Steed jumped up and held out a hand to me. "What do you say we water the horses?"

I didn't have to ask my horse to kneel because Steed grabbed my waist and threw me up there. He was mounted before I had settled into the saddle, and our horses took off, galloping north synchronously. I looked back for Chevelle. He was leaning forward, his legs nearly straight in the stirrups as his stallion raced to catch us, entirely displeased with the both of us, if I were to guess.

We were covering distance so quickly that I could barely take in the new surroundings, and it wasn't long before we came up on a wide creek. I assumed Steed had control of my horse—I was simply concentrating on staying in the saddle as we ran beside him. The horses edged closer to the creek, splashing along the muddy bank then in the shallows of the water. Silt and cold water sprayed my face as we ran, and I wondered if it was what it felt like to fly like the fey.

We followed the creek until it turned west, and we kept north, slowing to a walk. I tried to catch my breath. Steed was watching me, smiling appreciatively, and I realized I was wearing a huge grin along with about three pounds of mud.

The slower pace gave me time to take everything in. The ground had leveled out again, clearing to open meadows of low grass and a few scattered trees. Large gray rocks dotted the landscape. There was a haziness on the horizon, but as we rode, it began to clear, revealing a mammoth lake ahead. It was a hundred times bigger than the tiny forest ponds I was used to and as smooth as glass. Behind it, the haze thinned just enough that I could see the outline of mountains.

The image was like a punch in the chest. Chevelle rode up beside us. "The hills of Camber."

I looked at him, my watcher, and thought his features were peaceful for the first time. Junnie had said he was from the North, and I wondered if we had reached his home. Maybe that was why he'd brought me here, for a much-needed vacation from the duties of Council and the task of being a watcher. They would never know, as long as he got me back soon.

When we reached the lake, the horses stopped, and in the quiet shadow of the dreamlike setting, I forgot I was riding. The mountains and lake were almost too much to take in—none of it seemed real. Chevelle edged in next to me before Steed had the chance. As my horse knelt, he held out his hand, and I stepped down beside him. The three stallions followed Steed to a nearby tree, where he fed them small green-skinned apples from its branches.

I glanced back at Chevelle. He was watching me. I wanted to ask if he was from there but was afraid to set off any conversation that might end with me being hauled back to Council that much quicker.

I looked over the lake to the mountains. If I was incarcerated for a thousand years in the village, I would want this memory. I breathed deeply. The air was cool and moist and smelled so unlike the harsh floral scents that saturated every part of the village. I could sense the deep-green moss covering the rocks at my feet and the fir trees that edged the east bank. Even the soil smelled richer. My eyes were closed as I took it in, and a soft touch brushed my cheek. *Chevelle.*

I opened my eyes and realized he had swept debris from my face. I wiped a hand across my forehead, and dried mud crumbled away. I looked down and realized it was caked on the fabric of my pants and splattered nearly everywhere.

Moving to the edge of the bank to walk in, clothes and all, I waded out until I was waist-deep then relaxed, falling back and gliding under the dark water before it lifted me to float at the surface. The water covered my ears, lapping at my mouth and chin, and I stared upward, marveling at the size of the mountains as they seemed to dissolve into the blue haze of the sky. I wondered if it would ever seem real.

Eventually, I made my way back, wrapping my arms around myself to control the shivers. I was surprised and more than a little grateful to find that a shelter had already been set up for me. The idea of being drenched hadn't mattered until the cool air cut across the lake. Chevelle nodded toward the hut as he prepared a fire, and I found my pack along with a pile of dry clothes on a bed of birch branches.

As I tugged off my soaked pants to exchange them for the new ones, I wondered if Chevelle had brought both sets or if they'd been packed by Junnie in that small, strange village. I couldn't fathom why I hadn't considered he would so easily be able to follow me when I'd run from there or how I'd been oblivious to the dangers of being caught. It was not my aunt Francine I was dealing with. It was Council.

The shirt was fitted to my shape but of a heavier fabric, and a pair of boots was at the bottom of the stack. *It must be much colder in the mountains,* I thought. It reminded me of stepping out of the cold, wet gown on the bank of the creek then finding the scroll and the map. Chevelle's words echoed in my mind. *I'm sorry, Freya. I let my guard down at the creek. I was distracted... should have been paying closer attention... should have prevented this... too late now.*

The smell of cooked meat cut through my thoughts. I ran a hand through my wet hair and walked out to the fire. The scene wasn't any less impressive than it had been the first time, and I sat on one of the large, flat rocks facing the lake. Chevelle brought me a plate of food, settling in beside me. There were berries, roots, and a rich, savory meat that dripped onto my hands as I tore into it. It was a feast compared to what I'd been eating. And even though he was my watcher and my captor, I had to admit I felt less alone with Chevelle there.

Steed pulled his own ration from the spit and sat on my other side in companionable silence as we all watched the surface of the lake and beyond it, mountains.

THE MOUNTAINS at dawn were much more intimidating, and I was hesitant to leave our camp. I felt as if I'd finally found some solace there, safe and far from my punishment by Council. I'd been eager to follow the map on my palms and leave behind everything I'd ever known, but I was staring at the possibly of a strange new land, and the reality of what I was about to do came crashing in. I tried to distract myself as we rode east around the lake, attempting to name the species of plants as Junnie might have made me, but there were so many I had never seen that it started to remind me of the difference rather than distract me from it. I bantered with Steed about horses and imps and everything I could come up with to keep him talking. He didn't seem to mind. Chevelle rode quietly behind us, scanning our surroundings. I wasn't sure if he was enjoying the scenery or playing lookout. Maybe I wasn't the only renegade he was after.

We rode a few days into the base of the mountains. One night, we had stopped to camp when over dinner, Steed announced he would be leaving us the next morning to head east. His easy humor had become a reprieve to me during the long days, and our quiet evenings were a comforting pattern I knew I would miss. The disappointment must have shown on my face.

He reached a hand up and brushed my hair behind an ear. "Don't worry, sunshine. I will see you again."

I smiled a little, and he winked at me. Chevelle stiffened at my side, as he often did when Steed touched me so casually, and I couldn't help but think of being alone with him after that night. My stomach tightened, and suddenly in comparison, the mountains didn't seem like such a big deal.

The next morning, Steed said goodbye privately to Chevelle then came to where I stood with the horses, stroking one's neck. "You'll remember me, butterfly?"

I smiled in return. "Always."

"Yes, well, at least as long as he's yours." He patted the horse.

"Mine?"

He smiled and swung onto his horse, nodding farewell as he spun and galloped east.

My horse knelt, and Chevelle offered his hand to help me get seated. My grin widened as he mounted his horse, and he looked back at me questioningly.

"I'll name him Steed," I announced proudly.

Chevelle pressed his eyes closed, shaking his head as I patted the horse's neck once more.

7

───────

We rode through the morning hours. Chevelle seemed content not to talk, but I was wound up in anguish, trying to decide whether I was brave enough to ask him questions. I had no idea how much he would put up with before he called it all off and hauled me back to the village for sentencing. *You're being paranoid*, I reminded myself. Chevelle had done nothing to cause me harm. Despite being a member of Council, he'd never treated me the way the elders had.

But there was something dark about him that sent warnings from deep within me, and I was alone with my watcher in a place that set me on edge, unable to stem the tension inside me. Our path became more defined, pushing us through trees and between rocks, trailing upward so minutely that I didn't even realize how far we'd gone until I glanced back and saw the base of the mountains beneath us. I appraised the narrow path ahead, snaking high through a vast, rock-strewn mountain, and turning back didn't seem so bad after all. Fists clenched, I pushed out the question I'd been most afraid to ask. I was so tied up, it twisted into something of an accusation. "Watcher."

My skin flushed when the word came out harsh. Regardless of how he'd treated me, Chevelle was still a member of Council. I was on dangerous ground. He spun on me, but I couldn't place the expression on his face.

Panicked, I tried to recover. "You're my watcher." It still sounded wrong, so I added, "Why?"

He hesitated. "Frey…" His voice was unexpectedly gentle, and I had the strangest feeling he was searching for an answer. But I had no right to question someone of his station, and his face turned hard, his tone formal. "The Council was concerned after you tried to choke Evelyn of Rothegarr."

I drew a sharp breath, caught off guard. "What are you talking about?" Then I was offended. *How could anyone believe I choked Evelyn?* I bit down against the reply I wanted to snap at him, mindful of the trouble I was already in with Council. But that brought on images of the speaker's discolored face as he struggled for air and the blackened thistle in the back room at Junnie's. Evelyn's expression as she'd run from our argument had been accusing, and it suddenly seemed right.

I swayed, my vision losing focus. I didn't even realize I was falling until Chevelle's arms were around me—he was quick, catching me before the rocks did.

He was kneeling, cradling me in one arm as my back rested against his leg. "I'm sorry, Freya. I thought… How could you not know?"

Humiliation flooded through me. He was right, and not only had I wished her to choke, I had been too much a fool to see I had caused it, just as I had caused the speaker to do the same. I squeezed my eyes closed in misery, rolling away from him to curl onto a rock. He let me, stepping away to unsaddle the horses and settle onto a seat of his own. I felt sick.

We were both still until nightfall, when he retrieved a blanket from the pack and laid it over me. I didn't thank him, fearing what would come out if I spoke.

THE NEXT MORNING was quiet as Chevelle saddled our horses. I had plenty to think about besides the questions that had seemed so important the previous day.

I'd been convicted of practicing dark magic. I had thought it was a mistake. But the images rolled through my mind as we continued up the mountain: the lifeless body of a small gray bird. A garden of weeds with roots as black as soot. The faces of Council as their speaker struggled to breathe. A thistle growing in Evelyn's throat, slowly choking off her airway. Chevelle's face when he had asked who had showed me to fuse the crystal with blood. His expression as he'd looked down at me the night before. *How could you not know?*

That image haunted me the most. It seemed familiar somehow. He'd let his guard down, and though strained with concern, there was something else there, sadness or maybe just plain pity.

"This is a good place to stop for the night," Chevelle said, breaking my trance. I'd barely noticed the day pass. A glance at the path behind us showed the lake far in the distance below. It shook me from my stupor.

I climbed down from my horse to stretch my legs, facing the mountain top instead of the view below, some part of me unable to accept the distance and height we had traveled. Chevelle led the horses to a thickset tree, its limbs stretching low and wide above the rocks. His hand spun to form a trough from the bark and tinder scattered beneath, and the horses drank as he used the same method to gather grasses from the sparse patches on the incline.

Movement up the mountain caught my eye, and I looked to Chevelle in alarm. Though he appeared calm, he was staring in the same direction. A dark, cloaked figure advanced in the dusk, the full cape covering every part of its owner, the drawn hood shielding their face.

Chevelle nodded in greeting as I scanned the area for others who might approach. The stranger seemed alone and reached Chevelle first, since he stood nearer to the horses than I did.

The newcomer whispered to him, and Chevelle's eyes flicked in my direction more than once. Curiosity burned through me. And then a delicate hand reached out to pass Chevelle a package. Her fingers lingered against his during the exchange, and my chest felt like it was blistering inside. They were whispering about me, my watcher and this woman. Chevelle's gaze brushed mine once more, and I hungered to hear what they were saying. I was fixated on it, my mind spinning, convinced that if I were as invisible as everyone thought, if they truly couldn't see me, at least I could get closer and finally know.

As I shook my head at the idea, my eyes fell downward. A small scream escaped. My arms were covered in tree bark, blending seamlessly with the stump on which I sat. I bolted upright, batting at them as if my shirt were on fire. Chevelle and the cloaked woman ran toward me, and I looked up in panic. When my eyes fell again to my arms, they were normal. *Had I imagined it? Am I losing my mind?*

When my head came up, the woman drew a sharp breath. It was Junnie. Her cloak had fallen, and her golden curls were a welcome sight.

Relief flooded me, and I forgot all my previous resentment. "Junnie!"

"Frey," she murmured, reaching out to stroke a strand of my black hair.

The shock of seeing her disappeared at the reminder of my changed appearance. "Are you here for Council? To collect me?" My voice was colored with the shame of being a criminal, a bird-killer, an elf-strangler.

Surprised, she glanced at Chevelle then back to me, forcing a smile. "Are you all right, Frey?"

I stood there, baffled, then remembered screaming. I cleared my throat. "I was covered in bark."

Her eyebrows ticked up as she looked again at Chevelle, who was mirroring her concerned expression. "Maybe it's time to allow her a few small lessons."

Magic. I was ashamed by how long it took to realize I'd unwittingly camouflaged myself. That whole thing was going to take a while to get used to.

"Tomorrow," Chevelle answered. He glanced at the darkening sky. "Dinner?"

Junnie grinned as she reached an arm back, her cloak moving aside as she drew a bow from beneath. "I'll get my own, but thanks."

He nodded, a knowing smile stretched across his face—and not entirely the friendly sort. They turned in opposite directions, each disappearing behind the trees and rocks that strewed the mountain, as I stood alone and confused. I sat on a fallen tree, shaking my head as I stared down at its rough bark.

Chevelle returned quickly with two small, furry animals slung over his back. As his gaze reached the log that lay in front of me, it burst into an orange flame, thin branches forming a spit as he skinned and attached the animals. The process was so smooth, I couldn't say exactly what had happened.

Chevelle was changing. Or, more likely, he was becoming more himself. He wasn't as formal. Away from the village and council, he seemed relaxed, and apparently quick and powerful magic was intertwined into his every routine. He didn't need to do much by hand. I would have spent hours trying to build a spit and skin an animal.

As he wiped the blade of his skinning knife, his strong hands deft and clean, an old question came back to me. "How do you hunt?"

"Hmm?"

"You don't have a bow," I explained. "What do you use to hunt?"

He hesitated as if deciding what to tell me. "I use magic, Frey."

He looked like he was waiting for me to be upset. "Oh." I contemplated his answer. "I thought maybe you had a throwing knife."

He smirked. "Yes, well, that would have been easy enough."

"And Junnie prefers to hunt... for sport?"

He had that look again, and I wondered why he would be so cautious. *Because I'm dangerous? A practitioner of dark magic?* "No. Some prefer the meat not to be tainted by magic. They feel it is more... pure." He pronounced "tainted" with an edge.

"Is it? Tainted I, mean?"

"I have lived on it for"—his words caught midsentence. "Well, it doesn't seem to be, but to each his own." He turned to the fire.

Junnie came back into view, a large animal slung over her shoulders, bow in hand. She dropped her burden on a smooth gray rock near the fire and whispered a short thanks before removing the arrow to skin the animal. My gaze moved between the sizeable carcass and her lithe form.

"I'll be traveling fast and far, and don't intend to stop and hunt. I will pack the extra with me."

I managed a sheepish smile. It seemed like I needed things explained a lot lately. "Where will you go?"

"Back to the village."

"To Council?" I breathed. "They sent you to find me?"

Her bright-blue eyes flicked to Chevelle and back. "No, Freya. They will not know I saw you."

"Are they looking for me?" Terror crept into my voice. I was Chevelle's captive, but he'd given me some sort of reprieve. The thought of Council brought the danger of my situation to the forefront.

"No. They will not risk it."

"They are afraid," Chevelle said from his spot by the fire. Junnie shot him a warning glance.

"Afraid?" I asked, doubtful. "Afraid of what?"

"The mountains." Junnie's answer was curt as she returned to her work on the gazelle.

THEY WERE quiet the rest of the evening, but as I dozed by the fire, their conversation restarted in hushed voices. I tried to listen, but exhaustion won out, and their words began to meld into dreams.

I could hear them as I was drifting, floating in a great shadowed lake. My white gown spread around me in the water, my dark hair swaying with the ripples on the surface. I rose above, peering down at myself, and the image turned into my mother before the dark water went black and the ripples transformed into wind. I recognized the scene as her pendant began to glow. The wind howled, and screams piercing my ears.

It was the same dream, but different. I glanced around to find a village I didn't know. Someone was coming toward me, an expression of concern on his handsome face. His familiar face. He reached out to me, and I stepped toward him, tears streaming down my cheeks.

He wrapped his arms around me as I turned again to see my mother. A howl of rage escaped her, and I started to go to her, but he held me. He was restraining me. I thrashed against him as I tried to scream, to tell him to let me go, but I had no voice. She reached her hand out, and I could not move, could not help her, though I knew she was dying. I was imprisoned there, unable to move, unable to scream, and unable to save her.

Then I couldn't see her anymore. Something was covering my eyes. I struggled yet again, but my body felt like lead, heavy and useless. Darkness enveloped me, and I was underwater, struggling to reach the surface, desperate for air.

"Frey." A husky voice woke me. It must have been early dawn. The faint light revealed concern on Chevelle's face as he stood over me. His *familiar* face. The memory smashed into my chest like a battering ram, stealing my breath.

"You," I hissed. He backed away as I sat up and glared at him with fire in my eyes. "You. You held me back as my mother died. You held me and made me watch her die." I could almost taste the acid in my voice. He was still backing away, holding his hands in front of him with his palms out. A wordless hiss escaped my throat as I felt the fire coursing through the light in my hands. He would burn for this. *Burn*.

I was standing, walking step for step toward him as he backed away. He said nothing, his face calm as the fire flared, and I raised my hands to strike.

Then everything went black.

I heard chanting. My ears had been roaring with anger, but all that was left was a soft recitation: *"Gian Zet Foria. Gian Zet Foria. Gian Zet Foria." Junnie.* Junnie was chanting something.

I was engulfed with an empty, lethargic feeling. My eyes batted open, and I was lying on the ground, looking up at my tutor and the watcher. Junnie's words ran together as Chevelle mumbled. "Gian Zet

Foria Gian Zet Foria Gian Zet Foria." It seemed so familiar. Like *Geor-giana, Suzetta, Glaforia*. They stopped simultaneously.

"Frey." Junnie was talking slowly. "Stay calm and lie still." I tried to convey my incredulity as I lay there, unable to move. "Explain to me what happened."

All the anger and excitement had turned into numbness. What came out sounded no more than a statement of fact. "Chevelle held me back and made me watch my mother die." Junnie didn't have the outraged look I expected. I sifted through the dream—the memory—searching for a way to explain so she would be as stunned and infuriated as I was.

They stared at me, and I was abruptly certain that they were the reason I was lying on the ground, incapacitated. They had control over me. My thoughts shifted, and I ran through it again, going backwards from where I was... Their faces, the chanting from behind me, Chevelle backing away, the dream. *The water.* I remembered being trapped underwater just before waking, but I hadn't been drowning. And it wasn't a dream.

I grew horrified as more of the memory returned. The cloaks who had surrounded and killed my mother had been circling me too. I knew they'd intended to destroy me, though I couldn't see why. Chevelle had held me, pulled me into the water. He had tried to keep them from finding me as they attacked, tried to keep me from calling out to her. His fear, his sympathy was clear. He'd held me back to save me.

Tears streamed down my face, and my body began to release from its prison, no longer dead weight. Chevelle had saved me from my mother's fate. *How long has he been my watcher?* In the memory, he'd fought to keep me from seeing and tried to cover my eyes. And later, he'd pulled me from the water and dragged me away as we fled.

I shook with sobs, and that same pair of strong arms wrapped around me, supporting me as my limbs became heavy, my body and mind spent from the stress or whatever trauma the spell had caused. I couldn't say which, because I was pulled from consciousness into a black, dreamless sleep.

CHEVELLE WAS STILL HOLDING me when I awoke, the sun high in the late morning sky. I wondered if he'd slept at all. Cradled in his arms, I reached up to rub my bleary eyes. As I glanced up at him, it struck me how close we were. His dark eyes were on me, a blue so strange and still, and yet something seemed to boil beneath them. Something dangerous, something I should not have felt drawn to. My hand dropped from my face to fall against his chest. That didn't help. Heat rose in my neck as I felt the corded muscle beneath his shirt.

I had to look away. He must have thought I was searching for Junnie. "She left just after dawn, when she knew you were safe."

"Oh," I breathed. *Perfect. We're alone in the middle of nowhere, and I'm sitting in a council watcher's lap.* My flush deepened, and I hastily stood to straighten my clothes.

He watched me fidget.

"So I guess we should get going?" I stammered.

"No."

My breath caught, and I forced myself to look at him, still edgy from the closeness the moment before. I convinced myself I was just imagining the way he studied me as he sat against the downed tree, that he had no idea what I was thinking, that it was the furthest thing from his mind. "No?" I asked, unable to mask the tremor in my voice.

"Magic first."

That wasn't exactly a relief. It was obvious he saw my anxiety, but I couldn't be sure he wasn't enjoying it.

He just remained sitting there.

Practice it was, then. "What should I do?"

A sly grin crossed his face, and he rolled his hand out in front of him. "You are only limited by your imagination, Freya."

Great, so if I screwed up it was just a problem with my mind. I considered that, recalling what Steed had said about feeling it, thinking about what I wanted to happen. But I didn't know what I wanted to happen. I had to catch that line of thought before it spiraled out of control, so I concentrated on finding something small.

A tiny pebble lay on the ground at my feet. I focused on it hard, willing it to rise. When nothing happened, I looked for Chevelle's reaction.

He watched me, his serene mask back in place. "Do you need motivation?"

I was afraid of the kind of motivation he would provide, remembering the fireballs flying at me in the meadow. "No." My answer was too quick, and he laughed. I knelt closer to the gray rock. I thought it moved a little, as if trembling in fright, and the notion had me shaking my head.

Chevelle stood. "You're trying too hard, Freya. Let us play a game." He held out his hand, and a stone flew from the ground to land in the center of his open palm. He closed his fist around it, and when he opened it a moment later, the stone was floating half an inch above his palm, slick, black, and shaped to form a tiny hawk sculpture.

"It's beautiful," I said, moving to touch it.

He held up his other hand up to stop me. "Take it."

I wanted to hold the trinket. I reached forward and concentrated on moving it from his palm to mine. It floated shakily across the space between us, which seemed so odd that at first, I thought Chevelle must have moved it. I squeezed my fingers around it, as if to verify that it was real, but when I opened my hand again, it was only the dull gray rock.

I didn't hide my disappointment as I looked back at him. He tilted his head toward the stone, and I understood I would have to make the sculpture myself. I closed my fist around it, mostly because I had seen him do the same, and instantly, I knew what I wanted. I opened my palm, grinning triumphantly, and exposed my creation for Chevelle to see. Balancing there was a slightly misshapen but undeniable sculpture of a small black horse. Chevelle rolled his eyes, apparently not impressed with my preoccupation with the horse I'd dubbed Steed.

Still smiling, I looked back to the stone, but it had returned to its uninteresting round shape. Chevelle answered my unspoken question. "Yes, it's... tricky." He smiled a little as he used Steed's word, the expression softening his face. I liked the tilt to his lips, the way it eased that constant strain he seemed to hold at the back of his jaw. "You can't change something's makeup, but you can change the way it appears. You can move it, but only if you're near. You can stop someone's heart, but you can't make them feel happy about it."

He hesitated after that last part then continued. "You can manipulate the elements, move water, draw it from the ground, but you cannot easily make it appear from nothing... though one can usually collect moisture from the air. Fire is easier. It spreads so fast. You can pull a small spark from anywhere to create a flame fueled by the air and..." He trailed off as I leaned closer to him, listening intently.

Chevelle looked into my eyes his explanation ceased. *How well does he know me? What else can I not remember?*

I didn't know what he saw in my gaze, but he blinked and shook his head. "Let's keep working." He stepped a few paces away as he spoke, as if there wasn't a tension between us, an odd sort of friction in a strange situation. "You'll need to think clearly and stay calm. The best fighters are the best thinkers."

"Fighters?" I asked, confused by the direction of the conversation.

He shook his head again as if clearing it. There was a long pause as I waited for his answer. "I'd like you to practice, just for protection."

"I have fire."

He picked up a fallen branch, long and jagged, and snapped the smaller twigs from its side. His knuckle was marked with a short scar, a thin white line clearly faded with time. "Yes, but you should learn to think more openly. It is an important resource that should be familiar to you. You should have years of experience by now."

He was my watcher. He knew things about me I didn't. "Why don't I?" I asked.

He stopped fiddling with the branch. I could tell by his expression that he hadn't meant to say so.

"Why can't I use magic?" I asked. "Why couldn't I use it before?"

There was another long pause before he spoke carefully. "You were bound."

Bound. The word was so foreign in that context. All I could think of was the young children in the village, binding themselves to play the games of fey children who were unmagical until coming of age. I recalled seeing it in the documents in the briar patch—*Francine Glaforia, bound against using all but practical magic.*

I had been bound.

They must have known not to trust me. They must have known. My knees gave out, and I crumpled to the ground. *How many times can the earth be pulled from beneath my feet?*

Chevelle took a step toward me, but I held up a hand to stop him. *Bound against using magic. Assigned a watcher.* My swift and unforgiving anger toward him returned. He had been a volunteer.

He stared at me, his outstretched hands curling into his palms. His thumb twitched, and he opened his mouth to speak. My glare cut him off.

Something flashed in his expression before it finally settled to resignation. Whatever fellowship had been growing between us was gone. I had been lied to again.

"Let's just go," I said coldly, looking up the mountain.

WE RODE WORDLESSLY on as I stewed over the new knowledge. As my watcher, Chevelle probably would have been involved in the binding by Council. Maybe Fannie should have been punished for whatever she had done, but I couldn't figure how they could have assumed I would follow in her footsteps. So what—I'd killed a bird and stolen a few papers from the council library.

My argument faltered, so I went back to anger and betrayal that Chevelle and Junnie had kept this from me—and it hadn't been only them. The entire village must have known I was bound and that I couldn't perform magic, even as they sat and watched me try. They'd sent me to a special tutor for lessons, allowed Evelyn to taunt me without recourse, and pinned the blame on me for everything that happened, all because they expected me to turn, to resort to dark magic.

The horses slowed to a stop, irritating me further. I didn't even have control over that. If I'd wanted to run away immediately, the beast carrying me would have ignored my commands.

Chevelle stepped down and started a fire. When he walked away, I recalled what he had said earlier in the day, that one could stop someone's heart. It hadn't occurred to me then, but that might have been how he killed his prey. I'd not seen him speak over a weapon or even over his prey, and both he and Steed had seemed to use magic for whatever they did. *Are their clans so different?*

Chevelle made his way back over the scrubby brush with two small rabbits in hand. He dropped them and a branch covered in fat, blood-red berries by the fire, and I posted myself on the edge of an uneven rock to watch.

He didn't speak, but I couldn't tell if he intended to give me my space or was just indifferent. I had, after all, apparently been guilty of something. In his eyes, I was a criminal.

I'd choked a council elder right in front of him. Surely, there was no other way he could see me after that. But there must have been something before, some reason he'd given himself to be my watcher and that made him agree to bind me from reaching my magic.

I was too dangerous. Not to be trusted.

I felt sick. I blinked away hot tears before they could fall, silently wishing Steed was there to build me a shelter, so I could crawl in and hide until morning. I wasn't about to attempt to build one on my own, not when I'd barely been able to mold a tiny sculpture.

A gust of wind pushed the flames beneath the spit, causing them to writhe and jump. They formed shapes that pulled at my memories. I tried to follow them but couldn't seem to get my thoughts to cooperate. I could remember my dreams, the wind and fire surrounding my mother. But the memories that came back when I woke from those vivid nightmares were dull. The harder I clutched at them, the more they faded away.

When recognition dawned, I leapt from the rock, cursing Chevelle. He turned to me as I yelled, "Give it back!" He didn't appear to know what I was talking about, but I was so angry that I was having trouble forming the demand. "Give my memories—my *mind* back!"

Chevelle's confusion seemed to clear, but he didn't offer a response.

My hands trembled. The fire in me itched to burn. "Unbind my thoughts."

"Freya." His voice was smooth. "You don't understand."

I fumed. "Well, I'm sure that has nothing to do with you rummaging around in there."

He shook his head, and his complete lack of agitation caused me to pause. I supposed it was possible that he actually *couldn't* free my thoughts. If the council had bound me, it was likely that all of them would need to reverse it, and they wouldn't do that because they had convicted me. To make matters worse, I'd run away.

I might have asked how the process would work, but I was too furious to pursue conversation with any kind of composure. And it didn't matter, because they'd already counted me guilty. I was staying bound, and there was nothing in that realm that could change it. I let out a frustrated growl, clenching my jaw. He was one of them, and I had to remember that, even if being near him made it so hard.

It didn't matter if he wasn't the sole person responsible for my binding. It hurt worse, mattered more somehow that it was him. I might have run back to the village right then, just to get away from him. But Council would never release me. I had nothing. I glanced down the mountainside. I couldn't have found my way back even if I'd wanted to. I had no idea where I was.

I stared at my shaking palms and the spell-bought map carved into my skin and was hit full force with the knowledge that I didn't even know where I was going.

I was about as low on options as I could get. If not for Chevelle's desire to skip out on Council business for a few days, or whatever we were doing there, I would already have been imprisoned. I could hope that with the dreams, the mountains, and wherever the spelled map from my family's vault was taking me, I could remember more and could break some part free. But as it stood, it was the mountains or nothing. I could see no other way.

IT WAS days before I spoke to Chevelle again, though he didn't seem to mind the lack of conversation. He simply rode as he always did, with intermittent glances in each direction, as if I wasn't even there. In truth, he hadn't appeared to notice my behavior at all.

When I finally broke the silence, we were navigating a narrow pass. "How long will we be riding?"

I wasn't specific in my question, not wanting to reveal that I had no idea where we were headed. If he'd really been under the false impression that he had to take me where the map led, I wasn't about to mess that up only to be dragged back to the village, especially after everything that had happened. But I presumed he'd been doing it for other reasons, to delay his own return to the village.

My horse quickened his pace to ride alongside his, and I made a mental note to learn how to control him on my own. The constricted path forced us close together, our stirrups and legs brushing as we rode. Chevelle nodded at my hand, and I held it out, palm up.

Chevelle indicated a spot on one of the mountains. "We are here."

I tried not to let my disappointment show. The information would only have helped if I'd known where I'd started on the map or its endpoint. But at least I knew we were closer to... something.

When we came through the pass, our path widened, but the horses didn't separate as I had expected them to. I decided I'd had enough of that. "How do I control Steed?"

I could see the humor in his eyes at my phrasing, but he kept a straight face. "Think of where you want him to go and lead his head so."

I concentrated on turning left, and we were instantly spinning, the unexpected twirl throwing me half from my saddle.

Chevelle caught my arm and righted me on my horse. "Maybe not so severe next time."

My face heated, but I focused on the horse's head again, turning him back to our course as I gave a small nudge with my heels.

I was cautious after that, but it became easier to control his movement as we rode. I practiced guiding him, eventually even maneuvering him back and forth between the misshapen rocks and spiky brush on our way. I was still afraid to have him kneel when we stopped for the evening, though—I imagined him rolling on top of me if I tried. I slid down awkwardly and stretched my legs, glad for a rest after the hours of tensing every time the horse changed direction. The air was brisk, and I ran my hands over my arms to warm them.

I started as black swirled around me. Chevelle had thrown a cloak over my shoulders, and he moved in front of me to hook the clasp, his dark eyes piercing mine as he stood so close. My heart stuttered when he leaned in, our faces unbearably near. Just before he touched me, his cheek slid alongside mine, his mouth at my ear. I froze as he spoke low, his breath on my neck sending a shiver through me. "Stay. Still."

Then he was gone. He moved so fast that it took a moment to understand. The hood of the cloak was drawn over my head, and Chevelle stood a good distance away, facing the trees. I was watching him as two men drew near. I hadn't seen them—they must have been concealed or camouflaged by magic, as I had been days before. The tassels decorating their long robes identified them as members of Council, but I wasn't familiar with the two. They mustn't have been from the village.

As they approached Chevelle cautiously, I examined their insignia. Even if they weren't from the village, I still needed council members to unbind me, and I had a sudden urge to go to them. But I remembered Chevelle's warning that I be still.

"She's not going back." Chevelle's tone, level and uncompromising, caught my attention.

I pushed the hood back to better hear, and the taller figure glared at me as he hissed, "You're protecting her when you know what she's capable of?"

I flinched at his words, but something else had caught my eye.

The robes were ornate, the tassels interwoven with color. He was Grand Council, the order above those who had convicted me.

I studied the other newcomer, who acted as if I wasn't present. He was incredulous, staring at Chevelle when he spoke. "Her mother slaughtered your clan, your family. Why release this terror—"

The man's words were cut short, his face contorted in pain. Chevelle had gone rigid, and I could see that every muscle was tense. The councilman struggled, suffering from some unseen force. Blood poured from his nose, and I gasped. Chevelle's head jerked toward me, and I couldn't catch my breath—his eyes were as black as onyx. When his focus returned to the men, they eased away, the first supporting the other by an arm as both bowed slightly, stepping and stumbling in their retreat. Chevelle watched them until they spun to disappear then turned to me.

One look at his face, and I knew the cause of the devastation. I still couldn't remember, but I knew what I had heard was truth.

My mother had killed his family, his entire clan. He'd been there in the village in my dreams and memories. He had saved me. His family had been there as well—the people running and screaming and dying were his clan. I suddenly knew the cloaks in that vision too. They were Grand Council, just as the men had been. Council was circling my mother to stop her from killing the northern clans. I didn't know why. I didn't know how I knew, but I was certain I didn't want my memories back. What I had was already too much.

I couldn't fathom the pain Chevelle had suffered, which was surely a hundred times mine at the loss of my mother. *His mother... his father... each member of his family? How much loss had he endured?* Tears streamed down my face.

Chevelle took a step toward me, and I was struck by fear. *He must despise me.* That was why he'd become my watcher.

He gave a curt nod at my reaction, his head still dipped as he walked away. I wanted to speak, but the words choked me. I wrapped myself tighter into the cloak as Chevelle constructed a hasty shelter.

I was his responsibility, but surely, he loathed me—I couldn't fathom how he could feel any other way. I thought back to the scenarios I had envisioned after the memories of my mother being killed came back to me. What I would do to those men if I were ever to find them.

But then I remembered the truth. They were saving the North.

I couldn't say I didn't still want revenge, though, and I contemplated what he must have felt about me for taking so much from him. My mind was reclassifying every look he'd ever given me, everything that had happened since I'd met him, why he hadn't looked at me as I'd lain under the tree in the meadow, explaining why Fannie had struck me, why I'd wanted to learn transfer magic... to get my mother's things. The look he'd given the pendant on my neck... my mother's pendant. Of course he'd volunteered to be my watcher. I had taken everything from him.

My thoughts began to muddle as my mother, my dreams, and my own life twisted together. I still couldn't retrieve my memories—I only had the last years, which suddenly seemed a haze. The only parts clear to me were the days since Chevelle had walked through Junnie's door.

I thought of how I had cursed him when I'd found he was my watcher and the hate in my voice when I'd demanded my memories — the memories of his family's murder—back.

My mind writhed with anguish through the night. As I emerged from the shelter late the next morning, I was resigned to continue my journey with him and let him return me to Council without resistance. It was all I could do.

I found him sitting near the shelter's entrance, distress apparent in his features.

"Thank you," I said, indicating the shelter.

He nodded, but his face didn't quite return to the serene mask he usually wore.

My stomach knotted. I hadn't eaten since our ride the day before.

"I'll get you some food," he said. A fire lit beside us as if of its own accord. He strode off in search of food, and I sat close, tucking my cheeks into the material of the cloak for warmth. A moment later, he was back and roasting our breakfast over the flames. We ate in silence then mounted the horses as we had each day before, but it was obvious that nothing was the same. It never could be.

I was racked with guilt as we made our way up the mountain. I purposefully rode behind him, glad to be able to control the horse on my own.

Small patches of snow had started to dot the landscape, and the vegetation had turned a darker, sharper green. Occasionally, the sun would break through the mist, making me squint, and I would appreciate the calmer, hazier atmosphere—gloom, as they called it at home, in the usually sunny village where I would spend my eternity. I wondered where I would be kept as a captive, if there would be windows, if I was unfit for public view.

Chevelle picked up speed after we passed through the more difficult part of the trail, and we rode fast for the rest of the day. I struggled to keep up. I was sure I knew the cause of his hurry. He'd decided he wanted to get the journey over with, end it, and return me to Council for punishment. He wanted to be done with me.

We rode long into the evening, well past sunset, and I began to wonder if he would stop at all. Maybe it was that torturous to be near me. I was contemplating possible ways to sleep on a horse when he finally stopped. We were riding through a small pass, the moonlight barely lighting our way, and Chevelle's horse disappeared. My head swiveled, searching for any sign of them, and then my own horse turned beneath an overhang and stopped in a cavern so dark I hadn't seen it until we were there.

Chevelle tossed out a small flame, giving us enough light to dismount. The horses walked to one end of the cavern, their hoofbeats echoing softly as we remained in the other.

"Frey." Chevelle turned to me as he spoke. "Yesterday... the council trackers..."

Trackers? I tried to focus on what he was saying and not let my mind run wild with new information. "They will send someone for what I have done." I thought of the councilman's face, distorted in pain.

"We should continue your training."

"Training?" Even I could hear the dread in my question.

"Practice. You should be able to protect yourself."

I remembered his words from before the revelation that had ended my magic lessons. *Fighters.* A chill ran down my spine at the word, at the remembered violence in my watcher's gaze. I nodded my assent, biting back my questions. I'd skinned out of a few run-ins with Council, and it was no secret how they operated. I might be safe enough with Chevelle, but if the others retrieved me...

"We will work again at first light and possibly as we ride."

Part of me wanted to argue. *As we ride?* But I knew how serious it was. I was a fugitive, and it appeared that even Grand Council was looking for me. I had no idea what my punishment would be. We weren't in the village. It would be far worse than anything High Council could have planned. I'd heard the stories of prisoners thrown into holes dug deep into the earth and void of light and air, trapped in too-small cages while they awaited trials that never came, taken into the depths of the ancient council chamber system never to be seen again.

And that wasn't even counting what might happen before my captors delivered me. "What will they do if I can't protect myself?"

His face was grim. He didn't reply, and I suddenly didn't want him to.

We settled onto the floor of the small den, our backs against the wall, the rocky overhang blocking the light of the moon.

"That is my flame," Chevelle said. "Try to extinguish it."

My training began.

8

Early the next morning, even before first light, Chevelle woke me for training. Gone were the games we had played—the lessons were intense and stressful. I'd been unable to generate magic on demand, so he'd started lunging at me with weapons, sticks, and fire, forcing me to respond to protect myself. After each attack, he would come right back at me, and if I tried to repeat a tactic for defense, he would overpower my magic and push me to find a new maneuver.

I was beat, winded, drained.

"Mount up," he announced.

When I started to climb onto my horse, the horse shot off like an arrow, almost knocking me to the ground. I glared at Chevelle's back, but he was already galloping away.

I reached out with magic, drawing Steed's head around to press him back to me, climbed up, and clicked my heels hard to catch Chevelle. He was riding too fast again, and I was not looking forward to the day, sure it would be worse than the miserable morning. I rode up beside him, planning a snide remark about the trick, but I was distracted by a black stone in his hand. It was oddly shaped and just smaller than my balled fist. *Onyx,* I thought, though I'd never seen an onyx that big.

His gaze was intent. "Be prepared at all times. This will come at you from every direction. It is the only way you can learn to respond quickly. You need to get past that block and to use your instinct as defense."

I really didn't want to play anymore, but before I could protest, a black rock hurtled toward me. My hand jerked up automatically to swat it away, but my arm hit an invisible wall. The rock slammed into me. I was fairly certain there would be more than a minor bruise from the impact. I tried to slow my horse but no longer had control of him.

"Again," Chevelle said.

The rock came for me a second time. I tried to duck out of the way, but the wall was there once more, blocking me from moving. I cursed as the stone glanced off my arm.

"This isn't fair," I complained. It seemed he was holding me in place just to strike me.

"It's the only way, Freya. This is for your protection."

"I highly doubt they will pummel me with rocks," I spat out.

"No," he said, "they will bind you and burn you alive."

I felt sick. A vision of the Grand Council cloaks circling me was convincing enough.

But he continued. "You will not know their thoughts. You must be ready for any attack."

I nodded, even though part of me was certain there was a less painful way.

The rock came at me again. I couldn't respond quickly enough, couldn't counter and hold onto a galloping horse in the instant it took him to decide. It wasn't dangerous, but it was like being slapped—the irritation had me itching to burn something. The volley continued, and whenever my anger showed, the rock came harder and faster, so I tried to control the emotion or at least hide it. That was the hardest part. Eventually, I found the best defense was to block the attacks by deflecting them with other objects. His magic was too powerful to counter directly, and he'd prevented me from ducking.

When I was blocking about half the strikes successfully, he pocketed the stone and progressed with sticks, water, fire, and anything else he found on the trail. We were still riding too quickly, and I was exhausted from the mental and physical exertion when he switched to full-body attacks. By nightfall, I wasn't able to fend off anything that came at me, and he mercifully stopped the horses beneath another hollow in the mountain. I was practically asleep before I slid off my horse.

THE NEXT MORNING, I woke to the sound of rock against rock. There was no sign of Chevelle or his horse in the dim stone hollow. I sat up, rubbing my sore legs, unable to believe he'd left me. And then the rock wall struck me in the face.

I cursed, my voice hoarse from sleep. The wall came at me again. "Okay, okay!" I shouted. "Let me up."

Chevelle's camouflage dissipated, and he stared down at me, disappointed. His short hair was smooth, his face clean. He did not look nearly as bedraggled as I must have.

I frowned. "Where's your horse?"

He smirked as the beast nipped at the back of my head, yanking my hair. Grumbling, I swatted the horse away and ran my hand over my face, sure it was mottled with bruises and scratch marks.

"Drink this." Chevelle offered me a hide flagon.

I took it, swallowing a mouthful before the taste hit me. I gagged, losing half a mouthful onto the rock.

Chevelle chuckled. "It will help with the healing."

Why bother? I wondered. *It'll be another day of bombardment with mountain fixtures... maybe whole trees this time.* My face pinched with annoyance.

Chevelle threw me a piece of dried meat, barely holding back a smile as he jumped on his horse. "You'd better get started," he said, "it's going to be a long walk."

As he kicked his heels, I spun toward the corner where my horse had been. The beast was galloping up the mountain, just over a hundred yards away. I tried to think quickly and to keep the anger from slowing my response. Using magic to pull Chevelle's horse by the tail, I ran after him, hoping to leap on. A tree branch came from nowhere and smacked me flat across the face. Chevelle's horse grunted as they rode away.

"Why the face?" I yelled at his back.

I winced as a second branch, young and green and more like a lash, struck me from behind. A fierce growl escaped me, and I took off, running at full speed in the direction my horse had gone.

By midday, I was completely spent. I had eventually caught my horse, but the training hadn't let up. I was too exhausted for any anger to remain, but I had the sneaking suspicion that Chevelle was enjoying my lessons.

We stopped by a patch of snow that had gathered in a rock basin, warming it to water for the horses. Chevelle jumped down from his horse as I melted off the side of mine and onto a rock, my limbs like molasses.

He came to sit across from me, and I flinched, expecting another attack.

He smiled. "Well, at least you're anticipating assault."

I didn't have the energy for casual banter, but I did manage to glare at him.

He pointed northeast. "The village is a few hours' ride from here." He retrieved a fresh set of clothes from his pack and handed it across to me. "Go ahead and get cleaned up. I'll be back in a few moments."

I tried to pull myself together as he strode away, but I felt so drained. I stood, easing my clothes, soiled and tattered from the days of battering, off. The damage on my bare skin was minimal. I had imagined much worse, as I'd failed to block so many of the strikes. I satisfied my ego by giving that nasty elixir more credit than was probably due, but some part of me knew the training had not been hard because it was physical. It had been the use of magic that made it grueling.

I put the new shirt made of soft black leather and corseted tight around my waist, on. Slim, dark wool pants and tall boots went on next, and I wondered at the village we'd be entering, where black was appropriate. I could think of no one at home who had worn black—I envisioned the dainty blond elves dancing around in dark leather and giggled.

I glanced up to find Chevelle wearing an unfathomable expression. It was likely I looked as if I was having a breakdown. I hastily finished lacing the boots, throwing the cloak around my shoulders as he left more rations as Chevelle readied the horses.

I stretched out on the ground to eat, examining the carved medallion clasped to my boot. Chevelle stepped away again, disappearing behind the rocks that had become more jagged and taller along our way.

When he returned, the sight of him stole my breath. His worn traveling clothes were gone, exchanged for dark gray and black, a leather vest covering his shirt, the laces loose at his chest. A long, dark cloak was clasped at his shoulders, the material thick, coarse, and so unlike the soft robes the rest of Council wore. I knew I was gaping at him, but there was something so strange about it.

He caught my eye, and I let my gaze fall to his sword belt, struggling to gather my composure. I had to remind myself that he despised me.

By late afternoon, our path opened to look down on the village nestled in the rocks of a narrow valley ahead. Chevelle stopped on a ridge to allow us a better view, which made me rethink calling it a village—I couldn't count the structures from our vantage point, but it must have been ten times the size of home. The buildings were the dull stone of the mountain. None were made of trees. There was really no vegetation at all, no greens, no browns. The entire layout was made of dark, ashen stones and aged wood that seemed to melt into the bluish gray of the mountain. The cloudy mist filtered the sun, and I decided it was beautiful.

"Where are we?" I asked.

Chevelle nodded toward my hands as he started down the path.

The map on my palms was gone. My skin was unmarked, with no indication whatsoever it had even been burned. *Is this our destination?* My gaze shot up to find the village, then I hastily clicked my heels when I realized I was being left behind.

As we advanced, I could see movement among the elves. There was much activity, but it was nothing like home. There were no flags of quilts and rugs blowing in the breeze, no bright sunlight on a rainbow of colors, no dancing in the village center. A raucous sound traveled up to us, and Chevelle waved a hand, his magic bringing the hood of my cloak up to cover my head before he did the same with his own. At once, my stomach was a knot again.

We rode into town at a walk. Chevelle sat straight and tall in his saddle, but his arm hung casually, his hand resting on his leg. I was more comfortable watching him and looking for a reaction than I was with the passing elves.

Two men walked by in the opposite direction, their dark eyes on us. My cape blew back, exposing the shape of my leg, and they hissed indecent comments. I gasped, shocked, and my horse picked up its pace to ride beside Chevelle. Chevelle lifted two fingers slightly to silence me.

We hadn't ridden more than a quarter of the way into town when he turned the horses to a medium-sized structure, stopping before a water trough. He dismounted effortlessly and pulled me from my horse and into the building in a few quick steps, closing the door behind us.

It was dark inside, and his fingers lingered on my arm. I felt him shift as he waved a hand, and several lanterns around the main room lit, giving off a soft glow. He indicated a door on the rear wall. "Your room."

I drew back my hood, nodding.

"I have some business to take care of before we move on."

Move on? So this isn't our destination. Or does he mean back to the village?

He continued, apparently not noticing my perplexed expression as my mind ran through a list of possible scenarios. "The pouch from the vault. There was a stone in it."

It was clear he was asking for the ruby, but I wasn't sure why. I didn't think I had much choice in the matter, given that I was a criminal, but I could come up with no real reason to fight it. Standing in the center of that strange room, in the middle of a mountain, had me thinking through fog. I was going to be returned to the village for punishment or worse, since I was being tracked by Grand Council. I was completely ignorant of where I was. I had apparently lost part of my memories and magic because I had been bound—I was still bound.

I realized Chevelle was watching me, waiting for the stone. Shaking free of the thoughts, I removed the pouch from my pack to untie the lacing.

I reached inside, wondering momentarily what else might be written in the ancient language on the scroll. I handed the dark-red stone to Chevelle, who only nodded as he took it from me, not examining it before he slipped it into a pocket to hide it. There was a sound at the door, and his fingers slid over my lower back, urging me into my room. I was closed in just as the main door opened, giving me no more than a glimpse of someone's deep-red curls.

I tried not to be annoyed about being closed in a room—I was a prisoner, after all. Chevelle's voice was barely audible as he spoke to his visitor in a formal tone. "Ruby."

Ruby? Before I could stop myself, I was at the door, peering through the frame. A tiny crack of light allowed me a partial view of Chevelle's back and all of his guest. Ruby looked to be a little shorter than me, a little smaller, but she seemed larger somehow. I thought I knew why. Around her petite face, by some means both wicked and charming, was a mane of deep crimson hair flowing in curls.

I considered her name, given that mass of hair, but any sympathy disappeared as she reached out a hand toward Chevelle. There was something sinful about the way her hand turned seductively in the simple task of retrieving the stone—my stone—from him.

Anger swelled in me. I wasn't sure if I had given it to Chevelle because I'd trusted him or because he was my captor, but I couldn't shake the feeling of betrayal. I couldn't fathom why he would be giving my family heirloom to that woman. The ruby had been in the vault with my mother's possessions along with the map that had taken us there, and he was giving that Ruby *my* ruby. I shook my head. There must have been a connection, some reason it would end there.

Ruby drew a package from her cape and handed it to Chevelle, smiling a temptress's smile. It was about two hands in size and wrapped in light-brown cloth. He slid it under his cloak, and it disappeared from my view. I couldn't imagine what she had given him, but it must have been in trade for my stone.

As I peered through the gap in the doorframe, the stranger's eyes flicked to mine, and I was sure she somehow saw me. I held my breath and jerked away from view, plastering myself against the wall. When she didn't speak up to expose me, my pulse began to slow, but I wasn't brave enough to look again.

I stared into the room and noticed that the space was relatively large and ornate compared to my bedroom at home. There was a stone-framed bed wide enough for two with dark-olive blankets in layers on top. A side table held a few trinkets and a decanter set, and there was a hickory wardrobe in the corner. A full mirror lined the east wall.

I took a few steps forward, staring in disbelief as my figure came into view. I had seen the reflection in the water and knew my hair was dark and my eyes a strange shade of green, but as I gazed at the woman in my reflection, I could not reconcile the two. The dark silhouette, her figure emphasized by fitted clothes, her black cape draped behind her—the woman was breathtaking. I moved closer to examine her, nearly reaching out to touch the windblown sable hair. Her eyes—my eyes—were dark. That muddy fog was gone, and under my black lashes waited deep emerald jewels, flecked with the darkest of browns. Chevelle had been right—it did suit me. The image in the mirror was stunning.

It felt odd to marvel over my own reflection, but I couldn't pretend I didn't like it. The changes were still unnerving, though, and I tried to remember what I looked like in my oldest memories and to see who I was before, to see my mother's face.

The door opened behind me.

"Ah, yes," Ruby purred as she looked me over. "Lovely."

Her inflection left no doubt that the word was not a compliment, only that she found it lovely she'd discovered me. I could see Chevelle through the open door behind her, still in the main room and evidently annoyed.

"I, of course, am Ruby," she said. "I'm pleased you'll be staying with me during your visit."

Staying with her? This is her house? I was sure I was wearing the same irritated look as Chevelle. I was also certain, by the way she watched me, that Ruby had seen me spying. Her mouth was twisted in a smile, loaded with false honey. I noticed her eyes then, looking past the heavy paint they wore, to dark green jewels—emeralds. They were so like those I had just examined in the mirror that I had to look away.

"Frey," I replied softly. "Thank you for the room."

She seemed disappointed that I had no further comment. She flitted her hand in dismissal as she swirled out of the room and back to Chevelle, the metal bracelets around her wrists tinkling like chimes.

"I'm off to town, then. You *know*," she sang at him, "a handsome hunk of horsemeat was asking about you this morning."

My ears perked up. *Someone was asking about Chevelle? That must be why we're here.* And then I realized she had called someone a hunk of horsemeat, and I had to stifle a laugh.

Chevelle nodded but made no remark on the inquirer. Ruby winked at him on her way out, and the gesture lit a burn in my chest. I turned back to my room and climbed into bed, angry at myself more than anything else and determined not to let him see. I covered my head with a corner of the blanket, suffocating my fractured thoughts with the absence of light.

I was unsure how long I'd slept. The house was quiet when I slipped from bed, trying not to make a sound. I peeked into the main room, finding Chevelle sitting against the front wall, a small window above his head. He leaned over, working on something in the palm of his hand, a steady scratching accompanying the movement of his wrist. I started forward, and my boot scuffed the floor, alerting him to my presence. As he glanced up, he slid whatever he'd been working on into a pocket at his hip.

It dawned on me then that the main room had only the entrance and two other doors. If we were staying with Ruby, then the second room must be hers. I meant to offer Chevelle my room to sleep in, but the look on his face was so unnerving that I could not stop myself from offering something else. "You don't... You don't have to protect me." I hoped it was true. "I can turn myself in, take myself to the village, or"—I was trying to say Grand Council, but the words stuck in my throat.

No part of me wanted to surrender to my mother's killers, but I could not make Chevelle suffer more than he already had. My hands trembled, and I tightened them into fists. He was my watcher, and he must have felt he needed to fulfill his duties, to keep his honor. I knew he would finish our journey and return me to the village.

"Freya." He said my name as if it were tearing at him, and my chest ached. "You don't understand." His eyes closed for a long moment before they found me again. "You can't submit to Grand Council. You can *never* submit."

He was right, I didn't understand. *Does he intend to return me to the village, to High Council? Or will he keep me safe from the others?*

"You remember what they did to your mother?"

I felt my face pale. I'd known they were dangerous, but I wondered whether he meant that to submit was to accept her fate. The image of flames and a circle of cloaks surrounding her was there again, and I had to force it away before it turned to an image of me. "Protection," he'd kept saying as we worked on magic. *They're going to burn me.* "They would kill me because of the pendant, the library?"

"No, Frey. You have broken some of your bonds. They will not risk trying to bind you again."

I struggled with an intake of breath.

He stood and started toward me, about to speak again just as the door swung open. Chevelle's face flushed with anger.

"Elfreda!" Steed was through the door and to me in three long strides. He grabbed me at the waist, picking me up and spinning me so that my cloak swirled behind.

The shock and exuberance of his greeting was too much, and I couldn't help but let out a breathless laugh.

He put me down but kept me close, his hands still at my waist. I stared up at him, taking in the clean version of someone I'd come to know as a bit dusty and wild. His short, dark hair was straight and clean, his clothes of a more casual sort.

"Steed," I said, very nearly winded. "What are you doing here?"

He glanced at Chevelle, who was still plainly annoyed, and his carefree smile dissolved. "I was heading to Bray and ran across some trackers."

Chevelle's eyes flicked to my face and then back to Steed.

Steed dropped his hands from my waist as he winked at me. "I saw the horses out front and couldn't resist. I knew you'd be missing me."

I tried to smile, but the thought of trackers had taken the thrill out of the unexpected visit. The vision of flames was threatening again, and I swallowed hard.

Chevelle threw on his cloak and put his hood up. "Stay here," he ordered me. He gestured toward Steed, who turned to follow him outside.

I wasn't sure how long they'd be gone. I went to one of the narrow windows on the front wall and peered cautiously out. They were nowhere to be seen, but the sights of the village distracted me quickly enough.

It was so unlike home. Night gave the gray stones an even darker appearance, the firelight glinting off their ragged edges like polished onyx. Torches lit each walkway and building. It seemed late, but several villagers, loud and boisterous, were still outside. Nearly everyone was dressed in black, a few of the men bearing large silver breastplates or wrist cuffs. Most wore leather, laced tightly against thick, muscled frames. Few were as thin or petite as the elves I was used to seeing. These were strong like Chevelle and Steed. All but one had dark hair—*Ruby*.

I cursed. She was approaching the house, and I was alone. Part of me wondered if I was fast enough to get to my room before she came in. I hadn't made up my mind before the door opened beside me.

"Well, well. Alone, are we?" she purred, smiling wickedly as she neared, coming uncomfortably close. "Let's talk." She leaned in farther, and something glistened in the air between us.

I froze, unable to move away.

"Stop." Chevelle's voice was sharp as the redhead was whisked away from me, laughing. Her curls brushed my face on their way past, taking my head on a dizzying spin.

"Just having a little fun, Vattier," she said.

It sounded too far away or as if I were in a tunnel. Chevelle was reprimanding her, and then they were gone. My head swirled, and I felt off-balance. I started to stumble, but a strong hand caught my arm.

"Easy there, honeysuckle." Steed's voice beside me drew me from the stupor.

"What happened?" I asked. My mouth tingled.

"A little fairy dust. Breath of the siren."

"What?" My tongue was thick.

Steed chuckled. "Intoxicating, isn't it?" I could hear the smile in his voice. "It won't hurt you."

My nose tingled, and I scrunched it up, giggling at the feeling. I shook my head, trying to clear it. "Fairy breath?"

"Red. She's a half-breed. How do you feel?" Steed asked.

"Weird."

"Yes, that's normal."

"Hot," I said, unclasping my cloak and tossing it off behind me. I swayed.

"Maybe you should sit down."

That sounded like a good idea. "Half-breed?" I asked, unable to form full sentences.

"Half fey, half elf." He sat in a chair as he started to answer, and I kept moving past the bench where I intended to land and crawled onto his lap, curling my knees to my chest. His voice was mesmerizing as he continued. "Her mother was a fey from the West. Fiery one, her."

I wrapped my arms around my legs, holding my knees tightly, and placed my chin there to rest my head. "Tell me more." It was all I could do to pay attention to his words, but I was fascinated by their sound.

"Her father was a dark elf. When her mother died during childbirth, he left Ruby here in the village. I suppose it was for the best, really, since she can't fly. The fey would have tormented her. She's still a bit of an outcast, though." He was still talking as I struggled to catch up in my head.

I interrupted him, unable to stop myself. "My mother died." I had no idea why I was speaking. I batted my eyes and tried to shake it off, concentrating on Steed again.

He seemed to notice I was back and continued his story. I leaned my head on his chest, snuggling into his warmth. My face felt numb.

Somewhere in the distance, the door opened, and the vibration in Steed's chest quieted as his words stopped. Still in a daze, I turned my head toward the door, keeping it steady against Steed. Chevelle's furious gaze flicked to my cloak piled on the floor before returning to us. *Us.* I was curled in Steed's lap.

Chevelle stormed toward us. The arm wrapped around my back loosened, but Steed's body didn't seem to tense. *His body.* I giggled a little for no apparent reason then tried to straighten myself so I wasn't cuddling with him. Chevelle held his arm out, and I wondered foggily if he intended to strike one of us, which made me laugh again. He shook his head, plainly disapproving, and a flagon landed in his open palm. He knelt in front of us. "Drink."

I was so thirsty. I took a long pull then another. I couldn't seem to quench the thirst. He took the container from my hand. "Enough."

My stomach roiled, and I realized what I had drunk. "Ugh, blah." I thought I might vomit. *How much of that healing crap did I drink?* I heaved once, and Steed shook beneath me with laughter. I glanced up to find him looking at Chevelle. For some reason, it angered me, even though I knew Steed wasn't laughing at him.

I was talking again without regard to thought. "His mother died too. We killed her." It sounded so matter-of-fact, and my head bobbed along with the words. I couldn't seem to stop. My mouth opened to speak once more, but I was suddenly swept off of Steed's lap and into Chevelle's arms. I managed fear for half a second then lost the feeling to dizziness, followed quickly by only dull numbness.

Chevelle was lying me on my bed. "Stay here. It will pass." His words were gentle, the anger gone.

"I'm sorry," I whispered. He didn't respond. He leaned over me to straighten the bedding, his face close to mine. I stared at his mouth, wondering briefly what it might taste like.

I felt a sharp pain and realized I was biting my lip. The thought made me giggle again, but Chevelle's eyes shot to my face, and all amusement ceased.

The back of his hand brushed lightly over my cheek. "Sleep."
And I did.

My dreams were vivid. Crimson curls brushed my cheek and bounced as a slender fairy danced across the floor, flitting her painted fingers. Stone houses stood in the night, the glare of fire glinting off the rock. Massive stones rose high above. Dark leather was tight against my skin. Cloaks flowed in the wind, forming a circle and then massing together ominously. Black hair glistened with sweat in the moonlight and rolled in rhythm as the horse ran, its mane rocking hypnotically with the motion. Its heavy equine smell was unlike any other. I clung to Chevelle's strong back as we rode at full speed. The wind and rain cut at my face, and my eyes grew sore, my cheeks streaked with tears and ash.

I AWOKE STARTLED by the sound of laughter. It took several minutes to gather my thoughts enough to know where I was. *In bed... at Ruby's. Ruby, the half-breed.*

I was drenched in sweat. My head throbbed. Something had happened to me. Fey dust, Steed had said. Voices echoed through the open door. He was in the main room. Chevelle was there too. My mouth tasted sour. I tried to sit up, but my head spun. Before I'd moved an inch, I was back down. My pulse pounded in my temples as I struggled to recall what had happened during the evening. I hissed out a low oath when I remembered Ruby leaning toward me, blowing her glitter in my face.

My eyes opened again to find Chevelle offering me a glass. I winced, unsure of what I had said to him. I knew it was bad but couldn't quite piece it together. I glanced up at him timidly. "Thank you," I croaked as I took the cup, my hand trembling.

"Shouldn't have left you alone," he said quietly. There was a tinkling laugh in the front room, and I groaned. She was there too. The water helped. I was able to sit up with Chevelle's assistance.

Ruby swirled into the room, dressed in a red frock of sorts. The color hurt my eyes. "Here, a bath will help. Come with me, dear." Her hair was tied halfway back with a scarf, its tattered ends mingling with her crimson curls. I felt dizzy again. She hauled me off the bed, supporting me as I stood. She was much smaller than I thought and slipped easily under my arm. I kept my head down as we walked, mostly trying not to get ill but also unable to look Steed in the eyes. I watched Ruby's heeled boots as she led me through the main room and to the door of her bedroom.

"A bath?" I asked, confused.

She laughed. "Well, yes. A little cold for lake bathing here." She led me to a large basin in the corner of her room. Water streamed in to fill it halfway. "I've laid out some clothes for you, and there are some lovely soaps on the table." She spun and glided out of the room, closing the door behind her. *Lovely soaps.*

I examined the room as I undressed. A large bed, twice the size of the one I'd been using and topped with decorated pillows and colorful blankets was centered on the opposite wall. A tall rack in the corner was draped with material, deep-violet and emerald-green silks, dark wools, and a rainbow of patterned scarves. Shelves alongside were filled full with curiosities, and a few books lay on the bedside table near a lantern.

I stepped into the tub, sinking down as lavender-scented steam rose to dampen my face and hair. I breathed deeply. It seemed to be helping, so I closed my eyes and relaxed.

The water started to chill several times, but I was hesitant to get out. At the risk of boiling myself, I used to reheat the bath.

Finally, I felt well enough to stand. I picked up one of the soaps, washed quickly, then pulled the water from the tub to rinse the suds away. I'd not had much opportunity to practice with water, and I added it to the list of things to work on. It had been a long journey, and the bath was refreshing. The soap left a light fragrance in the air, smelling like morning and cold, and I wondered if the fairy dust was still affecting me.

I dried off and dressed in the clothes Ruby had put out for me. They were a little snug, but not enough to have been her castoffs. The room had its own full-length mirror, and I chuckled at my reflection. It was certainly not an outfit I would have chosen for myself, though I couldn't say it looked bad. I turned away, still painfully unaccustomed to my new appearance, and tugged down the hem of the short leather top.

Steed let out a whistle as I entered the main room. Ruby sat beside him, a warm smile on her face as if we were old friends. Chevelle was near a window on the front wall, leaning on one shoulder, his body turned toward me and his expression impossible to read.

"Better?" Ruby asked.

"Yes, thank you." I was polite, but it burned a little to thank her after what she'd done.

Steed smiled, shaking his head from side to side with exaggerated slowness. "Some night." He looked like he was trying to keep a secret. Heat crawled up my neck as I remembered climbing into his lap the first time and then again, the second time I'd gotten out of bed.

Ruby grinned at him conspiratorially. "Yes, so educational."

Had I talked in my sleep? Could this get any worse? Yes, it could. It came back to me then. I dropped into a chair, my head falling into my hands to cover my face.

Ruby started to say something, but Chevelle cut her off. "Won't you offer your guest breakfast?"

She sniffed. "Lunch, maybe." A plate of food landed on the table in front of me with a slap.

"Thank you," I managed. I was hungry despite the embarrassment. I grabbed the plate and started eating.

Ruby and Steed were sitting across from me. She was reclined, her bare legs showing where the material of her skirt was pulled to the side. When I looked up, she resituated herself, leaning toward Steed and talking quietly about some nonsense. She walked her fingers up his chest as she talked, glancing at me for a reaction.

She was trying to make me jealous. I was suddenly furious. She'd poisoned me, and now this. I wanted to burn her right then and there. I caught Chevelle's expression as I glared at her. He had seen what she was doing and most likely knew her motives, but I could tell he thought it had worked. He thought I was jealous.

Perfect.

I smelled something odd and glanced down. The meat I was holding had burnt in my hand. I cursed, dropping it onto the plate.

When I looked back to them, Steed was watching me, smiling. I tossed the burned meat onto the table and considered going back to bed.

Ruby laughed, and it made my hair stand on end. *No, I'll stay.* She might have been our host now, but I knew I would get my chance. I would fix her. She shifted, and the markings on her leg caught my attention. A thin, painted vine trailed up to her thigh.

She noticed me looking. "Well, Frey, I feel like I know so much about you"—she smiled slyly at Chevelle—"but you know so little of me. Let me tell you a few things, since we will be traveling together."

I felt my head jerk to find Chevelle, not believing what I had just heard.

Ruby continued without pause. "I'm sure you've heard by now that I'm an amalgamation, a half-breed." She said the last part with distaste and glanced at Steed. "I will give you a short version of events, so when the subject comes up—and believe me, someone will ask—you are not overcome by curiosity and forced to seek less than honorable venues to discover the facts."

I chose to ignore the jab about my eavesdropping.

"My mother was a power-hungry wench seeking notoriety. She was an elemental fey and, like me, she sported a fine head of red hair." She ran a hand under the curls for emphasis. "She heard a story one day of a mixed-species birth and got it in her head that she could breed a more powerful magic. Apparently, she thought she could control her offspring and use the magic to her advantage... I suppose she thought she could rule the realm." Ruby smirked.

"She studied various species for a few moons and decided her best chance at conquest was a dark elf. She made her way to this very village and happened across my father, the poor, unsuspecting sap." Ruby flitted her fingers, and glasses of wine appeared before each of us as she continued. "So there he was, and she, just a wisp of a woman, flew up to him and blew a little fairy dust... You know about that."

I narrowed my eyes at her.

Ruby grinned. "He was putty in her hands. It was all over before he even knew her purpose. She kept him under her enchantments and lies as long as she could. She thought she was safe, hiding here in the village, but as you know, an elf birth is a hefty event. Upon the hour of my birth, the entire village had gathered to see the newcomer, at my father's request, of course. Can you imagine the shock when they found that my mother was his intended?"

She laughed, but her audience was quiet. Chevelle, wearing an uncomfortable expression, turned to look out the front window.

"Needless to say, it did not go as she had planned. At her death, my father was released from her bonds. He was horrified by what he had done, by what had been done to him. But he hadn't the heart to destroy his crop. He simply left."

I felt a tug in my chest at her story, but Ruby's eyes were dry and clear. I wondered how many times she'd told it.

"I hear he wanders the mountain, probably killing fey." Ruby laughed again. That time, it sounded like genuine humor. The tension in the room eased a bit.

"Ruby." Chevelle's tone was respectful as he turned from the window.

"They're here?" she asked.

He nodded, and she rose gracefully from her seat. "Well, looks like we have some gathering to do. We can finish this later." She smiled at me as she followed Chevelle out the door.

9

Steed sat quietly across from me, seemingly lost in thought.

"Seems so sad," I said. I was thinking of Chevelle's loss, of my own, and of Ruby's, wondering how we could all be without family. "Your mother..." I trailed off.

He sighed. "My mother died years ago with a large part of the northern clans."

I cringed. His mother had died because of my mother, same as Chevelle. I was almost afraid to ask. "And your father?"

His smile was arch. "My father wanders the mountain, killing fey."

My jaw dropped. "You mean Ruby is your sister?"

"Half-sister," he emphasized. He let me roll that around for a while before he spoke again. "You know, Ruby told me she'd had dealings with the infamous Chevelle Vattier, but I didn't believe her. One can never be too careful with the tales of a fairy."

Infamous?

"But imagine my surprise when he walked out of the trees, following a green-eyed beauty." Steed smiled at the memory before his mood turned serious. "When I ran into the trackers, I had hoped Ruby had told the truth and might know where to find you." He laughed. "She tried to hide you, but I recognized the horses out front."

"She tried to hide us?"

"Ah, yes. Fey are full of treacheries and wickedness. Always meddling in the affairs of others, causing trouble whenever possible. They have quite a time. At least Red's only half wicked."

His sister. I was having trouble wrapping my mind around it all.

"Don't worry. She's had her fun with you. She'll be helpful now." He grinned, and I wasn't sure if it was sarcastic. "Besides, it sounds like you're the biggest trouble going. She would do well to stick around you."

I frowned.

"I'll keep an eye on her," he promised.

"You?" I asked, remembering Ruby's announcement. "You're traveling with us?"

"You don't mind, do you?"

"No, of course not," I gushed. I was too eager. "Chevelle's been training me."

"Well, we can certainly help with that."

I grimaced at the thought of what Ruby's training methods might be.

"Don't fret. She's actually very talented." His smile warmed. "An asset, you'll see."

An asset?

Ruby came through the door in a movement that could nearly have been classified as whirling. "Come on, Steed. We need to set you up outside of town. Chevelle is afraid we're causing a scene in the village." She laughed lightly. It seemed as if she was enjoying herself. I wondered if that meant she was causing trouble. "Don't think he trusts you with the girl," Ruby added, smiling playfully.

"I prefer the outdoors anyway." Steed dipped toward me, his hand folding his waist in a bow as he stood to go. "Sunshine."

MY HEAD WAS NOT up for this at all. *His sister. Traveling with us. An asset.* I rested my forehead against my knees.

"Are you ill?" Chevelle said from beside me. I hadn't even heard him come in. He was sitting forward on the bench next to me, and when I jerked up in surprise, it put us too close. I tottered, and he steadied me but didn't move away.

He leaned closer. "You smell... like morning."

I bit my lip, heat rising up my neck, but he lingered, breathing in the scent. "Ruby," I said.

He looked confused.

"Soap." I had been reduced to one-word sentences.

"Oh." He nodded, leaning back. "She does have a way with potions and such."

"I enjoy the mixing," Ruby said, startling me again as she entered the house. "But not to worry. I keep it contained to elements and minerals, no breeding. I leave that to Steed." She laughed at her own words as she passed us on the way to her room. I found myself reevaluating her as Steed's sister.

Chevelle noticed me watching her. "Do you mind staying with Ru—"

My expression cut him off.

"I have some business to take care of outside of town. She has given me her word she will behave." He eyed her with what looked like a warning as he spoke.

She replied from the open door of her room, "Yes, yes. No naughtiness." And then, under her breath: "On my part."

"No qualifications, Ruby."

"Just teasing. Now go. We have stuff to do."

My stomach knotted. *Stuff.*

Chevelle appeared reluctant to get up. For a moment, it seemed as if he might reach out to me, but then he stood and left without another word. It ached. I didn't want him to hate me.

Ruby whirled into the room and grabbed me around the waist from behind, spinning me up, over the back of the seat, and through her door before I could process what was happening. She plopped me down in the center of her bed and swung around to sit in front of me. My head was reeling from the spin as she grinned at me, waving her hands and bringing a plethora of bottles and canisters flying toward us to drop on the bed. I thought with disappointment that I hadn't responded to her attack as Chevelle had taught me and laughed at the image in my head.

Ruby gave me a genuine smile as she began twisting the lid on a small metal canister. "No mother to teach us the tricks of the trade," she said, sighing as she leaned in.

I jerked away from her, wanting to be angry about the comment, but Ruby had just told me her own story, which was no less tragic.

She mistook my reaction. "Oh, don't be silly. I wouldn't play the same design twice. No more dust."

I relaxed, but only a little.

"Besides, I will let you in on a little secret—fairy breath isn't really breath. Can you imagine if it were? Why, everywhere we go, we'd cause a terrible ruckus. It's a blend, is all. We keep it in a tiny capsule in our cheek, and when we need it..." She chomped her teeth together with a click, the look surprisingly feral. Then she smiled, her face melting into something very near adorable as she held a finger to her lips, protecting the secret. "Old family recipe, you see. My mother left a diary." She was thoughtful for a moment. "Ah, what a thing, a mother's diary."

Ruby went silent for too long, and I wondered if she would be returning to this one-sided conversation any time soon.

Her eyes flicked back to me. "It was very fortunate for me that she'd kept a journal, you see, for I would have no fey knowledge without it."

I felt my brows draw together and tried to smooth my face.

"No, don't feel bad for me. With you in such a position..."

I didn't know what she meant, exactly.

"And my dear brother has been there for me all along, helping me with the elf parts."

She kept talking as she leaned forward, seemingly unaware I'd not spoken a word in response—not that she'd given me much opportunity. I contemplated whether it was her usual behavior toward strangers or if she felt we had a special motherless bond.

She ran a finger through the substance in the canister, and it came out coated in a deep, dark green. She smeared it across the base of my eyelid. She continued rambling as she coated various parts of my body with lotions and powders, smoothed my hair with a sweet-scented cream, and painted my lips with a soft balm that smelled of spice.

When she was finished, she opened a tall glass container with black liquid inside and dipped a cut braid of hair into the bottle. She drew it out, using the tip to brush an intricate design on the inside of my wrist. When she was finished, she leaned over and blew gently on the paint. *Or is it ink?* I was oddly anxious to see the finished work. I waited impatiently for her to raise her head again and hoped whatever it was wasn't permanent.

She finally glanced up at me, smiling easily. I looked nervously at my wrist, but it was magnificent. A simple outline of a bird with outstretched wings marked the delicate skin at the base of my palm. Unbelievably tiny runes surrounded the bottom of its wings, making a pattern appear.

I smiled as I praised her. "It's beautiful."

One eyebrow shot up, and she jumped from the bed, grabbing my wrist and pulling me with her. I hoped she hadn't smudged the design. I checked it as soon as she stopped in front of her mirror and let my arm go. "And this." It wasn't a question. She was proud of her work.

The eyes that stared back at me in the reflection grew large as they took in her mastery. Gone was the girl I'd been in the village. This woman, dressed in leather and dabbed with war paint, was striking, even imposing. Her dark gaze might have been fierce if it wasn't round with astonishment.

Ruby was thrilled by my response. She bounced twice and clapped her hands at her success. Then she was over it. "Let's eat. I'm famished." She fired a look back at me, her hair flipping in the process. "Hmm. I'm not supposed to take you outside. Not supposed to leave you."

I stood, waiting.

"Food," she said. She yanked two cloaks from the corner and tied them on, covering our heads, and led me to the wardrobe by her bed. I couldn't imagine how we could get any more clothes on as she opened the door and started to throw them onto her bed. But she leaned out of the wardrobe door to whisper, "Come on." She stepped into the cabinet, dragging me with her.

We were standing outside the rear of her house. She slid the false wall back in place and grabbed my arm again, our heavy cloaks moving like shadows as we ran from the village.

We didn't go far before she stopped and jerked me to squat beside her. There was movement a brief distance ahead, a rabbit weaving from the cover of one rock to the next. As I watched, a stick shot from the ground and speared the animal through the chest, killing it instantly. I gasped, and Ruby giggled at me before she grabbed her quarry and rushed us back to the house.

We went to the main room, and she started a fire as she easily skinned and gutted the animal. The entrails went into an urn beside the fire, and I wondered what she used them for before remembering all the containers on her bedroom shelf with a shudder. She stretched the pelt to dry while the meat cooked then dipped her hands into an ornate basin to wash them clean.

She poured us wine and handed me half of her plunder. "It's not much, but game close to the village is sparse. Overhunted. When we get to the peak, we can trade. It is the strangest thing—they herd the animals to town then corral them to eat at their leisure." She shook her head at the absurdity. "But you haven't eaten until you've tasted a fattened beast."

"The peak?"

She looked concerned. "You don't know where we're going?"

I drew a breath, uncertain how to answer. I never would have trusted her, but she was traveling with us. Still, it was probably best not to tell her, of all people, that I had no clue where I was or where I was going. I needed to stay on my path more than ever. Chevelle's warnings rolled through my mind, and I wondered whether he'd told Ruby and Steed that he'd protected me from Grand Council.

An idea nagged at me, but I couldn't quite drag it into form. Ruby waited while I searched for a response, but then Chevelle opened the door, and I was saved from at least that much.

When he saw me, he became still. I had forgotten Ruby's treatments until she squealed in delight at his response. He composed his face again, but she'd already marked him. "Oh, you like it. She's fabulous, isn't she?" She was so proud of herself, but Chevelle only frowned at her. It might have pleased me too, except that I couldn't tell what had caught him off guard, how I had changed or the resemblance to my mother.

Ruby offered Chevelle a drink, and he sat in a chair beside mine. She prattled as she enjoyed the wine, and I tried to focus on her stories instead of the occasional glances he threw my way. Then he grabbed my arm. I flinched, afraid of the quickness and strength of the move, but he only trailed an index finger gently down the inside of my wrist, over the bird design, stopping in the center of my palm.

I relaxed into his grip. "You like it? Ruby did it. It's beautiful, isn't it?"

His finger stayed on my palm as he looked up at me. His eyes, piercing beneath dark lashes, lingered on my mouth for a moment then met mine. "A hawk?" It seemed like an accusation, but I had no idea why.

I sat staring back at him, blank-faced, and he turned to Ruby then gave her the strangest look. "A hawk?"

She appeared abashed for a moment then simply shrugged, smiling. "Seemed to fit." That apparently answered his accusation, and he released my hand, easing back into his chair.

"Well, now that you've returned..." She hopped off her own chair and bounded toward the door. "I can't wait to visit with our new guests." She frowned a little. "Too bad they can't stay inside with us. Frey can have my room—I'll be out all night—and you can take the spare." She took one last look at me before she rushed out, apparently satisfied with her project.

I was alone with Chevelle again. My pulse quickened, and I had to remind myself he was supposed to hate me. He was my watcher, and he was fulfilling a duty.

Then I realized what Ruby had said, and I wondered if my brain would ever be quick enough to keep up. "Guests?"

"We will be traveling with some friends," he said, hedging a bit.

He was so vague. A formless irritation started to crawl its way to the surface, but I had to remember I had no right to ask. They were my captors. My fingernails cut into the palm of my hand where the map had been. We would be traveling to the peak, Ruby had said. I couldn't guess what waited there, but that didn't stop the hope that it was something of my mother or my family. But even if it wasn't, at least I would be that much farther away from the village and Council.

The second bit of Ruby's parting comment registered, so I excused myself to her room with a yawn and a short goodnight. I closed the door behind me, and though tired, I didn't think I could fall asleep after all that had happened. I walked to the back window and stared out into the night.

Moonlight glinted off Ruby's figure in the distance as she headed away from the village. I didn't think. I just pulled a cloak from the pile on her bed, put it on, then walked out the hidden door behind the wardrobe.

I ran in a crouch, praying no one spotted me as I gained on her. I only once glanced at the house in fear that I wouldn't be able to find my way back. If I wanted to catch Ruby, I wouldn't be able to take the time to mark my path. Her cloaked form leapt over a tall rock and disappeared. I hurried forward, sure I was about to lose both her and the route. When I topped the rock, I froze, taking a heartbeat too long to drop to my stomach. Just over that ridge stood a group of elves, though I didn't think they'd seen me before I'd fallen back. My pulse settled.

I wasn't quite close enough to hear, but I didn't see a better vantage point. I squinted, examining the figures. Ruby's red curls gave her away. She had tossed back the hood of her cloak and was laughing with a large elf. I was almost sure it was Steed because of his stance. I scanned the darkness and found two others. One was about the size of Steed, and the other was thinner and appeared restless, even in the darkness. They approached Ruby and Steed, and out of the shadows I could see their dark hair. The thinner one's hair was long, his bangs falling over sharp features.

I couldn't understand what they were doing out there or why the "guests" would be traveling with us. Chevelle had called them friends, but I didn't know if I trusted that assessment. They'd been secretive, and since we'd headed into the town, Chevelle had been wearing a sword. Weapons weren't uncommon, especially among council members, but he'd not taken it off, even inside Ruby's home.

I studied their gestures in the moonlight, occasionally catching a few words. It seemed as if they were planning something, but I couldn't be sure. There was movement again in the shadows as more figures approached. I inched forward, anticipating when they would come into view. One of the forms was a mass, low to the ground. I squinted to see better, and—I almost screamed as a hand wrapped around my left biceps with fierce strength, jerking me to my feet. I tried to see my attacker, to think of the magic to protect myself.

"What are you doing?" It would have been a yell it if wasn't hissed. The tone was harsh, and I recognized it at once.

"Oh," I managed. Part of me was saying *calm down,* but the other was screaming that I was still in danger. "Chevelle, I-I-I..." I didn't have an answer. *What am I doing?*

He released his grip just a fraction. "I went to your room, and you were gone." He shook his head. "I thought I had to come out here to get a search party."

"I... uh... You were in my room?"

He straightened, his expression making it clear he hadn't expected that response.

I took my chance and pressed. "Why?" I heard movement behind me, and the fear returned tenfold.

Chevelle didn't tense. He only let out an exasperated breath. "It's fine," he said. He released me, and I turned to see whom he'd addressed. Four figures stood in a line, almost formally, before they relaxed at his words.

My arm tingled as the blood returned to the limb, freed of his harsh grip. I flexed my fist, certain he despised me. There could be no other reason for him to have reacted so strongly.

"Ah, she escaped," Ruby purred. "And you didn't trust *me* with her."

The formation broke as Steed came to stand beside me, the corner of his mouth tipping into a grin. I stared at the group. I had no idea who they were, but from the way they spoke, it was apparently no secret that I was Chevelle's prisoner or his property.

"Frey," Chevelle said, "this is Anvil." He nodded toward a giant of a man who bowed his head respectfully. "And Grey." The wiry man bent and straightened, his movements quick.

I drew in a startled breath as two more figures came into view. A pair of slender elves stepped in sync then stopped just outside the group. They were tall and lean, dressed in robes the color of ash that only accentuated their shocking silver hair. I was convinced the moonlight must have been exaggerating it. And then I jumped again as, on either side of them, two beasts walked forward to stand just in front of the twinned elves.

Steed brushed an arm against mine, mumbling under his breath, "Yeah, they're not from around here."

I felt myself leaning on Chevelle for support. "Rider and Rhys Strong," he said from behind me.

They nodded, and I was surprised that the small gesture also seemed synchronized. A strange whine emanated from one of the beasts at the elves' sides as the animals shifted to sit on their haunches. By their size, I might have guessed they were wolves, but I'd never known a wolf to be tamed. Their fur matched the robes of their masters, down to the black trim. I couldn't be certain in the light, but I thought there was even some silver showing. Surely, they would have been less frightening in the light of day.

Ruby broke the tense atmosphere with a curtsey. "And Ruby Summit," she said.

I attempted a smile for her, not missing the silent exchange between Steed and Chevelle. They were trying to decide what to do with me.

"Since you're apparently not ready to retire for the evening, I suppose we will resume your training," Chevelle said.

I sighed.

"Ooh, let me!" Ruby shouted.

Chevelle gave her a doubtful look then glanced at me, apparently deciding I deserved it. He nodded once and walked toward the rock ledge. Ruby bounced from foot to foot, celebrating her victory.

As Chevelle moved past Anvil and Grey, they turned to follow him. The silver-haired elves and their dogs were nowhere in sight. My gaze caught Steed, who was watching me. I always forgot how striking he was until I looked right at him. He wore a thin, loose shirt, rolled at the sleeves and covered by a leather vest. It matched the long cuffs on his forearms, made of the same dark, worn leather of his saddles. He stepped closer, taking my chin in his hand to examine my face in the moonlight. He said something to Ruby about her decorations and gave me a wink as he walked off in the direction Chevelle had gone.

Then Ruby and I were alone, and I was sure it was going to hurt more than my other training. She untied her cloak and tossed it to land with a muffled clatter on the rocks, its hidden pockets apparently stuffed full. She was smiling a touch as she reached a hand across her waist, closing her fist around a black hoop I'd not seen before. She drew it out and around as a long black trail curved in its wake and came to rest at her side.

My mouth went dry. *A whip. Oh, this will hurt.* I loosened my cloak and pitched it aside then lowered myself into a defensive stance, my hands out and ready.

Crack!

Okay, I was *not* ready. "Ow! Mother Earth!" I yelled. Blood trickled from the strike point.

Ruby giggled. "All right, so we start slower." She paused for a moment. "Maybe we work on your attacks instead of defense."

I relaxed my stance. "I don't... actually... have any attacks."

"Well then, I suppose we had better focus on getting you some. How to begin?" She was talking to herself.

My mind started to wander as I listened for sounds from the men below, trying to decipher what they could be up to.

"I'm afraid we will have to use your anger," she said, a smile creeping into the corner of her lips. "It seemed to work with your lunch."

I remembered the meat I had burnt and flushed.

"Yes, this will do," she hummed with a sly grin. "Let me see... Yes, I've got it." She began stepping in a slow circle around me, talking as she moved, suddenly cat-like. "The dreams you had after the fairy dust—do you remember them?"

Oh.

"I have a few questions, you see. You had plenty to say about someone as you slept. You mentioned how his mouth tasted and something about muscles under his shirt. And, well, I was curious just who you meant."

No.

"It couldn't have been Chevelle—you should have seen his face. He was livid."

No.

"Steed was certainly enjoying it, but, my dear, he won't spill the secret to me. Whose strong back were you wrapped around, whose dark eyes—"

I was mortified. There was nowhere to go, it was too much, and it turned to fury as she continued. I snapped. The flames that had been coursing through me burst in my hands.

She laughed and tossed her head. "Oh, you should have heard it. You gave us such interesting details!"

The image of Chevelle hearing my dreams, the sound of their laughter when I woke... I knew what she wanted, and I gave it to her. Fire shot from my hands toward her, hotter than any I'd ever produced. The warmth hit my face, and Ruby's heeled boots sloshed as snow melted beneath her feet.

She batted away the flames and grinned. "Come now, you'll have to do better than that." She kept circling. "Let me try harder." She flicked her wrist, and the end of her whip caught my ankle before I even realized it was moving. She jerked, and my leg came out from under me, my hip slamming flat on the ground. The pain stole the heat from my anger, and I struggled to stand.

Crack! The whip struck out toward my head, forcing me back down. She circled me, cracking the whip every time I attempted to right myself. I couldn't get a foothold.

"Come now, Freya, you must defend yourself. Fight me. Stop me." *Snap! Snap! Snap!* She was going faster, cracking the whip above me and at each side, moving again and again, closer and closer.

I had to think of something, but my mind could only concentrate on the snap of her whip. Her boots splashed in the melted snow again, and I sent the icy water racing up under the material of her skirt to her bare legs. Shock crossed her face, and I hoped it would buy the time I needed.

The cold water had thrown her for no more than a fraction of a second, but it was enough to right myself and execute one quick attack. I volleyed a nearby rock, which struck her in the back and threw her balance off for another instant. I knew I was larger than her, so I gritted my teeth and lunged, grabbing her as I tried to figure out my next move.

She raised her face, and when her eyes met mine, they narrowed. Part of me was aware that I should have been scared, but I was enjoying myself. Whatever pain I might have to endure didn't factor —I had wanted to hurt that wicked little redhead since the first time I'd seen her, since her hand had reached out seductively toward Chevelle and collected my ruby. My palms lit where they wrapped around her arms. I would finally burn her.

She cocked one eyebrow at me. "Half *fire* fey, silly."

I flew through the air to land with a heavy thump, yards away.

"Well, it was a little unconventional, but at least you're thinking on your feet," she mused, straightening the material of her skirt. Then she cackled as she realized I was, in fact, not on my feet.

My body ached as I stood. My best skill was useless. I desperately wanted to ask her to show me the way, but my ego stubbornly refused. Not her.

She must have picked up on my mood. "You see, most of us choose one particular favorite. We focus on that and practice constantly. That way, it becomes easier and uses less energy, you know."

I didn't know.

"Maybe we should see what your strong suit is," she said, motioning for me to follow her as she walked to the rock ridge and jumped over, hurrying down to the men.

"Sorry to interrupt, gentlemen," she announced. "I was wondering if you'd mind a little demonstration?"

They broke their circle to give her their attention.

"Frey here hasn't found her rhythm yet," she explained. They seemed to understand, and she bounded back over to me and drew me to sit beside her on a large rock facing the men before cueing them to begin.

The largest, boasting deep-brown hair and eyes, stepped forward. He wore plain clothing, but his broad shoulders and massive size made him seem regal. "They name me Anvil, but I am Reed of Keithar Peak." His voice was thick, though it was impossible to tell whether it was an accent or he had difficulty speaking. He was huge, frighteningly so, but something about him drew me in.

I wanted to be his friend for no reason I could rationalize. He walked to me and reached out his hand in greeting. As I took it in mine, a tingle ran up my arm, the fine hairs standing on end.

Anvil smiled. "Apologies. I will try to avoid touching you."

"It's fine, really," I said, though I didn't understand. It was like a static charge. Meanwhile, I had decided the thickness was a drawl. "I don't know your accent. Where is it from?"

"North Camber," he replied. A snicker slipped from Steed, and

Anvil glanced at him before amending: "Well, that is where they cut out part of my tongue."

I recoiled, wrenching my hand from his. The tingle remained. He didn't seem offended—he simply took a few steps backward to start his demonstration. I brought my arm back to my side, and it brushed Ruby, shocking her just enough to make both of us flinch. She only smiled as she returned her attention to the start of the show.

The other men drew back, some sitting, some standing, but all giving him their full attention and space as he raised his hands and braced himself, taking one deep breath before shifting forward ever so slightly. There was a thunderous crack, and excruciatingly bright light flew from both of his outstretched hands, slammed into a tall pine, and snapped the top third of the tree off. Several limbs splintered and popped as it crashed its way down.

I stared in open-mouthed astonishment. Sweat glistened on the large man's forehead, and his breath was a little labored, but still, he stood. Understanding came slowly. He had shot lightning from his hands. The others nodded appreciatively, but I was having second thoughts about friendship with him, though not being his friend was probably more dangerous.

I was shaking my head in disbelief as he turned back to me and bowed.

He stepped back, taking a seat as the wiry man stepped inside the circle. He nodded to me. *Grey.* He was thoughtful for a moment, likely deciding the best way to display his skill, before finally approaching to offer his hand. I reached forward, placing my palm against his, and then he was gone. His entire body had vanished. I half expected to feel his touch—perhaps he'd merely camouflaged himself—but my hand was empty. I looked around, baffled. The makeshift audience wore easy, amused smiles. They watched me, not the vacant space from which Grey had evidently disappeared. And then I noticed someone beside me who hadn't been there before... it was him.

"How..." But he was gone again. I'd been staring right at him and still had no idea where he'd gone.

I was just beginning to doubt whether I'd seen him at all when I spotted him standing across the circle, grinning fiendishly while he dangled an object from his hands. It was the feather Ruby had tied in my hair. I'd forgotten about it. I reached up to feel for it, but it wasn't there. I started to get irritated, but then the feather was in my other hand, and he was back, his hands empty. And then, for no apparent reason, he did a few somersaults and landed in the center of the circle with his arms spread. I could only shake my head as Ruby clapped beside me, clearly thrilled with the show. I thought I must have missed something.

Grey bowed out of the circle and was replaced by the two tall, silver elves. I found myself unsettled again because I hadn't seen them sitting with the group or anywhere else. For some reason, it was much more eerie than the little wiry man who blinked in and out of my vision.

Chevelle leaned forward to speak low in my ear, startling me. I glanced up at him, and something in his expression made me feel as if the words should have meant something to me—maybe he was waiting for my response.

Finn and Keaton, he'd said, the names of the beasts with the twinned silver elves. Feeling as if I'd failed some test, I turned back to the show.

One of the men spoke in a formal tone. "We will not demonstrate their full power at this time, in fear of shorting our forces a man for mere display." I assumed he was probably joking. "As you can see, they can be frightening, however, without attacking."

At that, the dogs walked into the circle. They came forward to snarl, one regarding Ruby and one Steed, and I could only be glad it wasn't me as their muzzles pulled back to expose vicious sets of teeth, complete with meat-tearing fangs. The hair rose on their backs, and I was suddenly positive that they were larger than Ruby. A horrific growl ripped from their chests in unison, and I cringed. Then, at once, they settled back into relaxed seated positions as if they had never been angry.

"We also do not do *tricks*." There was humor there, and I was relieved to see that the intimidating pair might not be as strict as I'd imagined. "We will return to watch." They inclined their heads and walked out of the circle in unison, disappearing from view.

I twisted the feather in my hand. *How remarkable it must be to master a beast. I wouldn't have to be battered during training then,* I thought, and winced at the idea of Ruby cracking one of those wolf-dogs with her whip.

10

The next morning, Ruby was in the main room, waiting for me. She impatiently instructed me to bathe and change, explaining that we would be spending the day training. I followed her directions but couldn't decide whether to be grateful or worried when the clothes she'd laid out for me—utilitarian and unadorned with her usual baubles—were plainly meant for a hard day. It was still early as we stole out the back, cloaks covering our heads as we made our way to the ridge.

Steed, Chevelle, Grey, and Anvil were already there. I imagined the others—the silver twins, Rhys and Rider, and their dogs—were somewhere nearby, though I couldn't see them. *Watchdogs*, I thought, *all four*. It was comforting, but Ruby wasted no time in getting to training. She immediately trounced me repeatedly, cracking her whip, besting me with fire, and even overpowering me despite her slight frame. I felt defeated before we'd gone even an hour.

After watching us for a while, Steed stepped in to save me. "Frey"—he'd adopted the nickname the others used in place of the sunnier ones—"why don't you take a break for a while? Let us spar so you can watch. We'll give you a few pointers."

I didn't know if I liked the idea of the group sparring, whether it gave me a break from the torture or not, but Grey stepped forward, and my opinion no longer mattered.

"Just watch and learn," Steed said.

I backed away and sat cross-legged on the ground. Ruby joined me, and I could tell she was excited. It seemed everything excited Ruby—everything that made me nervous, anyway.

Steed and Grey stood opposite each other in the center of the clearing. Both were tall, and though Steed easily had him in breadth, I'd seen Grey move—he was fast. A cursory nod at one another signaled the onset of the bout, and both tensed and crouched slightly into a ready stance. I found myself leaning forward as we waited. Chevelle moved to stand beside me, also intent. Grey wagged his eyebrows at Steed, taunting him to make the first move.

"Come on, blossom," Steed teased back, "let's see what you've got."

At that, Grey disappeared, and then, in a flash, he was behind Steed, reaching up to smack him in the back of the head. The instant before he struck, Steed ducked into a squat and spun, taking Grey's legs out from under him. I flinched. Grey was gone again, that time reappearing midair in a flip above Steed's head, reaching down to tag him with a loud smack on the way by. I was sure it had stung. Steed stood still, focused on the spot where Grey had landed and was flickering in and out of view. I made an effort to consider possible responses in my head but was coming up blank.

The nerves were gone. I found myself wanting Steed to win and leaned with his strikes, tensing as if they were my own. Grey bounded through the air once more, showing off, confident in his evident lead, and then a small rock rose at chest height in front of Steed. I was trying to figure out who had lifted it when Grey flashed back into view, hesitating only a moment as he considered the rock. At once, his face changed—he knew he'd been beaten. As he'd paused to study the floating rock, Steed had immobilized him and, just like that, the match was over.

Ruby leaned into me. "Steed is stronger than Grey," she said in a soft voice. "He only needed to catch him."

Grey conceded, his walk slower and his movements no longer restless as he made his way out of the makeshift ring. Steed threw me a quick wink.

Anvil approached next, stepping into the same starting position Grey had used, and Steed shifted several paces back before he readied himself and nodded toward his new opponent. I remembered the tree and was suddenly afraid for him, wondering whether Anvil would use the same method on a person.

A thunderous crack answered my unspoken question. The lightning bolt was faster than my eyes at such a close distance, but by the time I looked at Steed, there was nothing but a wall of water. He had constructed a barrier of sorts, caught the strike, and redirected it around himself by melting the snow that spotted the mountain. Anvil was winded, though the strike wasn't as severe as his previous show. Steed would unquestionably be the winner, and as he took aim to retaliate, his opponent raised his hands in surrender.

"Quick thinking, Mister Summit." The large man grinned, and I had no doubt that they were old friends.

Chevelle stepped forward eagerly. I had a feeling he'd been itching to spar with Steed in the way I'd been itching to burn Ruby. Steed smiled in acceptance, but it wasn't the same smile he'd given his last opponent. They stood across from each other and readied themselves. Both tensed, but neither took the low, wide stance the others had used.

As their eyes fixed on one another, I felt myself, and Ruby beside me, lean forward in anticipation of the action. Both men went taut, their muscles corded and jaws clenched tight, wearing determined stares that focused only on each other. I saw nothing happen but knew there must have been something, some unseen force, causing them pain and draining them. I couldn't look away as I stammered to Ruby, "What's happening?"

"They are trying to overpower one another." I could hear the pleasure in her voice. "No silly games—just power."

The way she said it had some part of my mind wondering whether her statement about not having her mother's ambition was true, but I could only concentrate on the struggle in front of me. There was still no visible action, so I tried to judge by appearance who might be winning. Chevelle's jaw was set, his eyes dark. Steed flinched, but I had no idea if it was from pain or magic. The only thing I was sure of was that neither intended to lose. Their stances, right down to their gazes, were absolutely unwavering.

A sound behind me drew attention to how quiet and still the valley had grown as we watched that unanimated brawl. Steed and Chevelle broke their stare, turning to the noise—dogs, I thought—before the entire world shifted into action. The elves around me ran, swords drawn and weapons ready as I was whisked from my seat. Ruby was gone, vanished from beside me, and I only caught a glimpse of Steed and Chevelle as they darted past. I didn't know who had hold of me, but in less than a heartbeat, I was standing over the rocks in the opposite direction, Ruby before me, her red curls blocking my view and her arms outstretched in readiness. Steed and Chevelle were at opposite angles in front of us, both even more tense than they had been in their bout. I peered around Ruby's mane to see what they were focused on.

In front of our triangle, directly ahead of Ruby, stood a reedy, blond elf draped in the long white robe and tassels of Council. I felt sickened as I absorbed the idea that a council member—*is he a tracker?*—had been behind me as we were all engrossed in a trivial match. He was frozen, unmistakable agony distorting his features. I didn't know which of the group was restraining him, but Anvil and Grey flanked him, and Rhys and Rider were a short distance behind with their dogs.

The man seemed to be attempting to speak but couldn't get the words out. His hair was so pale, his robe so stark in the moonlight, that I became aware of how quickly I'd grown accustomed to the dark features of my new companions. Chevelle mumbled something, but I couldn't make it out. My ears had begun to buzz, not with the all-out siren that had crippled me before, but with a constant, crackling hum. I worked my jaw and tugged at the lobe of an ear. The stranger's lips moved—apparently, he was able to speak again—and Anvil approached him, dwarfing the captive with his mass.

Anvil exhibited remarkable menace when he addressed the frozen councilman, who mouthed another reply. I couldn't decipher their words through the ringing in my ears, but somehow, I did hear the breaking bones. A grotesque crunch accompanied the snapping of the councilman's thigh, and he dropped nearly to the ground. Anvil leaned over him, somehow even more intimidating as he spoke directly to the man as if they were the only two there, as if the councilman hadn't just suffered a traumatic injury. And, evidently, Anvil didn't like the answers he received, because the councilman's other leg snapped, dropping him to rest on the stumps of his broken, mangled thighs.

I should have turned at the sight, but I couldn't keep from wondering how it was possible that he remained upright at all. Anvil bent down to keep his stare close and threatening, and the broken man looked at me. His glare turned accusing, his mouth suddenly moving with heated, determined words, but my ears only rang more loudly, engulfing all other sound. I cringed but couldn't stop myself from watching the scene play out, even as my head turned down and I wanted to look away. *Why is he fixed on me? What are they saying?*

Ruby remained protectively in front of me, her posture lowered and her arms tensed tighter since the stranger turned his eyes on me. His face twisted in agony as his right arm was dislocated from its socket, leaving the limb hanging limply at the shoulder. I was glad I didn't hear that sound. He turned back to his questioner, his mouth a grimace as the words, unmistakably a curse, came out, and his other arm was wrenched from its place as well. He winced, apparently not yet numb from the damages, and then his face went hard, his lips pressed together, his jaw clenched tightly. He wasn't going to scream or talk.

His back twisted, and he fell into a motionless heap on the ground. His body was bent out of recognition. It was over.

My ears had stopped ringing the moment he'd hit the ground.

Ruby relaxed and stepped away from me. I wanted to catch up with what had happened, but no one was talking—the mountain was silent. Rhys and Rider were gone from sight once again.

"Aren't you going to perform the death ceremony?" I asked as the other elves began walking away.

Anvil spat on the mangled body. *The corpse.* "It's done."

I stood staring at the crumpled mass as the others gathered, arguing.

A council member—

"It's time to move," someone said.

Came for me.

"No, not yet," someone else replied.

They killed him. I was glad.

"There could be more," Grey insisted.

That brought me back, no matter how disturbing my realization was. "More?"

Chevelle gave the bickering group an admonishing glare as he approached me.

I could hear the alarm in my own voice when I repeated, "There are more council members coming for me?"

He tried to calm me. "Frey—"

"I won't let you all pay for my crimes." Confusion passed over everyone's faces except Chevelle's.

"We aren't. You don't understand..." Something flickered in his eyes. "Besides, they are pursuing me for choking the tracker."

Grey shook his head.

"Because of me," I argued. "And now you've killed one." But I didn't know who had killed him. Anvil had stood before the man, but any one of them could have snapped his spine.

"Frey"—Chevelle's tone was solemn—"you know what they did to your mother."

I could hear what he didn't say: *You know what they'll do to you.* I didn't have a counter for that, and he had to have known it. He took advantage of the silence and gave orders to Ruby. "Take her to the house."

She had me at once, towing me beside her as she retrieved our cloaks.

Chevelle was still giving instructions. "Steed, watch the front. Stay inside. Grey, take the rear, out of sight. Anything, no matter how trivial, signal the wolves."

Wolves. They *had* been wolves, not dogs. I immediately had more respect for the tall, pale-haired elves. They were men who had tamed wild wolves.

We were back at the house in what seemed like a heartbeat. Steed watched the village from the front room, and Ruby sat with me on her bed with the door closed.

"This will calm you," she said. A sprinkle of glitter hit my face before I had the chance to protest. "Just a touch," she assured me.

It was too late. The dust had already taken effect. I relaxed onto the bed, just as Ruby did the same beside me. We stared at her ceiling, not speaking for an immeasurable amount of time. I rolled onto my side toward her, dimly irritated that she'd poisoned me again, though it was much less severe than the last time. I was simply enveloped in tranquility.

"Ruby..."

Her curls had tumbled back, and my complaint fell short as I was distracted by her ears. "Hmm?" she answered.

I reached up to feel my own ears as I considered hers. I had always hidden mine behind hair, never braiding it back or putting it up to expose them, not that I could have pulled off the intricate braiding and designs of the other elves. But my ears were clearly more rounded than everyone else's, almost blunt. Ruby's were different too. Hers were more angular, though, long and almost pointed at the tip. Neither of us matched the norm. Hers were one extreme, mine the other.

She turned to look at me. "Feeling okay?"

I remembered I was going to ask her something. I said, "Mm-hmm," and got lost in the hum of my reply. She smiled at my satisfied trance.

I faded off to blackness then, though my dreams were vivid and wild.

I was a hawk, flying high above the mountain. My wings stretched as I soared through an endless and open sky. Through keen eyes, I watched below, surveying a massive structure of dark stones.

Then I was a wolf, running through those stones, hunting, searching, protecting. My muscular shoulders tensed and released with each long stride.

I was myself again, though strong and confident. Two statuesque elves, twinned in white, glided past me. Lightning struck around me, cracking the dark stones of the walls. Reed of Keithar stood before me, and suddenly I was on a pedestal, looking down as he wagged his tongue at me. I scorned him, burning a chunk of it off, and he smiled.

I jolted awake, the smell of burning flesh still lingering in my senses, and stared at Ruby's ceiling. *Curse her.* I was alone in her bed but could hear an exchange of low whispers from the open door as she and Steed conversed in the front room. I wasn't about to announce that I had woken. My head didn't throb as before, and I had no sour mouth. Overall, it was overall a much better experience, but I wondered who could stand the dreams. I rolled onto my side, rubbing the sleep from my face.

There were a few books on the bedside table, and I reached over to draw the top one near. I flipped idly through the pages until I recognized that it was detailing different aspects of magic. I hurriedly scanned through, getting caught on a section marked Exchange. It claimed that using magic consumed a person's energy, and not just immediately available energy, but *life* energy.

I'd never known a book to lie, but I couldn't imagine its applications otherwise. *Ruby was giving part of her existence to draw me a bath? Chevelle and Steed forfeited time for a silly instructional match?* It couldn't have been right.

I tried to recall the magic I'd seen in the village, though it was still clouded with fog. The youngsters played carelessly, often until they collapsed from exhaustion. But the elders were reserved. I couldn't remember them using it for anything that could have been done with less physical energy. They hunted with weapons, wrote with their hands, and worked as if they took pleasure in it—maybe there was no energy left for magic, or maybe it was unimportant until one reached the close of one's years and realized it was almost gone. I remembered how long a thousand years had seemed to me before I planned on spending it in a prison.

Ruby walked in, and I snapped the book shut, positive I shouldn't have taken it from her table without permission. One glance at her stifled reaction told me that I would not be able to ask her about what I'd read.

"Sleep well?" she asked.

"Oh," I said with a start, my voice hoarse.

She handed me a glass of water, which she smoothly traded for the book.

"Dreams," I complained.

She smiled as she sat on the bed beside me. "Some seek out the breath. They say it is foresight."

"Foresight?"

She nodded. "What did you see?" She raised an eyebrow questioningly.

"Not the future."

She laughed. "Have a bath. You'll be good as new." The water was filling the basin again, and I wondered about what I had just read. Surely the dust and fog were meddling with my thoughts. "Chevelle will be swapping with us for the evening," she explained.***

The bath refreshed me, but unfortunately, it also cleared my mind. *No wonder Ruby drugged me.* I tried not to think about the tracker as I dressed. The smell of the cold morning hung in the air, and I felt a pang of guilt at using the fragrance again, knowing Chevelle would be there. I appraised myself in the mirror and smiled then shook my head, certain the dust was still influencing me.

When I walked into the main room, Chevelle was sitting on the bench seat, leaning over as he worked on something. He raised his head as I approached, closing his hand around whatever it was before sliding it into a pocket. He seemed mildly anxious.

I was still feeling peculiar, so I climbed into the seat beside him, curling my feet up close. He watched me, his eyes lingering even after I had settled. It felt as if he yearned to say something.

The tension became too much, and I broke. "Ruby drugged me."

He gave me a half smile. "She told me. She was worried about your sanity." The last word cracked. He appeared to regret saying it.

"Did she tell you"—I wasn't sure I should be admitting it—"I read her book?"

"Yes."

He wasn't offering any information. I would have to ask. The dust must have given me courage. "It talked about exchange." Still nothing. "About energy... life... for magic."

He cleared his throat. "Yes."

"Can you tell me about it?"

"Today, after Anvil sparred with Steed, you saw how the strike drained him. This is something you'll need to know for a group conflict. The tactics are different than one on one." He hadn't answered my question at all, but he was talking, and I would take it. I nodded for him to go on. "A single opponent allows you to use more energy and focus only on that and let yourself..."

My thoughts were wandering. *Cursed dust.*

"... but with a number of opponents, you have to conserve your energy so you don't leave yourself too weak..."

I was watching his mouth move as he spoke but lost the words. I couldn't focus.

"... tactics that do not drain your energy. Protect yourself..."

I was leaning toward him, my gaze tracing the lines of his face.

"... even hand-to-hand combat or choose a weapon. Ruby's whip, a staff..."

Cursed Ruby.

"Frey."

"Hm?"

He shook his head. "Never mind."

I was angled toward him and could feel myself moving. A voice in the back of my mind was screaming *stop,* but it was too late. I had closed in on his lips. I was close enough that my intent was unmistakable when he grabbed me, wrapping both arms around my biceps in a too-tight grip. "Freya—"

There was a howl. *A wolf.*

He let out a deep breath, and it tickled my nose. *Oh. Oh, no. No, no, no.* My head cleared, but Chevelle still held me around the arms. My neck flushed, my eyes shooting to my lap. I couldn't look at him. *What am I doing?*

The door opened, and Chevelle's hands dropped as he stood to face the newcomer.

"They are here." It was Steed's voice, but I didn't raise my head. The blood was still hot in my cheeks.

"Take her to the ridge. I will meet you after—" Chevelle stopped midsentence.

After what?

Steed must have been concerned, because Chevelle explained. "Ruby gave her a little dust to relax."

"Frey," Steed said from beside me.

I glanced at the door. Chevelle was already gone.

"Are you well?"

"Ugh."

He snickered. "Come on." He swept me up, clearly planning to carry me.

My head spun. "No. Please let me walk."

"You don't tolerate that stuff well. You're going to have to lay off the shimmer."

"It's not like I chose to take it," I complained.

He laughed.

THE COLD AIR HELPED A LITTLE. I was back in the circle—the group of us sat around a small fire. Ruby was telling stories. She related the tale of Bonnie Bell, a blue fairy from the East. "He hunts the human children, luring them in with glitter and lights, and eats them, beginning with their tiny little toes. Though he gives no choice in the matter, in exchange, he allows the mother one wish."

I scoffed. "Humans aren't real."

"Even so," she continued, smiling wickedly, "you'd be surprised by how many don't think to wish for their children back."

Raucous laughter floated up around the ring. *Fey tales, indeed.*

It felt good being there, surrounded by my new companions, a fire and stories, and laughter. It felt like more of a home than Fannie's had ever been. But I was also under the influence of a fey.

"Better yet?" Ruby asked.

I grimaced.

Grey approached. "Ruby, dear, won't you allow us to partake?"

"Speak for yourself," Anvil cracked from across the fire. "Last time, I lost a bit of tongue." I cringed and remembered my dream. I thought I could still smell burning flesh.

Ruby laughed. "Ah, well... I suppose just this once."

Grey sat, his rough brown boots resting among the stone, and she leaned over him as if for a kiss. Her lips stopped just short of his, and their eyes connected as a glint of firelight caught the shimmer. Grey breathed it in. As she pulled away, his fingers trailed slowly off her arm, and I felt I was intruding, so I averted my eyes.

Steed gave me a gentle smile beside me. *I like Steed. He's a good guy.* I shook my head to clear it. *Cursed dust.*

Ruby joined us.

"Do the effects last longer sometimes?" I asked.

"It depends."

"On what?" It seemed like an obvious follow-up.

"Your mood."

I was irritated all over again but got distracted when she licked the point of an arrow. "What are you doing?"

She grinned. "Look, Frey, I don't know if you're up for this story right now." I didn't think she was funny. She sighed. "All right, but you'll probably regret it."

"Just give her the short version, Ruby," Steed interrupted. "No gory details." His eyebrow cocked meaningfully.

"Oh well, yes, that would do." She smiled at me as she licked another arrow, her tongue sliding carefully along the blade. "You see, my dear, being a one of a kind—well, as far as I know—has its benefits. Though they weren't always benefits. In the beginning it was bad, but, well, that's the long version, isn't it? No gory details." She winked at Steed. "I am, how should I put it? Venomous."

I gasped.

It was obviously the response she expected. "Yes, yes. I know." She held her tongue out for me to examine. As she pressed another arrow against it, tiny slits opened up and released a translucent liquid. "Not really venom, per se. All fey have it, a chemical to help break down their food. It's just that mine is toxic to many. Not to worry, though. I have pretty good control of it now. Nasty, poisonous stuff." She laughed again. "You know, that's what Chevelle thought I intended the first time I dusted you."

I recalled the panic in his voice before he whisked her away. As disastrous a night as that had been, this one wasn't much better.

"Ruby, please take Frey back to the house." Chevelle was standing behind us. I was too exhausted to jump, but Ruby merely glanced back at him, not at all surprised he was there.

Her face crinkled. "Didn't go well?"

He didn't respond but was obviously frustrated. I couldn't tell if it was with Ruby or whatever hadn't gone well. *Or the idiotic offspring of his parents' murderer who tried to seduce him in a drunken stupor.* It didn't matter. I was being removed again.

Ruby rambled about all of the difficulties with and uses for venom on our way back. She'd gotten so involved in her stories that I thought she must have forgotten I was there. Her last words confirmed it. "No one knew to check. How would they? I mean, a new species. A new breed. And lethal. Poison to her mother. They couldn't even know that was what had happened until the others. Until the pattern became patent and they found the source."

I stared at Ruby, imagining the nameless others who'd been taken by her venom before they discovered its root.

But it was not the idea of those strangers that tightened my chest. *Poison. To her mother.*

My dreams were wicked that night, all venom and wolves, snakes and beasts, death and fire. I awoke in my bed, light filtering in through the window. The door was open a crack, and I could see Chevelle sitting in the front room. I was hesitant to face him.

I lay there, running back through the events of the night and the stories. Embarrassment flooded me again, and I turned my head to bury it in the blankets, but something strange on the side table caught my attention. I picked it up and examined it—it was a small bird carved of stone. A hawk made of onyx.

I knew at once that it was what Chevelle had been carving. And then I recognized the stone, the large black stone that had pummeled my body for days, and I couldn't help but snicker. I remembered the tiny hawk he had made with magic and my disappointment when it had turned back into a dull gray rock. He had carved me the symbol with his own hands.

I was completely ashamed of my actions the previous night.

I closed my hand around it and noticed the painting on my wrist of a hawk. I knew I had to face him. The carving might have been a peace offering, and it might be my last chance. I stood and walked into the main room, clutching the figure in my fist for courage.

Chevelle was not alone.

A statuesque elf with pitch-black hair and eyes rose as I entered, not in the respectful a-guest-has-entered-the room way, but in a way that led me to believe he wasn't happy to have me, or anyone, find him there. He gripped a long staff so tightly that his knuckles whitened, and he was dressed in casual traveling clothes that didn't seem to fit his posture.

I found myself questioning whether it was a disguise, then I chastised myself for wandering around in ridiculous thoughts so often. They were watching me. *Cursed brain fog.*

I stood there for a moment, unsure if I should leave the room after I had so obviously interrupted or pretend I had a mission and make my way to Ruby's room. I clearly wasn't welcome there. Neither Chevelle nor his guest spoke, so I lowered my gaze to the floor and took the shortest route to Ruby's door, closing it hastily behind me.

Chevelle said something to his guest, and I groaned internally, wishing I'd heard their low voices earlier. Asher, as Chevelle had called the man, was apparently leaving. It sounded as if Chevelle was trying to persuade him in some way, but the man was short and cold in his responses. Quiet, too. I imagined he didn't want me to hear them. My mind accused me of paranoia.

I heard the front door close as I flopped onto the bed only to jolt upright when Ruby's door opened a few seconds later. It was Chevelle.

My courage was gone again. He seemed to be waiting for me to speak. I tried. "I'm sorry I interrupted…"

He nodded, but I didn't know if he was acknowledging my interruption or pardoning it.

He walked slowly toward the bed, glancing at Ruby's things on the shelves and walls, then sat on the bed beside me. I forced myself to continue breathing and kept my gaze down, knowing a flush was coming.

He reached out and placed a hand under my chin, bringing my

face to meet his. The flush that followed was not from embarrassment. Heat flooded my neck, and I felt it might engulf me as he spoke my name.

"Frey."

"Yes." It was all I could manage.

His eyes held mine, and I could swear he was searching for something. He opened his mouth to speak, but the door of the wardrobe flew open.

"Oh." Ruby giggled a tiny bit. "Excuse me. I didn't mean to interrupt." She seemed pleased that she had.

Chevelle's hand dropped, and his face was hard.

Ruby continued, "Steed said you had a guest, so I just used the back..." She trailed off when his stare didn't soften, but she smiled. "You know, you do have your own room."

He stiffened and stood, not at all amused by her implication.

Ruby began gathering things as she spoke, pretending she hadn't noticed his attitude. "So how did it go?"

He relaxed a little, but his mood didn't seem to rise in the least. "We shall see."

"Indeed," she purred. "Indeed."

He didn't look back at me as he left the room, simply directing Ruby to take me with her when she'd finished. She seemed more than happy to comply, and didn't doubt that we would be training again. I slid the hawk sculpture into my pocket.

She hummed as she gathered her things, throwing a cloak at me in the process.

I tied it on and drew the hood up. "Want me to carry anything?"

She eyed me as if I was entirely absurd. "Well, if you would like to, I can find something for you." I glared at her back, and she turned to grab my arm beneath the cloak, yanking me behind her as we left the house through her closet. She replaced the cover that hid the entrance and snatched a quiver of arrows from the ground before pulling me forward again.

"What are those for?" I asked, afraid they would somehow be used in my training.

"They are arrows, Frey." She was really on a roll, in a delightful mood. I shook my head, certain that it didn't bode well for me, and she laughed. "We are leaving them for Rhys and Rider to find."

"Are they poisoned?"

"Yes."

I considered that. "Did they use all the ones you prepared last night?"

"You're silly, Freya. It's fun." The way she pronounced my name, like it was dear to her, made it harder to be angry with her.

But I made the effort. "It's not entirely my fault." I huffed. But then I was sorry I'd said anything. I didn't need to defend myself to her.

"I know," she said, "but it's still fun."

I wondered if she did know, as everyone before had. I pushed the thought from my head and stepped over a pile of loose rocks. "I thought the dogs were their weapons of choice," I said, cringing a bit as I remembered their demonstration.

"Wolves, Frey. And they aren't weapons."

"They don't use them to attack?"

She spoke like she was explaining something simple to a child. "Yes, the wolves attack, but not as weapons and not by command of the elves. The wolves attack who they want. Protect who they want."

"They don't control them?"

"No, silly. No one can control animals." She cocked an eyebrow at me speculatively.

"But—"

"All right, well, sure, you can lead an animal. You can turn your horse and guide him on the path, but that is simply pushing their heads and encouraging them with the click of your heels. You can't make them choose to take you—it just doesn't work that way. You can't get into an animal's mind and make them behave the way you want them to."

"But the dogs—wolves—follow them. They had them do a demonstration, and—"

"No, Frey. The wolves do not follow the elves. The wolves protect them by choice."

"By choice?"

"Yes. And I have seen them tear an elf apart as quickly as defend them."

I shivered.

"Rhys and Rider were saved by the wolves once. They think the animals understand. They follow the wolves, you see. That is why they are here." We topped the ridge. Jagged rock and loose dirt shifted beneath our feet, and Ruby dropped the quiver by the edge before climbing down with a deftness I had yet to master.

Steed, Anvil, and Grey greeted us before we resumed training. I tried to keep my mind off the wolves, off the reason I was learning magic, off the encounter with Chevelle, and off all of the terrible things it kept returning to, and I was grateful for the fog that clouded my thoughts.

Though I wasn't exactly winning matches, I was getting better. I'd learned to use my fire with more precision, and I'd improved immensely moving objects, mostly in defense and to shield strikes. The battering continued, and long days of constant fighting were making me tired. We took a break, and I leaned back on a rock, staring at the sky as I rested.

CHEVELLE WALKED me to the edge of a tall peak. The rock mountain ended in a sheer cliff, straight down into haze. He looked into my eyes as if he saw something there, as if he really knew me. We gazed out over the cliff at the endless horizon. I felt his hand on my back and closed my eyes, relaxing into the comfortable, familiar feel of it.

He pushed me with full force. I flew off the cliff, falling straight down. I stared back at him as he stood, watching me fall, with nothing but open sky above and below. I couldn't imagine why he'd throw me from the cliff, couldn't think of the magic to stop myself, and couldn't see when I would crash into the rocks below.

My arms flailed as I jerked awake. The group stared at me.

"Frey?" Ruby asked.

I grappled for breath. "Just a dream." A few chuckles moved through the crowd.

Ruby was more interested. "What about?"

I glanced at Chevelle, a few paces away. He had the same concerned expression as they waited for my answer. I only shook my head.

My chest still ached from panic. I sat up and took a drink of wine from the flagon, wondering whether anyone drank water anymore.

When Grey sat beside me, I tried to mask my surprise. "Ruby a little hard on you?" he teased. I smiled. "She's only trying to help, you know." He spoke with tenderness, and I recalled how they'd touched each other nights before.

I made an effort not to be too obvious about my real curiosity. "You've known her long?"

"Forever." The way he gazed at her when he spoke left no doubt.

She noticed us watching her. "Ready to get back to it, then?"

I grimaced, struggling to my feet. "Ruby, how long will the effects of the dust last?"

"Depends." It was the same answer she'd given me before.

I couldn't decide if I was truly that out of it or if everyone thought it was funny to make me drag answers from them. "On?"

She laughed. "Don't worry. The dreams will get better."

"They will get better or they will go away?"

She laughed again. "Depends."

WE WERE FACING each other once more, ready to begin another round. "Want to try a weapon?"

I was pretty sure I didn't, give how much the weaponless training hurt. I opted for a delaying tactic. "Why use arrows if you have magic?"

She had that Frey-you're-an-imbecile look again. "Magic uses more energy the farther away you are when you try to focus it. And it is less accurate. And you are more visible. And—"

I held up a hand. "All right, I have it."

She smiled. "Any more questions, or can we begin?"

"Fine. What sort of weapon did you have in mind?"

Her smile widened. Her hand stretched out to the side, and a long, silver sword came from the pile of gear to land in her palm. She righted it, twisting the blade for me to see.

My stomach dropped.

"There are a few things you need to remember when using a blade," she instructed. "First of all, always go for the fatal attack. If you merely wound someone, well, someone with magic will use the last of their power to stop you. Cut off their head or puncture the lungs and heart. Never mess around."

I imagined myself decapitating someone. I laughed as I realized my mind placed Fannie on the other side of my blade.

Ruby didn't look like she could think of anything funny about what she'd said, but she continued. "Secondly, don't cut yourself. These things are sharp."

She moved to toss the sword to me but reconsidered and handed it over, making sure I had a good grip. There were intricate designs carved on the handle and runes etched in the blade. It wasn't as heavy as it appeared. I moved it around a bit, slashing wide arcs though the chilly air. It was pleasant, nicely balanced in my hand. That didn't mean I could actually cut through someone's neck, though. "Ruby, how do you intend to teach me with this? I mean if there's no messing around, just lop your head off and all?"

She laughed. "Don't worry, Frey. I think I can handle you."

"I'll do it." Chevelle's voice startled me. I'd been absorbed in our conversation, unaware that anyone was listening. I glanced around and realized *everyone* had been listening.

It dawned on me what Chevelle had said as they all circled around to watch. Ruby smiled at him, making me instantly suspicious that she had set it up. A long sword was already in his hand as he approached. He raised it, expertly gripping the hilt with both hands. My mouth went dry, a vague part of my brain only managing a weak *uh-oh.*

Fear rushed through me, and I wrapped my fists around the grip of my own sword, praying I could protect myself. A smile was the only warning Chevelle gave before his blade cut the air. Instinct took over, and I flung my arms up to block his swing with my own. The metal clashed, and I felt the shock vibrate through me even as the peal pulsed in my ears. He struck again, and I pulled the sword back, twisting to block another shot. I straightened and raised it again, surprised at how powerful I felt the moment before releasing my blow. I smiled as I swung at him, sure he would stop me but reveling in being attacker instead of victim.

He wound his blade around mine, a metallic screech filling my ears as he knocked my strike aside before coming back at me. We continued, blow after blow, the repetitive clank forming a pattern in my head. Chevelle seemed to be enjoying himself as the exercise increased in intensity. I found I was as well. I'd taken no direct beatings like my other training, and I wasn't getting exhausted the way I did when I tried to use magic. I could see why they all carried weapons.

Chevelle pushed harder, assaulting me with faster and stronger swings. I was able to defend myself if I focused. Murmurs of approval floated in from our audience, and I enjoyed that more than I probably should have. I concentrated hard and began throwing a few good hits of my own in with the blocks. Our swords clashed repeatedly, neither of us hitting the mark. Certainly, he could have, but I felt confident that I was blocking well.

We continued until I became winded, then Chevelle lowered his blade, smiling with approval. Our audience commented on the show, and I glanced around to see that it was evening already—the sun had begun to set. I wondered how long we'd sparred. I could suddenly feel the ache in my arms, the sword hanging limp at my side.

Ruby took it from my hand. "We'll get you fitted with a sheath."

I stood there, facing Chevelle, breathless but grinning. He was smiling appreciatively. I realized we were still being watched and sheepishly turned from him to join the group as they prepared a fire for dinner. The evening was filled with stories and laughter. Chevelle's eyes fell on me often, and he seemed in better spirits in general, which made me wonder again about his morning guest.

Rhys and Rider approached, and most of the group went to meet them. Steed moved to sit beside me. "Very nice today, Frey," he observed. "You seem to be a natural."

I snorted.

Across the fire, Grey leaned over to speak in Ruby's ear. Steed noticed me scrutinize them, so I asked, "Are they... together?" I was confident in Grey's affection, but they didn't act like a traditional pair.

Steed sighed as we watched them. "No."

There seemed to be more to his answer. "But he..." I wasn't sure how to phrase it.

"Yes." Steed glanced back at me when he spoke. "But you can't always have the one you want, Frey." His voice was soft, yearning.

I could never tell if he was teasing. "I heard once you could die from grief."

He smiled at my subject change. "It's true. I've seen it myself."

"Tell me about it."

"No, too sad." He was thoughtful for a moment. "I worried... about my father." His eyes returned to me. "After my mother died. Sometimes, I'm grateful for the fire witch's seduction. He was grieving so hard..." His expression lost all trace of its usual cockiness as he brought back the memory. "Her enchantments numbed him. Then, when he woke from them, the tragedy gave him purpose." A shadow of his smile returned as he looked away. "The irony is that her tragedy gained roots from the idea—"

"Frey." Chevelle was suddenly standing between us.

I gaped up at him, the trance of Steed's words broken. "Huh?"

"Time to go." There was anger in his voice. I didn't know what I had done, but I stood obediently. Chevelle pulled me away from Steed.

"I'll take her," Ruby offered.

"No. I'll do it myself." I sensed a lot of anger.

"We'll both go," she pushed, biting the words out. The rest of the group was quiet, watching us, and Ruby eyed Steed as we turned and headed toward the house.

As soon as we were out of earshot, though I was still being dragged by the arm, I asked Chevelle, "Did something happen with the twins?"

Ruby laughed. We both stared at her. "Twins," she said with a scoff.

"Right, well, you know what I mean," I said, embarrassed.

Chevelle's tone softened. "No. Everything is fine."

Ruby chimed in: "It *is* fine," and I knew it was intended for him. He relaxed his grip on my arm and slowed our pace as he directed an almost imperceptible nod at Ruby. I relaxed, too—*fine* was better than anything I'd thought in a long while.

Chevelle stayed in the front room that night, watching through the small windows. When I closed my eyes, I could see the glint of swords making patterns as they crossed again and again. Ruby's hummed tune was sad, the sound drifting through the walls between us as I fell into an easy sleep.

Chevelle and Ruby's voices, low and confrontational, woke me. I rubbed my tired arms as I rose to join them in the front room.

"What's going on?" I asked, though I could tell they'd been arguing.

Ruby grinned at me. "Just planning for the trip."

"Trip?"

"Yes, you know, to the peak." She was scheming.

"Oh." I decided I'd let them work it out, heading instead to Ruby's room. "I'm going to take a bath."

As I closed the door, Ruby said, "It's time to tell her." I didn't hear a response. I was soaking in hot water, my eyes closed, not even considering getting out, when there was a knock on the door.

"What, Ruby?"

She giggled. "How did you know it was me?" She didn't wait for me to explain that no one else was that annoying before asking, "Can I come in?"

"No."

The water streamed from the tub, and I swore. "Fine, I'm getting dressed." I dried off, gathering clothes from a pile I assumed was for me, as they were too large for Ruby's petite frame.

I opened the door and knew right away that I would regret whatever they were about to tell me. Ruby commanded me to sit.

Chevelle straightened, clearing his throat. "Frey, we need to talk with you about something." I waited uneasily, and he proceeded carefully. "You know you are partially bound."

"Yes," I agreed, even though I wasn't clear how that worked. I could use some magic, and I had lost some memories. I couldn't really remember anything from before the village except the dreams.

"And I'm sure you want to be unbound?"

Why is that even a question? "Of course."

He nodded as if he were going down a checklist. "We know Council has bound you."

I waited for the next detail, my fingers curling into my palms.

"And we know they must be the one or ones to unbind you."

Some part of me realized the seriousness of the conversation, but all I could do was listen.

"They are obviously... unwilling."

The breath I drew was too sharp.

"I know some about the binding. I've studied it."

When he stopped, I said, "All right." I didn't know what he was getting at.

"The problem is... meddling with the bindings, meddling with your mind is... well, it's dangerous."

And there it was. "Dangerous," I repeated.

They let me consider that for a moment. They were being careful with me, obviously not wanting to upset me. I tried to ease them. "So we go back to the village and..."

They shared an uncomfortable glance. "Not High Council, Freya. *Grand* Council."

Oh, right. The ones who are trying to capture me. The ones who want to burn me.

Their cautious demeanor made more sense all of a sudden. Council had sent trackers—the pair Chevelle had choked and released and the other, the broken, limp corpse in the clearing by the ridge. We had killed him. *And they're worried about my stupid binding?*

The circling cloaks from my dreams were back, filling my head. My thoughts were twisting out of control. They would be hunting us all down. They would kill us. That was why I needed training, to protect myself, because they intended to kill me, not capture me. They intended to kill us all. And without magic, bound as I was, I didn't stand a chance.

My anxiety must have shown. Ruby shifted her jaw.

"No." I held up a hand up to stop her. "No more dust." I stood. "Let's just get back to training."

They didn't argue, though they were plainly concerned.

We went to the ridge with the others, but we didn't train. In fact, I was fairly certain Ruby and Chevelle were avoiding me. I waited through the morning, and finally, around midday, I gave up and relaxed onto the ground, staring up at the sky. The earth beneath me was warm, the sun shining brightly. I watched as a bird flew high overhead. It was gliding slowly and steadily on the wind.

As I shielded my eyes with a hand, I noticed the ink on my wrist and smiled. I suddenly knew the soaring creature above was a hawk. I closed my eyes and relaxed my arm at my side, imagining flying. I breathed deeply and conjured the image it would see, looking down on us.

The picture was sharp, even at that distance, but the colors weren't as clear, the outlying shapes not as defined. I laughed at myself for adding that detail to my daydream, imagining a bird seeing differently.

My vision sailed over us, past the ridge, south. I imagined seeing the twins, perched in two trees, watching. Hardwood bows rested high on their backs. The wolves were mostly concealed on the ground, vigilant. One glanced up at me, at the bird. Someone approached, robe and tassels blowing in the cool breeze. The second wolf looked forward. He saw it too and abruptly pointed, calling out.

But the howl echoed in my ears, not in my imagination, and I jolted upright. The field was in motion, rushing in response to the warning. In seconds, they were set again in the same protective positions they had taken the last time a tracker had found us.

It was all I could do to steady myself as the councilman was brought forward, because he was the same one from my vision. I was in shock as he knelt, not under his own power, and was frozen there before us. *How could I have seen him?*

Chevelle mumbled something, and my ears began to ring, distracting me from my bewilderment. After only a few stuttered heartbeats, recognition came.

"Stop!" I hissed. All eyes turned to me, but I glared at Chevelle. "Stop," I repeated.

He understood. My ears ceased ringing, and my hearing cleared. I stepped forward, the rage still fuming. I felt like a fool for not realizing before. He had been the cause of my hearing issues, and he was the one holding the tracker there. Chevelle had bound the man from magic for questioning. He had studied it and said he knew something about it.

I was so furious that I forgot my own situation. It felt untethered, as if I was outside myself, watching as I approached the kneeling tracker and daring anyone to stop me. "Tell me what you know about binding."

He didn't answer, his jaw tight in defiance. The sword sat in my newly acquired sheath, and I drew it out, taking a peculiar sort of delight in the *ssshk* that sounded when the steel passed through. The others watched me, silent and wary, but the tracker only smirked. He wasn't afraid of a sword. The last tracker hadn't given at broken bones, not even before the threat of certain death. I would need something dreadful, a new tactic to convince him.

A tiny snake sunning on a nearby rock caught my attention, and I smiled. Even in my denial, some part of me knew what had happened before. I had felt it and knew I could do it again.

I slipped the tip of the sword down to the tracker's leg, just above where his knee met the ground, and sliced his trousers up to the thigh to reveal bare skin. Drawing the snake close with magic, I took it in my hand, its thin green body writhing over my left palm, the sword grasped in my right. The prisoner watched me, almost smug.

It was a small snake, its white belly confirming it was nonvenomous, its frame no thicker than my pinkie, but it would do. I slid the tip of the sword across the skin above the man's knee, making a narrow incision. His expression did change then, giving way to uncertainty. I smiled at him as the sword tip rested against his leg. In measured movements, I placed the snake on the base of the blade, letting it slide toward its mark. I closed my eyes to relax and settle into the snake, as I had the bird.

My knees buckled as I released too much, and I had to back off, giving myself just enough to control it. As it entered the wound, the tracker gasped, and my smile stretched wickedly. I wormed my way blindly up his leg, intent on getting the information I needed.

They're getting closer. They've found us a third time now. They'll kill us. I wanted to free my mind, free my bonds. *They won't take me.*

Something about that last thought didn't seem right, as though it wasn't mine, but I couldn't follow it. The tracker screamed—it had reached his thigh. My eyes flicked open. The body of the snake made a lump under the skin of the tracker's leg. His face was contorted in agony, but that wasn't what had made him shout. It was the fear. He had cracked. Chevelle released the tracker's hand long enough for the man to scribble a few words of a spell but didn't allow him to speak or cast magic.

He slumped after his surrender, clearly confident the worst was over. I reached the sword tip back to his leg and made another incision to release the snake. It jerked and coiled free of the wound, flicking blood over the tracker's pristine white robe. Behind me, a low voice ordered, "Kill him."

I glanced down at the sword, still in my hand, the sword I was supposed to take someone's head off with. I didn't know who the order had been intended for, but it wasn't me. The man was going to die. I knew he didn't have more than a moment before their magic broke him. They would take his life because he was after us, after me.

I didn't hesitate. I pulled my arm up and swung hard, backhand. The blade cut cleanly, and his head rolled backward, hitting the ground with a sickening thud.

I looked away.

The others stared at me, stunned. I couldn't blame them.

Steed's voice was low and wary. "He didn't mean you, Frey."

I turned, unable to stand the blood in my peripheral vision. The tracker's words waited in Chevelle's hand. "All right," I said, feeling detached from myself. "Let's try it."

Chevelle's disbelief was more than evident as he shot back, "No."

Ruby spoke up. "It could be a trick. He'll need to try it on someone else first."

Someone else? Who else was bound?

She could see I was prepared to argue. "It isn't safe."

"And if it doesn't work?"

She didn't answer. I remembered the story of her father then, and how he'd been released after the fey woman's death.

I faced Chevelle. "If the council member who bound me dies, then will I be released?"

He plainly regretted what he'd divulged that morning, but something else rested just below his reluctance, something hopeful that burned beneath my skin. "Yes."

"Then we kill them." *And if we don't know which ones?*

"We kill them all."

I glanced around the clearing as the others watched me. The atmosphere had changed, and I realized only then the uncertainty I'd grown to expect from them. It was different. It was reverence.

Anvil smiled. Something had happened that I didn't understand, a wave of sentiment at my actions, and it was far from condemnation.

A movement at the tree line caught everyone's attention, and I turned to find Chevelle's onetime guest, Asher. He stood in the shadows, his staff in hand, as if allowing us to see. The air was still as he inclined his head toward Chevelle then turned, a long, dark braid whipping behind him as he disappeared into the brush. It seemed to mean something to the group—they seemed relieved.

I stared after him, but Anvil stepped forward, thumping his balled fist against his chest in a gesture I didn't understand. Grey followed, repeating the action and adding a single nod, and Ruby clasped her hands, bouncing excitedly from heel to toe. I felt myself drawing back together, tied by the knots in my stomach and mind. A tandem wolf howl sounded in the distance.

My stomach swam in unease.

12

The councilman's body was disposed of, and the group bustled around the clearing. I slid my sword into its sheath, careful not to touch the blade. I hadn't comprehended what the flourish of activity meant until Ruby grabbed my arm to conduct me. "Come on. We have to pack."

She dragged me along as she rushed back to her house. She threw things around her room, sorting and gathering. I didn't have anything to assemble. There was only the pack I'd acquired months ago with nothing in it but that stupid white dress and the pouch... *The pouch.*

I hurried from the room, explaining to Ruby that I would be getting ready for the trip.

"I already put your pack in the front room for Chevelle."

"I'll just check it," I said. "Thanks."

I found the pack with some of Chevelle's things in it. As I started to open it, I knocked one of his bags over then went to pick it up. The flap was loose, and a piece of familiar fabric hung out. I glanced over my shoulder to be sure Ruby wasn't watching and opened the bag to find the fabric-wrapped package she'd handed to Chevelle our first day there, the package he'd traded my stone for. I pulled the material back to reveal a leather-bound book. Afraid Ruby would catch me, I slid the book into my own pack and took it to my room.

I'd already been in trouble for stealing one book, but this was technically mine. It had been swapped for my ruby. I was careful anyway, pretending to lie down and placing the book where I could quickly cover it if I were caught. I ran my fingers over the dark leather cover, tracing the scripted V etched there. *Vattier?* The first pages had been torn from the bindings, so I flipped through, finding several more damaged sections, some torn, some by water. I sighed. It wasn't any more than I expected. It felt like everything I touched was destroyed.

I returned to the first page and began reading.

TODAY WAS the solstice celebration for the fey. They are such fools. They got hopped up on dust and raided the castle. We had to kill at least six of them before they sobered up enough to reason with. That was before Father killed two more just for fun. He said he had to prove a point, but I could tell he enjoyed it.

I STRAIGHTENED AND BLINKED. *What* is *this?* I shook my head and continued.

MY STUPID SISTER was mad because he didn't let her help. She started to throw a tantrum, and he stiffened her tongue. It was stuck like that for hours. I laughed so hard I kept having to wipe the tears from my eyes. She tried to yell at me, and it came out, "Thut uhp! Thop iht!" Which made me laugh harder, and she got so mad she screamed and busted a bunch of glass.

I KEPT READING, enthralled. It seemed to be a journal written by a girl, but I had no idea who. It could have been someone in Chevelle's family, but I couldn't figure out why he would have a young girl's diary. It was filled with pointless stories as far as I could tell, but after a few pages, it seemed to jump several years, and the writing matured. I wished it had been dated.

I TIRE SO EASILY of the formalities here. The only thing I have to look forward to are the few breaks I get to go out on my own into the pines. Father has increased my work periods to every other day. Combined with my other duties, I am stationed in the castle almost all week. The magic practice exhausts me, or I would sneak out at night, the way I enjoyed as a child. It doesn't seem fair. My sister is practically ignored. Father clearly prefers me, but sometimes I wonder if that is really better. She wanders idly around the castle, no practice, no duties, no formal gatherings.

MAGIC PRACTICE, castles—*who is this girl?* I read the entries for hours while Ruby gathered supplies and made her arrangements. I had no idea what in this journal could have been of interest to Chevelle unless he knew the woman, and that kept me reading. For as much time as I'd spent with him, it still felt as if I knew very little, as if a part of him was missing. It continued with her father's rigorous schedule and their distaste for her sister, and then the entries got more detailed and frequent.

MOTHER HAS BEEN TOO ILL LATELY for guests. I have not been able to see her. The tedium of my duties is getting to me, and Father has been relentless with my studies, pushing me harder and harder to strengthen my control.

My sister has been exploring the mountains. I see her bring in all sorts of interesting finds, but she refuses to tell me where she got them. I wish there were a way to sneak out. I would follow her or force her to show me, but Father is keeping a close eye on me, making certain I stick to a strict schedule.

This morning, he brought in a detailed list for Rune, giving him direction through a series of tasks. Rune is supposed to grade me on them and see which I excel most at so they can pick a specific field to concentrate on. I don't know how extensive it was, but I saw "wind," "water," "growth," "transfer," "fire," and "foresight" written as it passed between them.

We had already done months of fire. Pass it through water, see how large a flame I can create, see how hot I can go, test me on this, test me on that. And now, he asks Rune to test me in the impossible, to see the future.

He expects too much. Merely because I am different. My sister is different too. But she never has to practice. He doesn't expect her to stay in the castle, not even when we have guests. No doubt he prefers her not be seen, embarrassed by her light hair and features. It is infuriating! I wish I were as strong as he hoped. I could do what I wanted, then.

THERE WAS a clank of metal in the front room and talk of horses. Ruby complained of a delay—apparently, they were waiting on a meeting before we could leave, and from that meeting came some sort of guarantee. Ruby did not seem to have the patience for it. I yawned and rolled over, flipping another page of the book.

I ATTEMPTED SLIPPING in to see Mother this morning, but the doors were protected. Father found me trying to break through and sent me directly to Rune for practice. At least I got out of my duties in the throne room. We started with water. I was so exhausted that I had to sleep through most of the afternoon before they brought me back to work again in the evening. Every muscle in my body throbs. I think I hate Rune.

A SERVANT BROUGHT a letter to my room this morning. It was from my father, informing me I'm to prepare for a banquet. I've put on my formal attire. I wonder what sort of tricks he'll want me to perform for our guests. How will he display my talents this time?

I understand he needs to show strength in his position, but it seems as if he's being a bit obvious. "Look at my aberration. See what she can do?" I'll be too tired for anything but sleep tonight, or I'd try sneaking out when he's occupied with visitors. Maybe he'll give me a break from training tomorrow.

~

Father hasn't left his room this morning. No one has seen him since the conclusion of the festivities. My sister has sealed herself in her room. No one will tell me what has occurred.

~

Late last night, a servant brought a note from my father. It was four words long... "Your mother has passed."

I am still in my room. I guess I am waiting. I don't know what will happen.

I heard a noise in the front room and slid the book under a pillow, dropped my head, and pretended to sleep. I'd been so absorbed in the book that I had no idea how long I'd been reading. There was a light rap on my door.

My voice was hoarse. "Yes?"

"Frey, I'm on my way to the ridge. We will be leaving in the morning." Ruby's words confused me. I must have read well into the night.

"All right."

"Steed is here. You can stay with him or go with me."

"I'll stay." I listened to her footsteps recede. When I was sure she was gone, I slipped the book into my pack and hid it inside the material of the white gown. We would be leaving soon, traveling to the peak. I laughed to myself—no matter how many times I said it, I had no clue what it meant, but I suddenly felt a sense of urgency. No matter if it held safety, no matter if it held my family secrets, it held my escape from the bonds. It held my only chance.

I hadn't slept, and I knew I would have to sneak a nap in at some point, but I had priorities. It might be my last opportunity for a real bath. *And lovely soaps.*

I SAT with Steed for a while after I'd bathed. He was reclined on the bench, his feet propped on a low table. He didn't seem as excited as Ruby had been about our coming trip, so I asked him about it.

"I'm just riding the wind, Frey."

"Oh, so you don't know where we're going either?"

He laughed. "No, I know where we are going. It's only that I don't know where we'll end up."

I didn't know what was going to happen, either. I thought of the tracker and realized what a good distraction the book had been. "Steed?"

"Frey?"

I smiled but it fell away quickly. "How will we get to Council? I mean, how do we find them?"

His smile dropped too. "Well, there's a good chance they'll be looking for us."

Of course, and they'll all come together. It was clear we were too strong for one or two—they would need to attack as a group or pick us off one by one. I wondered how large their force was.

"Frey?"

"Steed?" It wasn't as funny this time.

"How did you do it?"

I raised my brow, unsure what he was asking.

"The snake," he clarified.

"Oh. I-I don't know."

"Was it transfer magic? Did you simply push it there?"

I didn't know how I'd controlled it, but it wasn't from the outside. *Should I tell him?* "How else?" I asked innocently.

He nodded. "Some of the others, well, they seem to think you encouraged the snake to go under its own power. Silly, I know." He was watching my response.

I tried sidetracking him. "Ruby says no one can control animals."

"You've been talking to Ruby about it?"

I had never been great at lying. "Well, Ruby just talks."

"Mm-hm."

"So, some of the others... Who, exactly?"

He smirked. I'd given too much away. "You couldn't tell by the way they looked at you in the clearing?"

I *had* noticed Anvil and Grey. It brought back a memory. "Who was the old guy with the stick?"

"Staff."

"Staff." I waited.

"Shouldn't you be preparing for the trip?"

"Shouldn't you?" I countered.

"*I* am minding you."

I stuck my tongue out at him. Tired, I settled back into my seat. "Steed, tell me about breeding horses."

He sighed. "How much detail do you want?"

I giggled, and he smiled as he started into the subject, explaining what he'd been taught about breeding techniques and dominant traits when he was young. His father had imparted to him all he had learned in his lifetime and all their ancestors had passed down before him. They bred the animals methodically, striving to combine certain traits and bring them together in a single horse. With each generation, they strengthened the line, even bringing in new breeds from other lands to add to the list of desired attributes, such as smoother gaits, better endurance, stronger health, and longer lives.

I faded off somewhere during the part about bloodlines.

I woke in the early morning when Ruby switched places with Steed. She had brought some meat back with her, and we shared a strange pre-morning meal together before I headed off to bed. Ruby didn't question why I seemed to be sleeping so much. She was busy being excited about her upcoming trip.

I didn't share her enthusiasm, so I retired to my room to read more of the journal. There were many sad passages after the passing of the writer's mother, though their bond didn't seem traditional. It seemed more... formal. And there were several complaints about the additional workload, both with the castle duties—which were described in more detail—and her training. I couldn't be sure how much time had passed without the entries being dated, but her mood had definitely shifted.

Father has been merciless in my practice and testing with Rune. Unrelenting sessions are wearing on me. I can barely concentrate. I don't have the energy for the simplest tasks, let alone the new and wild trials he's created. He thinks he has to test every possible idea he has, or else he won't know what I might be capable of.

He's gone much more often lately, but Rune doesn't let up in his absence. I wish there was a way to handle him, some way he'd give me a break when Father was away. I can think of nothing short of begging, and that would only result in punishment.

Sometimes, when Father's away, I remember my mother. I try to see her room, but it is sealed. I am sorry that I destroyed the only thing I had of her, this insignificant journal—tore her pages out and tossed them away to make it my own, like a silly child.

I remember most of it, though I can't recall the tone of her writings, whether she was happy in the beginning. My father's indiscretion was no secret. The entire kingdom knew of his notorious action, stealing a light elf for his bride, though the stories vary. Some insist he was overtaken by love, and she came willingly. Others say that he raided her village and took her in the night. A servant once told me he heard of her extraordinary powers and beauty and sought her out, bargaining with her parents. I scoffed at that. What kind of person would trade their child? But now that I am older, I see. I see what power and greed can become. My doubts about the more outlandish stories, those about the obsession with power and ideas of breeding a stronger line, are gone.

But maybe they were in love. Maybe she was impressed by his station, maybe she had her own ambitions. Or maybe she lived a nightmare and only hung on so long for her children.

I WAS able to piece together some things about her life. She didn't go into much detail about the magic, which I would have found useful, beyond the fact that she practiced often and was apparently unusually talented. But she did describe her duties in the castle. Her father must have ruled a vast kingdom, and she was his second.

I heard someone in the front room and hurriedly slipped the book into my pack and pretended to sleep. Ruby woke me minutes later to head out to the ridge.

13

―――――

The group was waiting for us when we crossed over the ridge and went down to the site where we had spent so many days and nights. If I hadn't been so exhausted from lack of sleep, I would have probably been nervous. As it was, I blindly followed Ruby as we gathered and eventually mounted to leave.

Chevelle, Steed, and I were back on our mounts from the earlier leg of the journey. Ruby, Grey, and Anvil each rode their own black horses, though Anvil's was larger—I assumed to accommodate his massive frame—and Ruby's was decorated with tendrils of red and gold in his mane. Though it wasn't unusual, I didn't see Rhys and Rider or the wolves. I wondered if they had their own horses and preferred to stay out of sight or if they ran with the wolves. I felt slightly comforted either way.

Once we were on our way, I didn't mind so much. I was enjoying being back in the rhythm of the ride, not to mention the break from training. Conversation flowed easily as we made our way farther up the mountain. I had been thinking about my discussion with Steed but hadn't decided how to respond if I were asked again about the incident in the clearing when I controlled the snake. No one knew about the hawk, and I wasn't sure how I had done it to begin with, so

I couldn't exactly explain it. Like Steed had said, "you just do it." But it had been easy for me, much easier even than fire.

I drew my cloak tighter around my shoulders and yawned as I considered my horse. I'd had so much trouble learning to control him, trying to push him from the outside. Falling back from the group only enough not to gain notice, I tried to settle into his mind as I had with the snake and the hawk. I closed my eyes, trusting him to avoid running into anything, though a low limb was the more likely problem. It was more difficult and... different. I was there, though, leading him and seeing what he saw. It felt odd and uncomfortable, not like the hawk.

The feeling reminded me of something, and I drew back, opening my eyes to focus on remembering the small gray bird on the lip of the library window. For a fraction of a second, I had been there inside that bird before I dropped it. I hadn't realized. The moment had seemed insignificant in the course of things. I shook my head at myself as it dawned on me that I probably simply could have made it stop singing. And the frog that had exploded on my white gown—I had been there for a mere instant. Their minds were so small, so simple, it was like nothing. The horse was different. It was watching for predators, concentrating on the path and its steps, carrying a load.

I tried to find another animal to experiment on. Our group wasn't exactly small or quiet, so I was sure we'd frightened most of the larger animals off. I wondered if I could figure out a way to locate them without seeing where they were first. I thought of the wolves. If I had an animal trained, I could call it to me to use at my leisure. I had no idea where they were now. Besides, the thought of entering those massive, vicious-looking animals made me uneasy. Maybe I could get in on the hunt later and find something away from the clatter of rocks under horse hooves.

At the lack of options, I closed my eyes again to fall into Steed's horse. It felt similar to my own, though I could tell he had more power, a more confident stride. I pulled back and experimented with each of the other horses. Anvil's seemed slower, fatigued. The others were about the same, though I noticed Chevelle's horse was skittish. I was sure Steed had done that on purpose.

"Frey?" Ruby was talking to me.

I pretended I'd been alert. "Yeah?"

I hadn't fooled her. "Doing all right?"

"Uh-huh." I decided to take the opportunity—I had a dozen questions since reading the diary. "Hey, Ruby, are there any castles around here?"

The caravan stopped as everyone turned to stare at me. I had no idea what I'd said wrong. I must have given away the fact that I had no clue where I was. It wasn't my fault. I'd never left the village. I didn't know anything about anything.

She glanced to the watching eyes and again to me. I was sure they were waiting for something.

"Well, it's just that I remember reading in the village about castles in the North." *Was I supposed to have read that? Had that been in the documents I had pilfered from the library?* It was probably well past time I stopped talking.

They seemed to relax a bit as Chevelle shook his head and brought his horse back to pace. I thought I knew what they were thinking. *Imbecile.* Ruby answered, "Hmm," with a cocked eyebrow as she turned to follow the group.

They were mostly silent the rest of the day, until we stopped to make camp. The group split after dinner as Anvil and Grey positioned themselves on rocks at the perimeter of our site. Ruby hung out by Grey, and Steed busied himself as Chevelle paced stiffly around the camp. I was bored again, with everyone entertaining themselves, so I leaned back against a rock and pulled my pack to my lap. I wrapped my cloak loosely around me and positioned my legs so I could place the book there and hopefully not be found out. I wondered how many more days of traveling we had. I didn't see a peak and didn't even know if we were going to the peak of the mountain we were on, but I was too cowardly to ask, to think about what had happened, so I distracted myself with the journal.

. . .

MY SISTER HASN'T SPOKEN to me since our mother passed. I wish she was... different. Not merely a different personality, but different altogether. I can remember the stories in my mother's journal about her own sister. They were so close. That was, of course, until my father. But I suppose my sister might be different as well, if not for him. He's taking a journey, they tell me. He'll be gone a long time. I'll be here alone, except for Rune. He's to continue my practice.

CHEVELLE APPROACHED DURING HIS PACING, and I slid the book into my pack, pretending to examine the beading on the material of the dress, which seemed to disturb him. He avoided pacing near me for the rest of the evening but threw me odd glances now and again. I shrugged it off and went back to reading.

FATHER HAS BEEN GONE for weeks. Rumor is he's searching for a new mate. Someone unique, someone powerful, I'm sure. I can't stand it anymore. He thinks I'll sit here and exhaust myself practicing while he's out running around. All the servants are gossiping, and I know nothing.

I have had it. Mother's room remains sealed, but I was able to obtain some of her things from Father's study. I am only to use them under Rune's supervision, so I took the books out and returned to my room with them in secret last night. I have scoured through them, and though I don't know all the words of the spell exactly, I think I've found a way to escape. I'll have to practice on a servant first.

"PRACTICE ON A SERVANT" brought back something Ruby had said. Chevelle would have to practice the unbinding spell on someone else first. I wondered whether he would use one of our group and what would happen if the spell went wrong.

I glanced at the others as they stood at intervals around the camp. Gone were such usual habits as sharpening a blade or casual banter. Their eyes were on the surrounding landscape, their postures giving the impression they were more worried about staying alert. I could only imagine they were waiting for trackers, and the thought made my stomach turn. I swallowed hard, going back to the book.

I TESTED the spell on Rain last night. I'm not sure what went amiss, but she convulsed for hours before she fell into a sleep. She finally rose late this morning, but she couldn't remember who she was, and she kept scratching at her face until it bled. At least she'll not be able to tell anyone I did it. I'll have to catch another servant tonight.

No, I had a feeling he would not be using one of our group. I was starting to get sleepy but didn't want to put the book down. The others didn't seem to notice, though they never slept as much as I did.

I'd positioned myself near the light of the fire, and across from me, Ruby sat watching the darkness, occasionally tossing some bit of dust onto the flames that turned their glow from orange to blue. I could see the outline of Chevelle's form near a large rock, the jut of his shoulder and his hand on the pommel of his sword. I wondered where he had studied the binding spells and how many other spells he might have learned.

THIS ONE WORKED. Dree's nose bled for the first few minutes but after that she slept soundly and woke just before noon not knowing she had missed anything. Tomorrow, I try it on my watcher.

WATCHER. I tucked the book into my pack and fell asleep with her words in my thoughts. My imagination had filled in all the blanks and let the fear I'd been suppressing creep in and take over. It turned her words into my nightmares. Watchers and trackers, tassels and robes, Chevelle's furious gaze as he pushed me from the cliff again. *Chevelle. My watcher.*

"FREY." Ruby woke me at dawn, urging me to stand for a few moments before we were back on the horses.

I was exhausted again, so I hung back from the group as we rode. Steed slowed to ride with me as I watched Ruby and Grey banter ahead. "Steed, why *aren't* they together?"

He sighed. I didn't think he enjoyed discussing his sister's personal life. "Ruby doesn't believe she can get close to anyone... that way."

I considered the way she was with me, as if she wanted us to be friends, the way she touched Steed, sat near him. "Why?"

"Past experiences."

She'd killed her mother, and I wondered how many others. *What had she said, "until a pattern became noticeable?"* I shivered at the thought. "Poison."

He nodded in silent acknowledgement.

"In the village, some of the elves never paired up." I thought of Junnie's family. "But I guess most of those had received the calling."

Grey scoffed ahead of us.

I hadn't realized he could hear us. I was embarrassed but couldn't stop myself. "What?"

His horse slowed to fall in with ours as he spoke. "The calling?"

I didn't understand. It had been a thing of honor, but he spoke of it as if it was a joke.

"Do you really believe such nonsense?"

"What nonsense? It isn't real?"

He let out a harsh laugh, and I flinched. "Oh, I suppose it's real. The service is real. Honestly, Freya, don't you see?"

"See what?" I cursed my bound brain.

"Grand Council."

I drew a sharp breath at the words.

"The calling is simply service to Grand Council. A hundred years of servitude under the guise of duty and honor. What is honorable about doing their bidding?"

"So you don't... answer the call?" I stumbled, searching for words.

His laughter was a roar. "No. We do not answer." It settled, and he added, "They do not call." At that, Steed joined in, chuckling.

It didn't make sense. I knew I had been assigned a watcher from the North. "No one?" I asked.

"No. Council does not attempt to rule the North."

I considered that and considered my watcher. He was a volunteer. I seethed for a moment, but flashes of my mother and council cloaks flooded my thoughts, and I had to block them.

"So the North has no council at all?"

His answer was uncomfortable. "No. No council." He paused while he formed the rest of his reply. Steed watched him intently. "We are... unruled."

"Unruly," Steed added with a half laugh.

"You've never had a council?"

Grey shook his head.

"No rulers?"

He gave Steed a sidelong glance. "Not anymore." I could tell he intended to end the conversation with that, but it only made me more curious.

I was tired of having to make everyone spell things out for me. "No council ever. No rulers anymore? So what, then?"

Steed flinched at my tone but didn't answer.

"Frey," Chevelle called from the front of the line.

I glared at him.

"Time to resume your training."

They had me work with Anvil, trying to anticipate when he was preparing to send a small current of electricity toward me, which meant I spent the day getting shocked. I was grateful when we finally stopped to make camp.

I was afraid they would resume training after dinner, so I found a place off by myself and pretended to rest as I went back to reading the diary.

.   .   .

Today was exhilarating. For the first time in I don't know how long, I was out of the castle and free from practice, free from duties, free from walls.

Though tricky to set up, the spell worked on Rune. I showed up at practice early and whispered the words in case something went wrong and he heard. I can't imagine what my punishment would have been, though it might have been worth it. He fell asleep quickly, and I ran as fast as I could, my pulse pounding with excitement.

I spent the entire day away from the castle. Without the drain of practice, I was thrilling with energy. I could feel the trees, the mountain. I hope Father never comes back! I am sure I will try again tomorrow and every day I can spare after that.

An owl hooted from far away, echoing off the jagged stones. I'd not heard much in the way of wildlife the farther north we'd gone, and I had assumed it was owing to the size of our group. But the elves of the North were not like those I'd grown accustomed to, and I wondered if more than a few of my assumptions had been wrong. The answering call came, another owl in some far away tree, and I glanced at Steed where he spoke quietly with Grey. He winked at me before falling back into his conversation, and I returned to reading.

Rune was completely unaware of any foul play yesterday, so I had full confidence in the spell this morning. Not that I wouldn't have attempted it again anyway, but at least I know I'm safer now. No worries when I'm out of the castle.

My sister is out every day, but I can never seem to find her. She keeps bringing back the strangest treasures. I have run for two days now. I think tomorrow, I will follow her. She refuses to tell me where she goes, neither under threat nor for a bribe, so I'll have to use stealth.

Grey walked into the darkness outside of our fire, and in the shifting shadows, I saw the broad form of Anvil. He carried a sword at his hip, like most of the others, but I'd rarely seen him draw it. I supposed since he had lightning, he didn't always need steel. I glanced at Steed, his back to me, and then Ruby, who only offered me an encouraging smile. I wasn't certain what it meant, but she busied herself with tying a thin braid into her curls, so I carefully turned the page where the diary was tucked against my cloak.

Today was brilliant. I left a sleeping Rune just in time to find my sister sneaking from the castle. I followed her all the way to her secret spot. It took us half the day to get there, but it was worth it. It's so far away from any kind of traffic, I have no idea how she even discovered it.

Nestled in a patch of trees outside the forest was some sort of camp. I watched her at first. She scoured the area searching through the things she found there. But I couldn't observe for long. I revealed myself and inquired about her previous finds and all the questions that were plaguing me. She was furious! She screamed and cursed and fumed. She was no help with my queries, so I was forced to look around myself.

Whatever had been there lived a little like the imps. And there were imp tracks there, but it appeared only one. A massive number of bowls and jars littered the camp. I have no idea who would need so many. The fey like containers, but not of this crude sort—the craftsmanship was almost that of a troll. I tried to stay on the opposite side of the camp from my sister's wrath, but I found tracks and had to follow them near her, stirring up another fit of rage. The prints were shoed, about the size of elves, but the treads were irregular. Whatever stayed here, there were a lot of them.

Near the center of the camp, the ground was beat down with tracks circling a ring of stones. I found remnants inside and ashes. A crude fire pit. Around that, several feet out, were various logs, I assumed for sitting around the pit for warmth. A few huts were situated about the camp, but their construction was unlike anything I'd seen before, very poorly built. I ducked inside one and was shocked to see it was full of possessions. Clothing, bedding, so much left behind. I had thought they'd departed suddenly, but I was confident then that it was not of their choosing.

I went back outside and examined the tracks again. I followed the imp's this time and found my answer. Outside of the camp, I uncovered blood and drag marks. The imp had killed what appeared to be three of the camp's inhabitants and dragged them off, likely by stringer and tow. Whatever was there had run away because of the attack, and recently.

I questioned my sister again—she'd had some time to cool down—but she was no help. I immediately knew she had not even considered that whatever she had been so interested in was still out here, probably close. I didn't clue her in. After a little more time there, I acted as if I'd lost interest and headed home.

Tomorrow, I will follow the tracks. I will find whoever was there and solve the mystery of their rudimentary tools and strange huts.

I YAWNED. After a quick glance around, I slid the book back into my pack. I rolled over and fell asleep listening to Ruby's quiet tune.

THE NEXT MORNING, the group seemed in unusually high spirits. I had no idea why the mood had shifted, but I enjoyed the laughter and joking anyway.

We rode past a waterfall, the roar of water making me curious. I figured Ruby was my best bet. Chevelle gave me no answers, and though hers were sometimes cryptic, I knew she'd been reading books on magic. "Ruby, is there a way to harness the power of things like that waterfall?"

Grey glanced at me. The look of concern for my intelligence was not exactly uncommon, but it was something I'd yet to get used to.

"Not that I know of," she said. She got her mischievous grin. "Though I did read once that there was a way to steal life force and use it for yourself."

Chevelle shot her a stern rebuke from the front of the pack.

She continued as if excusing herself. "But it was merely a fey tale and probably not entirely accurate." Then, in a lower voice: "It is fun to speculate, though."

I wiped at my cheek to clear the dampness from the mist, mirroring her low tone as I questioned her. "How would you steal life force?"

"Well, like I said, probably not accurate... But you would have to take the other's life in order to gain their power. Take it in a specific manner." She noticed Chevelle glaring at her and clamped her mouth shut.

I waited until he turned back around before I whispered, "Ruby, did you bring the magic book with you?"

She smiled.

"Can I read it?"

She winked at me.

I started to share her grin, but before I could, Chevelle was in front of us, his horse blocking my way. I was almost thrown from my saddle when we stopped to avoid running into him. He was angry again. "Frey."

"What?"

"Do you remember the last time you used a spell?"

I recalled the smell of burning flesh as the maps cut into my palms. "Yes," I muttered, defeated.

The look he gave Ruby was clear. There would be no magic study for me.

But I did know she had it. Maybe I would be able to steal it...

Lost in thought, I began to fall behind the group. The higher we rose up the mountain, the more treacherous the jagged rock became. I felt every step, holding the reins tightly as the horse's hooves slipped and jumped. The haze thickened, keeping the view both ahead and behind close. It gathered in my hair, leaving it a matted mess with the single braid—Ruby's handiwork—dripping condensation over the shoulder of my cloak.

I decided to practice as we rode, closing my eyes to sink partially into my horse, still alert to my own self and the outside world.

It was there, leading my horse and seeing through his eyes, that the pain struck. It came on instantaneously, hitting me like a blade, cutting, shearing. It was accompanied by sharpness of sound as well.

My ears were in excruciating pain. The horse dropped, and his head smacked to the ground. I watched through his eyes as he hit. The animal's senses stilled, not panicked as my own. I didn't understand what was happening and couldn't quite form a thought.

I yearned to retreat into the horse, run from the agony, but the severity of it tore me back and kept me there in my own head. It felt and sounded like metal bands inside my mind, screeching in my ears. I hadn't opened my eyes again, and I found that I couldn't. I couldn't find my body. I wanted to bring my hands to my head, cover my ears, but I couldn't feel anything aside from the pain in my mind.

I focused all of my energy on unearthing feeling somewhere, and finally, though the terror was unrelenting, I felt my body again and knew it was there. It still didn't respond, but I knew I hadn't fallen with the horse. Something had caught me. Not the ground, not a rock. Someone was carrying me. The horror must have stretched time, making the few seconds seem like minutes.

I struggled to bring myself back. I could hear nothing but a piercing squall. I willed my eyes open, though only a fraction. I was looking at the back of a horse from my position slung over someone's shoulder. My eyes closed once more as the pain doubled, and I lost my body again for a moment. I concentrated until I got it back then realized I was bouncing. I worked my eyes again, using every ounce of control I had left. I was on a horse, running. Not my own. Chevelle was holding me in front of him, my body limp and useless. I fought to focus on more but was overtaken by pain. *Are were running away?*

I could control nothing but my mind, and that just barely. As my eyes closed again, I reached out and found my horse as he lay motionless on the ground, my steed. He wasn't dead. I asked him to stand and tried to impress upon him to follow. I hoped it had worked as I faded into blackness.

14

I regained consciousness very slowly. I was hit with blurry images first, sights and scenes that melded into hazy dreams. Eventually, they became clearer, though they didn't make much sense. After a time, it occurred to me that the problem was that the images were mixing with the wrong sounds... real sounds. Panicked sounds.

I thought I recognized Chevelle's voice and tried to focus on it, to understand the agony. "Frey," he said, and something brushed my cheek, warm and feather light.

The distant impression that it might have been the brush of lips had me drawing in a sharp breath, and I coughed, gasping to fill my lungs. The air shifted as those surrounding me moved in response. I forced my eyes open and found Ruby, Steed, and Chevelle. They looked for a moment as if they were suffering my pain... and then I realized the pain was gone, and the siren was silenced. My breathing steadied, the fear abating, and their faces relaxed. Relief washed over their expressions, but their postures remained stiff and alert. I pushed up to find the source of the danger, and dizziness incapacitated me.

They rushed to kneel beside me, and I could see that was how they had been before my gasp had moved them to standing. My throat was too raw to speak, so Chevelle gave me a canteen. I would have taken anything, but I was glad it was water, not hot wine or that foul-tasting elixir.

"What happened?" I finally choked out, but they were tight-lipped.

"How do you feel?" Chevelle asked. His tone was off, a little shaky. I couldn't tell if he was cross or something else. There was something so familiar about the way he leaned over me, but my thoughts weren't working right yet.

I tried to clear my head before answering. "I don't know." It was the best I could do.

"Are you hurt?"

"No."

He glanced at my hands wrapped tightly around the neck of the container then back at me. "Do you know who I am?"

Something about that was funny, and I laughed, but it came out hoarse.

He looked torn and tentative as he posed the next question. "Can you tell me your name?"

I wondered how badly I was messed up for him to approach me with such a line of questioning. "Frey."

"Your *full* name?"

I rolled my eyes then wished I hadn't as the room spun. I pressed a hand to my temple. "Elfreda Georgiana Suzetta Glaforia."

They all drew in a deep breath.

"What?"

Chevelle's sigh seemed to have let the air out of him. His fingers rested on the edge of the cloak beneath me. "Are you in pain?"

"No. Not anymore."

He nodded. "What do you remember?"

"I was—" I faltered. I didn't know why, but I felt protective of my secret. I didn't want to tell anyone I was in my horse's mind. I started again, aware of my annoyed tone. "I don't know. I was following all of you and suddenly"—I threw my hands up in a vague gesture indicating the attack. It was the best description I could give—"just pain and screeching."

Ruby and Steed bolted to their feet as someone came in, but it was only Grey. "What is it?" Chevelle said, still kneeling over me.

Grey hesitated, rubbed a palm awkwardly over the woven material of his shirt. "A horse is at the door."

Chevelle glanced at me, and I hoped he didn't see my smile. I knew it was my steed.

Grey waited. "Well, should I let him in?"

Chevelle nodded once, and Grey left as quickly as he'd entered.

I realized he'd walked through a door. I glanced around, confused about where I was. Gray stone walls surrounded us, but I'd been staring at an open sky, nothing but the cloak between my prone form and the cold earth. "Where are we?"

"Fort Stone," Steed answered.

I snickered, and Chevelle's irritation resurfaced. I didn't know if it was for me or Steed. "Fort Stone?" I asked anyway.

"Named for Lord Stone," Steed explained.

Chevelle's gaze caught the other man, leaving no question as to the source of his crossness.

"A lord?" I tried not to sound too impressed as I took another look around, reassessing the walls. I wondered how old it was.

Chevelle stood, directing Ruby to stay with me until he returned. Steed followed him without another word.

Ruby must have known I was curious. Or she just wanted to talk. It was hard to tell with Ruby. "It's been abandoned for centuries," she offered, making me a bed as she recounted ancient stories.

She helped me move onto the blankets, and the dizziness improved, but my muscles were weak and drained. I asked, "Why are we here?"

Her mouth twisted to the side as she considered her answer. "We were in need of shelter after your... episode. It was close enough to work. Are you cold?" she asked, tucking me under a blanket.

"I'll get it," I said, waving my hand to form a fire beside us.

Nothing happened.

The vertigo was almost gone, and I was feeling close to normal, just a bit fuzzy. I tried once more, but it would not light. I pressed down the panic as I concentrated on pulling the burn together.

But nothing happened.

I sat up, holding both hands in front of me palms up, as I focused on lighting a flame, any flame.

Nothing.

I reached out to move a rock from the floor. It didn't budge. I concentrated on a pebble beside me. It didn't shift in the least.

"Ruby? It doesn't work." I held my hands in front of me helplessly.

Panic was taking me when she laid a hand on my shoulder and leaned forward. I expected her to calm me, explain it would come back, it would all be all right. Glitter was in the air before I could stop her.

By the time Chevelle returned, I was loopy with it. He and Ruby sat facing me. She must have filled him in on my problem.

I resisted the urge to touch him. I always wanted to touch him.

"Frey," Chevelle began in a measured tone.

I cut him off, trying to sound calm. "What happened?"

"It would seem that Council has attacked us."

I was too numb to draw in the quick breath I expected. My cheeks tingled. I didn't think I could feel my hands.

"Attacked *you*," he clarified.

Something came out of my chest that sounded like a moan. I blinked too slowly. "Attacked?"

"They must have tried to strengthen your bonds."

I knew I should have been shocked, but I couldn't produce the feeling. "They succeeded," I complained.

He nodded. "It seems they may have taken your magic completely this time."

This time. I concentrated on keeping my head straight and looking like I was listening properly, acting properly. My attempt at concentration must have come across as anxiety.

"You found a way to break their bonds before. You will again."

I nodded. My nose was itchy. I wiggled it.

"Rest now," he said. "We have time."

I reached forward, ready to ask him to stay, but he wasn't leaving. He only settled in. Both he and Ruby were staying with me. I was happy... downright blissful. *Stupid dust.*

I watched Chevelle's face as my eyes fluttered closed with exhaustion. My dreams brought him close in a much-too-vivid kiss on the cheek that burned like fire. My skin was blistering—I could feel the color. It swirled around me and shocked me awake again.

I lay on the floor with wide eyes and an unmoving body. I was weak, tired, and still under the influence, but I heard voices. I didn't move as I listened to discern if they were real.

They seemed to be close but were muffled—maybe in the next room or down a corridor—as they echoed off the stones. I thought I'd picked out Anvil's deep voice. "Trapped here like rats... cowards..." He sounded outraged.

Someone else, Grey maybe, worry coloring his tone: "We can't just leave them out there."

I knew Chevelle's voice, interlaced between the other comments. "She's not ready... we can't... too soon."

And a voice I couldn't place: "... another setback..."

They seemed to be in disagreement, but I couldn't find the interest to stay with them. I faded back into sleep.

These dreams took me further. My sight was off, not as clear, distorted. But as I lingered there, I knew the cause. I was seeing from a horse.

We were outside the stone walls of the fortress, finding sparse greens to eat, which bored me even in a dream. I encouraged the horse to run, and he responded immediately, taking flight down the mountainside. The rocks streaked past us as we ran faster and faster, the wind whipping his mane. A great bird perched on the dead limb of an ironwood tree, and I jumped to it just as it dropped from the branch and flared its wings out to catch the wind. We flew still farther as I watched the mountain pass below. There was a scrubby patch of trees ahead, and I could see movement there, inside. I tried to focus on it, the familiar silver and white.

~

Commotion brought me back, and I sat up, startled. My head spun. Ruby caught my arm to steady me. Her smile was strained as she handed me a drink of water.

Chevelle was near the entrance of the stone room with Anvil and Grey. They appeared to be preparing to leave. "What's going on?" I asked.

"Nothing to worry about," Ruby assured me. "Just a hunting trip."

I was still muddled, but I knew it wouldn't take three of them to hunt. Then I remembered the bits of conversation I'd heard when I woke. "Someone's missing?" I took stock. I'd seen everyone but Rhys and Rider and the silver-and-white wolves. "The wolves are out there."

Each person in the room turned to me. Ruby finally spoke. "What do you know about the wolves, Frey?"

"Are they hurt?"

"We don't know. They did not return."

"Rhys and Rider?"

"They are attempting to locate them. They will not rejoin us until they do."

I started to draw a map for them with magic then cursed when I realized I was no longer able. *Bound.* Ruby had been right to drug me —I couldn't have handled it otherwise. They were watching me, unsure what I was doing as I sat helpless and swearing. "I need something to draw with."

Ruby pulled a piece of charcoal and scrap of paper from her bag. I rushed to sketch the path I remembered from my dream, focusing on the ring of trees with the most detail. "They are there."

The men stood motionless and staring until Anvil crossed the room to retrieve the map. He bowed a little as he took the paper from my hands then hurried out. Grey followed. Chevelle stayed.

Ruby turned to him and breathed a deep sigh, but he didn't respond.

My head throbbed, and I groaned as I pressed the bridge of my nose. He was beside me in a flash, unspeaking. Ruby handed me another drink.

It helped, but I was still irritated about the binding. "Does this mean we'll have to train again?"

Ruby snickered.

Chevelle answered slowly. "There has to be a way. You broke them before."

I tried to remember how. The first magic I could recall were the thistle and thorns. It seemed so far away.

Ruby was speaking to him. "Maybe it was just the length of time…"

What does she know about how long I was bound?

"If we can find a way to test without endangering—" He stopped. "Don't worry about it, Frey." I wondered if I'd looked frightened. "We will figure it out."

How reassuring. I meant to smile at him but only succeeded in pressing my lips into a flat line.

"Rest now. There is plenty of time for tr"—he thought better of saying *training* again—"to test the bindings." He smiled, and again, I had the feeling he wanted to reach out to me. But he did not. He simply stood and walked from the room.

Ruby saw me watching. "He's right, Freya. Rest now. Plenty of time to get you straightened back out." She stood and walked to the front wall. I hadn't noticed the narrow window before, which was no wider than the flat of a hand. Ruby positioned herself in front of it, watching whatever was outside.

I sighed. *Plenty of time.* I fiddled with the blankets for a while, tried a couple of times—futilely—to move tiny specks of loose rock on the floor, then gave up and decided to read the journal again. I rolled away from Ruby and pulled my pack into the curve of my body, settling the book open but able to be quickly hidden.

This morning, I extended my spell, giving Rune an extra day of sleep. It was a good thing too. I found the camp right off and followed the tracks easily. The occupants must have run in panic initially but then gathered back together and walked in a line, some two by two, some dragging sleds. They made temporary shelter in a cave, likely for just one night, and continued again. They must have moved slowly, and I could see they stopped often to rest. It didn't take long before I'd found their new camp. I slipped into a tall tree to watch them.

To my shock, I found something I had never seen before. I watched for hours before I was sure, too stunned to believe it possible. I had heard stories —the fey were always puffing dust about it—but I'd never believed it. Was I really watching humans?

I WAS PULLED FROM READING, confused. Humans weren't real. *What kind of book is this?* She had mentioned fey stories. I wondered if it was fiction, a fey ruse, given to Chevelle by Ruby. Or maybe the dust was still playing havoc on me. I glanced over my shoulder at Ruby still watching anxiously out the front window. I shook my head and found the line again.

BUT I COULDN'T DENY it. Their size was about that of an elf, but all were different. The men were thicker. Not necessarily with muscle, some more bulbous. The women were varied as well, some thin and wiry, some stout like the males. Their hair was in all shades—light blond like the sun, brown as a fall tree... One even had rusty red, his plump cheeks peppered with light-brown spots. And there were so many children! They were loud and ran round the camp all afternoon. And they were just as varied as the adults. I examined their wide noses, rounded ears, and stubby fingers. Those who wore no shoes had short, thick toes like trolls. The men had patches of hair curled on their chests and forearms, and some even grew it around their chins like goats. Their clothes were tattered and ill-fitting rags.

They moved about the camp slowly. Clearly, they had no magic, and they definitely were the owners of the crude tools we had found. They spoke to each other often, their voices like the protest of an old hound. I watched until nightfall, when they settled into tents and lean-tos. They seemed to assign a watchman, wielding only a torch lit from the central fire. I slipped down from the tree and returned to the castle. I am dying to see what I can find of them in the books of Father's study.

LAUGHTER BROKE MY CONCENTRATION. Anvil and Grey were back. I looked to the front wall, but Ruby was gone, having moved to the entrance of our room. She seemed to be waiting there excitedly for something. I slid the book into the pack and sat up to watch.

Chevelle came in, and Ruby greeted him. "It's fantastic," she breathed. He smiled at her.

Steed was following. "Almost unbelievable," he added, shooting me a speculative look.

They turned to me as Rhys and Rider entered. They didn't approach but stopped just inside the room and dipped into a bow. "Our gratitude, Elfreda."

I blushed. I had forgotten the wolves. They must have found them. "Were they hurt?"

"No. And our thanks to you for that as well."

I wasn't exactly sure how that was due to me, but I smiled, glad they had found them and everyone was safe. They turned to leave, and Grey entered with two spits of meat and wine. It almost seemed like a celebration. Almost. Their high spirits from before hadn't quite returned.

I wondered how long I had been out. I wondered where the councilmen who'd attacked us were now.

The wine flowed. Steed took some food to Anvil, Grey and Ruby made their way to the front window, and I found myself sitting alone with Chevelle.

"How do you feel?" he asked.

"Better. And worse." Better because the dust was clearing. Worse because I was fuzzy and bound again.

He nodded. He was closer than before, sitting opposite me, and I had the disconcerting feeling that I'd lost the bit of time when he'd moved there. He reached out and took my hand in his, his fingers gentle as he turned it palm up to place a pebble there. "Can you do anything with this?"

"No." Frustration was clear in my voice. I had already tried.

"And no fire?"

"No."

"So nothing works?" The implication was there, but I didn't know what it meant right away. And then it occurred to me: the horse. I had thought he had shown up because I'd impressed upon him to follow before I blacked out, but I had already been bound again at that point.

I wanted to tell him, but I didn't. I didn't know why I felt so protective of the secret.

Chevelle drew a section of moss from one of the stones on the wall and it replaced the pebble. "Try this. They shouldn't have bothered binding you from growing."

I concentrated on it. Nothing. But I was never good at that, anyway. I shook my head.

He nodded, giving up, but our hands still lay together, connecting us.

"Where are they?" I asked.

He'd been looking at our hands, but his eyes returned to my face at the question.

"Council," I explained.

"They have retreated. They were able to briefly incapacitate the wolves, giving Rhys and Rider less warning of their approach before you were attacked." He hesitated. "When we heard the alert, I turned. Your eyes were closed." I didn't comment, so he continued, "I was able to catch you just before your horse dropped. I've no idea why they attacked him. They should have been focused on you."

I wasn't sure they *had* attacked the horse. Maybe it was because I'd been there, in his mind, controlling him. "What happened to Rhys and Rider?"

"They broke to keep from fighting such a sizeable force alone. They circled back to meet us. In the disorder, they lost track of the wolves."

"But the wolves weren't hurt?"

"They had been strung up by vine among the trees, but alive."

I winced at the idea. "Why?"

A wry smile crossed his lips and I couldn't help but focus on them for a moment. "Because the wolves would have fought to the death, and Grand Council does not kill animals with magic."

I remembered my mother. "Only elves?"

His mocking smile widened. "Only elves."

They thought killing an animal with magic was evil and dark, but they were hunting us down to burn us. I considered the alternative—pierced through with arrows, blessed with a prayer—and laughed.

His eyes were intense as he reached to cup my neck, his fingers resting gently at my spine. His thumb grazed the base of my ear as I felt him urge me forward. My breath caught, heart stuttering into a broken lope.

And then Ruby was beside us from out of nowhere, her words startling me back to the cold, dull room. "They're coming in."

Chevelle leaned back, his fingers brushing my collarbone when he pulled away. I bit my lip at the tingle that ran through me, and the corner of his mouth turned into a different kind of smile.

He stood to walk from the room, and I stared at the stone entry, struggling to keep my thoughts from spinning out of control. Too much had happened. Too much was wrong. My life had flipped, twisted into some strange reflection of itself, and I couldn't reconcile the fragments. It caused me physical pain to think about Chevelle's touch, about Council, and about what was happening, and I knew it was the bonds.

When Grey walked out, my trance broke, and I noticed Ruby by the front window, wearing an odd smile. I flushed and turned from her, rolling into a ball on my blankets, remembering no more than the feel of his skin on my neck, the quirk of his lips.

I had to keep distracted, and there was nothing for it but the book.

· · ·

I WASN'T *able to find much regarding humans in the study's library. But I had been right. Illustrations and descriptions matched what I had seen.*

I know I took a risk extending Rune's spell further, but I did not want to get caught, definitely not followed. I wondered if my sister was still at the original camp. Surely, she wasn't bright enough to figure it out. And apparently, she wasn't willing to tell anyone.

I was returning to the spot where I had found the humans the previous day when I ran across one of them alone. I hid myself behind a patch of brush to watch him. He had a lovely complexion with a hint of bronze and cropped dark-brown hair with a few tiny streaks of blond just around his face. He looked less like the others I had been watching. He was built like the elves, strong and muscled, but still lean. He wore plain pants and tall boots. His light cloth shirt was unlaced, moving around him as he walked. He carried a small blade in his hand, but I couldn't imagine what he was doing there unaccompanied.

There was a rustle from the brush several yards in the opposite direction from where I was hiding. He rushed toward it, and I followed, unsure why he was running. The noise was made by a small boar, and the human was chasing it. He ran after it, gasping for air, and I followed close behind, thrilling at the clumsy spectacle. The boar approached a ridge of rock and turned, giving the human the advantage. He leaped after it, blade held wide, and landed, slicing into its side and twisting the blade back out. He was leaning over its small, motionless body, heaving for breath, covered in blood. I laughed, shocked at myself but filled with excitement and amusement.

He stood, whirling to face me, bloody blade held out. I had to stifle another laugh. I managed to keep my reaction calm, with only a smile.

He seemed disoriented for a moment, and then his breathing slowed, and his arms relaxed. He stared at me as if I were a delusion, a dream looking back at him. He was speechless, and it occurred to me that perhaps elves were not a part of this human's knowledge. I wondered if he would recover soon. I considered abandoning him and returning to watch the others, but his face was so interesting, the emotions so plain and readable there. But he wasn't afraid. It was awe.

I decided to have a little fun with him. They couldn't possibly be dangerous. "Hello." I spoke to him slowly, but it appeared he didn't compre-hend. He merely stood gawking at me. I tried again. "Do you wish to speak with me?"

"Yes," he finally stuttered. "Uh... hello."

"I am..." I hesitated, unsure if I should tell him my name—I was on the run, after all. I decided on a replacement. "Lizzy."

He seemed to like that. "I'm Noble."

I was confused. "You are noble?"

He shook his head. "Noble is my name. Noble Grand."

"That is a large name. You are a ruler among your people?"

He laughed. "No, no. Noble is my given name, passed down for genera-tions. Grand is the family name."

Generations? I was surprised again. I stepped closer, enthralled. "What are you doing here?"

"We are searching for a good place to start over," he explained. I was scrutinizing his blade. "Oh—well, I'm hunting."

He wasn't as slow as I had thought, quite capable of conversation. I couldn't help but wonder. "You were a bit... stunned before?"

He flushed a pleasing shade of red. "Yes."

"Why?"

"Well, it's only that you are quite beautiful. Surely the loveliest thing I have ever seen." I smiled in spite of myself, and he continued the flattery. "And then when you spoke, your voice... it's like a melody."

"And you are seeking a new camp?"

"A more permanent settlement, actually."

"You have found it here?"

"We are undecided. Days ago, we were attacked." Pain washed over his features. "A horrid creature took several of our men."

I nodded. "An imp."

"I'd never have believed it to be true if I hadn't seen it myself." He was clearly lost in thought as he continued. "We may move again. The risk seems too great."

Suddenly, I didn't want them to relocate. I wanted them to stay right there, where I could watch them. I tried to make him feel safe. "You know, I could protect you."

He was incredulous. I decided to show him.

I stepped forward, noting his unease at my movement, and faced the boar that lay on the ground behind him. He turned to see what I was focusing on. I was afraid to scare him too much, so I decided on a small gesture. I held my hand out in front of me, emphasizing the action as I twisted my wrist in the air, the boar's head spinning, the sound of its neck cracking in tandem with my movement.

He gasped and stepped back from me. I was afraid for a moment that I'd shown him too much. He looked at my face, searching, and finally let out a breathless, "Magic."

His expression was filled with wonder. I had seen many impressed with my talents but never with such an effortless show. I laughed to myself. It was refreshing to have someone so genuinely awed. He didn't ask to see what else I could do. He wasn't sizing me up for battle. I smiled at him, and he seemed to think that alone a reward.

He was still speechless.

"Well, shall you stay, then?"

"Forever," he gushed. It was a curious response, but I had begun to think he wasn't that different from me, aside from the obvious lack of magic, skill, and grace. Moreover, where many of the others lacked beauty, he did not. Unconventional, yes, but nonetheless... interesting.

I led him to a set of stones to sit, wanting to get answers to all the questions that had been burning in my mind since I had spotted them. He had forgotten his prey, so I offered to help him with it. This befuddled him, so I simply skinned and spitted the animal while he sat, staring in amazement. It was as if he'd never seen fire before. It made the magic fun again. Like when we were children, before Father's ridiculous schedule. I shook off the memory of practice and focused on the human.

"So, how old are you?"

"Twenty-two," he said, almost shamefacedly.

At first, I was shocked at the number and thought maybe I'd misunderstood. But I remembered reading the human lifespan was very brief. By his manner, I'd have guessed twice that number, were he an elf. "Why the hint of embarrassment?"

"They tell me I should have a family by now."

"You have none?"

"A mother and father but none of my own. No wife, no children."

"You are expected to have a wife and child after just two decades of life?"

He laughed for some reason I could not see. "Then you have no family of your own?"

"I am not expected to pair for quite some time, if ever. And children? Ha!" He was visibly perplexed, so I kept talking. "I have a family as well, though my mother died recently."

Sadness washed his features. "I'm sorry. Was it an imp?"

"No." I laughed at the strange idea. And for no apparent reason, I told him the truth. "She died of sorrow."

His brow furrowed.

We shared the boar and talked further, casually, as if we were old friends. He resituated himself on the rock, coming closer to me, and his shirt moved to expose a different color skin where it opened at the chest. I reached out to pull it aside and his eyes grew wild at the touch.

"Your flesh is a different tone here."

He smiled, as if I were being coy. "Yes."

"Why?"

"Sometimes I work with my shirt on, to avoid the burn of the sun."

"The sun?"

He laughed but then realized I was earnest. "It is a tan... from the sun." He pulled the laces and lifted his shirt over his head, throwing it aside to show me his bare chest. The bronzed color of his face extended there but was a lighter shade. I examined him closer, taking his hand and turning his arm. The inside of his wrist was lighter still, close to the shade of my own skin.

I was still studying him when he spoke softly. "May I kiss you?"

His breath hit my face. I hadn't realized how close I had gotten. It surprised me, as did his request. I had a perverted desire to let him. I smiled thinking of it. He took that as an invitation, leaning closer, his hand raised to touch my face. His thumb caressed the line of my jaw as he reached for me, fingers tangling in my braids as he drew me to him. He started gently, teasing, then crushed our lips together, his strong hand holding me there, his breathing ragged.

At some point, I became aware of what I was doing and drew back. "I have to go now."

He looked devastated.

"Goodbye, young Noble."

"Can I see you again?"

I smiled. I couldn't seem to help it. "I will return."

He took a deep breath, satisfied. "I'll be waiting."

As I turned to go, I realized I hadn't asked any of the important questions that had been nagging me. I'd have to try harder tomorrow, stay on task. I ran back to the castle at full speed.

RUBY CLEARED HER THROAT, and I shoved the book into my pack. I glanced over at her, but she was still facing out the window. A moment later, Chevelle walked in, and she threw him a wicked grin. I brushed the length of my hair forward, hoping to cover the heat that had risen in my neck and ears.

"Ready to resume training?" he asked.

That cooled the flush, and I grimaced, moving to stand. I hadn't done so since the incident, and my head spun. I wobbled, and Chevelle was suddenly there, steadying me. I shook off his look of concern. "I'm fine. Really."

He shifted closer, and I became wholly aware of his hands at my waist. The grip he'd used to steady me became softer and yet, at the same time, his fingers tightened around me. My breath hitched as he pulled me against him, the length of our bodies touching.

My throat went dry, and black spots swirled in my vision. I fought to stay focused on his face, which was so close. His eyes grew troubled, and then he blurred out of vision as I went limp in his arms.

"FREY..."

I opened my eyes to the darkening sky. "What happened?"

"You seem to have blacked out," Chevelle said, a hint of some emotion under his reassurance.

I blushed. He must have seen that coming and held me because of it, simply to prevent me from falling on my face. I was a fool.

He helped me up, holding me only by one arm. I took a deep breath. "I'm all right now."

His lips twisted again, but I couldn't make out the expression. I could barely look him in the eyes.

I attempted every type of magic he could come up with, to no avail. I was beyond frustrated. Worse, I could tell he was being gentle on purpose, afraid I would break. I thought of what he'd said before about the dangers of messing with the bindings.

He must have read it on my face. "That's enough for now. Rest, Freya."

I didn't argue.

Ruby came in as if on cue, and Chevelle excused himself. I lay down, but irritation kept me from sleep, so I returned to the book.

I SPENT *the next several weeks visiting him. I had forgotten about the rest of the camp. He had become infatuated with me, and I couldn't keep myself from indulging him. I was thoroughly enjoying it—reveling in it, if I was honest with myself.*

He persisted in trying to touch and kiss me anytime I was close enough to allow, and I let him sometimes.

He surprised me one evening, when he knew it was time for me to leave, grabbing my wrist and holding me there. I was stronger than him, but I didn't resist his pull as he spoke. "Don't go."

"I will return tomorrow," I promised. "Early."

"No," he said, flush with emotion. "I don't ever want you to go." I laughed and he drew me closer. "Stay with me."

I started to pull away and he reached up, placing his hands on either side of my face, feverish now. "Marry me, Lizzy." I had long since gotten used to the name, but I wasn't sure he was talking to me at first. It seemed ridiculous.

I stopped myself from laughing, knowing from previous experience it would hurt him. I had come to realize he didn't know what I was. He knew I was different, of course, knew of the magic, though I'd shown him nothing of my real power. But he didn't understand I was an elf. I hadn't explained, knowing it would do nothing but perplex his simple mind. He merely thought I was something special, extraordinary. But did he actually think I was human, someone he could wed? I was incredulous.

But he was obsessed. The moment it slipped from his lips, he became more focused on that than anything else. Making me his bride. I couldn't understand.

He tried to explain. "I want you forever. I need you, Lizzy." The yearning in his voice was clear, and I was surprised that I ached for him a little, felt his pain and need. He touched me then, and I thought I understood when he continued, "We could be together..."

Marriage. He wanted to join us. I bit my lip, undecided. Curiosity was there too. And I couldn't help but imagine. He was unmagical. He had no idea what I could do to him, for him, in such an intimate setting. What could it hurt, really? Sure, I could marry him. It wouldn't be real. But the other part, well, I could do that without the marriage, couldn't I? Harmless fun...

I smiled as I leaned closer to him. This was the first time I had initiated a kiss, and he was grateful—more than grateful, he seemed overwhelmed with pleasure. I laughed to myself at what was to come, if this small, insignificant gesture brought him so much happiness. Our lips touched, and he gasped, and then the breath turned to a low moan.

I RUBBED the back of my hand over a cheek, trying to clear away the blush of color. The encounter was very *descriptive*. I threw a wary glance over my shoulder, making sure Ruby was still at the window as I continued.

. . .

THE DAYS *we had spent coupling had done nothing to diminish his desire. If anything, they had enflamed it. And his obsession with marriage increased tenfold.*

I had not met his family, but one morning when I arrived at the patch of forest where we met, he proudly presented his mother's wedding gown, a gift for me. He wanted me to wear it in our ceremony. I had never agreed to the union, but I avoided telling him it was not possible. It would only be valid in his mind. But then again, what would that hurt?

I accepted the dress from him and looked it over. It was poorly made and ill-fitting but had potential as a design. I sat, using magic to work on the seaming and to arrange the scant pearls and beading in a more pleasant pattern while deciding how best to deal with him.

He was watching me intently. "We will have such prosperity. Think of it, with your magic, we will be able to conquer anything. Whatever we need, whatever we want, it will be nothing but a flick of your wrist."

I froze. It was irrational, I knew, but anger seethed inside me. I couldn't stop myself from thinking he was just like everyone else, interested only in my powers, my magic, and how it would benefit him. I turned to him, glaring, and he drew back, startled. "Is that what you want, why you are so intent on marrying me? For my power?"

He shook his head, mystified. The rage had overtaken me, though. The weeks of drugging Rune, sneaking out, my father being missing while he searched for a new wife, I was sure—all of it was too much. I slipped. A small crack in my stability let out enough magic to hurt him. I didn't hit him, but the surrounding trees and rocks were pulverized, and I knew I had done too much. He stared back at me... afraid.

I turned and ran, without another word, straight back to the castle. In these few short weeks, I had started to think of it less as a home and more as a prison. My limited freedom made me ache for more. My time with this human had felt like living.

It was wrong. I will return to him tomorrow, set things right. As I ran, I realized I was still carrying the dress with me. I couldn't understand why I had bothered dragging it along, but my grip on it was tight. I rolled it up, tucking it under my arm as I approached the castle. My prison.

. . .

Prison. I pushed the book into my pack and finally slept.

When I woke, I felt better, stronger. I was hopeful that would apply to my magic as well. Chevelle sat against the dark stone wall, watching me. He seemed to recognize the change in my mood.

"Feeling well?"

I nodded. "I think I'd like to train again."

"That is probably a good idea. We'll be leaving soon."

I didn't know if I was *that* much better.

"Don't worry. It is safe. They will not attack again so soon."

"When?" I could hear the worry in my tone, despite his assurance.

"We will protect you, Frey."

Sure. I might have rolled my eyes.

"We knew they were following before. Our mistake was in assuming they meant a physical attack. We will not allow them so close again."

"So they're still following?" Panic set in.

"No. Not now." He paused. "They have accomplished what they came for. Now, they will regroup and return, which is why we need to move."

"Why would we leave a fort?"

He chuckled. "Trust me, Frey. We have a more secure location." I must not have appeared convinced. "Please," he added.

I sighed. I didn't have much of a choice. Then I laughed because I couldn't even trust myself.

I expected him to look at me like I was mad. Instead, he looked as though my behavior was... endearing. He stood and walked over to me, taking my hand to help me up. When he touched me, I tried to fight the heat that ran up my neck. I couldn't, and embarrassment caused my cheeks to color as well. I peered up at him through my dark bangs and could have sworn it amused him. I laughed at myself. The silly romance I'd been reading in the diary must have been affecting me.

I tried to stop my thoughts from returning there as we practiced, but it was near impossible. He kept working closely with me, touching me. I knew I should have been focusing on the magic, but it was useless. Each day ended with nothing but frustration and exhaustion, with naught to look forward to but leaving the safety of the fort. Only the book provided escape.

The moment I entered the castle, I knew something was wrong. I had gone in through the servants' quarters, desiring to keep a low profile. When they saw me, fear crossed their faces, and they disappeared from sight. My heart sped. I wondered if something had gone wrong with Rune's spell this time. I decided to go check on him. I realized I was running.

As I rounded a corner heading to the practice rooms, I ran into something hard. The impact didn't knock me down, but the shock almost did. It was one of Father's guards... one of the guards he'd taken with him.

He had me by the arm, dragging me along before I could think. I couldn't decide whether to run or fight. And then we were in the throne room. My father's face was indescribable, his fury almost tangible. I couldn't bring myself to look away from him, but I saw Rune standing in my peripheral vision. I was caught. I frantically searched for some explanation. But he didn't speak. He flipped his arm, dismissing me.

The tension showed in that small movement, and I blanched. I started to pull away from the guard, but he didn't release me. I realized then I hadn't been dismissed. It had been a direction for the guard. He wrenched me beside him, jerking unnecessarily, then shoved me through the door to my room. I listened, but his steps did not recede. I tried the door, but it was already bound.

I threw myself onto the bed. I felt absolutely wretched. Actually, I felt worse than that. I felt as if I'd been poisoned. The room turned, and I heaved over the edge of the mattress.

When I woke late the next morning, I was covered in sweat. My head spun as I stood, but I steadied myself and moved to the basin to splash my face. As I looked in the mirror at my pallid complexion, my features twisted in horror.

Understanding came suddenly and would not be denied. I scoffed at myself humorlessly as my words taunted me—just harmless fun... what could it hurt? For half a second, I wanted to scream. And then my hands found their way to my stomach and rested there.

I DREW IN A SHARP BREATH. I hadn't noticed I had gotten so deeply involved in the story. I needed to rest, finish my recovery, and break the bonds. But I couldn't seem to step away.

I WAS UNNATURALLY CALM when they finally came for me. I knew they would recognize the signs. But it didn't matter now. I walked forward, resigned to my fate.

What I didn't expect was their response. The throne room was full. They all gasped when comprehension hit. But my father, and each of those present, seemed almost pleased when they saw me. They had no idea there was a human growing in the belly my hands cradled. I listened as their voices began and then rose, clamorously discussing the news and what it could bring. I cringed as their words turned to the possibilities, the power I might pass down, the strength the new one might bring.

"WE WILL LEAVE AT DAYBREAK," Grey informed Ruby as I read. The news brought on nothing but worry, so I went back to the book.

EVENTUALLY, my father did seek to find out who the father was. I refused to tell him anything, and he could not force me in my condition. I could see his plans already forming. I was almost happy it would not be powerful—it would be half human and unmagical. I wondered if it could even be brought to term, I was ill so often. The elders discussed it constantly—it was so unusual to be sick, but it must have been a result of the pregnancy. Several of them were assigned to watch me, and I had to listen to their incessant chatter. They seemed thrilled not to know how or when I had gotten this way, carrying on about young elves and their quests.

Ruby's hand was on my shoulder, shaking me awake. I hadn't realized I'd fallen asleep. I jerked up, hoping she hadn't seen the journal. It wasn't lying there. I grabbed my pack, pretending to get ready, and sighed when I felt it tucked inside. I didn't remember doing it, but I was grateful I had. I was really getting into the story.

I yawned and stretched then followed her out of the room. I was surprised by the size of the fort. We went down several corridors and passed a few doors before finally coming to a large, open arena where the others waited for us. Chevelle favored me with a smile as I passed him on the way to my horse. I started to command the horse to kneel, but Steed grabbed me about the waist and threw me up. I took one deep breath before we kicked the horses into a gallop and ran from the fort in a pack.

Our pace finally slowed as the way became too treacherous. Massive rock formations loomed over us, loose stones underfoot causing the horses to stumble. The haze was so thick I couldn't see anything but the riders in front of me. I only knew from the strain on my legs that we were heading up, climbing higher into the gray sky and biting wind.

Chevelle rode beside me throughout the day. When we stopped for the evening, he pulled me down from my horse and stayed near as we sat on large stones around a fire. Ruby was telling stories again, and everyone gave her their full attention—everyone but us.

"How do you feel?" he asked.

I shrugged. "Fine, I guess." He seemed unusually concerned. He was also sitting uncommonly close.

He spoke in a low voice, though the others didn't appear to be listening. I had to strain to hear. "I've been thinking about the bindings." I turned to face him, his deep-blue eyes on mine as he continued, "I was thinking there might be another way." He was hesitant for some reason.

"How?" I demanded, keeping the volume as low as I could, my palms pressed to the smooth rock beneath us. *What is he hedging around?*

"If... Well, it seems you may have more control over your thoughts than you realize?" He phrased it as a question. He had to be talking about my secret, but I couldn't figure whether he was trying to be respectful of it, or trying to keep me from getting upset.

I wasn't sure how to answer. But if it helped, if there was a way to unbind me, free my mind and get back the magic... I settled on an "Mm-hm?"

He nearly smiled. "Well, if you were able to... move about..." It seemed to make him uncomfortable, searching for words. "Then perhaps you could find a way around it."

I bit my lip, and he reached up to gently pull it loose. His hand lingered, his thumb tracing my bottom lip. I was definitely not imagining that. Warmth flooded my neck and cheeks, and his gaze followed the flush.

His hand dropped to my shoulder. "Please, Freya, try."

All I could do was nod.

He stood and walked away. I sat unmoving for a moment then finally glanced at the group. They were deeply involved in their conversations, seemingly unaware of the encounter that had my heart in my throat. I closed my eyes and took a deep breath, attempting to move about in my mind.

It was completely frustrating, fuzzy, and wrong. Nothing worked. None of it connected the way it should have. It made me angry and tired, and the maddening fight against it gained me nothing but a buzzing headache.

I sighed and threw myself onto my blankets, away from the group. It was still daylight, and I tossed and turned, unable to rest. I decided to go back to my favorite distraction.

THE TIME CAME SOONER *than any of us expected. Looking back, I suppose it was fortunate. I can't imagine what might have happened if a full birth ceremony had been prepared and how many would have been present. It makes me cringe to merely think of it.*

The elders were there, though. My father and the others waited in the throne room, arranging a celebration. I had read everything I could obtain on the process during my pregnancy and imprisonment in the castle, even finding a few books and scrolls on humans. But nothing prepared me for what happened.

I had been walking—pacing my room with worry, if I were truthful— when the pain struck. It hit suddenly, a stabbing, ripping, horrible thing. My screams called everyone to order, but then it subsided. However, it was only long enough to catch my breath before it was back tenfold. I writhed in agony. Nothing they did would help. I could not control my magic. and it shattered most of the things on the nearby table and twice caught the bedding afire. The elders were frantic, which only frightened me more. I had never seen them agitated.

This carried on for hours. My hair and clothing were drenched in sweat, and I was near surrender. And then, with no more warning than when the first pains came, it was over. A small, sweet child was in my arms.

I drew in ragged breaths as I cleaned her face. I wiped her eyes and they came open, an unbelievable shade of dark green, sparkling like emeralds. She was a beauty. I wasn't aware the room had grown silent until I wiped her ears and heard my own gasp. They were slightly rounded at the tips... almost blunt.

I REALIZED I had stopped breathing as I read, completely engrossed in the story. I reached up absentmindedly to stroke the tops of my ears.

I LOOKED UP, then, at the elders who surrounded me. Their faces were astonished. "She is... human," they said.

I took a steadying breath and spat out, "No." They stared at me incredulously. I spoke deliberately. "She is elf. I name her... Elfreda."

. . .

MY HEART STOPPED THEN SURGED as blood rushed to my face, my neck. My ears rang. I must have been speaking or cursing. I could hear the sound, but could not make sense of it. Nothing made sense.

I was standing before I knew I was surrounded. Fury and fire swam in my head, my chest, my hands.

I heard them through the buzz. "Frey, what's wrong? What is it? Frey... Frey." And then, more clearly: "Elfreda!"

My jaw tightened, and my teeth ground together.

Comprehension crossed Chevelle's face as he saw the book on the ground between us. He reached for it.

"Touch that book and you die," I hissed.

He froze, staring me straight in the eyes. I was fighting for control, struggling to find my thoughts.

Then I saw him flick a glance at Ruby, and I knew. They knew. And it was all true.

Suddenly, I couldn't catch my breath.

"Please, Freya, stay calm," Ruby pleaded. They were circling me, their arms outstretched as if to catch me... or cage me.

Black spots floated in my vision. My head screamed. The sound of metal bands snapping echoed through a scraping, screeching noise inside my mind. I pressed my palms against my temples. I didn't know I was going down until my knees hit the hard rock. I held myself there, refusing to give in.

They argued frantically. "Knock her out. Do something. She's going to crack."

Yes, crack was a good word for it. I felt as if I were breaking in half. No, I was being torn.

I sensed someone close to me, Ruby no doubt. She would drug me. I didn't want that. I didn't want that ever again. I slid from the pain, reaching out. I found nothing but the horses, but I would take it. I left my body completely.

My entry was so furious that it startled the horse. I held him there, but when he raised his head from grazing, he was facing them. They were standing, kneeling, surrounding my limp body. I watched them and the horror on their faces for an immeasurable moment. It was too much. It was all too much.

A raw, unbearable ache crushed my chest, and I gave in to it, accepted it. There was nothing else I could do. I sighed, melting back into my own mind. It was quiet there, and I wondered if I had cracked. But then it occurred to me that maybe I had been the cause of it. I was resigned—the fury was gone, and so was the screeching, the pain. They had said the binding was dangerous...

There was a collective sigh as they realized I was back. I heard someone beside me, and a flash of anger swept through me, lighting a flame at whoever it was. *So maybe the fury wasn't completely gone.*

I suddenly remembered the pages I had burnt in the briar patch so long ago—I'd burned them before I'd read them. My eyes flashed open. I sat up, ignoring my spinning head, but the book was already gone. I glared at Chevelle. It must have been dreadful, because he nodded and backed away, his mouth tight.

"Oh, Frey." Ruby's voice was low and soothing.

I grimaced as I turned to her, not at all wanting what I was about to say. "Go ahead." I closed my eyes again as her jaw shifted.

15

———

The dreams I had then were the most dreadful of my life. I jolted awake and shuddered at the images I could not beat down, my mother screaming in agony, her body tearing and breaking from the magic inside, fire, blood, betrayal.

Ruby was there, waiting for me.

"Where are the others?" I asked, my voice hoarse.

"They've set up a perimeter."

It was all I had to say. I felt empty, alone. It was dark—even with the dust, I'd not slept through the night. I sat up, curling my legs against my chest, and wrapped my arms around them, pulling tightly.

Though I didn't speak, I occasionally glanced or glared at Ruby. She sat, immobile, watching me.

It was morning before she broke. "You have your fire back."

It hadn't occurred to me. I held my hand out, flicked a flame above my palm, then promptly extinguished it. I tried moving a stone from the ground to no avail. *Just fire.* I sighed. But Ruby looked hopeful.

The group approached warily, keeping their eyes on me. Chevelle hung farther back, avoiding my gaze as he hovered near the edge of the mist. Steed led my horse to me. I didn't think I blamed him—he seemed to be involved by chance—but I hadn't fully decided yet. I was too occupied by my anger at Chevelle. It might have been irrational, but it felt as if he lied to me again. He'd been there before, when my mother was killed. He had known all of it, and he'd kept it from me. He had bound me from using my magic because I was dangerous, a deadly threat. I wasn't even wholly elf.

As we rode wordlessly through the cold stone landscape, my thoughts twisted and writhed as they were a pit of vipers. In the end, I'd decided I wasn't really that shocked about being half-human. It explained so much about myself, my clumsiness, lack of skill, and the fact that I never quite fit in. What took me by surprise was the betrayal I felt. In all the years I'd lived in the village, I'd never counted on anyone the way I had done with the group, and especially Chevelle. My chest was heavy.

The rest of me wanted everything to burn.

Struggling with my reactions kept me distracted from the ride. It was steep and rocky, with a haze hanging in the few spiky trees. When we stopped for the evening, the men quietly set up a perimeter, except for Chevelle, who was watching me as I glared back at him. I chastised myself for expecting more from him. He was my watcher. He'd volunteered to help council bind me. He owed me nothing. But it didn't stop the hostile glower I was sending his way.

Ruby stepped in front of him. "I'll stay with her."

He didn't reply but merely turned from her to walk into the haze.

I was still fuming when she faced me, wearing a self-satisfied smile. She practically danced forward to plop down in front of me. "I have something for you, Frey."

I simply stared at her. She was harder to stay mad at. I expected her to be a pain—it wasn't as difficult to accept that she'd kept the truth from me.

She extracted a small package from beneath her cloak and passed it to me. I pulled the material aside and saw the V etched into the cover. I wondered what Chevelle would do if he knew she'd given it to me.

She answered my curious gaze. "It's yours, and I think you should be able to read it."

I could do nothing but nod. It didn't matter. Her expression made it clear that she considered herself forgiven. She faced the direction Chevelle had gone and left me to my discoveries.

I EXPECTED *fury from my father. He never failed to disappoint me. He saw the child, as he called her, as an opportunity. I shouldn't have been surprised. After all, had he not stolen my mother for precisely the same purpose, to experiment with power? He did, however, concern himself with where I'd found a human.*

I refused to tell. The only gift I could give Noble was his safety. I laughed bitterly as I remembered that was how I'd convinced him to stay. I'd promised him protection, but it was a false promise.

Eventually, one of the servants slipped, revealing they had seen me following my sister. And just like that, she was to blame for the entire ordeal, even though she'd never known. She'd been still searching the empty camp for trinkets and trifles. At least I was off the hook.

I SURPRISED myself by being so slow. Of course, her sister would have been Aunt Fannie. For a flash, I felt sympathy for Fannie, but it passed. Just because life had given her sour grapes didn't mean she had to stomp them into wine and get drunk.

I wondered whether Fannie had known all along, but that was hard to discern. I did know that she had been bound, as I was.

THE ELDERS WERE a different story altogether. My father had given them orders to protect me and the child, and even though they followed through with them, they persisted in chattering about their concerns. The humans frightened them unreasonably. They constantly fretted, wanting to keep her—and me—from contaminating anyone else.

I attempted to reason with them, but they turned on me. "You don't understand. You never will! They will consume you. The humans will consume us all." Their hands shook as they spat out the words.

I didn't argue after that. I wouldn't have been allowed to leave the castle, anyway. Besides, it kept her from being paraded in front of so many visitors.

I STOPPED AGAIN. I had been born in a castle. I sat with the journal for a long moment. There was no way to reconcile that information with my own thoughts, no way to fill in what the bonds had taken. It hurt to read the diary, but there was no *not* finishing it. I decided the only way to keep going was if I did it as I had before I'd known it was my mother. I had to be an uninvolved reader.

MY FREYA HAS GROWN into a stubborn and willful child. She's prone to fits of screaming or crying. The emotion frightens the elders. It comes from her father, yes, but I can't see how it will harm her. The humans seemed to live their lives fine, controlling it well enough.

I FROWNED, hating that I felt like crying or screaming and that I could not step away from the story because it truly had been written of me. By my own mother. Then I remembered the tales of elven grief, how it could become strong enough to overwhelm one enough to take one's life. I felt sick, but I continued.

I RECEIVED a visit from my mother's sister today. News of the child had reached her, and she felt she needed to call on me, now that my mother is not here to guide me.

I was in my room when she arrived. I heard the two quick raps and then one loud knock from her visits during my childhood and instantly knew it was her.

I gushed as my Aunt Junnie came in, grateful for someone who actually felt like family. She wore a simple hooded cloak, seemingly unafraid as she passed the guards at my door. She walked as though she ruled the castle, not as if she were a light elf in the center of a dark lord's rule.

She confessed to me a secret her family held, a power I had not known from my mother. They had kept it from my father, though he had stolen her after hearing a rumor of it. She passed to me many details of her sister, of the family... my family. She'd risked so much by coming here to help me, to help my child. I would owe her.

I HAD to stop reading as betrayal ripped through me again. *Junnie.*

Ruby laid her hands on mine, which were trembling, but I would not take the dust again.

Tears streamed silently as I drifted, the ache in my chest only dulled by exhaustion. I felt weak when I woke, but I was silent about the pain as we continued the journey. Yearning to avoid my thoughts altogether, I spent much of the day in the mind of my horse.

IT WAS evening again when we stopped. I barely noticed the group's mood—though quiet, they seemed anxious and kept the perimeter close. Ruby brought me the book again, and I took one long, deep breath before I started back to it.

FREYA IS GROWING AND STRONG. She has amassed a following of sorts, though I suspect it is somehow connected to her frailties. There is something endearing about it, but some of it worries me. She doesn't seem to be able to hear as well as she should through her rounded ears, and her voice is oddly alto. She is a beauty, though, her unusual features earning her extra atten-tion. The elders express their anxiety again that the humans will consume us, but my father is already discussing arranged marriages, even mentioning Rune's son, of all people. He'll do anything he can to gain power from her.

. . .

IT WAS hard to read my mother's diary. I had so little memory of her, but it had not diminished the loss I had felt all along. Her writings went on until they became more erratic, answering questions I didn't want answered.

MY FATHER HAS TAKEN Freya from me. He has assigned her tasks, and Rune watches over her, testing her. It's just as Junnie feared—just what he'd done to my mother. I will find a way to stop him.

THE ELDERS ARE KEEPING Freya now. Guards have been assigned to me. Like a prison.

I KILLED three guards to get to her. We only had a moment before I was torn away from her, yet I feel I got the message through.

SHE CAME to see me last night. I don't know how she got past the guards. But I begged her to keep our secret, for her protection...

AND THEN SEVERAL pages were torn from the diary before it continued.

IT WAS AN ACCIDENT. A product of her temper, her human emotions. They were testing her, a servant told me. Anvil was holding her back physically, Rune with magic. She snapped, and they saw her power. Some denied the possibility, but not my father. He has attained his prize, that which he has always coveted. I will stop him.

THE PLAN IS FORMING, *but I am unsure whether it will work. I know I cannot defeat him and his guard alone. But I must protect my Freya. I must protect us all. It is the want of power that will consume us. The want.*

THE SCRIPT WAS SHAKY, many of her words hard to decipher. It felt ominous.

I HAD no choice but to escape. I would need a distraction to have any chance. I went to the village to find my young Noble. I didn't expect what was there.

On my way in, I found the spot where we had met on so many days. I almost didn't recognize it, bare of growth, the dirt patted down from years of wear. And then I saw him, the man in tattered clothes, hunched over with his face in his hands. He heard me approach and raised his head, the awe all that was recognizable.

"You're back." His voice was trembling, feeble. It was my Noble, young no more. He had been waiting for my return.

He was an outcast of the village—no one believed his tales of magic, the mysterious woman he claimed to meet here. He confessed to spending years trying to find me. He'd thought I was angry with him and that was why I'd not returned. He was afraid to leave this spot in case I were to change my mind and forgive him for whatever he'd done.

I pushed the guilt aside when I recalled why I'd had to come here. For my Freya, to save her. What my father had done to me, to my mother, I would not let him do to her.

I approached the grieving man and reached out to him. As I held his hands, I closed my eyes. I could not watch as I snapped his neck, the way I had with the small boar as my first show of magic to him so long ago. I placated myself by remembering he would soon be gone, his life so short.

I held him until the daylight began to fade then carried his lifeless body into the village as proof they would be attacked and killed, proof they must fight the elves. It was not hard to incite a riot. They were fearful creatures. I convinced them to raid the castle and gave them direction.

And then I returned. I knew I would have time to prepare. They would be slow to gather and make the journey. I was thinking of Noble as I resolved to wear the dress meant for our wedding, with its dramatic shape and deep meaning. I remembered when he'd given it to me, explaining the white stood for innocence. I had stifled a giggle then. I could find no humor now. Yes, it would be fitting.

I KNEW WHAT WAS COMING, but what I had read so far was much more horrifying than I'd expected. I didn't want to continue. I couldn't believe that I had been so stupid as to forget it was my mother who had destroyed the Northern clans and taken the families from everyone I knew. As they stood protecting me, the betrayal I'd felt before was gone. In its place was a new hurt, a heart-rending sorrow.

They heard my sobs. I was aware of their eyes on me before they uncomfortably turned away again. Chevelle approached me warily as I lay curled in a ball on my blankets, the book positioned in front of me. He tossed it aside, but I no longer cared. He sat behind me and pulled me into his arms, holding me as I wept. It felt more right than anything had been in a long, long time.

I AWOKE WITH NEW RESOLVE. I stood, prepared to make things right, but something was off. The group surrounded me, tense. I glanced at our surroundings but couldn't see why.

And then, from nowhere, I was thrown into the air. I landed hard against my back. I slid down a wall of stone, barely managing to stand when my feet hit earth. Ruby was suddenly in front of me. I threw my hands back to steady myself on the stone barrier behind me. I didn't look to see where I was, though, because just as I'd regained my footing, I heard the howls.

Before the next breath, a new sound—a closer sound—filled my ears: *shoosh, shoosh, shoosh*. It took longer than it should have to realize they were arrows. My mind couldn't seem to process the scene quickly enough. Before I could distinguish the threats, they changed. The hands I'd splayed against the wall for support were in bonds. I forced myself to look away from Ruby's back, and her arms stretched out defensively, to see what was holding me.

My breath came then, fierce and gasping as panic took over. Long vines were wrapping tightly around my wrists and reaching for my legs. I burned my right wrist free, fighting to reach my sword before they grew back. Large thorns burst from the vines on my legs and pierced my skin like daggers. I barely had the capacity to hope they weren't poison. I sliced at them furiously, but I wasn't fast enough. There was a flash of lightning, though no storm was near.

A vine wrapped my shoulder, jerking me back. I was trapped. I looked to Ruby, but she could not help me anymore. Beyond her, a line of long, flowing robes marched through the mist. They were coming for us.

The sight gave me strength, or courage, or blinding stupidity. I didn't know, but I gave everything I had. I was trapped against the wall, unable to move, but there was one thing I could do.

The sun broke through the clouds, and I saw precisely what I needed. A shadow crossed the ground in front of us as a hawk flew overhead. The corner of my mouth pulled up in a smile as I closed my eyes to join him.

The scene from above was just as incomprehensible. I focused on one thing at a time. Directly below me, I saw Grey. He was caught, wrapped in vines as my own body was, but there were flames circling his feet. I followed his gaze to find his opponent then dove.

I hadn't planned what I was doing, still running on adrenaline. I decided the fastest course of action was pecking the council fighter's eyes out. It worked. He threw his hands up, covering his face, screaming. But he did not attack me. As I rose to find my next target, I saw the wolves. They were also not being attacked and were fighting with no opposition. I remembered what Chevelle had said. They would not kill the animals.

As I laughed, the hawk screeched, and Chevelle and Steed glanced up at the sound. They were fighting, almost back to back, the bodies of council fighters strewn around them. I surveyed the land, searching for a stronger animal to jump to, something more harmful. I ran through my options, but I wasn't able to find anything nearby. Evidently, the fight had cleared the mountain, so it was just the hawk and the horses. I quickly passed through their minds, urging them to stampede before I returned to the sky.

When I entered the bird again, something was wrong. It wasn't only the bird—someone else was there. The shock of it threw me back to my own mind. My eyes shot open, and I scanned the scene again.

I forgot what I was looking for when I recognized a face hooded in a cloak, fighting against her own. *Junnie.* She stared back at me for one brief moment before she turned to fight some invisible foe.

That moment of shock took the last of the borrowed courage from me, and I drew in, afraid as my body remained encaged in vine and thorns. My legs were wet with blood, arms deadened to the pain and cold. I became aware of an unbroken chant, a voice I didn't recognize, and I turned, stunned again, as I saw Asher. He wasn't in the battle. He stood back, seemingly a bystander as the words flowed from his barely moving lips. Then he ran.

Confusion hit me again as Junnie chased him.

Ruby's whip cracked in front of me, and I knew the advance had gotten too far. And I was tied to a wall. *Why haven't they killed me already?* I waited for the flames, but what came instead was far more excruciating.

I expected to collapse as my body disconnected from my mind, but the vines held me in place. I saw a few final flickers of the battle before my eyes looked toward the sky, rolling back into my head. I had no way of forming a coherent thought, or I might have been afraid.

16

I was surprised, in my dreams, that I wasn't already dead.

For a long time, there was no sound, only those disjointed images. When the sound came, something else was wrong. It was like I wasn't alone. Someone else was there, dreaming with me, and I could see their dreams. They mixed with mine, creating chaos.

There were faces I didn't recognize and those I did.

I dreamt of Steed, winking conspiratorially, which was mine.

A large and frightening dark-haired man in leather and armor was not.

My room in the old tree, my mother's pendant casting rainbows on the bed was.

A long, damp stone corridor lit with torches was not.

There was Junnie, her blond hair shining in the sun as she greeted me at her door on the west side of the village. And Junnie, mysterious under a hooded cloak, fighting with magic and weaponry, killing members of the council guard.

We sat around a fire, telling stories. Someone was ribbing Ruby. Her eyes narrowed when she replied to him matter-of-factly, "Your mouth is very small. It's unattractive." And her head bobbed side to side as she smiled, pleased with herself.

Anvil laughed, and his tongue wagged. He was holding someone by the arm, preventing them from running away. Suddenly, my vision changed, and I was a hawk, attacking, tearing a piece from his tongue.

Chevelle was in many of my dreams. We were sparring sometimes, clashing with our swords. Sometimes, he was pummeling me with rocks. Other times, the moments would have surely made me blush if I could have felt my cheeks. He held my face in his hands, declaring his need for me. "I have wanted you since the moment I first saw you." But the word burned. *Wanted*. He'd used the wrong word.

Occasionally, I watched as a third person. My vision would change, and my perspective went off. When I saw Francine, she was razing the village, slowly tearing it apart. There was fire and wind and destruction as she cackled and taunted the villagers. She dropped them as they ran, sometimes snapping their necks, sometimes breaking a leg so they would have to stay alive to watch their homes burn and their families die.

There was a large man who forced me to do magic, testing me until I was on the brink. He was fierce, with a long scar crossing his brow to touch his cheek. He kept his hair cropped short, probably not wanting to hide any part of the damage.

And my mother was there, though my dreams gave her two names. Her dark hair blew in the wind, her arms outstretched, the pendant hanging at her neck glowing fiercely. Fire, flames, burning.

And then water. Drowning. Over and over and over. Being away from the repetitive drowning almost made the dreams of being shoved from a cliff more bearable.

I swam around in these impressions for what seemed like eternity. Eventually, they became so familiar that they all started to seem like my dreams, not someone else's.

Then the dreams stopped. No images flickered behind my lids, yet my eyes did not open. The muffle in my ears from the drowning dreams was gone. I could hear more clearly than I'd ever heard. I hadn't found my body yet, but I heard conversations among voices I knew. They were whispers, but they were clear. I listened, hoping to gain clarity, but something was still wrong. Nothing fit. They discussed Junnie and Anvil and Fannie, but those felt like two sets of people now.

They were worried. I could hear the stress in their tones. *How long have I been like this? It seems so long, trapped here.*

I remembered the vines. I tried to feel my arms to see if they were still there. *Is that why I can't move? Am I still tied to a wall? No, no, I'm not tied. Had the thorns been poisoned? Am I dying now?* I worked to calm myself. No—I was getting better, not worse.

I felt light pressure on my forehead, and my eyes flew open instinctively, though I'd had no response from them all the hours I'd struggled to force them open.

It was Ruby. She sighed with relief. "Oh, Frey."

I was suddenly surrounded, and the sight made my head spin. I closed my eyes tightly in an attempt to stop it. "Get her a drink," someone commanded. I felt the hand in mine then, as it was pulled away and replaced with a glass. I grimaced. I doubted I could hold a glass up, let alone myself.

"Don't worry, it's only water," someone reassured me.

At the word, I realized I was parched, bone dry. I forced myself up, keeping my eyes tight as I concentrated on getting the glass to my lips. They were rough and cracked—I could feel them against the rim of the glass. I wondered if it was dried blood or if I had been down so long that they'd simply split. I drank the full glass and felt it exchanged for another.

I finished it and started to lean back. There was suddenly a pillow behind me, keeping me in a sitting position. It was soft. Everything surrounding me felt warm and smooth. I opened my eyes gingerly. I was in a bed. A very nice bed.

I looked up to see several people leaving. *Steed? Grey?* I fought panic as I wondered if they'd all made it. The worry throbbed in my head, and it felt as if my mind could splinter. I checked the faces close to me for stress but could see none. Ruby's smile was soft. "How do you feel?"

I was having trouble forming a simple answer. There didn't seem to be a word for it in the disorder of my brain. My silence was answer enough.

"It will pass."

I hoped she was right.

Chevelle was watching me anxiously.

"Is everyone all right?" I asked. My throat was raw, my voice gravelly.

"Are you?" he replied in a low tone.

I couldn't be sure.

He hesitated, almost not wanting to ask the question he knew he must. "Can you tell me your name?"

"Elfreda," I answered immediately. He waited for the rest. *I have two answers, don't I?* "Of North Camber."

It must have been the right answer, because he grabbed me, exultant, sighing and kissing my skin. He held me with a fierce gentleness that took my breath. His lips trailed my cheeks, murmuring words, careful of wounds as they swept to a temple, my eyelid, the corner of my mouth. He lingered there, unable to resist touching the broken skin of my lips, even if it was only feather light, the barest brush of skin.

He drew away slowly, probably feeling my shock or seeing it in my eyes and realizing his mistake. His expression fell, but he didn't take his hands away. He swallowed hard, waiting for my confirmation.

But I wasn't the other Elfreda, not the long list of binding words that had been my identity for so long. I couldn't seem to reconcile the two lives.

"I-I think I'm just Frey."

Chevelle's hands slid to my shoulders with tension in his grip.

"That's all right," Ruby assured me.

"We will find the others," Chevelle promised, his jaw tight. I couldn't tell if the pledge was meant for me or himself.

The others. I had forgotten, lost for so long in my dreams, the bonds I'd hoped would break, the councilmen we needed to free me. I wished I could think clearly. I tried to remember what had happened but could only see flames.

A FLICKER of movement caught my eye, and I turned to find a hawk perched on the ledge of a balcony. Suddenly, I needed fresh air more than anything.

Chevelle helped me to my feet, and I walked, a little wobbly, to the door. I had been dressed in a vest of dark leather and slim pants with carved medallions adorning my chest, but my feet were bare as they crossed the polished stone floor of the bedroom, at ease in a place they seemed to know. I stepped out into the sun, and I had to steady myself on the stone ledge, not because of the lightheadedness, though I was feeling faint, but because below me, before the steps to what I now realized was a castle, a thousand elves watched me. I sucked in a harsh breath, unable to get my mind to accept what I knew was happening.

I had been so oblivious reading the diary, learning of my mother and her ties to the throne. It had told of my own life and of what I was to become, a reality that would not be put to rights in my broken mind. But as I stared down, the assembled pieces of my shattered self held together by no more than tattered bits of string, I understood.

It was my place. It was part of what had been taken from me.

I heard Ruby behind me. In a low voice, she said, "They have heard of your return. They have come to see for themselves."

Their rulers had burned along with so many of their families. After the massacre, there had been no one. From the dead, it seemed, I had returned.

Chevelle stepped to my right side, placing a familiar weight against my palm. A sword. *My* sword.

I knew what to do, then. I took a deep, steadying breath as I raised the blade into the air. There was a faint pause, the briefest tick before the bird took flight, its wings hitting wind as the shift began, and then nothing could be heard but my name, roared in the song of the crowd below.

BOOK II: PIECES OF EIGHT

THE
FREY SAGA
BOOK
2

PIECES of
EIGHT

MELISSA WRIGHT

1

There were only three certainties in my new life.

The first was that I couldn't be certain of anything. The bonds that kept me from my memories hadn't been fully undone. The shattered images from before the binding didn't fit together the way they should have. I had tried to force them, but my bonds held me from reconciling the two lives: the years I'd lived as a dark elf, strong and powerful, and the more recent part—the part that seemed more real—where I'd been trapped, living as an untalented, unmagical light elf.

There weren't many memories of the first years, the ones spent in the castle where I was born, in line for the throne. Most of the information I had about that life came from reading my mother's diary after she was gone. The few memories that returned later were scattered. Attached to them was a feeling of strength, a power and confidence that was nothing like my second life.

For all that time, I'd thought I was a graceless light elf, an outcast, unable to use magic, but it turned out that my magic had been taken from me. I was still ungraceful, but at least I had a few special talents all my own. Not that I could even think about where that left me. My power and lineage would put me at the head of the dark elves' realm.

Everything I'd known had been proven false, and I was still struggling with reassembling the broken pieces.

The bits that *did* fit were my new family, the seven other elves who had fought to save me. We had only spent a short time together, but I had become dependent on them—honestly, I had been dependent on them all along but simply hadn't known it. They'd protected me from Council, who had bound me from magic and stolen my memories. Council, who had burned my mother and wanted to burn me.

"Frey."

Focus. I had a bad habit of getting lost in my thoughts. It was confusing there, foggy.

Ruby cleared her throat.

"I'm listening," I insisted, shaking out my hands to ready myself for another assault.

"We have to continue your training, Frey. It's important."

I narrowed my gaze on Ruby, not convinced my safety was really the issue. I had my suspicions that she enjoyed the training more than she let on. But Chevelle had insisted, and they'd been working with me daily since I'd woken in the castle with my memories partially restored. He'd assured me it was not a good idea to reveal that my bonds were still in place, for my own protection. I'd barely seen him in the days since we'd arrived.

Ruby's whip cracked beside my head.

Grey, who had a tendency to drop by on the days I trained with Ruby, chuckled at my expression, moving to stand. "Give her a break, Ruby," he said. "Frey, why don't you rest for a bit, go get something to eat?"

I didn't miss the glance she shot him. I waited, hoping she would agree.

"Fine." She waved a dismissal, bracelets clinking at her wrist.

I hurried to the door, wanting to make my escape before she changed her mind, but I had to turn back. My fingers played over the leather of my new breastplate. "Ruby?"

Though I'd been there for weeks, I still got lost any time I tried alone to traverse the maze of corridors. With an exaggerated sigh, she pointed me in the right direction.

"Thanks," I said over my shoulder, not giving her a second chance to stop me. The castle was massive, and that section of corridor was wide enough to accommodate a half-dozen men. I hung along the edge, feeling comfort in the closeness of the cool, dark stone, and tried to decide whether to eat in the dining area or just raid the pantries.

My steps were soft, the leather soles of my boots making no noise in the empty hall, so the echo of voices caught my ears well before I realized whose they were. I followed them, coming to rest outside a chamber a few doors down.

Chevelle saw me standing in the doorway and dismissed the slim, dark-haired man he'd been speaking with. The stranger—a castle guard, I thought—inclined his head as he passed me, his eyes skirting my own to follow the line of the floor. I waited, watching Chevelle as the sound of the man's steps receded. Chevelle had always been striking with his strong jaw, dark hair, and eyes of the deepest blue, but there was something more there too. Lingering at the back of my mind was some half-remembered dream I couldn't quite pull into focus. Those hazy memories felt as if they wanted me to reclassify every single look, every momentary break in his expression, but they weren't truly my memories, not yet.

When the hall was finally silent and he could let down his defenses, Chevelle smiled at me. It was nothing out of the ordinary, simply the same greeting I received from any of my guard, but because it was him, I flushed. I always flushed when I saw him those days, whereas before, it had been sporadic. Before he'd thought I was her, Elfreda of North Camber instead of Frey from the village, when he'd thought I was *that* Frey and he'd kissed me. I fought the urge to touch my lips at the intensity of that remembered kiss, but it had only lasted a moment.

Because he'd realized I was not the forgotten girl inside of me.

I worked to push the thought away, but no matter how I tried, I couldn't. In fact, it was almost all I thought of with any kind of clarity.

The second thing I was certain of was that I wanted him.

The moment my cheeks colored, Chevelle's smile fell back into his standard, stern expression, and he asked, "Shouldn't you be training?"

My jaw flexed, and I pressed my palm against the carved stone framing the doorway. "They said I could take a break, get something to eat."

He nodded and went back to his work, and I turned from the room without another word. I sifted through my thoughts as I went, still trying to find some kind of order. Reaching out to trace the interlocking lines of the stone wall, cool and smooth beneath my fingertips, I let my steps slow to listen for echoes through the corridor.

I couldn't say what I was missing in the memories of Chevelle, what dark secrets our past held, or why he'd kept his distance until he'd thought me restored, but other memories called to me. The recent days of training seemed eerily familiar, and it wasn't just that some part of my mind recognized the practice rooms—the feeling of being forced, of being trapped, was something I had experienced before. I was stronger—there was no question of that—but I still wasn't fully in control. However, they all insisted that I be prepared for anything. They were worried about someone finding out I was weak, confused, and unable to lead.

I was in danger in my own home.

Fingers still trailing the wall, I turned into the door to the kitchen and cursed. It was not the kitchen. I stood in the entrance to an enormous open space with high, arched ceilings. It was ornate, but not like the council buildings of the village. The dark walls were wreathed in deep burgundy and velvet, and intricate stone constructs bore the flickering light of so many torches. A raised platform stood in the center of the back wall, holding a grouping of elaborate chairs, the largest of which was unquestionably meant to be the focus.

My mouth went dry. I was standing in the throne room.

My feet moved toward it automatically. I gave no mind to the warnings I'd received from the others. They'd not mentioned it specifically, but of all the things I'd been advised against, I was pretty sure what I was doing would fall into the not-a-good-idea category. It was one more place in the castle I shouldn't have been exploring alone, one more thing that wasn't safe for me until I'd recovered.

A shiver crawled over my skin as I reached out to touch the design along the crest of the throne. Again, I remembered the day I'd woken from the battle. I'd been more than a little slow to understand. I'd spent weeks reading my mother's diary, her words spelling the whole thing out, but it hadn't crossed my mind once that I was in line for the throne, as she had been.

But I'd seen the gathering outside my window. Chevelle had handed me my sword, and I'd raised it overhead to claim my place as Lord of the North.

I smirked. That hadn't lasted long. Since I couldn't remember my previous life and didn't have the slightest idea how to rule, I'd been kept from public view, "just until we straighten things out."

I hadn't caught up with the details, but apparently no one had truly ruled since the massacre my mother had started so long ago. Since there wasn't exactly a set routine, the seven elves who had returned me were calling themselves my guard and had taken to setting things in order—privately, so no one could guess I was out of sorts. But it was my throne. I felt myself smiling as I rolled the idea around in my mind.

"Looks like the cat finally got her canary," Steed teased from the doorway. I reined in my grin as a hawk swooped through the door, flapping a wing inches from Steed's shoulder then drifting to land on the carved pedestal beside the throne. It shook out its feathers, their snap reverberating softly through the hall. I thought I remembered the bird from some of the memories that weren't quite mine—it must have been a pet of sorts. But it couldn't have been the same hawk. I'd surely been gone too long for that.

Steed was still looking at me, waiting for a reply while I was lost in thought. "Steed," I gushed, and he looked pleased. I choked back the enthusiasm, clearing my throat. "You and Anvil have been gone. I thought the pair of you had left."

He leaned a hip against a side table, crossing his arms in front of his chest. "Just checking on some things nearby. But we will be going soon."

Despite my best efforts, I knew disappointment was plain on my face. I flopped down on the chair, forgetting it was a throne.

Steed stepped forward, coming close enough to brush my cheek with a knuckle. "Frey, someone has to get the rest of your magic."

My stomach twisted at his words. They would hunt down the other council members, the ones who had bound me. They would have to kill them to release the hold on me, but it wasn't just that. I couldn't bear to see our group of eight separated. "I don't want you to go," I confessed, and for some reason that made him smile.

"What would you have us do, Frey?" Chevelle's voice from the doorway made me jump. I became intensely aware of the intimate distance between Steed and me. I straightened.

I'd assumed the question had been rhetorical, but Chevelle waited for my reply. I didn't know if it was because of who I'd been before or who I was supposed to be now, but I certainly didn't feel like I had any authority. Nor did I feel like that other Frey, adored and spoiled, second to the throne. But the idea only made me realize where I was sitting and what my chair symbolized.

I huffed out a frustrated breath, fighting the urge to argue. I wanted the bindings released, needing my magic and my memories, but I couldn't stomach the idea of staying there if they left. "Why can't we all go?"

Chevelle nearly rolled his eyes but caught himself. We'd had that conversation more than once. "Frey, we just got you back here. We can't leave. The North will be back in chaos in a short time. We've just given people hope."

I laughed at the idea that they had hope because of me then shook my head. Steed and Chevelle gave me a look that said they thought I could crack at any moment. It wasn't a look that I could get used to, though I'd seen it regularly enough. I ignored them, thinking of a way to leave the castle without giving the kingdom doubts about their leader, without revealing my condition.

Suddenly, something occurred to me. Steed's comment about cats and canaries replayed in my mind. I sat back in the chair and closed my eyes, falling into the mind of the hawk resting beside me. It was the one magic the binding had never taken from me, the one talent that made me unique. I flew from the castle and over the mountain, searching for what I needed.

I was aware of Chevelle arguing with Steed. "Why do you insist on making this more complicated?"

"She's not as weak as you think."

"You know the bindings are dangerous. And you've seen what the stress can do to her."

"She's safer with us."

"Is she?" Chevelle asked icily.

"They won't hurt her."

"You know, I can still hear you," I said, a moment before my eyes flickered open.

I could tell by their expressions that they did not know. I stood and walked down the steps in front of the throne. "It doesn't matter now," I said. "I've taken care of it."

As I walked from the room, Chevelle's expression turned, his fingers curling into the palm of his hand. I picked up my pace.

Eventually, I found one of the servants to guide me to my room. I was fairly certain her name was Ena, though I couldn't be positive because she looked peculiarly similar to another of the servants, whose name I couldn't remember at all. They both had long, dark hair woven into intricate braids that accentuated sharp features, but one of them was definitely taller.

There'd been no shortage of servants moving about the castle during the weeks since I'd woken, but I hadn't tried to remember them, not because I wasn't interested, but because of the way their gazes dropped or they found a new task just as I took note of their presence. It seemed awkward. But it wasn't as if they didn't know me, even if I couldn't remember them.

"The staff is in on the secret, Freya. It's not a formal thing. None of the details were laid out for them, but they would have seen clearly enough. Anyone in the castle would have known something was wrong," Ruby had explained, flipping her scarlet curls. "Not to worry. They've proven their loyalty. They waited here, stayed in this empty castle, anticipating their lord's return." Her eyes had leveled on mine. "It's what they wanted." And then she'd lit up the practice room with fire and demanded that I fight my way through it.

I bit down hard against a rush of irritation when I realized that Ena had stopped outside my door, but I'd kept walking at least a half dozen more steps before noticing. It baffled me that I still did not have any idea where my room was. It was beginning to get under my skin, and it didn't help that the lost feeling wasn't any better inside the room. Sure, I could tell it was the room I'd been sleeping in, but it didn't feel like mine—not that the tree I'd lived in back in the village would anymore, either. That life felt so far away that I couldn't even grasp it.

I sighed. How bizarre it was that sleeping outside with a group of strangers had begun to feel like home.

I ran a fingertip across the table by the door. It was near bare, holding only a few books of no real interest, an empty marble dish, and a jeweled pin in a style I couldn't imagine ever liking. The whole room felt impersonal. I wondered if someone had removed my things, maybe in the years I was absent, or perhaps if it was all I'd ever had. I glanced around the room and focused on the nightstand, which held no more than an assortment of blades and a boot clip. My stomach tightened, and I walked past the sheer silks draping the wide, pillow-covered bed, heading to the window to look out over the mountain.

The sky was a clear, sharp blue that melted into the mists hovering over the land below. The view was comforting, more so than anything else in the castle, but still, it was only a moment before my thoughts turned once more to Chevelle. It was obvious he was avoiding me, keeping a formal distance, but I didn't know how to change that. I'd tried, a few days after it became apparent what he was doing, but that had ended in disaster.

We'd been alone in the practice rooms, trying to develop my control. I had decided that I could break his resolve, but I had been concentrating so hard on my seductive face and the look in my wanting eyes that I'd forgotten to pay attention to my cursed feet. I'd been moving in for the kill when I tripped, falling flat on my face. He turned away when I looked up, and I was sure I saw him smile. A flush tore back into my cheeks at the memory of him fighting that smile, that laugh, and I flopped on the bed, buried my face in the pillows, and prayed for sleep to come quickly.

I vowed to myself that I would keep my dignity, but that was forgotten early the next morning, when Ruby woke me for training. I found myself groaning and complaining as she dragged me to the practice rooms to work with fire. She'd given me the it's-for-your-own-protection speech again, and I had to choke down further comment while she threw bits of flame toward me.

We hadn't been at it long when the cats showed up.

"Frey, Chevelle would like a word with you," Anvil spoke in the tone of official business from the doorway of the massive, open room. Still, I thought I saw a smile tease the corner of his mouth.

"What is it?" I asked, dropping my defenses to stare at my most solidly built guard.

"Best you come," was his only answer.

I took a deep breath as I followed him out with Ruby and Grey behind me. We went through the lower levels of the castle, where the staff carried on with their daily work, their heads down and their attention glued to their tasks. Anvil led the way as we wordlessly passed a group of sentries doing repairs to a block wall and another on patrol. Near the entrance to the castle, we found Chevelle, Steed, Rhys, and Rider.

Chevelle did not look happy. "Can you please explain to me why there is a pride of wild cats waiting for entrance to the castle, Frey?"

There should have been more than a simple clowder. I'd found as many mountain lions as I could and lured them to the castle. I tried to see past Chevelle then subtly raised to my toes to see over his shoulder. I barely caught a glimpse of golden fur glistening over a sleek, muscular body before Chevelle stepped forward, blocking my view.

It was more than evident that he wanted to put a strong hand on my shoulder to flatten my feet and keep me still. Instead, he peered into my eyes in an apparent attempt to force the answer from me with sheer will.

I sighed. "The cats will watch the castle for us." *Obviously.*

Ruby cracked a laugh, and everyone spun to glare at her. "She's right," she said, gesturing toward the cats. "I mean, who's going to doubt her powers now?"

They didn't exactly argue, but a silent chain of smirks and glares passed through the group. After several agonizing minutes, they apparently decided Ruby was right that the cats would leave no doubt as to my power. Chevelle shook his head and dismissed us to go back to training.

As Ruby and I left, Steed remarked in a low aside, "The wolves are going to love this."

I felt a pang of regret—I hadn't considered that. I'd barely seen the wolves since we'd arrived. I assumed they were outside, guarding us as usual.

Ruby elbowed me as we walked side by side through the corridor. I smiled back at her. We were all going together.

Within a day, we gathered, ready to leave the castle. The plan was to depart before dawn, drawing as little attention as possible. I'd made arrangements with Dree from the kitchen staff to feed the cats, and I fervently hoped none of them would attack the servants. *Except maybe that big one who offered to give me a bath*, I thought, the shiver of revulsion making me twitch.

Everyone was staring at me. I managed a timid smile and got the collective look that said they were waiting for me to lose it.

But I didn't care. Shrugging it off, I mounted my horse, so glad to finally be doing something. All we needed was to find one more council member, and I would be that much closer to having my mind back. I wouldn't have to worry about how the bindings stole my memories and my magic, or when they became overtaxed, even affecting my ability to simply stay upright.

That was the worst part. The harder I tried and the closer I came to breaking free, the tighter they bound me, bringing me to my knees —or worse. At times, I had been lost to darkness for I didn't know how long and had woken exhausted from a dream-filled sleep. I had heard whispers since our return, and I understood that the others had not been merely concerned for the amount of time I had spent lost to that darkness, but also because of the violence with which it took me.

I kicked the horse up, leading the others through the gates.

Chevelle was beside me in a moment, his expression amused.

"What?" I asked defensively.

He merely tilted his head toward the others, who were heading in the opposite direction. *So much for doing this with dignity,* I thought, turning to follow them.

We made our way down the mountain on a path that exited the castle from behind. I wondered briefly if we would wind around to where we had come from weeks before, or if we would be headed somewhere new. But it was all so new to me. Such a short time ago, the village had been all I'd known, the whole of my world. None of the land was familiar to me. Everything and everyone were just shadows of memory.

I scanned the landscape, trying to distract myself from the journey I'd been so adamant about taking. I couldn't see much in the dimness, but the haze eventually thinned, and light from the rising sun started to peek through, allowing me a better view of the area. I spotted a pen of what looked to be boar in the distance. Ruby had explained to me how the elves there herded the animals and kept them until they were needed. The game on the mountain's peak was too sparse to keep up with the population, and there was very limited foliage. I didn't see anything I would have called vegetation amongst the rocks, but she assured me it was there, and despite an apparent aversion to growing, the castle held at least two gardens that I knew of.

I'd read about the feasts in my mother's diary, and I knew it must have taken a fair number of animals to sustain the castle's needs. There would be more pens and more corralled beasts, and it reminded me of an idea I'd had before the battle: *I could keep some animals handy for whenever I needed them, in case we get attacked...*

I shuddered at the thought. We weren't about to get attacked—we were on our way to *find* a fight. I suddenly wondered why I hadn't waited until I had trained more. *Why hadn't I kept my big mouth shut?*

"Cold?" Steed asked.

"Um, no. I'm fine." The conversation I'd been missing was about the horses, and I jumped in, trying to cover my lapse. "What's your horse's name?" I asked Steed.

His eyes met mine, and in a casual tone he answered, "I've named her Elfreda."

Heat flooded my cheeks, and he grinned. The jangle of Ruby's bracelets behind me gave me no doubt that she was the one who'd told him I'd named my horse Steed, which I probably would have thought twice about if I'd known how things were going to turn out. I shot her a glare, and Steed leaned forward, patting his horse's neck to cover his laugh.

The way was rough, and I found that I liked riding up the mountain better than down. Maybe the old Frey was a good rider, or maybe it was only my nerves, but leaning back all day to avoid being tossed over the horse's head wasn't exactly enjoyable. Plus, we had not, as far as I could tell, swung back around toward the south side of the mountain. The stones were darker on the north side, less traveled, and kind of eerie. When we finally stopped for the evening, I slid from the horse and walked through the jagged rocks surrounding the trail while I waited for dinner and a fire.

The others were in an official-sounding conversation that I clearly wasn't expected to be a part of, so after a while, I busied myself by investigating what Ruby had packed for me. When I opened the first bag, my stomach knotted—it was full of weapons. I told myself they were for training, not for what lay at the end of our journey, and pulled out two knives. The blades were shiny and disturbingly sharp. I gingerly slid them back into the bag and took out a less offensive looking weapon, two sticks connected end to end by a thin metal chain.

It looked fairly harmless so, satisfied with my find, I stood to try it out. I had a hand on each end and gave them a pull, as if I were testing the chain. I had no idea what I was doing but figured it looked right. The contraption seemed to be pretty sturdy, but I couldn't decide how to use it in both hands, so I went with one. I'd seen Grey spin a staff and I thought I would try that method, holding the end of one stick in my right hand and swinging it carefully in a circle. It worked out nicely, so I swung it in a figure eight that wrapped around my sides. I found it went better with momentum, so I sped up a bit.

I really liked it. I got brave and tried out some new moves.

That was when the free end cracked the bridge of my nose.

Eyes watering, I risked a glance at the group to see if they had noticed.

They had. To their credit, they were trying to hold back their laughter, but it didn't matter. I had to save the embarrassment for later. My face hurt too badly to think of much else.

Pressing the base of my palm between my eyes, I sat blindly on one of the rocks behind me. I scowled beneath my forearm when I heard a low chuckle, sure it was Steed. Our journey had barely begun, and I'd already proven I was in over my head, which stung worse than the bridge of my nose.

I COULDN'T REMEMBER FALLING asleep, but I knew I was dreaming because I was the other Elfreda again. I was younger and braver, and though I couldn't lose the confusion even when dreaming, I was in control.

We were outside, but the ground was rocky, and the trees were low and spiky. We hid as we waited, pleased with ourselves as we watched our plan play out perfectly. Aunt Fannie had found our decoy. She was younger too, but old me still disliked her.

She spotted the scroll and checked to see that she wasn't being followed. She'd not seen us. Her eyes widened at the words on the page before she softly whispered them aloud. Beside me came a stifled chuckle as Chevelle worked his magic, burning lines into her palms. She dropped her prize then froze as she took in the image on her skin. It was false map that would lead her in circles for days, giving us time.

.   .   .

I JERKED AWAY from Ruby's touch as she tried to wake me. It was dawn. I was covered in sweat and muddled, confused. All I could see was that image burned into Fannie's skin.

Had it been a dream? It had to be that I had taken the real memories of the map I had found, which had led me north—led me to the castle—and combined them into a dream. Nothing else made sense. It could not have been memory.

But Chevelle had been with me as we tricked Fannie. I couldn't believe it. It must have been a dream because I could not fathom why he would have deceived me in the same way. I shook my head, hastily grabbing my things as the others waited.

The images nagged at me all day. They would not be quieted even as we rode down the mountain, farther and farther from the castle.

I tried to remember the words that had called up the magic to draw the lines on my flesh. I was almost certain of them—it had been such a shock at the time to find a map burnt into my skin. When I couldn't resist any longer, I held back from the group as we rode and whispered the spell: "Fellon. Strago. Dreg."

Nothing happened.

Maybe I'd used the wrong words. But no, I was sure. Maybe it was a spell that only worked once. But I'd never heard of that, either, not that I knew that much about spells.

Spells had been forbidden in the village, to be used only by Council. They were certainly not for the likes of me.

Maybe I was already there, so there was no reason for the map to appear burned into my palms. However, the lines had disappeared before—I'd been riding into the village where we had met Ruby.

My mind returned over and over to that point and to the idea that it could be a memory, not a dream. But my hands were clean, and I held fast to the one shred of evidence I could muster: no one had the power to heal.

We were stopping before I realized it was evening. I was exhausted from worry.

Ruby must have been able to tell something was wrong. "Ooh, you should have put some snow on that." She giggled, pointing to my black eyes from the previous day's self-taught sticks-on-a-chain lesson.

I managed to glare at her, but it hurt more than it was worth.

We sat as Chevelle lit a fire, and I tried not to eye him suspiciously. I'd once marveled at how good he was with a flame and thought that maybe he had some sort of reversible burning power. *Now you're just making things up*, I chided myself. I considered the incident at the creek again, when the map had first appeared on my palms. He'd been so sincere later, when he'd said he had to take me north—once I saw the map, I was compelled to follow it. He regretted that he hadn't been paying closer attention. *I'm sorry, Freya. I let my guard down.*

He couldn't have burned the map into my palms. He'd said he'd been distracted. He'd had his own agenda—I'd watched him the night before as he snuck into a strange village and through a window for a secret meeting.

I froze as I made the connection. "What about Junnie?"

Ruby shot a quick glance at Chevelle, but his eyes didn't stray from the fire. She looked away, busying herself by rummaging in her pack as he answered, "What *about* Junnie?"

"I saw her when we were being attacked." I swallowed hard at the memory, forcing myself to stay on track and not to think of the day I'd nearly lost myself to the bonds in my mind.

Chevelle did look at me then, but I had my own answer about Junnie. My voice was weak as I talked myself through it. "She's a member of Council. She received the calling just before I left the village."

He let me digest that, but I was sure the fog in my brain and the breaks in my memory were keeping me from being able to make sense of it.

For all of those years, Junnie had been my only friend in the village, but it turned out that she hadn't been merely a friend at all. As my mother's aunt, she was my family. I'd read in my mother's diary how Junnie had come to see her, to warn her. I replayed my memories of the days in Junnie's study, of her lessons. She'd been kind to me.

There was no question about that. Even though she would never have let on that she was any more than my mentor, it certainly wasn't the only thing she'd kept from me. She might have helped me with my studies, but she'd never truly taught me about magic.

I hadn't been sure then that I could even do magic. I had fire, though, and one morning, Chevelle had shown me how to control the tiny flame I'd been using since I'd arrived at the village.

"Frey?"

Ruby's voice pulled me from the spiraling thoughts. I looked up at her, away from the warmth and flicker of the camp's fire. I could feel the tension in my face.

The pity in her eyes made it easy to believe that our group was as important to her as it had become to me. It was all either of us had. She was alone but for a half brother and a missing father, and my only family were my two aunts, although I couldn't be sure whether I could count either. Thoughts of Fannie replaced my stress over Junnie.

And then something gnawed at the edge of my memories, a forgotten dream of Aunt Fannie, glorious in her anger—

"Frey." Ruby's voice was harsher than before. "It will be dark soon. We should continue your training." I had the feeling she was trying to distract me. Someone always interfered when they saw the strained look on my face as I fought with the bonds and the memories. A chill wind cut across my skin.

Ruby choked out a laugh as she scrutinized my bruised face. I narrowed my eyes at her when she said, "I'm guessing you don't want to try weapons today."

3

Training was as brutal as always, but I had a harder time than usual because I couldn't stop my mind from returning to Junnie and Fannie. I wished there was a way to retrieve my memories and stop the ridiculous eddy of dreams and recollections. I cringed as I realized the most likely way was the one we were taking: hunting down and destroying those who'd bound me.

Instantly, worry set in. There was no guarantee it would work and no guarantee that no one would be hurt. It was why they'd had to be so careful with me before and so valiant in their watch against Council. I was determined to keep working and not to think of the flames.

But I did have that memory of the fire that had taken my mother, and it made me reconsider what I'd read in her diary. I hadn't wanted to finish it after the revelation that my father had been human, the description of my mother's own father and his wicked plans, and her depiction of the madness that led her to destroy the North.

I glanced around the camp as I sat alone with Ruby beside me, her legs curled beneath her, giving her a bit of height. The others spoke in hushed tones across from us. It didn't make sense that they'd survived. The reports I'd seen of the Northern clans had claimed extinction.

"Ruby?"

She smiled as she answered, always anticipating something entertaining. "Hmm?"

It was hard to find the words. "What happened when my mother..."

Her brow tightened as I trailed off. "We don't have to talk about this now, Frey."

"I want to know," I said, but it didn't sound convincing.

She shook her head, light glinting in her emerald eyes. "You *think* you do."

"Would you be happier if you never knew..." I lost my words, unable to finish or to point out that she'd poisoned her own mother and who-knew-how-many others by accident.

Her reply was cool. "Wouldn't I?"

I sighed, scooping up a rock only to toss it aside. Ruby was probably right, but not knowing was torturous. "But she couldn't have... I mean, you are from the North, as are Steed and Chevelle." As I waved toward them for emphasis, I noticed Chevelle watching me. Staring at me. My throat went thick. My mother had killed his clan. "She didn't kill them all?"

Ruby's face flashed with sympathy and then irritation before reaching a third emotion that I couldn't quite make out. "No, Frey," she said, "but most remained scattered until things settled a bit."

I let out a deep breath, gaining at least some relief.

She eyed me suspiciously. "Frey..."

Uh-oh.

"What made you think she'd killed them all?"

I bit my lip, forcing my gaze to stay on hers. "Um, I read it?"

Her eyes narrowed. "That wasn't in the diary."

I hesitated, not wanting to admit anything about my research project but unable to skirt the truth. My thumb slid over the sharp edge of another rock. "It was in some papers from the village."

Her eyes flicked to Chevelle then back to me. He was still watching, but his face had gone hard.

Ruby's words were very nearly an accusation. "I thought you burned those."

"The ones from Council, yes. These were from the library." I glanced from Ruby to Chevelle, seeing that it troubled them but unsure why. Suddenly, my brain caught up, and I turned back to Ruby. "Wait, *you* read the diary?" It came out a little sharper than I'd intended.

She almost blanched. Instead, she answered matter-of-factly, "It was of interest to me."

Before I had time to respond, Chevelle was beside us. I was startled, and then I flushed because it was the closest he'd been since my failed seduction, and I couldn't seem to rein in even my minor reactions.

He seemed oblivious. "That wasn't in the documents you found at the library."

I flushed anew. He *had* seen the documents at the library and knew I had been researching him.

He waited for my answer.

"Um, I found these before."

"In the library?" He was still serious.

"Yeah." And then I remembered, pointing vaguely upward despite the fact that we were currently not in the village or the library. "Actually, they fell from a higher level."

They were staring at me as though I'd missed something obvious, something they didn't like. Ruby interjected, "Frey, are you sure you didn't pull them to you with magic?"

"I don't think so," I said, leaving the "how would I know?" implied.

They stared at me.

"What?"

Chevelle was close and in careful mode, the one they used to protect my delicate brain. I nearly snickered at the thought but didn't —it clearly wasn't the time for that. "Were there any other documents, papers, *anything*, that you found?"

The way he said "found" confused me. "I don't know."

He waited while I reconsidered.

"There were those, and the ones in the library the day you helped me study..." He hadn't been helping me study, he'd been watching me. I huffed out a breath. "And then the ones in the council library."

"Nothing else?"

"Only the scroll."

They both glanced away, almost flinching, before Chevelle turned his focus back to me. "Are you sure?"

"Yes, but it didn't matter. They were all messed up, anyway."

His fingers tightened against the hilt of the sword at his hip. "What do you mean, 'messed up'?"

"They were all out of order, just loose pages." His eyes narrowed, and I couldn't stop myself from talking. "The stuff about the Northern clans was mixed in with stuff about Fannie and you—"

I stopped suddenly when it looked as though he might have paled. I couldn't be sure because before I could get a good look, he was gone. I watched after him for a moment then turned to Ruby, who was expressionless.

"What is it, Ruby?" I whispered.

She composed a polite smile. "Nothing, dear. You should get some sleep."

I glared at her, not for the first time, and received no response. They weren't going to tell me anything. They were too worried about my fragile brain.

I flipped a blanket out a few feet from the fire and flopped down onto the hard earth, frustrated and annoyed. I wondered if I could get someone else to tell me, maybe Steed. It could be worth a try, but I didn't know about the others. I liked Grey very much, though I had my suspicions he hung around more for Ruby than anything else. Rhys and Rider were always on the periphery, watching and guarding. That only left Anvil.

I glanced in his direction, finding only the vague outline of his form among the mist. There was definitely something about Anvil— I'd been drawn to him since the first time we'd met, wanting to be his friend. It didn't seem right, though. He was massive, not to mention the fact that he could shoot lightning from his hands, and he should have been frightening. The feelings I had toward him, that inexplicable pull, didn't match my dreams of his tongue wagging then being burned and torn away.

I groaned, rolling over as I tried to remove the image from my mind. There had to be another way. Maybe there was more in the diary. I should have kept reading it, but I hadn't wanted anything else to do with it once I'd found out. I wondered where it was. I couldn't remember seeing it after I woke. The last time had been the night Chevelle had tossed it aside, when he'd held me as I wept. There were so many images I had to banish from my mind.

And then inspiration hit. Surely, we were still close enough...

I closed my eyes and concentrated until I found what I needed. My new talent seemed better all the time. I was in the mind of one of the mountain lions I'd left in the castle, seeing through his eyes. His vision was clearer, but it was harder to stay focused than with the horses.

He didn't cooperate as well as I would have liked, but I was able to get him to move from his comfortable spot. I couldn't discern exactly where that spot was, but when I tried to look around, the cat became distracted by the sight of blood, and I had to focus harder to keep him moving. I really hoped that was whatever Dree was feeding them and not Dree herself.

The cat had been lounging high on a ledge, possibly in the throne room. I was still confused by the layout of the castle and not sure how to get the cat where I wanted, but I could embody its mind and thought I knew where we needed to search: Ruby's room.

As we wandered through the corridors, my head began to ache. The halls of the faraway castle were unusually empty, and I didn't know if that had anything to do with the presence of the cats. I tried several rooms, but most that were open held nothing of interest.

I was wondering how I would ever find Ruby's room and the diary when I came to a set of double doors I'd never seen before. They looked more ornate than the others, with intricate iron details and arched stonework around the frame, which showed promise, proof of their importance. With some effort, I reached a heavy paw up to pull the lever that released the latch. The cat was bigger than I'd realized, and his weighty body pushed the door right open.

He slinked forward toward the sheer-curtained bed, and I let him, looking around as we went. It seemed easier to ride along than to constantly try to control his movement, but I couldn't decide if that was due to the distance or the animal. He pounced on the curtains, pulling them loose, and lazily plopped down on the end of the bed to survey the room.

I wasn't sure how to know when I'd found Ruby's bedroom, let alone where to look for the diary, but it was definitely a woman's room. There were rich fabrics everywhere and dresses draped over the wardrobe door, but they were dusty. Upon closer inspection, I realized it couldn't have been Ruby's room—it obviously hadn't been used for what seemed to be an exceptionally long time. I wondered why the servants hadn't cleaned it.

An annoyed rumble rolled from the cat as I tried to move off the bed to get a better look at the items on the vanity. We didn't budge. My head was throbbing, but I pushed harder. He refused to behave as I wanted, and I wondered if the cat's resistance to my direction was why so many fewer than I'd planned had shown up at the castle.

Suddenly, his muscles tensed, and he turned his head at some commotion nearing the door. He moved too quickly, and I struggled to concentrate on making out the shouts over approaching footfalls.

"The seal has been broken... Miss Vita's room... No, no, by one of the cats..."

I didn't know whether it was the pain in my head or recognition of the name that brought me back, but I was gone from the castle in a heartbeat, the link broken. I sat up on my blankets, rubbing my temples as I attempted to focus on what I'd heard.

Vita was my mother's mother, according to the diary. She'd died from grief, it had said. My mother had tried to see her and her room later, but it was sealed, kept from her by her father.

Ruby was watching me. "Headache?"

Having an audience had become unsurprising. I opened my

mouth to speak but was too exhausted. Instead, I only shook my head and lay back down. It was nearly impossible to examine the memories between the exhaustion and pain, so I tried to not think as I drifted off to sleep.

I FELT BETTER when I woke but was still foggier than usual. It was late morning when I remembered I was mad at Ruby for keeping something from me. I shot a glare in her direction, finding only her back as she rode. I focused on the drape of her cloak and her bright-red curls knotted into a scarf.

Steed noticed my scowl. "Don't be sore with Ruby."

I raised an eyebrow at him, drawing my own cloak tighter around me as the horses stepped over loose stone.

"She had her reasons for the invasion. She's very interested in your... lineage."

I realized he was talking about her having read my mother's diary, and my irritation flared. I had forgotten that part.

Steed had stopped talking, so I composed my face and waited for him to continue, trying to appear patient. He smiled at my attempt, and we fell back from the others.

"You know some of her story, that she's a half-breed," he said.

Patience was a hard thing.

He could tell I was struggling and winked. "I should start from the beginning. It will be a long ride, after all." His grin died as he began what I knew would be a somber story. "My mother and father had a happy life. Their differences fit nicely together, and their bonds were strong. But the horses couldn't thrive on the mountains that my mother loved, and my father traveled often to find new blood to bring in for the line. He was gone sometimes for months at a time, as was I, once I began to learn the trade." His hand fell automatically to the shoulder of the beast beneath him, and he ran his fingers over the smooth dark hair. "Which is why we were both absent during the incident in which she lost her life."

I stifled a groan, sure the "incident" he referred to was the massacre single-handedly caused by my mother.

"We returned separately, as I was detained in another matter, so I was not there when he received the news."

I realized I was holding my breath and focused on matching it to the rhythm of the hoofbeats. I wondered if Steed's father had the same short dark hair and easy smile, if he had the same way with the horses.

"When I finally saw him, he was beyond distraught. He was not himself. I was fearful for him, but I too was in mourning. Likewise, I had my own duties to fulfill. So I was gone again when the second tragedy befell him."

Ruby's mother.

"The fey woman found him in such a condition that it was effortless to sway him with enchantments. All this you know. What Ruby has left out is the root of the issue. Yes, you are similar in that you are both from unmatched parents."

I very nearly laughed at his term.

"But the real reason she was interested in your mother's diary was because... Well, you were what sparked the idea in her own mother's twisted mind."

I was lost, and he could tell.

"You see, Frey, your mother was bred"—he paused, pursing his lips as if changing his mind—"*created* for uniqueness. But you? You were born with it."

I couldn't think of my own mother or of myself, labeled a crossbreed, so instead I thought of Ruby. *Uniqueness.* "Well, she got it, didn't she?" I knew we were both thinking of her venom when we looked at her.

She turned back with a half smile and shot us a wink. I could see why Steed had helped her, despite everything. After all that her mother had done to destroy his family, it almost gave me hope. It seemed that the group had forgiven me for my mother's actions as well.

I wondered how clearly those actions might have been detailed in the diary. "I wish I'd finished reading it."

"Why don't you?"

"I don't know where it is."

"I'm sure Ruby has it. She carries everything she values with her."

The possibility almost had me clicking my heels to catch her, but she was riding near Chevelle. He tended to get annoyed at this sort of thing, and I still had an odd feeling about him, given the dream, the memory, and the strange lines that had curved over my palms. I tried to shake it off but stayed back with Steed.

I had a lot to avoid thinking about as we rode, so I bantered with him like we had when we first met. It was nice to be out of the castle, to breathe the cool mountain air, to be away from so many shifting eyes, and to have a purpose, even if I had to keep from questioning what our purpose was so that I didn't make myself sick with worry. When Steed and I talked, laughter came easily, and soon, the group's pace slowed as everyone joined in the conversation.

The casual mood continued throughout the day, and all seemed in good spirits when we stopped earlier than usual for the evening. I groaned when Ruby suggested training before dinner, so Chevelle offered to spar with me. He knew it was something I enjoyed—it was the only training that was tolerable, mostly because I didn't get hurt, though it also wasn't as tiring as practicing with Ruby. Nothing about it taxed those bindings in my mind and on my powers. Everyone gathered around to watch as Chevelle and I clashed swords, a rhythmic clinking the only sound besides the occasional comment or murmur of approval from the makeshift audience.

As it often did when I trained with Chevelle, time slipped by faster than I'd realized. It was getting dark when he straightened and lowered his sword. I tried to wipe the grin off my face—I knew I was improving immensely. Someone lit a flame, and our audience moved to surround it. I started to follow, but Chevelle stood still for a moment, simply watching me. His eyes were bluer in the waning sun, and he must have forgotten to mask his features.

He didn't speak, and the pressure of silence built in me, bringing all sorts of things that I shouldn't say to the tip of my tongue. He made no move to ease the tension, and I panicked, fearing something as disastrous as my last attempt. I blew out a nervous breath, hurrying past him to join the others.

Apparently, the tension had been all mine. He didn't guard his countenance, even as I glanced at him frequently during dinner.

It seemed he was watching me, too, but I'd been known to imagine things of that sort. After all, I was the one staring at him. I forced my eyes down, picking at my food, and the process of eating became daunting. Time passed, but I could still feel his eyes on me, even if he wasn't looking.

Wind cut through the sparse narrow trees, and Ruby came to sit beside me, smiling mischievously as she offered a small metal cup. I peered inside, suspicious of what appeared to be water, and she laughed, bumping my shoulder. When I raised it to my lips, she slipped a parcel onto my lap. It was the diary.

I glanced at her, knowing I shouldn't have been surprised that she'd heard, and she wiggled her eyebrows as she rose to play in the fire. The flickering light threw shadows across the leather binding of the diary. It was heavy in my hand, and I was suddenly unsure. Maybe Ruby was right about being happier not knowing.

I ran my fingers over the cover, etched with Vita's initial. I remembered once thinking it had stood for Vattier. I'd been wrong about so many things. I tucked it into my bag. After the day we'd had, I didn't want to lose the good feelings just yet.

I should have known better.

4

———

I'd fallen asleep thinking only of the patterns of crossing swords, choosing to avoid thoughts of Chevelle, so I was surprised to dream of Fannie.

It was a familiar dream, but I couldn't be sure why. I was taking in the scene from above, my vision slightly off. I could see her there, wild and violent. She was destroying the village around her, uprooting trees, burning them to ash. And she was laughing. As I watched the devastation, I recognized the villagers as my own, but even in my dream, that was not the worrisome part. Nor was it the broken bodies, the demolished grounds. There was something else, something I couldn't quite grasp...

I awoke unsettled. Although Ruby and the others remained in the previous day's elevated mood, I couldn't shake the feeling. I glanced around as we mounted and started back on our path. We'd covered some distance, and the terrain had settled slightly. It wasn't as steep or rocky, so I was able to relax in the saddle more. My thoughts kept returning to Fannie and the dream.

I suddenly realized I knew something about her that I was sure hadn't been explained to me by the others. I might have dreamt it, or it might have been there, unnoticed until I'd focused on the memory of her.

What I knew was that Fannie had been skipped. As the oldest daughter, she had been in line for the throne before her sister. Their father had, at least for all public purposes, disowned her, instead choosing my mother as his heir, his second. The details weren't all there in my mind, but I remembered from reading my mother's diary that from an early age, Fannie had been shunned for her light features, a product of her mother's heritage, and her lack of the power and uniqueness that her sister apparently possessed. She held more light magic, also like her mother, and he had disdained light elves.

It was disconcerting when the memories returned. Most of them came to me in dreams, which was confusing—parts of my previous life seemed strange enough to be dreams, while my dreams so often felt real enough to be memories.

Chevelle had once told me that he thought the memories found their way back more easily in my sleep because they didn't have to fight as hard to be released from their bonds while my mind was resting and unable to resist. It had made sense then, but I wasn't sure they couldn't just slip through at any time. Maybe they were already there, and I simply hadn't sifted through them enough.

A shiver ran through me, though I was wrapped in a heavy cloak, and when a rock clattered down the path, I flinched. It was only knocked loose by a horse hoof, and I was growing more self-conscious about how jumpy I'd become. I adjusted my position in the saddle and glanced at the others, who seemed oblivious to my jitters. Maybe they were just getting used to it.

The dream still shook me, so I closed my eyes and drifted to the one thing that gave me solace: the bird soaring overhead. I glided for a while in large, calming circles over our group and eventually scanned farther. I attempted to survey the path ahead, but I wasn't positive where we were going. My hope was that if I did a sweep of the land every morning, or maybe a few times a day, I would spot danger ahead of time.

Suddenly, I was back in my own head again, wondering what I'd gotten myself into with hunting Grand Council, scoping out the perimeter, and planning to capture animals for use in battle. Maybe I *was* nuts—maybe those looks I'd been getting were rooted in something real.

But in the back of my mind, I had to fight the thought that going mad wasn't as far-fetched as I might like to think. It had happened to my own mother, after all. I felt my face pinch and tried to smooth it before someone noticed.

I realized they were otherwise occupied when Grey began whistling a tune and asked Anvil to join in, provoking him about his inability to do so due to a damaged tongue. Anvil flung a metal stud from his vest at him in retaliation, and it must have been carrying electricity because the instant it hit Grey, he jerked, almost losing his seat. Steed laughed, and it wasn't long before a mêlée between the three ensued. I was beginning to enjoy the spectacle, though it looked painful. Before it escalated further, Chevelle called over his shoulder, "I can think of a better use of your energy, men." However, I thought I saw him smirk when, several minutes later, Steed and Grey were still twitching.

Out of nowhere, an image came to my mind. For no apparent reason, I remembered someone. There was a split second of astonishment before fear choked me.

It must have been audible because instantly, the others were surrounding me. "What?" someone said, but I wasn't sure who. My ears were ringing, but I couldn't bring myself to be irritated because I was overwhelmed with terror that was quickly turning into hatred.

I made an effort to focus when Chevelle was in front of me. I thought he'd grabbed me by the arms and pulled me from my horse, but I couldn't be certain because when I was finally able to bring myself back to the moment, he was all I could see. It was good he was close, because I was only capable of a whisper when I said, "Archer Lake."

An intake of breath swept through my audience, although I could only see Chevelle's face. It was a study in fury. The name meant something to him as well, but I couldn't tell if it was more than simple recognition. All I knew about Archer Lake was that he was a member of Grand Council, and I hated him.

Someone asked where Archer Lake was, and I forced the sick feeling down enough to explain. "It wasn't a vision," I said. "Just a memory." As if I had returned from nowhere, missing essential pieces. "I don't know how I know him." I'd no idea from when, though it had to be from my previous life, surely, and no idea why it had come back. "Only the image of his face." And the knowledge of his station. And the feeling that accompanied them.

"Does that happen often?" Grey asked, his brows knitted beneath short, shaggy bangs.

I shook my head. "No. Just today."

"There's more?" Chevelle said.

"I'm not sure. I remembered something new about Fannie this morning."

He blanched.

It seemed like less of a coincidence all of a sudden. The dream of Fannie that had bothered me so much was creeping into my thoughts again, along with the one before that included Chevelle. I looked down at my hands, at the ground, at anything but him.

After a few minutes, Ruby collected herself enough to keep me occupied, per usual. She offered me some powder for my headache—which I refused, having been subjected to her concoctions in the past—and fluttered around doing things. I didn't watch her too closely, partially because the flow of her clothes and swing of her bright-red curls made my head ache, but mostly because I was forcing myself not to hope—and at the same time, fear—that my memory was returning.

The group made like there was a good reason we'd stopped for so long in the middle of the day, busying themselves as well. Steed adjusted the packs on the horses, Grey sorted and cleaned weapons, and Anvil stood with his arms crossed over his broad chest, staring into the distance.

When we finally got back on the horses, they took it easy until early evening, when we stopped again to set camp. I was impressed that they managed to make creating a fire and situating themselves around it a seven-man task.

No one even mentioned training.

THE NEXT MORNING, I was groggy—they'd let me sleep in. Grey and Anvil looked itchy to get back on the trail, so I hurried to mount my horse, taking my cold breakfast with me. The extra time had allowed for better hunting, and our bags were packed with stores of food. I couldn't believe I'd slept through the smell of cooking meat. I remembered how I used to love elk, but it was everyone else's favorite as well, which made it hard to come by on the mountain.

I froze, the chunk of meat suddenly heavy in my unmoving hand. My love of elk was another new memory. I examined it, unsure whether to explain it to the group. It was nothing aside from a preference, so I decided to let it go. I could tell them if I remembered more. Chevelle watching me, so I kicked my horse up as if I'd only been daydreaming.

We rode at a more normal pace as the ground leveled off a bit where the mountain valleyed into a smaller ridge. The rocks were changing again, and I looked back toward the castle to see how far we'd come, but between the distance and fog, I couldn't see it. I wondered how the cats were doing. When they'd arrived, there had been more than one fight—they were extremely territorial, and I couldn't seem to convince them otherwise. They were complicated animals.

It made me curious about how other animals would react. I'd had pretty limited experience so far, but birds had proven very useful.

I recalled my plan and looked up, trying to find a vessel to scan the mountain again. There was a large red-tail, a nice one with good eyes. I briefly considered bringing it with us, in case I wasn't able to find one when the urge struck, but there seemed to be plenty available, so I took a brief survey of the land around us then let it be.

We continued that way for days, following the valley for more passable ground. Twice, I spotted the wolves. It made me feel more secure to know they were out there, but I still did a quick sweep from above at least three times a day. The feeling of foreboding grew worse the farther we traveled from the castle, and my paranoia increased as we closed in on our destination, wherever that was.

Then Ruby decided to start telling her fey stories, which, since I knew they were probably all true, only made things worse. I tried to ignore her by flying over the valley, gliding over a spectacular view. The gray rock was beginning to give way to vegetation, and deep-green trees had started to appear more and more frequently. I found myself counting them, marking their patches. *Dark green, dark green, dark green.*

"Does that not tire you?"

Where I might have jumped, surprise didn't have the expected reactions in the bird's body, but it pulled me back to myself. I opened my eyes to find Anvil riding beside me, watching.

I grinned at him automatically then remembered he'd asked a question. "Oh, um... I guess not, not really."

"That's good," he said, smiling, and I had to brace myself from reacting to the thought of his burning tongue. He was such a contradiction—part of me was so drawn to him, so trusting, while the other part reeled at the image in my dreams. I pushed the memory down, thinking instead of his talent and how it exhausted him of strength.

"The lightning tires you, huh?" I asked. Sometimes I thought I sounded like an idiot, mostly when I wanted to impress someone.

He didn't seem to notice, resting the heel of his hand on the pommel as he leaned forward. "Yes. But it's worth it, I think."

"How did you think to try?"

He laughed lightly. Apparently, I didn't get the joke.

I found myself wondering if I could do it and concentrated on my hands while we rode, willing electricity through them. Nothing happened. I didn't really expect it to, but then I saw Anvil's wide grin, and I grimaced at forgetting he was beside me. *Yep, usually just people I want to like me.*

But he did like me, and he was part of my guard. I lowered my voice. "Anvil?"

He shifted toward me, and I struggled to find the right way to ask. "What do you know about me?"

He stared at me while I waited for his answer. And then I was thrown forward in the saddle as my horse came to a sudden stop. Chevelle's horse was inches in front of mine, blocking us.

"Frey, we've been neglecting your training," he said. "You should work with Anvil as you ride."

I tried to hide my reaction, but it was too late.

Anvil chuckled. "Don't think she relishes the lightning."

Chevelle was undeterred. "Grey, then."

Anvil smiled as he moved forward, and Grey fell in beside me, our horses joining the group's pace automatically as he began his version of training.

He was outfitted in dark leather, the unadorned sleeves cut widely to allow extra movement. "You know what I find helpful?"

"Being able to disappear and reappear?"

He laughed, and I softened. His eyes glinted as he grinned conspiratorially. "Distraction."

Our lesson continued throughout the day, and he was good at both the teaching and the distraction. I forgot most of what had been worrying me and concentrated on retaining Grey's tricks, practicing sleight of hand and diversions.

When we stopped to make camp, I stuck by Grey's side, content to keep on task with the nontaxing occupation. I didn't let myself be concerned about the diary or what waited inside. I didn't think about what the coming days might bring or where we were headed.

THE NEXT MORNING, I kept silent, hoping no one volunteered to teach me about a new weapon or something equally painful. But Ruby had taken to telling stories again, and no one mentioned my practice. I happily returned to the sky to hide from her terrible tales and the constant threat of practice and our eventual destination, but it was impossible to deny when I could see that we were traveling toward the territory of the light elves and the Council that wanted to destroy me.

The chill had fallen off, the haze clearer, and I examined our new surroundings from above. The sun warmed the colors of a patch of dormant weeds to almost golden, and the new color was such a pleasant change to the scenery that I kept looking, trying to pick out more.

What caught my eye next was so wrong that I couldn't quite process it. The pressure on my arm was the only indicator that I'd gasped.

I opened my eyes to find Ruby grasping my arm tightly and wearing a concerned expression. "What is it, Frey?"

"I don't know." I tried to sort my thoughts and place why what I'd seen seemed so important. I knew what was wrong with the picture. "Blond hair."

Their faces reflected mine, I was sure. It wasn't a dark elf.

"Was it a council member?" Ruby asked.

"I don't think so. She... well, she didn't look like it. And there was a man with her. He had a dark cloak with a hood."

"Where?" Chevelle snapped from my other side.

I hadn't noticed how close he was, and it took a moment to find the answer. "About two miles." As soon as I pointed out the direction, he was gone. I kicked up my horse, racing behind him and trying to keep up, but the others were faster, finding our target well ahead of me.

The seven of them were surrounding the strangers before I had a chance to see anything. I threw myself off my horse, leaving him where a couple of the other horses stood, and stumbled blindly toward the group. I pushed through where they had gathered, determined to not be kept out.

Chevelle's hand flew up to keep me back. I pressed, but his grip was strong on my shoulder, restraining me.

Rhys and Rider had beaten us all there. The plain black cloak was a pile on the ground in front of them. The man I had seen lay crumpled beneath it, motionless. His hair was dark, the carved leather of his bracer familiar somehow. My eyes fell on the girl, and I knew she was next.

I yelled, "Stop!"

And they did, if only to look at me.

My outburst couldn't have bought me more than a moment, but I wasn't able to capitalize on it because standing before me, on the other side of Chevelle and the outstretched arms of the tall, slender, silver-haired Rhys and Rider, was a sight my brain could not process.

But there it was, right in front of my wide eyes. The blond hair that I had seen from above framed a soft face, flushed cheeks, full lips, and round blue eyes filled with fear.

It can't be.

When the breeze caught her shoulder-length locks and flipped them back, it was just enough to reveal rounded ears.

I almost fainted. All that saved me was that in the split second before blackness hit, I saw a nod.

I knew what that nod meant. Chevelle, standing inches in front of me, was instructing the pair of elves before the human to end her life.

"No."

It came out with more desperation than I'd intended, but it caused them to hesitate. Chevelle looked at my face for a long moment, and I stared back at him with a wordless plea.

The seconds dragged on agonizingly. *I cannot let them do this.* Chevelle's face was hard as he finally turned from me and called it off. I wasn't sure why, but for an instant, I imagined it was because she was like me. I felt my cheeks color and looked down.

Then I slipped off the edge.

WHEN I CAME TO, I was convinced it had all been a dream. I almost laughed at the absurdity as I tried to sit up, holding my throbbing head. Ruby steadied me, purring something soothing as she handed me a drink of water. It helped. I opened my eyes, and she was right there, trying to hide the concern in her gaze. I wondered what was wrong with her then realized Chevelle was beside me as well. Though he was angled away, he turned to look at me when he noticed I was awake.

It irritated me that this fainting thing was becoming commonplace.

Ruby was unusually quiet and looked as though she might have been biting her tongue. I hoped I wasn't about to get dusted for some reason that I couldn't see. She'd used the powder on me more than once when I'd been bound, anytime my mind became overwhelmed.

I started to scan my surroundings, but Chevelle was blocking my view of the others, who seemed to be gathered several yards away, huddled around something. I leaned, straining to see past him, and he put a hand on my arm to steady me.

"Easy, Frey. You should rest more. Don't get too excited."

What?

"Just lie here for a while."

He wasn't trying to steady me. He was trying to restrain me. When my glare hit him, he reluctantly released my arm and straightened, allowing me to see.

At first, I was only numb. When I realized my jaw was hanging open, I snapped it closed and clenched it so tightly that I wondered if my teeth might shatter. I felt the heat in my cheeks. I wasn't getting enough air. But I couldn't release my jaw. I knew from much experience that I would regret what I was about to say, so instead, I just kept staring.

The others noticed I was awake as they talked with her and turned to gauge my reaction. I was surprised they were speaking with her as if she was... well, as if she was one of *us*. That idea turned my stomach, but they seemed genuinely interested in her. Especially Steed.

I felt the flush of my cheeks brighten when I gathered that he was *particularly* interested in her. He sat close, leaning in, as he often had in our private conversations, his voice too low to hear.

Ruby's face appeared unexpectedly in front of mine, her eyes wide, and I realized I was making a sound akin to a growl. I should have been attempting some kind of control, but I couldn't bring myself to care. An actual human was sitting there. It was just too much. It made everything too real.

Somehow, I'd still believed they didn't exist, though I'd read in my own mother's diary that I was half human. It was hard to deny when I was staring directly at what was indisputably one of them.

She was surrounded by the only thing I had, my friends, my family. A fire lit in my palms, and Ruby clasped her hands around my wrists. I knew she couldn't be burned because she was half fire fey, a hard lesson I had learned during training, but I wasn't sure it mattered. I had been teetering on a ledge for months. I couldn't even say where that ledge *was* anymore.

I was standing before I realized it. A brief flash of memory, too quick to act on, told me the mumbling chant coming from Chevelle was a problem.

Blackness hit.

It was hard to say how long I'd been immobilized, but when I did finally regain control, I didn't want to move. My head throbbed, and my ears rang. I'd been down before. Chevelle wasn't causing the pain —that was me, fighting my own brain. I had to.

I knew Ruby was waiting beside me, anxious for me to respond, but I didn't. I couldn't manage any kind of composure.

Eventually, the ringing in my ears lessened enough that I could hear the girl's voice, which only agitated the turbulence in my mind more.

A human. I could not, would not, allow myself to be compared to *that*.

It was unreasonable, and I knew it, but the unbearable, unrelenting emotions tore their way through me anyway, tied to some darkness, some secret that I could not recall.

No one asked me to move or reminded me that we had a task to follow through with. No one did anything but entertain themselves with the cursed human.

Time passed. I had finally moved into a sitting position, facing away from all of them. A human in our camp felt too wrong—unacceptable—for a reason I couldn't quite identify, and it wasn't just that the others seemed to enjoy the oddity of her so much. True, Ruby and Chevelle kept their distance from her, but I had my suspicions that they were only staying near to keep me in line.

I stared down at my arms wrapped tightly around my knees, concentrating on picking at the dark fabric of my pants. When I heard a peculiar noise from her general direction, I wasn't able to stop myself from looking over my shoulder, a knee-jerk reaction. She was staring at me.

A very nasty thought crossed my mind, and I yelped when Ruby stomped my foot. Apparently, I'd said it aloud.

My toe throbbed, but Ruby was wrong if she thought I would be abashed. That girl had been eyeing me with pity. *Or like I'm mad.*

When the noise came again, I forced myself to ignore it, finding a spot farther away from the group. I mumbled under my breath that I should have let them lop her head off, and Ruby made a sharp sound, but I couldn't tell whether it was a laugh or a hiss.

The rest of the evening, spent on a rock well away from them, was hard, full of the bad feelings and foggy memories that haunted me. At nightfall, Chevelle came to get me. I didn't turn to him at first, imagining him smug—after all, he'd intended to be done with her right then and there. I'd been the one who stopped him. I hadn't wanted them to kill her.

That realization lessened my anger just enough to allow me to breathe. Irrational as it might have been, I was having serious trouble controlling my reaction.

Chevelle stepped beside me, standing to stare in the same direction I was. "We should continue tomorrow."

I glanced at him, unable to read the emotion on his face in the dying light. Honestly, I could really only be sure when he was angry, which he didn't appear to be. I nodded, and it seemed for a moment as if he might reach out to me to comfort me—or possibly to smack me for my tantrum—but he merely turned and walked away.

I sighed deeply before rising to follow him to the camp.

IT TURNED out I was able to cope with the human's presence by ignoring it completely. It might have been petty and childish, but it worked. It seemed that because I had spared her life before going into that lengthy sulk, she was now under the group's care, excluding, of course, Chevelle and Ruby, who were constantly throwing glances toward me... to check my stability, I presumed.

However, I had been a model of good behavior, except for one incident around the campfire. Once I was back with the group, it wasn't long before I saw the source of the peculiar noise. It was the yelp of a small, dark puppy the girl they'd been calling Molly kept tucked under her arm, hidden beneath her heavy shawl. When I'd proven capable of self-control, she'd given it more leeway, allowing it to romp and play for the delight of its new audience. *Her* new audience. At that moment, it inexplicably attacked, giving the girl a good, solid bite. Like I said, there was the one incident.

The girl had seemed baffled but had immediately forgiven the tiny black pup.

When we reached the base of the mountain, the overall discontent I'd been feeling since we'd left had spread through the group, building into stony silence. We were hunting down Grand Council. And we had a human... pet.

We made camp, and Ruby escorted the human from the group for privacy. It was Ruby's only real contact with her. I was glaring in their direction, wondering why she didn't just piddle on our blankets like the pup, when a catclaw seed smacked me in the back of the head. I whipped around but couldn't tell who had thrown it, so I gave up and sat on a low rock slab to wait for dinner.

That was when I realized they were talking about her. They were trying to be discreet, but I knew what they were saying. They were working out what to do with her, how to get rid of her. My chest tightened as I focused on the conversation.

"No," Chevelle said, his words making it entirely clear that he didn't trust Grey or Anvil with her. I couldn't understand why.

Grey shrugged. "What about the brothers?"

Chevelle's eyes shifted toward Rhys and Rider as he said, "They have refused."

Steed nodded once. "I'll do it."

I was talking before I could contain myself, the words sour. "Sure, you'll take her home." When they turned to stare at me, I realized I was furious. And that I was standing.

Chevelle's face was hard, and I had a flashback of the look he'd given me at Ruby's so long ago, when he thought I was jealous of her affection for Steed.

I swallowed hard, forcing myself to sit down, but it was too late. My outburst had cost me knowing their decision. I lowered my eyes to the ground as Ruby came back with the girl. I didn't know what was wrong with me, couldn't understand what it was about the idea of her that made me want to claw my chest out.

Am I truly going mad?

"Who's hunting tonight?" Ruby chirped, and the others pointed to anyone but her. They chattered as they prepared, as if nothing important was happening, as if it was just another day. For them, maybe it was. Maybe I was the only one who'd been blind to the existence of humans and who hadn't realized how much danger I was in.

After dinner, Ruby moved to sit with Grey and Anvil, telling more stories of the fey. I faded in and out of her tale of Violet Moon. "She came from the South," Ruby said, "farther than any area of record, and she possessed a wicked knowledge of the changelings."

Any chill faded, and I knew the flame twisted within the confines of the circle at Ruby's command. She would make it dance along with her words, make it flare and spark. "They say she was bored with her native land and traveled North, looking for those who would not know her disguises and deceits."

My head lay cradled in darkness, where my arms made a bridge across drawn-in knees, as Ruby began regaling us with Violet's seduction of a young fire fey, complete with plenty of unnecessary details of his physique, when Steed said my name. I looked up, across the fire to him, and I almost choked.

He hadn't exactly said my name. He'd used my nickname—well, my old nickname—on *her*. He'd called her Sunshine.

My face burned. Steed didn't notice my glare because he was still talking to her, laughing. He reached up to tuck her hair behind her ear, and I heard a loud pop, or maybe felt it. I was off balance for a moment before I realized it was fire.

I gasped, looking around to see if any of them noticed.

Everyone had, not that I could blame them. I had pushed fireballs out of my squeezed fists so hard it had actually been audible.

They stood motionless, staring at me until finally Ruby asked, "Frey, are you all right?"

I took stock. "Yeah." *What just happened?*

She took a tentative step toward me. "Have you been practicing your fire?"

I shook my head. I hadn't practiced at all since the girl had shown up. There was no way my power should have increased that much so suddenly.

"How do you feel?"

"Fine." I held up my hands, wondering if I should try to do it again.

Reading my intention, Ruby shouted, "No!" She pointed out into the night. "Please, Freya, if you must, then do it away from here."

Everything in a ten-foot radius was singed. "Sorry."

I started off in the direction Ruby had pointed, and Chevelle joined me before I'd gone two paces. He walked beside me in silence, and when we were much more than a safe distance from the others, he halted.

I stopped as well, giving myself a few extra steps. I couldn't place his mood as I glanced over my shoulder at him, so I simply faced forward and took a steadying breath. Through squinted eyes, I watched, holding my hands out to release the flame. The size and power of it was astonishing, and it hadn't even tired me. I turned back to Chevelle trying to gauge his reaction.

I thought his expression was hopeful. Or maybe he was just trying not to laugh. It was hard to tell. "How do you feel?" he asked. His features were lit only by sparse moonlight, filtered as it was by clouds.

"Good." I smiled. And then I felt like a fool, so I straightened to match his posture.

That almost made him chuckle. He stepped toward me.

I froze.

We were alone, and he'd positioned himself squarely in front of me, not even an arm's length away. He didn't speak—he merely gazed into my eyes as if he was searching for someone. *For her.* I was close enough that I could see, even in the dark, the faint line across his chin that years ago was a scar. He was so familiar, so much a part of my other life, that it was painful.

At that moment, standing alone in the night, I remembered touching him. I recalled looking at his strong hands and placing my fingers on his. So I did.

Before I could process what had happened, his other hand was pulling me closer for a desperate kiss.

His mouth was warm against mine, his grip drawing me up to meet his height. I melted into him, relishing the sensation of his touch, of the closeness I'd been trying to reach for so long. It lasted only a moment before he realized his mistake and gauged from my response that I wasn't her, that the touch must have been merely a coincidence. He drew back to look at me again as he asked softly, almost in a whisper, "Who are you?"

I only shook my head, but he understood. He pulled his hand free of mine, and I was suddenly ashamed—I had no excuse for my actions. I'd tricked him into thinking I was someone else.

But I had remembered that touch. I glanced back at Chevelle. "What's happening?"

His face was pained, but he didn't have time to answer before Grey and Anvil's voices echoed through the darkness. Chevelle took a step away from me as we awaited their approach.

My head spun. The three of them started an apparently serious conversation, but I couldn't keep up with any of it. I merely followed them, massaging my temples as we made our way back to the camp. Steed was still near the girl, but he was quiet. Ruby had my blankets out, and I went straight to them, lay down, and closed my eyes.

It was hard to find escape from the torment of my own mind.

My dreams were confusing. They were almost all about Chevelle, but some were horrifying and some were not. I dreamt of the touch, of *before*, but the dream included our kiss from hours ago. I dreamt of things fantastic and impossible. I had some of the old dreams as well, clinging to him as we rode away from the flames with tears and ash smearing my cheeks. There was the dream of the cliff too. I stood, looking out across the horizon, and he stepped beside me, placing his hand at the small of my back. But when he shoved me off the ledge, instead of me flailing the entire way down, wings spread out and caught the air, and I took flight, soaring in the empty expanse, free.

I woke to laughter and was irritated to find them surrounding *her* again.

I rode in silence through the day, savoring a couple of the better dreams.

Once we reached the base of the mountain, the terrain turned to level ground. The trees were wiry and jagged, but they were trees nonetheless, and there was grass. Instead of feeling relief at the more familiar landscape, I found myself wondering how big a mistake I'd made by leaving the castle.

We stopped for the evening under the sparse shelter of a patch of those trees. It was warmer, so I excused myself to change out of my heavy leather boots and wool pants and into something a little more suitable. I opened my bag to find that Ruby had packed me only black with leather or silver accents—I was Lord of the North, after all. *So much for something light. At least it isn't all wool.*

I threw on the first pants I found, switched my shirt, and laced the lightest corset over it. Draping the cloak over my arm, I walked back to the camp, muttering the entire way about the redhead in charge of my wardrobe.

I was already in a foul mood, so when I saw them, I had to bite the inside of my cheek to keep from cursing. Steed was sitting opposite the human, so close that it was nearly indecent. I focused on walking to my bags across the camp from them and putting my cloak and pack away. I took as long as I could, but eventually, I had to join the group. I thought I tasted blood.

I tried not to look at them, I really did. But he touched her cheek with the back of his hand, and she flushed. He grinned at her wickedly. It was the last thing I was sure of.

What happened next didn't make any sense. I was across the camp, looking at him, but I wasn't. I could see myself in the periphery, and my head screamed with pain. Steed moved across my line of sight as I swayed, and blackness came as my eyes closed.

When they opened again, my head throbbed, with a duller version of the knifepoint pain from earlier. Back in my spot, I tried to focus, staring at Steed and the girl, but something was wrong. She had fainted. I concentrated harder and discovered Ruby staring at me accusingly.

"What?" I asked, automatically defensive.

Her eyes narrowed. She suspected *I'd* done something to the girl.

I should. But then I looked back at Steed and the human, and suddenly I understood. I *had*—I'd been in her head, just like the birds.

The pain of it was horrible, and the girl was only just coming to. When they helped her sit up, she looked frail and exhausted. Her thin hands trembled, clutching at her cloak to wrap it tightly around herself.

I lay back and covered my head to think, or maybe *not* to think.

I was asleep so fast, I might have blacked out. My dreams were darkness. Swirling blackness surrounded me. Suddenly, there were voices. One was familiar, though I couldn't place who it belonged to. "They are like witless animals... weak... She could get through to them... Think of the possibilities..."

I knew he was talking about me, comparing me to a witless beast, an animal. Anger flooded me. The darkness turned to water as I struggled to reach the surface, unable to breathe, drowning.

I woke with a gasp, expecting to find Ruby there, watching me. What I saw instead was almost as shocking as the dreams.

"There, there." Steed brushed my bangs from my face.

I jerked away from his touch.

"Rough one, was it?"

I had the strangest feeling that he was teasing me. I must have managed to glare at him, because he laughed.

Sitting up gingerly, I looked for Ruby and Chevelle. They were several yards away, watching me but pretending not to. I wanted to groan when I saw Chevelle's tight jaw.

I wrapped my arms around my knees to bury my head. As I fully awoke, I wondered whether Steed had been teasing me all along, trying to irritate me for fun. He surely had no real interest in that human girl. I cursed the thought trying to surface that *I* was part human.

There was so much else to worry about, and it was unfathomable how I could have such distaste for someone simply because she was so like me. I lifted my eyes just enough to peer over my forearms, looking for the girl. I found her sitting with her puppy, as far away as from me as she could possibly be while remaining inside the camp.

No, I decided, *she is not like me.*

Out of the corner of my eye, I noticed the crook in Steed's lip as he watched me scrutinize her. I glared at him in response, but he only shook his head as he got up and trotted across camp to play with the puppy. I vowed not to give him the satisfaction of watching them.

But apparently, I wasn't one to hold to my word. Because when I saw him close to her, talking low and calling her my sunny nicknames, I found myself acting without regard to dignity.

Everyone in the camp turned to stare in astonishment as the small blond girl smacked Steed heartily across the face. I had already been focused on them. I had only a moment to enjoy it before the pain came again. My vision swam, my head pounding and ears ringing so that I couldn't focus on anything else. I lay my head down, and when I was finally about to open my eyes, Ruby was beside me.

The girl was sitting alone, looking completely confused and ashamed, rubbing her temples. Steed was standing across the camp, talking to Grey with his back toward me but angled enough that I could just see the edge of a bright red welt on his cheek.

I smiled with satisfaction as I let my eyes fall closed again.

I was quiet for the next few days. My attack seemed to have quelled the others' interest in the human, and I couldn't deny that it offered at least some relief. Silence was the easiest way to mask my contentment.

They would have to find a way to be rid of her soon, though I'd not heard any more discussion on the matter. I tried not to wonder how much longer I had before we found the council, or they us. I could see a few of them in my resurfacing memories, but I couldn't recall their names or anything about them—only random images had returned. I hadn't mentioned it to anyone because it seemed hardly worth the commotion it caused. Commotion made my head ache.

As we kept riding, the grass thickened, and the trees began to look more like those of the village, though not nearly as large without the assistance of a light elf's magic. We'd stopped near a pond to camp, and I was considering taking a dip as Ruby took the girl for her evening's privacy. The men gathered nearby, talking in hushed voices. I decided it wasn't worth eavesdropping and having myself act the fool again, so I looked out over the water, watching the dragonflies bounce just above the glassy surface.

The days had become warmer, but the evenings felt more of my new home in the mountains. It was cool and dark in the castle where I had apparently been raised. Even though I couldn't remember that time, there was comfort in the night that brought a relief from the heat and brightness that devoured the southern lands. As the sunlight faded, I sat on a rock near the water, and it was cool enough that I could close my eyes and almost pretend I'd never left the safety of the castle.

The group's discussion became heated, and I absentmindedly turned toward them. My eyes caught a flicker of movement in a tree line several yards behind them. Suddenly, Chevelle was gone, and Steed and Grey were posted in front of me protectively before I even had the chance to see what—or who—the movement was.

I couldn't understand why we hadn't heard the wolves signal. Panic flooded through me as I remembered the battle from before. The feeling of being tied to that wall and stabbed through with thorns as my mind was attacked was indelible.

Someone had come for us. For me.

I tried to calm down. Even if it was the worst I could imagine, if it was Council, that was who we were looking for. I cursed myself again for insisting that I come along. The seconds dragged as I waited.

After what felt like a few eternities, I recognized Junnie's voice. She was speaking with Chevelle in a rush, her tone low. As they drew near, Steed and Grey relaxed slightly in front of me, Grey stepping a pace to the side. I had been moved to standing. Steed's arm was so close that it was almost touching me as he stood half in front of me. I stared past him, the tension in his muscles making me wonder why he was still protecting me.

Then I remembered that Junnie wasn't just my tutor and friend. She was Council. She was my mother's aunt. My head swam, and I clutched Steed's arm in an attempt to focus. I had no idea how to react to her. She was still speaking to Chevelle in a flood of words that ran together. She hadn't even seemed to notice me.

When she finally looked in my direction, it was not at me or my guards. I barely had time to turn and see Ruby approaching before it happened. The spots in my vision came just as fast. Through them, I saw a flash of Junnie's cloak flying past as she picked up the limp body of the human girl, and then they were gone.

5

____

I should have caught on by then that the fainting was a protective mechanism, but I didn't always think rationally, and shock wasn't an easily controlled reaction. The bonds that held my mind captive shut down my body every time I struggled to get free. They refused to let me break out of the spells tangled within, tightening their hold with every strike I made, every stress I tried to endure. I fought them anyway, and I was barely able to hang on. It had taken me to my knees, but I wouldn't let it take me further, no matter the cost.

Before my eyes opened, I heard someone speaking: "The pup as well..." Recognition came, and then confusion returned. Junnie had seen the girl—the human—and her reaction was fierce, even worse than my own. I'd heard a low oath just before the girl's body had collapsed, hitting the ground with a chilling hollow thud. Junnie hadn't even waited for an explanation of who the girl was or why she was with us. If I'd only been able to tell her, I might have saved the girl.

My blood went cold. I hadn't even tried.

I lost my focus then, despite my resolve. My eyelids fluttered as the blackness came, leaving me with nothing but dreams.

I WAS in the practice rooms. A tall, dark-haired man with a long scar across his brow was threatening me, pushing me too far. Darkness creeped closer and closer, surrounding us. Then I felt alone in the gloom as it swirled around me, but I couldn't have been truly alone—I heard voices. My chest tightened as I realized what the voices were saying about me. They compared me to them, calling me a witless beast. It ached. *How could he?* I didn't understand. I ran to my mother. She had been right.

I AWOKE LONG before I could bear to open my eyes. When I did, everyone was quiet. I didn't question them, and I'd forgotten about the girl, about Junnie. All I could think of was the dream. It couldn't have been right. My grandfather had been killed in the massacre, and he hadn't ruled since. He *must* have been gone, but the man in my dream—Lord Asher, my mother's father, the one who had driven her to the massacre, the man who had pushed us both—was not gone.

I could not fathom how that man could have possibly been the same Asher who had met with Chevelle when Chevelle had been gathering the others—my guard—at Ruby's.

I remembered the first time I had seen the dark-haired man and the look he'd given me, the way his knuckles whitened as he gripped the staff, his shabby cloak. I remembered thinking it must have been a disguise because of the way he carried himself, then chastising myself for being so paranoid.

I realized I was staring at Chevelle as I recalled their meeting. He was watching me with concern on his face, and a thought flashed through my mind that maybe he knew I was on to him. It was all so wrong.

My head spun, and I closed my eyes, trying to find something to grasp, something to steady me before I blacked out again. I needed a way to fix the conflict. Asher couldn't have been my grandfather. It could not be true. I struggled to sit up long enough to reach my pack. I felt around for it, the only real thing I had. My fingers caught the edge of the binding, and I pulled the diary out, clutching it tightly, as if someone might try to take it from me.

I couldn't make myself look at the others, but I knew what they were thinking: that this was it, that I was finally falling into madness. It was a few moments before I could focus well enough to read. I flipped through the first pages, where my mother wrote as a child, her father's prize.

A tear tracked down my cheek, and I wiped at it distractedly. When I felt their eyes on me, I hardened, biting down, determined to keep another from escaping. I did not want pity, not from anyone.

I scanned, searching for mention of him, but I kept getting caught in the story. It was all so different now that it wasn't a stranger's. It was my mother's story, my story. *And Asher's?*

Page after page, I kept my nose buried in the diary. No one asked me to move, but they kept close. I could feel them watching, waiting. They were concerned about what had broken free inside of me and if it would be the thing that pushed me over the edge. Eventually, exhaustion won out, and the dreams were back.

BY THE NEXT DAY, I was almost certain that the dreams were not simply dreams—they were memories, and the Asher I had seen was in fact *Lord* Asher. What I could not reconcile was how he was alive, how he could have met with Chevelle, and why.

My thoughts were clearer, but that made them all the more distressing. It felt as though secrets were everywhere, swallowing me. It felt as if I was drowning, and the sensation was all too familiar.

I recalled more each time I encountered him. I focused on the day he had watched us from the tree line, the day I'd felt untethered from my own soul, remembering how they had reacted to his single nod and his seeming approval. I could see his braid swing behind him as he turned and disappeared into the brush. I struggled to understand, and I couldn't help but remember what had happened just before, a memory I'd not returned to willingly: the sickening thud as the council tracker's head landed on the ground, the sight of it rolling to a stop, and the blood on my blade.

Yet I could not understand, so I forced myself to stop thinking about it. It was the only way to put an end to the screeching pain in my head, to save me from the blackouts. However, when I finally calmed the searing pain to a dull throb, I could begin to feel the ache in my chest. It was tough to breathe. *How could they...* I couldn't even finish the thought before the other pain returned. I was balancing, and not well, on a narrow ledge.

Betrayal. Chaos. Loss. Madness.

It was some time later that I broke, unable to stand the conflict in my own mind or the pain it was causing me. *The pain they were causing me? No, I can't allow myself to think that.* When I finally gave, I found solace in the mind of the hawk as it hovered above us, floating on the current of the wind. I stayed there, void of all other thoughts until, exhausted, I had to surrender and return to my own body.

IN TIME, I found a compromise with myself. I would let go of the other concerns when possible and devote my concentration to the one thing I was positive of: we—no, *I* needed to find Council, to release my mind from the bonds that felt like they were killing me. I could only hope that doing so would release the memories as well, remove all of the unanswered questions, and erase the doubt that was constantly trying to creep into every thought I had. *How could they? And always, why?*

Finally, I was in control of myself enough to continue. Our task became my first priority: find Council. I focused on my memories of them, the images of their faces. It was all I had, but at least it was something.

Ruby scrutinized me, obviously concerned as we rode through a field of tall grass. I ignored her, pretending to watch my horse steal bites along the way, struggling to keep a steady pace as his head bent sideways, securing generous mouthfuls.

She couldn't stand it for long. "Frey?"

I looked at her blankly. Her eyes went wide, my gaze apparently not as blank as I'd intended. I tried to smooth it. "Hmm?"

She must not have planned for my response, because she said nothing, her expression tortured. I wondered what she was reading on mine.

She glanced forward at the backs of the others as they rode ahead of us then at me. "Was there something specific you were looking for in the diary?"

It struck me that she had no idea why I had been reading it again. I had not mentioned my dream or my new knowledge. She must have thought that I'd been upset about Junnie or the human. They must have all thought that. They had no idea that I had remembered anything new.

I realized that I was smiling. Some part of me, buried deep inside, was pleased. It relished the secret knowledge and wanted to protect it. It was not a pleasant character trait, I supposed, and not the first negative quality I'd found in myself. I spoke without thinking. "No, it was just a shock. I'm fine."

Her eyebrows knitted together.

"I'd been meaning to finish reading it. You know, for closure." I almost scoffed at my own words. She was staring at me hard, so I changed the subject. "So, where exactly are we going?"

It didn't appear as though I'd lessened her concern, but she looked forward and nodded at some structure in the distance. Tied up in my thoughts, I hadn't even noticed it.

We rode closer, and the shapes became more defined. I kicked up my horse to fall in beside the others for a better view. In a ring of yew trees, pillars of stone rose up in patterns around a massive amphitheater.

I gulped, cringing at the thought of what the place could be. "Grand Council?" I whispered.

"No," Anvil answered, smiling.

I let out a breath, the tightness in my chest easing by degrees.

Chevelle spoke from the front. "The Temple of Loelle."

Once I could see more clearly, it was apparent that the structure had been abandoned long ago. Here and there, the sandstone pillars crumbled at their corners, gangly weeds spiking up between the footstones. Faint outlines of carvings bordered the base of the columns, weathered away with time. The others stopped and dismounted, leaving the horses as they entered the central building. I followed behind, still cautious. I remembered my plan to sweep the sky each day—I'd forgotten that during the time spent agonizing over Asher—and I had to catch myself to focus on the present.

A light dusting of sand shifted beneath my feet, making me feel a bit more secure in my abandonment theory. Regardless of my concerns about the group's relationship with Asher, I was glad they were there. I knew I would be unable to stand alone to face Grand Council when the time came—soon.

I shivered, and Chevelle moved beside me, his hand sliding across my back. It did not ease the chill inside me, and I had to force myself not to look at him to avoid betraying my emotions.

"We will stay here until Rhys and Rider can locate Council."

Some part of me expected to stiffen at his words, but I became aware that I already was—I had hardened when he'd first touched me. He must have noticed, too, because he dropped his arm as he continued. "You will need to train."

He turned and walked off without another word, but as if on command, Anvil approached, holding two large metal rods.

We trained through the evening as the others gathered in small groups, planning, watching, or checking the perimeter. I was exhausted when we finally stopped for dinner, and almost before I'd finished my last bite, Grey was urging me to train again, to practice trying to stop his disappearing acts. It was well past dark when I finally gave up.

THOUGH I'D FALLEN asleep by the fire, I awoke inside my own small hut, complete with soft bedding. I dragged myself from the cot, only to find the day's training already planned for me. "Let's go," said Ruby. "We'll work on your control today."

I managed not to groan aloud, but internally I was doing more than my share of complaining.

"Now!" she shouted. "Here!"

That pattern continued, in the middle of that strange temple between nothing but forest and grass. Ruby drove me during the waking hours, her fire lighting around me so often that it swam through my vision even when my eyes were closed. Grey's training had me moving constantly, always too slow to catch his strikes. "Focus," they would command, as if it was even within my control.

By the third day, exhaustion was winning out. They pushed me relentlessly. I was too tired even to be miserable. It reminded me of something that I couldn't quite place, when I'd been forced to train, exhausted, and paranoid.

I cried out in defeat as Ruby's whip cracked at my shoulder. I fell to my knees, spent.

"Up!" she commanded.

I huffed out a breath, having no intention of following her order.

She stepped forward, her gaze trained on mine. "Up."

I forced a look of defiance, and her expression became heated.

"You will burn, Frey."

Not by her hand, by Council's. I convinced myself to stand, not for her but for me, to give myself every possible chance when the time came. On wobbly legs, I fought back.

When I could stand no more, it was Anvil's turn, but I didn't have much left to fight off electrical attacks.

On the fourth night, a new dream surfaced.

It was twisted and confusing, but I came away with an unmistakable feeling. I stayed inside my hut, pretending to sleep, and pulled the diary from my pack. I flipped forward to the pages in which my mother described her own training. Asher, her father, had forced her to train for his own benefit.

I was certain of their actions. The idea that had been nagging at me grew until it was fully formed. They weren't training me for my protection—I had no chance against Council in my condition. And it wasn't merely to keep me occupied. They were training me for Lord Asher.

I gritted my teeth against the hate that was filling me.

"Frey?" a voice asked from outside the hut.

The part of me that had relished my secret knowledge was in control again. I took a calming breath before answering, "Yes, Ruby?"

"We should probably get started."

I took two more deep breaths. "All right."

I stood, trying to get a handle on the tremor that was racking my body and praying that the madness would not split me in two. With one more deep breath, I stepped out into the sun.

I tried to keep my expression clear as I scanned the temple. I remembered Anvil before. He'd been in some of the older memories, helping the scarred man with training—no, practice. I continued, seeing Grey and Steed by a pillar. I couldn't decide on their involvement. They might have just been there for Ruby.

Ruby was the troublemaker—*could that be why she's involved? Merely for fun, her own entertainment?* Then I remembered what Steed had said: her interest in the diary was because of her mother. I wondered if revenge or some sick obsession because her fey mother had come up with a crazed plan because of me was driving her.

"Frey?" Ruby sounded concerned. She wrapped her hand around my arm, pulling me to focus on her. "Frey, what is it?" She sounded panicked, and I realized I was shaking again.

A strange part of me needed to cover for us. I couldn't think clearly, so I spat out the first reasonable truth I could give. "I-I just remembered something."

She waited.

"Council... a council member."

"Who?"

"I don't know. I only see his face. Nothing else."

She nodded and rubbed my arm. I played on her sympathy, and eventually she encouraged me to lie back down.

When I was alone again, the rush of thought and emotion tore through me. I struggled to hold myself together. I had no one but these seven companions. I didn't want to believe they would betray me, but I could not otherwise explain their association with Asher, the man who had ruined my mother, the North, and me. A wave of nausea hit, and I doubled over, sweat thick on my brow. I tried to wipe it away with a shaky hand, but found I needed to grip the cot to keep from falling. My eyes closed as dizziness took over. Someone was coming in, and I became aware that I had been moaning in agony.

I heard them talking. "What's wrong with her?"

"Get Ruby."

A few moments later, Chevelle's voice rang out. His betrayal hurt the worst. It pushed me over the edge, past that breaking point I'd been fighting so hard not to pass, and I couldn't focus on their words or find feeling in my limbs. I could only recognize the burning of my skin and the pain in my mind. Something was wrong, and it was much worse than before. I shut down completely.

FEVER DROVE my dreams to new heights. More irrational paranoia seeped through all of my old dreams, turning them to nightmares, but the new ones were most disturbing. Even the colors frightened me. Blood red and flame orange saturated everything in one moment, and then stark white swallowed me whole.

My companions, my guard, surrounded me in the long robes and tassels of Grand Council. Chevelle approached me, his face hard. As he closed in, his mouth twisted in a menacing grin, and he grabbed me, pulling me close for a deep kiss. When he drew away, I tasted blood. Then fire lit around me, and they gathered to watch me burn.

I wanted to scream, but my throat was grated raw by the fine sand of the surrounding pillars. The flames threw wicked shadows across the ground, which began to sway, and I lost my footing, falling down only to be kicked by the watchers. I laughed then, crazed by the flame, and I could feel my mother. I knew she too had laughed as she burned, and I began to scream.

MY OWN HOARSE scream woke me. I started up in a panic, but Ruby held me down, patting my forehead with a damp bit of cloth. I was drenched, shivering as my eyelids fluttered before falling back to closed.

They must have thought I was asleep again, as a groggy relaxation kept me still. I could hear their whispers as I silently took stock. "Maybe that's not even why... Maybe we overdid the training... No, let her rest..."

My body seemed to have recovered. My mind was rested but still in pain. I tried not to think of why, wanting to stave off the worst of the pains in case it was the bindings.

They gave me the rest of the day off, but that evening, after Ruby had brought me dinner, the makeshift door to my room was tossed open, and Chevelle stood there, staring at me. His impatience seared me through his tone. "Enough. Get up. Return to your training."

For just a moment, I was surprised. Then, in a flash of anger, I found myself responding without thought. "Why? For him?" I couldn't stop myself. That secret part of me that had better control was nowhere to be found. "How could you? After what he did. How?"

A small group had gathered behind Chevelle, seeking the source of the commotion. It only enflamed me more.

"All of you. My guard," I spat. They stared at me as though I had lost it, and maybe I had. "Training me at his command. Slaves to Asher. Your *Lord* Asher."

I had directed that last part to Chevelle, and his face went white. He wore an expression that I had never seen, and honestly, it frightened me. I ran from the hut, tearing brush free of the back wall to get away from them as fast as I could.

Breathless and with no idea where to go, I kept running until my shaking legs would carry me no farther.

Apparently, it wasn't far enough. When I finally rose from the ground to look behind me, Ruby was already there. I was pretty sure she'd been right behind me the entire time, silent. She appeared annoyed with her mouth turned down and a fist perched on a hip.

I turned my head away from her and dropped it to the ground. She let me stay there until eventually, I gave in and followed her back to the temple. I might have been embarrassed by my outburst, but no one had denied my accusations, so I felt justified, wronged, and bitter.

The fever was gone, so I continued to practice through that bitterness. No matter their reasons for training me, I knew I would not be able to face Grand Council without them, and they knew it too. I could only work to get better. Then I would worry about the others, about Asher, and about how I would have to face things alone.

Nights later, I woke with a start, remembering that I had abandoned my plan of sweeping the area. I knew Rhys and Rider were on guard with the wolves, but I hadn't forgotten the last time, when Council had bested them. I hoped I could locate a vessel as I closed my eyes and searched past the temple and the pillars into the surrounding trees.

An owl perched in a red oak near the temple, and I decided he would suffice. I started to take him off his branch to check the grounds when his keen eyes caught a group standing together not far from his spot. Focusing, I realized it was Anvil and Grey, close together and speaking, and Chevelle, who faced away from them with his arms crossed, giving his stance an irritated feel.

I was afraid to move any nearer, sure the flapping of wings would alert them. I considered checking for other animals close by but imagined Chevelle spotting a clumsy squirrel with his knowing eyes, catching me spying. The uncoordinated squirrel was taking over my thoughts, and I had to focus and try not to chuckle at my sleepy efforts.

I concentrated, finally hearing their words, but just as I caught them—"Fannie's doing our job"—Chevelle spun, facing them, his anger palpable. Grey held up his hands as if to say "no harm," but it didn't matter—Chevelle was beyond calming. When he scanned the clearing, I jumped back into my own mind, afraid that he'd somehow known I was there.

I couldn't fall asleep after that. I couldn't understand what they'd meant or why they were talking about Fannie. I wondered what they'd been referring to as their "job" and if it was something they were doing for Asher. But I couldn't fathom how Fannie could be doing that. She wasn't training me. It had to be something else, then. Maybe they had more than one task.

"What is it?" Ruby asked from the corner. I hadn't noticed her. She was apparently watching me even during peaceful sleep now.

I started to answer that it was nothing but decided, given my previous outburst when I gave the secret away, that I might as well ask. "Fannie," I said, sitting up to face her.

She leaned forward. "What about Fannie?"

I wasn't sure how to respond. She didn't know what I did or didn't remember, what I did or didn't know. I wanted to find a way to lead her into answers.

"Frey, did you see Fannie?"

Evidently, it was going to be easier than I thought. I remembered the dream and used that. She could decide what to do with it. "Destroying the village."

In the dim light, I saw Ruby's reaction, and I knew that it hadn't been a dream at all. I gasped, choking on the shock.

She moved to sit beside me on the cot, and in my stupor, I let her attempt to comfort me. "Freya, I'm sorry."

My skin crawled at the endearment. "Don't call me that."

She was stunned at my response. "I'm sorry I didn't tell you before. It's just that I know what it does to you when you get upset."

"As if you care," I spat.

The surprise in her expression twisted to hurt. "Frey—"

"Oh, come on, Ruby. You work for Asher. You read the diary. You know—"

"You..." She stopped herself. "Elfreda, you are the most ridiculous..." I didn't know what she intended to call me, but she grabbed my arms tightly and stared me straight in the eye before she started again. "I. Do. Not. Work. For. Anyone." She released her grip just a fraction. "Is that clear?"

I had no idea what my face gave away, but my mind was anything but clear.

She rumbled out an irritated growl. "Listen to me. If that is what you're thinking, then there is no danger of telling you now. I don't see how it could possibly make things worse for you." She took off on a side rant. "And all this time, I thought you were upset about that stupid girl!"

Guilt washed through me again as I remembered the human.

Ruby continued, "Frey, Fannie is after Grand Council."

My mouth dropped open. "What?"

"She's killing them."

I couldn't get my voice to work.

Ruby continued in a softer tone, "She was bound. Same as you."

Pain racked my mind, but I tried to stay focused.

She recounted the binding. "She was not considered guilty, as your mother was, and she was allowed to live, though bound tightly and under watch. You see, when we fought them before, as we tried to release your bonds... we inadvertently released some of hers as well."

My chest tightened, but I couldn't convince myself it was real. "How do you know?"

She looked at me as though I was missing something. I didn't see it. "Junnie."

Junnie. I'd never even wondered why she'd come or what she'd spoken to Chevelle about in such a rush before saw the girl. The cursed bonds kept me from facing anything, kept my mind in a constant maelstrom that pulled me under when the turmoil became too much. "Focus," they said, as if that wasn't the very thing that did me in. I still couldn't speak.

"I should let you rest for a bit. Are you going to be all right?"

"No," I begged. "Please, Ruby, tell me more." She didn't think I could handle it—I could see that. I probably couldn't, but it didn't stop me. "Ruby, I need to know."

"What do you want to know?" She hedged.

I wasn't sure where to start. My thoughts were in that current, and it was too strong to conquer. "Why? Why did she destroy the village?"

"We think she blamed them for the binding." Ruby shrugged. "Or maybe she just loathed them. Hard to say."

I shook my head. "Why would she blame them?"

"Somehow, apparently, she'd gotten parts of her magic back, and she was confused, though she knew for sure that she'd been bound."

I thought of my time with Fannie, her conspiracy theories and her hatred of all things Council. "How long had she known?"

"We can't be certain. She was secretive and probably didn't know who to trust. We don't think she knew of Junnie's involvement, though." Ruby looked sorry that she had mentioned Junnie. She straightened the edge of my blanket. "However, she did seem to know you were bound as well. At least at the end, just before you left the village."

"How did she know?" I ignored the dance she'd done around my choking a council leader and running off after I'd been accused of practicing dark magic. At the time, I'd had no idea.

"We aren't sure, but the documents you found had been taken from Council. And the ones that you"—there was really no other way to say it—"stole had been tampered with."

"Tampered with?"

"Mixed up, at the least. Unfortunately, we didn't get a good look at them before—"

"Before I burned them."

"Yes." Ruby attempted a timid smile.

"So you think Fannie used me to get the documents? Or do you mean she tried to frame me to get me into trouble with Council?" I could hear my voice shake.

"There is no way to know what she was thinking or what she was after, Frey. From what I understand, there was no love lost there." She touched my hand sympathetically.

I struggled to remember, but it seemed so far away, and none were memories I'd wanted to cherish. Something came to me, and I couldn't help but ask, since Ruby was being open with me. I pushed down the thought that was trying to scream maybe she wasn't being honest—maybe it was more lies. Instead of asking directly about the spell that placed the map on my palms or having to recount my dream of the trick we'd played on Fannie, I took a side route. "Ruby, what about the pouch? Did she know I had that?"

Ruby shook her head. "I don't know much about that, Frey. But I do know one thing: the silver medallion, the one you found inside, seems to match those that Fannie had secured from the human site you read about in your mother's diary."

I swallowed hard, wondering when Ruby had seen the medallion. In the castle, probably, maybe during one of the many times I'd been unconscious. I'd had no idea what the symbols meant, but I'd never made the connection to—it was still hard to think—*humans*. I pushed on. "And the ruby?"

She seemed almost embarrassed as she answered this time. "Yes. You see, that was payment. Please understand, that was before I knew you."

"Payment?" I was incredulous, but she only nodded. "Payment for what?"

"Securing some items, helping you, gathering the guard."

Bitter resentment wanted to rise, fire was waiting in my palms, and the ache was heavy in my chest, but I kept them all still. Some part of me needed the rest of the secret, in spite of everything. I hadn't forgotten her words from just moments ago: *I do not work for anyone.*

Lies. All of it was lies.

Ruby could see that I'd had enough. She moved aside as I rolled away from her to curl into a ball.

And, after a few hours of mental torment, I fell asleep thinking I had reached my limit and feeling certain that I was beyond surprise.

Somewhere in the depths of my subconscious, I knew that what I was watching might finally crack me, leaving me in separate pieces. But I couldn't make myself look away.

From a perch above, I could see Fannie slinking slowly toward a council member. He stood tall, his robe and tassels unruffled, murmuring words I could not understand. I couldn't decide whether to scream in warning or to root for his demise, for I knew that his death would release me.

The panther came into his view and sauntered closer, enjoying itself far too much. Then without warning, it launched forward into the chest of the council member Magnus White. It tore out his throat as they both landed on the ground, blood spattering down his clean white robe, tassels splaying out behind him.

The cat lingered above its prey, savoring the sight of blood flowing from the fatal wound. Then it turned, slowly and deliberately, to look directly at me, its dark muzzle wet with death.

Fear overtook me.

I woke to my own words, oblivious at first to my surroundings. "The animals. She's using the animals."

As a hand touched my shoulder, I realized I wasn't alone—Ruby and Chevelle were in my tattered shelter. My chest heaved, and Ruby tried to calm me. "Easy, Frey."

They had been watching me sleep, likely waiting because they wanted to talk to me. Ruby had probably explained our conversation about Fannie to him. A shiver racked my body.

"What is it, Frey?" Ruby asked, her tone concerned as her hand remained resting on my shoulder. From across the shelter, Chevelle's gaze narrowed as he gave her a knowing look. He must have blamed her for telling me, knowing my mind wouldn't be able to handle it.

I shook my head and sat up straighter. "She's using the cats." Even in my panic, I regretted that I had chosen cats for my own ploy in the castle. "She's taking Council out, one by one. She knows."

He stiffened. "How could you know that?"

I didn't answer his question, instead rambling about my dream. "She knows they won't kill the animals, knows she has free rein to slaughter all the council members if she uses beasts." I could hear the blind panic in my own voice.

He leaned forward. "Frey, it was only a dream. No one knows—"

"No," I cut him off. "I *know*. And she's coming after me."

My thoughts were frantic. Fannie understood that the light elves had reverence for nature and rules about killing animals. She knew they wouldn't fight back when she was in that form, not hard enough to truly stop her. And I was next. She was coming for me. I strived to hold on, to not let the chaos in my mind drive me mad. But I was swaying back and forth, curling my fists.

Eventually, the motion calmed, and rational thought returned. The further I got from sleep, the more the dream lost its potency. Ruby sat beside me, offering me tea and powders and anything else she could think of. It was quiet for a long time when I refused.

Then it struck me that they were too quiet. They weren't shocked at all. "You knew?"

Ruby didn't answer, and I looked at Chevelle accusingly for what seemed like the hundredth time.

"We could not be certain."

How? How could they have known? "Junnie?"

He replied with a curt nod.

I started to demand why they hadn't told me that my crazed aunt was coming to murder me, but as my mouth opened, I remembered the chain of events that had followed Junnie's visit. They couldn't have explained anything to me—I'd passed out, and when I awoke, I didn't speak. I'd been obsessed, doing nothing except reading the diary of my dead mother. They thought I was too fragile to include.

I closed my mouth, curling my fingers into sweating palms. *They might have been right.* I blew out a shaky breath. *Fannie is killing Council.* I felt like a complete fool.

"That's why I'm remembering." It seemed so obvious now. All I received was another nod. Just like Ruby had said, as we broke my bonds, we were breaking hers... and she was breaking mine.

Grey came to the opening in the shelter, and Ruby stepped out to speak with him. I watched her leave and kept my gaze on the doorway. I was alone with Chevelle.

The air was charged, as it always was when I was alone with him. *Always thick with anger or*—I stopped myself, embarrassed by the thought of how I'd acted the last time he'd been in my shelter. I had accused him of working for Asher.

I couldn't even think clearly anymore—there was so much wrong in my head. It was impossible to be rational or control my emotions with so much missing and disconnected. I let myself look at him.

It was a mistake.

He had been watching me, his gaze already trained on my face. I felt off-balance and briefly wondered if Ruby had drugged me again because without a conscious command to do so, I found myself moving toward him.

He was sitting near the end of my cot, on the stool where Ruby had watched me sleep. I felt how small the room was as I slid down to sit next to him in the dimness. I couldn't stop myself from wanting to be near him, no matter how wrong it seemed. I was entirely confused —I felt as though I knew him and he was part of my life, but at the same time, he was a stranger, mysterious in every way. I forgot all those strong feelings of betrayal as I sat inches away from him, looking into his eyes.

He was staring expectantly at me, but all I could see was a memory, a similar situation when his face was filled with something else, sadness or disappointment. I couldn't seem to pull it to mind, couldn't find the clear, solid memory, and I was overcome with frustration. My hands came up, knotting in my hair as the base of my palms pressed against my temples. I could feel myself rocking back and forth again, but I was too overwhelmed to stop.

Suddenly, I was jerked from the bed to standing. At first, my eyes shot to Chevelle's hand on my wrist. His grip was so tight that it was almost painful. But when I realized he'd pulled me close to him, our bodies nearly touching, my eyes slowly trailed to his face.

But he wasn't looking at me. I opened my mouth to speak, and he reached up, placing his fingers on my lips to still them. His head was turned away as he listened intently, so I concentrated to hear what had his attention. It was distant and slightly muffled, a strange sort of noise. Then the pitch rose, and I realized it was animals. Within seconds, a clearer sound came: the wolves sounded a warning cry.

I was wrenched from the tent so quickly that I could barely keep my footing. I tumbled forward, losing my last step, and Chevelle lifted me and ran away from the temple. Panic seized me, but I couldn't see behind us. He was intent on his path. The only way I could think of to see what was behind us—after us—was to jump to the wolves.

I managed to locate one, but even as I sensed where it was, I wasn't able to find its mind to learn why it had called out a warning. Confused, I searched for the second wolf and tried again.

Nothing. I didn't understand—it had never not worked.

"Frey." Chevelle's voice brought me back, and I opened my eyes to find his face in front of mine. We had stopped running. He gazed down at me, still in his arms. "Are you all right?"

I stared back at him. *Nothing had happened to me, had it?* I took stock, but aside from the frantic beat of my heart and labored breathing, I could find nothing wrong. I nodded to him in reply.

He put me down, and I started toward a nearby rock ledge to sit, still baffled that I'd been unable to get through to the wolves. *Was it Council? Had they bound me from the animals now?*

Chevelle must have seen my dread return as I stepped away because he grabbed my arm and drew me back to face him. "What is it?"

I couldn't answer. I knew my face had paled. They'd taken from me the one thing that made me revered.

"Frey." He gave my shoulders a quick shake to pull me back.

A small squirrel jumped from a limb in my peripheral vision, and I felt it automatically and fell into its mind with ease. Satisfied I'd not lost the ability, I finally started to relax, but my vision went black when the animal's neck snapped.

My eyes opened in time to see its body tumble to the ground. I was standing with my mouth hanging open in disbelief as Chevelle glanced back at me. Only then did I realize he'd been watching the squirrel. He had been distracted at first, but the noise had alerted him, and he'd focused on the squirrel a breath before it had dropped.

"Did you kill that squirrel?" I accused.

He answered in his careful tone, "Frey—"

The tone infuriated me, and I cut him off. "Tell me now."

He leaned back indignantly. "Did you have a personal relationship with that squirrel?"

He'd never spoken to me that way. It threw me off for half a second, and then I was incensed. "Tell me right now."

"Tell you what?"

We were suddenly arguing. I leaned forward, my hands in tight fists at my sides. "Tell me whatever it is that you're hiding from me. What now, what else?"

He twitched, the muscles of his forearm tensing. His jaw jumped too as he stared at me, tight-lipped for a long moment. Finally, he sighed and said, "We are simply taking every precaution. To protect you."

The words enraged me. "To protect me? How many times do I have to hear that? 'Oh, it's just to protect you.'" I had the perverse urge to strike him but arrested the thought. "What is it now? What are you doing to protect me now?" I spat.

He only looked at me.

I waited.

"The animals," he replied, watching me as though I'd missed something obvious again. My anger flared until I realized the implication.

The fury rushed out of me in a huff. I was as winded as if I'd been punched in the chest. I didn't understand how I could be so continuously oblivious. They were lining up in my head, the details I'd so blatantly missed. Some were more noticeable than others, but they were all there: the battle with Council, when I'd felt someone else in the mind of the bird, the glaringly obvious lack of animals on our path, and Fannie's apparent abilities, which I had seen so clearly in my dreams.

Fannie. Suddenly, my head was spinning, joining the images from my dreams with the last few hours and minutes. I was speaking before I was aware of it. "We were running."

Chevelle gripped my arm, and I knew he heard the change in my voice.

"Running from Fannie." I'd known she was coming for me. I hadn't known she was already here.

I looked into his eyes. I wasn't sure what he saw on my face, but he was abruptly trying to calm me. "Frey, she hasn't gotten near you at all."

I felt my features twist at his words.

"The wolves are taking care of them," he said.

The wolves. Taking care of them. *Not an animal,* animals. *How many times has she tried? How long has this been going on?* I opened my mouth to speak, but I couldn't process the anger and humiliation, the irritation. I growled in rage, throwing my fisted hands to my sides. The sound of shattering stone caught my attention.

I realized it had been me. I sighed, suddenly ashamed that I'd unintentionally exploded the rock ledge that had been my intended seat moments before. I loosened my fists, throwing my hands up in surrender.

I turned from Chevelle to walk toward the temple, or at least in the direction I thought it had been, unwilling to look at him. I heard his steps behind me, following my slow progress, and remembered his words from the time I had been attacked by Council, when they'd found me and rebound my magic. He'd said they had known Council was close, but they were mistaken in thinking Council intended a physical attack. They had been prepared for that, and I knew they were more than capable of defeating Council. However, they had not been prepared for the binding, the direct attack on my mind. He'd assured me that Council would not get so close again.

And now they're… what, destroying every animal that came near because Fannie was tracking me too? The wolves were my guard dogs? I was too far gone to laugh. I could see their first demonstration of power in my memory, hear their vicious snarl, see their jagged fangs. Ruby's words came back to me: *"No, silly, no one can control animals. The wolves attack who they want and protect who they want."*

I kept walking slowly over dirt and thick clumps of grass, attempting to process it all, struggling to find a place for it. Twice I spun on Chevelle, ready to fling accusations at him, but each time, his expression was such that I could only look at him before I turned and continued on.

Eventually, I came into a clearing, the hot sun directly overhead a clear indication that I'd been walking far too long. I couldn't decide if I'd passed the temple or gone in a different direction entirely. Sighing, I turned, finding Chevelle behind me, exactly where I'd expected him.

He waited.

I took a deep breath. "I don't know where I am."

His expression was pained as he took a step toward me. "I know, Frey. We are trying to help you."

I put my hands up in front of me. "No. I mean I don't know *where* I am." I waved toward the surrounding wall of trees.

He almost smiled as he took another step closer. "They will be waiting for us." Before I could respond, he pulled me up to carry me again, spinning and breaking into a run toward the temple.

I hadn't even been close.

Once I knew I was being hunted by the remaining members of Grand Council *and* my crazy Aunt Fannie in various animal forms, it was considerably easier to forgive the seven others who were willing to help me, regardless of their reasons.

It was in that state of mind that, upon returning to the temple, I resumed my training with Grey. The others were planning again, something about moving since Fannie had likely found us. I wasn't sure what "likely" meant, since the wolves had apparently slaughtered numerous beasts throughout the morning, but I ignored their discussions, confident that they would not have let me join in.

We found a quiet spot near the center of the temple. The sandstone floor was open, free of the pillars that bordered the outer walls, so I hoped I would have a better chance to follow Grey's movements as he flitted around in an attempt to lose me. Unfortunately, I was often disappointed. I readied myself, standing motionless with my eyes and ears on alert when he stepped in front of me, wearing a smile.

I scowled, certain he was making fun of me, though I had no idea why.

"I never thanked you for the assist," he said.

I was lost for a moment before I understood what he was referring to: the battle with Council. I'd missed the majority of it, at first tied to a wall then overtaken by blackness, but I had managed to fight some. A bird had flown over, and I'd jumped to it, able to see them all below in the fray. Grey had been trapped as my own body had been, vines wrapping him in place, long thorns piercing his skin, flames surrounding him. I had found his attacker and given Grey the few precious seconds he needed to escape. The horrid scene filled my mind anew, and as I looked at it with fresh knowledge, I couldn't help but wonder if they had actually been fighting to protect me.

Then the last little bit of the memory came back, the moments just before the blackness had taken me. Asher watched from outside the battle. I could see his lips moving, a flow of words.

"Frey?"

Grey had been talking to me, although I had no idea what he'd said. I answered anyway. "Yes, of course."

He laughed, and then he was gone.

I shook my head, trying to focus because I knew I was about to be smacked in the back of the head or have a leg pulled out from under me when he reappeared.

I was wrong. I got a punch in the gut. Yet to my surprise, he was still standing in front of me. We both looked down to see my hand wrapped tightly around his wrist. He was lightning fast, but I'd grabbed him somehow, almost unthinkingly.

We stood there, staring at the offending hands, unable to relax at first. Then I let loose a breath, and Grey opened his fist as I eased my grip on him.

We didn't speak.

"Frey," Ruby started as she bounced up to us. Noticing the uncomfortable atmosphere, she asked, "What's going on?"

Grey spoke up, smiling genuinely at her without looking me in the eye. "Hey, Red. Just finishing up here." He gingerly reached up to pat me on the back of the shoulder. "The girl's really picking it up. Impressive."

Ruby eyed me, perplexed. I squeaked out a nervous laugh, and she glanced back and forth between us a few times before shaking it off. "It's time to move. Frey, I'll get your things together. You can keep practicing until we have everything ready."

She threw one quick look back to Grey with an eyebrow raised before bouncing off in the direction of my tattered shelter.

When I turned back to Grey, he was watching me. I felt my shoulders come up in a shrug.

"Do it again," he commanded, and I wondered if I heard a hint of excitement in his voice.

Almost too fast to see, his fist was coming at me once more. It stopped as my palm came up to meet it automatically.

Grey smiled.

My hand still blocking his, he twisted to take my fingers, leading me by the hand as he walked from the center of the temple and farther from the others.

"When did your instincts return, Freya?" he asked in a low voice.

I stared at him, having no idea what he was talking about.

His smile turned apologetic but at the same time unrepentant, an expression I was sure only Grey could get away with. "Seems the wicked Francine is helping you out more than herself."

I shivered at the mention of Fannie. I had plenty of awful memories of her, cruel as she was, but nothing had compared to the look she'd given me in her panther form. It was only a dream, but the way she'd watched me...

The words came out almost as a thought. "What does she want with me?"

He looked incredulous, but I couldn't understand why. I must have been missing something obvious again. I wondered if she intended to punish me for what I'd done or because of my imagined part in her binding and imprisonment.

Grey turned to me, placing his hands on my arms. "Frey, you are the leader of the North."

I didn't understand what that had to do with it.

He could obviously see that he wasn't getting through. "Do you remember what you read of Francine in the diary?"

I glared. "Has *everyone* read it?"

He ignored my accusation, and I could tell he felt as if he was explaining something to a child. "Francine is in line for the throne, Freya. After you."

Anger flooded through me. There was no betrayal, only fury. "She plans to kill me."

Grey shushed me, but I couldn't be calmed. Fannie had been hunting me down in beast form to kill me. The idea hadn't even crossed my mind. I expected punishment, yes, or some form of prolonged torture, but she wanted to kill me. A hysterical laugh escaped. *For the throne.*

Grey glanced nervously toward the others. They wouldn't want me to know. My fragile brain wouldn't be able to take it.

"Wait... wait," I said. "This doesn't make any sense. Why am I even leader? Why isn't Asher?"

"It doesn't work that way, Frey. The leader can choose the next in his line, but in a conflict, power is the deciding factor."

I was lost again.

He threw another quick glance at the others before he continued in a hushed tone. "Francine is not as powerful as you are, Frey. You would have to be... out of the picture for her to rule."

"She's stronger than Asher? *I'm* stronger than Asher?"

"She's counting on Council disposing of him." I didn't miss that he'd avoided the other question.

My hands were shaking, so I tried to calm myself before the blackness came. Grey waited, uneasy.

"Why am I the leader? If Asher is alive, why would I be ruler?" My gaze bore into his, forcing him to answer. "Am I stronger than Asher?"

His tone was severe. "No one is stronger than Asher."

That threw me—none of it was making any sense. "Then why?"

"It's very complicated, Frey. Grand Council intends to remove him again—"

I cut him off. "Again?"

"Frey, just..." He trailed off as someone approached then

concocted a new conversation. "So you'll want to try and anticipate where I'll strike. Oh hey, Ruby. Are we ready to go?"

I had to work to conceal my growl of irritation, but Ruby was already eyeing me suspiciously.

WE RODE LATE into the evening, and the group became silent as darkness fell. When we finally stopped, we were deep in a forest, thick brush close against our camp. I slid from my horse and found a downed tree to lean against, its bark covered with soft amber-tipped moss. Ruby brought me a blanket, and I watched as she cornered Grey, something I was sure she'd been dying to do since the afternoon's practice.

I had started to doze off when Chevelle sat on the tree beside where my head rested, and I sat up, immediately alert.

"Sleep, Frey."

Unlikely now, I thought, sighing as I tried and failed to settle back in to the comfortable spot I'd been in before. It was a struggle to keep my thoughts from returning to questions about Fannie and Asher, about me. That was possibly the most disturbing part. It was starting to sink in that I was expected to be a ruler and that my throne was something people wanted enough to kill me. I had always disliked Fannie, but it was still hard to believe she would be so utterly ruthless, not that I hadn't wished her dead a few times.

And I didn't understand why it was so important that Asher not be the one to rule. At least he had his mind. But no one knew I didn't. My guard had kept it a secret for my protection.

DAWN CAME EARLY. I was wrapped in a blanket near the same fallen tree when Ruby urged me awake with her foot. "Come on, Frey. Time for practice before we move on."

I groaned, but practice was brief because it was only a short time before they were mounted, ready to set off.

We rode too fast, in and out of patches of hot sun and dense forest, the scents and sounds more familiar to my recent memory. The plots of forest were becoming longer, though, and by the evening of the second day, I was getting annoyed with being smacked in the head by so many limbs.

"Wouldn't it just be easier to walk?"

"We are conserving energy," Grey answered in a low voice. "The horses spare us the energy we would have used running while carrying our weapons and packs. We are taking every precaution."

My horse ran into the back of Anvil's as we stopped unexpectedly. I gave him a sheepish grin. He didn't seem surprised that I hadn't been paying attention.

As we stepped down off the horses, Ruby caught sight of all the scrapes and scratches I'd gained from the day's ride. It felt like every branch had hit my face. "You look terrible, Frey." It seemed to delight her to be furnished with a task. She gathered her supplies then cornered me, making repairs for a full hour before she tired of it. She admitted defeat with a sigh. "I shouldn't have let it go so long."

Grey laughed from where he'd been watching her toil beside us, and Ruby sauntered off on some other venture.

I took the opportunity while we were alone. "So how long have you known about Fannie?" I asked, indicating the group.

He only looked back at me.

"I mean, how long has she been stalking me?"

"Not so long," he answered in a hushed tone.

He was glancing around, placing the others, I thought, so I lowered my voice as well. "Is she only using cats?"

"I wouldn't know, Frey. We are simply being... over-cautious."

My brow knitted.

"Is there something else?" he asked.

"It just bothers me. The cats, I mean."

He laughed, shifting to rest an elbow on his knee. "They didn't seem to bother you so much at the castle. They are practically sleeping in our beds as we speak."

"That's different," I protested.

"Does it seem so far off that she could have gotten the idea from you? I'm certain your cats are the tale of the North by now."

My eyes narrowed, but having no defense, I shrugged it off, though it did bother me, tremendously.

Suddenly, the atmosphere changed. Grey stiffened, and before I could process the difference, he was gone. In his place stood Ruby, ready in her protective fighting stance.

I tried to stay calm and remember to breathe. I didn't know if it was what we'd been waiting for, Grand Council, or if it was the new threat of Fannie. I realized I was hoping it was the latter. I was standing, ready to face her. I wanted to tear her apart. My anger was staggering.

Then Ruby straightened slightly, relaxing her shoulders and adjusting her belt, but still watching. I followed her gaze to find Junnie. I didn't know how to categorize Junnie, but I didn't think she intended to hurt me, kill me, as Fannie planned, or burn me, as Council wanted.

But I hesitated, because Junnie *was* Council. My ears were ringing in a low buzz as I tried to concentrate. My focus wasn't on the memory of her chasing Asher, on the endless days we'd spent in her study, on her story in my mother's diary, or on the limp body of the human girl. I tried to hone in on what she was saying to Chevelle.

They came closer, and the ringing got louder. It was only a moment before I understood they were stopping me from listening. I didn't waste time being angry with them. I only closed my eyes and moved to the mind of my horse, where there was no ringing to be found.

"No, he is helping her. She's forgotten everything, or maybe she's just using him as well."

I could hear Junnie clearly, but Chevelle was harder to understand—he was speaking so low that the conversation sounded one-sided.

"Apparently, she's decided this was the better path. I doubt she trusts him completely, but for now, they are assisting each other."

Chevelle's face was furious. For a moment, I thought he must have realized I was listening, but he turned away, facing Junnie as he answered, anger bringing out a growl in his muffled voice.

"I don't think he sees it that way," Junnie said. "He may not even know that she's found a side occupation. Regardless, he's not to be trusted."

Chevelle's hand was clenched in a fist at his side—I still couldn't hear him as they spoke, only Junnie. "He's merely using her to eliminate as many of us as possible without risk to him," she said.

Us. I was back in my own head, where spots swirled in blackness. Junnie was Grand Council, and not only was she after Asher, he was after her, And Fannie was after everyone. I tried to stop the swirling, fighting to stay afloat, but by the time I had it under control, Junnie was gone.

The others spoke in guarded tones and clipped words, but I didn't try to decipher what they were planning. My mind was a mess, the strain on the bonds too much. I sat quietly, eyes closed, exhausted from fighting images of Junnie and Fannie and animals slaughtering Council one by one.

When my eyes finally opened again, they found Ruby, ever faithful at my side. She offered me a flagon of water as I considered the disturbing dreams I'd had the night before. I'd been flying overhead, in the mind of a great hawk, peering through the trees, and I'd seen the human girl—not her dead, limp body, but her previous self, the happy, laughing girl Junnie had taken. The girl they'd called Molly. I recalled the fluff of her puppy's lanky frame, now too large as it frolicked in the grass beside her. It seemed odd I would dream of her so close to Junnie's visit.

And then there were the dreams of Asher's voice, as he plotted the use of the humans and the sense of betrayal as he compared them to animals.

There had been more, though, something that hadn't been in the previous dreams. I was running to my mother. Two guards were attempting to stop me from entering her room, and they had the nerve to command me to leave. My eyes narrowed, and my jaw clenched tightly. The girl that I used to be pulled a deep breath through her nose as she drew her sword and killed them both with one swing.

I shuddered.

"Are you all right, Frey?" Ruby's voice was gentle. I tried to give a convincing nod, and she pulled my cloak tighter around me. I wasn't cold. It was actually too warm. I had an irrational urge to throw the thing off, tear everything away.

I spoke instead. "Ruby?"

She smiled. "Yes?"

"How do they find us?"

She looked back at me, confusion written on her face.

"Junnie, Fannie..."

"Oh," she answered, hesitating momentarily. "Frey, I know you're worried about Fannie, but don't be. We have you covered."

"I know. I only mean that Junnie just pops up sometimes."

Ruby didn't answer right away, so I waited, working to seem patient. She saw I wasn't giving up. "I suppose the same way you found the wolves... and the girl," she said.

I drew in a sharp breath. Junnie must have the same abilities as Fannie and me, and surely the same as our mother. Suddenly, I had a thousand questions. "Ruby, if Fannie was unique, why would Asher not want her? Just for her looks?"

"I don't know, Frey. I wasn't around then." Ruby's eyes flicked to Anvil before she caught herself. She made a show of straightening the bottles and jars inside her pack, tucking the flap down neatly before she fastened it. "And your mother's diary was not clear on everything that happened."

No, it wasn't, and there was one particular part that I was suddenly exceedingly curious about. I pushed up to find my pack, but Ruby was faster. She grinned as she handed it to me and stood to leave.

"Thanks, Ruby."

Her departing smile was enchanting.

As soon as she'd turned, I flipped through the pages to the back of the diary, finding the passage I was after.

"You're back." His voice was trembling, feeble. It was my Noble, young no more. He had been waiting here for my return.

He was an outcast of the village. No one believed his tales of magic, the mysterious woman he claimed to meet here. He confessed to spending years trying to find me. He'd thought I was angry with him and that was why I'd not returned. He was afraid to leave this spot in case I were to change my mind and forgive him for whatever he'd done.

I pushed the guilt aside when I recalled why I'd had to come here. For my Freya, to save her. What my father had done to me, to my mother, I would not let him do to her.

I approached the grieving man and reached out to him. As I held his hands, I closed my eyes. I could not watch as I snapped his neck, the way I had with the small boar as my first show of magic to him so long ago. I placated myself by remembering he would soon be gone, his life so short.

I held him until the daylight began to fade then carried his lifeless body into the village. Proof they would be attacked and killed, proof they must fight the elves. It was not hard to incite a riot. They were fearful creatures. I convinced them to raid the castle, gave them direction.

All that was still hard to read, but I'd found what I was looking for. My mother had impressed upon the humans to find the castle and attack. She must have kept it a secret from her father. She would have known the danger.

I thought of my dream again, how I had run to her. I could recall the emotions, the betrayal, but there was more. I had thought her ridiculous and hadn't stood by her as Asher condemned her. Yet she had been right. I'd run to her, slain her guards, and... *and what?*

I tried to force the memory, but pain seared through my head, so instead I focused on what I did have: Asher. He was still alive, and he was somehow connected to my group... my guard.

Comprehension came. I knew, not just from reading the diary, but intuitively, what he wanted. Power and control unique enough to ensure his line, his rule. He'd known her child was half human. He'd thought the humans dumb like animals, but he did not know she could control them until she had created an army.

"Frey."

Chevelle's voice startled me. I looked up, but he was staring at the diary on the ground beside me. "It's time to go."

I moved to stand, and he grabbed my arm to help me, a little too forcefully. Before I could protest, I realized I was standing too close to him. The feel of the length of his leg against mine caused a flush to tear through my cheeks. At my expression, he turned, letting me go to hastily direct the others to the horses.

This is it. It's time.

They mounted, and Anvil's massive black horse huffed heavy breaths as they brushed past me. I hurried, jumping into my saddle and nearly over the other side to catch him.

I fell in beside Anvil, who glanced at me suspiciously. "Do you mind if I ask you something?" I asked.

"Probably."

I ignored the teasing. "I was reading my mother's diary, and I was wondering, why would Asher shun Fannie if she could use the animals?"

I expected him to reply in a hushed tone or avoid answering altogether like everyone else. He did neither, instead answering as if he had nothing to hide. "Francine kept her ability a secret not merely from Asher, but from everyone. She was smarter than anyone gave her credit for and paranoid to boot."

I considered her conspiracy theories about High Council and the villagers. In hindsight, they had more substance than I'd imagined.

Then I caught sight of a familiar expression on Anvil's face. It hadn't been familiar before I'd regained part of my memories, but I could see his manner like a reflection all of a sudden.

I'd been impressed when I was younger with the way he'd regarded my grandfather not as though Asher was his ruler, but as if they were equals. Anvil had shown no formality—he was calm and undaunted. He would have never bowed to *Lord* Asher, and I found myself smiling at the memory.

8

———

It wasn't clear how they'd learned where the light elf Kore was, but I had my suspicions that the information could have come from Junnie, or the usually out of sight Rhys and Rider. Yet there we were, tracking him down and racing toward another confrontation with Council. Ruby had assured me it would not be like before because the council members who'd been involved in my binding had gone into hiding. Whether they were hiding from Fannie or hiding from us, I didn't know.

The absence of a larger force didn't stop the thrill of terror that shot through me or the strange tingle of anticipation that felt as though it belonged to that other me. I would not be the one fighting. I would no longer be allowed to wield a sword against a kneeling tracker to lop off his head. It was different—we would be facing council leaders, men and women whose abilities were far too dangerous to use as practice, or so I'd been told.

My guard intended to find more than just Kore, but information had been slim. No one on either side could be confident in who to trust, so we only had hope that his death would bring back enough of me that my mind would be recovered and would find its way to unity, safe from fracture.

We barreled through the forest, the trees getting thicker and more closely woven until the horses came to a sudden stop at an oaken barrier. My guard dismounted, Chevelle only glancing over his shoulder at me as he drew his sword from its sheath. He wanted to save the person who was trapped inside of me, the one who wanted to fight. He wanted her back.

I wanted her back too.

The others moved forward, cutting through and leaping over that barrier as Ruby and Steed stood with me.

They watched me, not the forest, obviously waiting for what might happen when another of the bindings that held me together was broken free.

Ruby took my hand and looked into my eyes.

"Stop," I whispered. "You're making me nervous."

She grinned, and then there was a flash of light from within the trees. Scuffling, breaking limbs. Ruby squeezed my hand. It was over that quickly.

"How do you feel?" she asked.

I shook my head. Nothing was different. Nothing had changed.

She frowned, relaxing her grip to straighten the mess of my braid. "No matter," she murmured. "You'll get there."

She'd repaired her work and plaited a new strand by the time the others returned. Chevelle looked to Ruby for confirmation and found only a small shake of her head that meant *no, still not her.*

He slid his sword back into its sheath without another word.

WE RODE without event for days, and I finally began to relax into the pattern once more. When we stopped one evening, I sought out Ruby for training, even though I knew I'd regret it after a few lashes of that whip.

She must have been taking it easy on me, though, because I didn't fare too badly, even besting her twice. She cut practice short, prattling something about Grey, and stomped off toward Chevelle. I watched her for a moment, but a chill caught me as I stood motionless. I picked up my pack and found an isolated spot among the trees to change into warmer clothes.

Ruby had taken to tinkering with my garments, so the strings of the vest I held were adorned with tiny beaded jewels and feathers. The latter reminded me of my strategy to sweep the sky each day, which I cringed at neglecting again. I stuffed the bejeweled vest back into the pack, and the next morning, as soon as we mounted, I found a black kite soaring above and closed my eyes, settling into its mind.

Though it had been a cool morning, the sun was bright, and the sky was clear. I could see the landscape far and wide, so it was embarrassing how long I drifted in that hawk before I noticed that something was wrong with the lack of trees and the abundance of rock. I didn't know exactly where we were going, but I had no doubt that wherever the other members of Council were, it wasn't back up the mountain.

I pulled back to my body and almost before I opened my eyes shot out, "Where are we going?"

Five of them turned to me. Ruby said, "Oh."

"Oh?" I repeated.

"Well"—she shrugged—"there was a change of plans."

"And no one thought to tell me."

She smiled. "You just swoon so easily these days, I didn't know if I should." At the sound of my teeth grinding, her playful tone disappeared. "Frey, please. Trust us."

I narrowed my eyes.

"Fine." She sighed. "We are going back to the castle."

We had been riding for days in the opposite direction, and I'd had no idea. I didn't know what irritated me more, the fact that they'd left me in the dark or that I'd been oblivious. "Wait, *why* are we going back to the castle?"

The horses slowed to a walk, and I could feel the tension surge. I swallowed hard. I really didn't want to swoon so soon after being accused of swooning.

Ruby explained, "Fannie has destroyed a number of Grand

Council members. Those who remain are not waiting for her to find them. They have scattered and are too well protected for us to simply stop by for a visit."

I wondered if Council was busy chasing after her, if they had given up on me for the moment. I wondered how many were dead by Fannie's hand, and I asked.

"We do not have an exact count."

"But several. And Ruby, I don't have my mind back." I felt my features contort, and I worked to compose them, not wanting more information kept from me in their attempt to protect me.

"We will take care of you, Frey. We will find those who remain and—"

"Ruby," I interrupted, "why haven't I recovered? How many of them were in on the binding?"

"It's not how many, Frey. It's which ones."

The information caused tumult in my mind, and I had to take a deep breath as I attempted to find order. Fannie was slaughtering Council at random, causing them to scatter or come after her, but we still had to find the right ones, those who had twisted the spell through my mind.

Then I recalled Junnie's part in the ordeal. She'd shown up out of the blue and, it seemed, informed on Fannie. I wondered if she was acting on behalf of Grand Council, trying to get us to stop Fannie's agenda for them, but I'd seen Junnie fighting against Council at that initial battle, before she'd gone after Asher.

My hand tightened on the strap at my waist as my head began to throb, and I had to draw back and blur my focus. It was near impossible, and in the end, I was forced to return to the sky to avoid the commotion of my own mind.

I circled overhead for a while, watching us ride below and contemplating the peculiarity of seeing myself. I started to play a game, jumping from the bird to my body and changing the view from above to below, but the flashes made me dizzy, so I stayed in the bird.

I was flying when I was attacked. Hooks tore into my back, taking feathers with them when they pulled away. The yellow curve of a beak flashed as I was assaulted again, talons tearing into my wings next. I tried to maneuver clear of my aggressor, but it was futile—I was struck again and again, claws tearing out more feathers. I fought to no avail. Somehow, I knew it was the loss of my feathers making it harder to fly, so I relaxed just enough to let the bird have control, hoping its instincts would guide us better than my efforts. We were being thrashed by the attacker, and nothing I could do seemed to be working.

Then I remembered myself. It wasn't my true body being assaulted—it was the bird's. The realization eased the alarm that was building, and I formed a new plan. I jumped to the mind of the other bird, but the second I hit, the tension increased tenfold. The shock threw me back into my mind, and my body jerked in response. I was only trying to breathe, but it came as more of a gasp as my head snapped up to find her in the sky.

"Frey!" Ruby's voice cut through my disbelief, and in an instant, I remembered I wasn't actually in danger.

I *was* incensed, however. My eyes narrowed on my attacker in the blue sky, but before I could pluck her head from her neck, both birds dropped from the sky. I watched them as they plummeted in a tangle, finally landing with a muffled whump on the ground. I had expected a softer touchdown.

I shook my head as I turned to look at the others, who were clearly waiting for an explanation.

"Frey?" Chevelle asked.

I sighed. "I was just up there"—I pointed to the sky for unnecessary emphasis—"and plague strike me, I was mugged."

"That's all?"

"No." I hesitated, but it was almost pointless. They knew so much. "There was someone there. Fannie, I assume."

The group was in an uproar. Confusion and anger eddied around me. Bewildered, I interrupted the commotion. "If you didn't know it was her, why did you drop them?" I asked, indicating the lifeless bodies on the ground.

"I told you, we need to kill all of them," Anvil said, his level words directed at Chevelle.

Chevelle nodded his assent as he looked at me. "No more birds."

He was telling me I couldn't fly. "What? Why?"

"We only left them for you," he said with a hint of regret.

It took a moment before I understood. They had been killing all the animals, leaving nothing but the birds. He wasn't asking me to give them up—he was telling the others to destroy them.

Fannie hadn't hurt me. She'd only irritated me. But she'd gotten my birds taken away. I suppressed a growl.

Chevelle and the others swept our surroundings as they set off again, and I just sat and stared at them. One of them must have noticed, because the horse beneath me took off without my command, nearly tossing me from the saddle before joining the group. I had to restrain myself from riding by crossing my arms, and I glowered intensely. I was tired of feeling helpless and impotent, and I couldn't believe they'd taken my birds.

Anvil was riding beside me, smirking at my scowl. By some means, it made me feel slightly less irritated. I couldn't fathom his effect on me. He was in some of the few memories I had recovered after the battle with Council. I could see him there, his magnetism strong even in a faded recollection.

"You feel familiar with the hawk?" he asked.

The easy question threw me, but I gave a short nod. Anvil smiled, and I tried not to think of the dreams I'd had of burning his tongue and the hawk tearing it out.

"You will be with him again," he assured me, tilting his head slightly as he clicked his heels to join the front of the pack.

I was unnerved for the rest of the day. It was still bothering me when I fell asleep, which was probably what brought on the dream.

I was engulfed in blackness again. I could see the large dark man with the scar and felt nothing but hatred toward him. He was focused not on me, but on something else, a strange lump just beyond my field of vision. I didn't know why, but the lump meant something to me. I concentrated on the dark man's face and grasped the detail that made the difference: there was no scar, not yet. I knew it was coming, though, when out of the periphery came a blinding strike of lightning. The shot was partially deflected by the large man, but it caught his brow, and his previously smug face became enraged. I felt my chest swell just as I heard the laughing response, and though I woke before I could see his massive frame, I knew it came from Anvil.

I SHOT UP, suddenly awake and short of breath, the way I felt when I was roused from the violence of the battle dreams. I surveyed my surroundings, not surprised to find the others watching me with concern. I attempted a weak smile, and most of them returned to their tasks.

I wasn't usually awake that early, so at the very least, my breakfast was warm. Sitting on one of the rocks scattered around the camp, Ruby inquired about my start.

"A dream," I answered. I glanced at Anvil, only a few feet away, as I recalled the dream. Almost without realizing it, I remembered the dark man's name. "It was Anvil. And Rune."

I heard a peculiar noise, and my gaze flicked to Chevelle, whose face had drained of all color. My chest constricted, though I wasn't sure exactly what I'd said wrong. No one spoke.

I could feel the flush in my cheeks. I opened my mouth, but nothing came out. There was nothing to say. I didn't know why he was staring at me like... *like what?*

Finally, Anvil broke the silence. "Ah, my little Freya has been dreaming of me." It was apparent he was going for humor, but no one laughed. He stood, and after a moment, Chevelle turned and left the group. My questioning eyes shifted to Anvil. He forced a smile but said nothing as he walked past me to his horse. I followed as the others mounted their own.

It was a quiet ride that day. Once, something passed between Ruby and Chevelle, but despite the fact that my hearing was better than before, I couldn't understand the whisper. I was afraid to bring it up again, to say something wrong, so I merely watched our surroundings, studying the passing rocks and saying goodbye to the greens and trees. I missed my birds.

We finally stopped for the evening, much later than usual. I was paranoid that it was because of something I'd said, and I had trouble stopping the images of the dream from making a continuous circuit through my thoughts. Steed brought an elk in, though, and I managed distraction for the entire time it cooked and the few short minutes it took me to devour my portion.

After dinner, Chevelle was nowhere to be seen.

I was surprised when the wolves showed up after dark. I lay waiting for sleep when the flicker of the firelight caught their silver fur as they sauntered into the camp. Their eyes roamed over each of us before their massive frames settled onto the ground and they relaxed into sleep.

I felt more secure in their presence, and when the dreams came, they didn't have the mood of nightmares. I felt assured—I was the strong, certain Elfreda that I sometimes knew. She smiled as the cloaks circled, beckoning them. She faced the panther with courage, defying her lord. And she laughed at Rune, fearless in the face of his might, at least until the dream focused again on the mass, the figure that lay on the floor, that he concentrated on. She was powerless to act, suddenly weak. She stared, and the shape took form.

I could see him now, his face contorted in agony. In answer to my wordless plea, there was a flash of light, a surge of electricity, and the torture ceased momentarily. His rigid body eased a fraction, and I was grateful for Anvil intervening and for the broken man, he who signified so much, who lay so near to me.

I choked on the breath I sucked in. My eyes darted around the camp, seeking Chevelle, but he was nowhere to be found. It was as if I needed to see him, to look upon his face in the flesh, not in the dream, to be positive it was real. But even without seeing, I knew.

Someone approached, and I sat up, shaken, to find it was Anvil. He knelt beside me as he inquired on my condition, and I surprised us both by wrapping my arms around his massive chest in a hug.

"Anvil," I gushed, the appreciation pouring through me. He patted my back, and I felt his shoulders come up in a shrug.

I looked behind me to see who he was gesturing to and found Ruby and Chevelle walking toward us. I awkwardly pulled my trembling arms loose and wrapped them around myself. I should have realized Ruby had stepped away from camp when Anvil had come to me.

I'd desperately wanted to find Chevelle moments before, but with him only feet from me, I couldn't bring myself to meet his eyes. The rush of emotion I had felt in the dream was swimming through me, the image of his pained face and besieged body stealing my focus. I forced my mind to accept it so I could function again.

A tear rolled down my cheek, and Ruby was there, brushing it away. She didn't ask what was wrong that time—she just sat beside me and waited. For an instant, I was overwhelmed and clung to her as I had Anvil, but eventually the chaos settled.

It was dawn by that point, and we shared breakfast once more, though I couldn't enjoy it with the ill feeling that had seated itself in the pit of my stomach.

We were back on the horses in short order, and I was sure that we must have been getting close to the castle. Dark-gray rocks spotted the mountain, and the haze was beginning to thicken. We rode through a familiar pass. I slowed as I surveyed the land, trying to shake the eerie feeling that I'd been there before, but it only worsened. I found that I knew what was coming, how the path would curve just so past the jagged rock that slanted toward us, as tall as a dragon, and how the shadows fell in the crevices where the rocks met. I knew all of it.

I'd started to turn almost automatically off our path when Chevelle called to me. I stared back at him, keeping my face deliberately blank, and he explained that we were nearing the castle and I would need to ride amid the group. That was enough to derail me from wherever the impulse had been taking me, and then Ruby rode away from us, picking a slender path that twisted through the dark and spiky rock, and I forgot the idea.

Anvil and Grey had fallen behind me, leaving Steed and Chevelle at the front. I turned to Anvil and asked, "Where's Ruby going?"

"The castle, same as we. She is taking an alternate pass, as it is midday."

He apparently didn't feel the need to clarify further. "Anvil," I said, "*why* is Ruby taking a different way because it's the middle of the day?"

He used an uncharacteristically low tone as his lips twisted into a smirk. "Truth be told, Elfreda, your previous self was not so keen on the fey."

"What do you mean?" I asked.

"It is unfair to place my rendering of the events upon you, but suffice it to say, you dealt with them quite sportingly." His laugh was almost wicked.

The memory that came to mind was not my own, but my mother's. She'd talked in the diary of her father, Asher, killing fey for fun. I felt the blood drain from my face.

Anvil saw my concern. "Do not fret. You have treated Ruby well. It was merely the nefarious you disciplined."

"How?" I asked.

He smiled again. "Rather publicly."

I didn't know whether that was reassuring or not. "Does Ruby know?"

He chuckled. "Everyone knows, I'm afraid."

I felt sick. She couldn't be seen with me.

Grey threw in from behind us, "You know, Freya, Ruby is not the only of us affected by your... aversion."

I spun in my saddle to see him, positive that I would not want to hear what he was planning to tell me but unable to resist. Grey smirked at Anvil as he began his reply, but Chevelle cut him off. "Silence until we are inside the walls."

It was silent until late afternoon, when we arrived at the castle and Dree escorted me to my room.

9

———————

I awoke famished, striding from my room, through the maze of corridors, and directly into the dining area. I had no idea how I'd found it.

I was surprised to see Anvil, Grey, Rhys, and Rider there. "Don't you ever sleep?" I asked.

They found my question amusing for some reason and beckoned to me to join them, which I did as soon as I spotted the display of food. They had already eaten and were enjoying drinks, the roar of their laughter increasing with each swig.

The food smelled delicious, and as I selected a piece of meat from one of the trays, I asked, "What are we having?"

"Mountain lion."

I froze mid bite, though I'd received a report on the cats from Dree only hours before. Grey chuckled and offered me a glass of wine. I took it because I was thirsty, but it wasn't long before I found myself matching their pace.

Anvil and Grey began an intense conversation at one end of the table, and I took the opportunity to speak with Rhys and Rider. The wine had loosened me up. "Where are the wolves?"

They smiled in unison, and for a brief moment, I was afraid that was their only reply. However, Rhys answered, "They are enjoying searching the mountains tonight."

I'd wanted to question them more about the wolves ever since I'd been unable to slip into the animals' minds, but I was certain I could not walk that line in my condition, not without giving away too much of my own. "Tell me about them?" I asked, settling on a general inquiry.

Rider said, "Ah, they are incredible beasts, but beasts we do not know. It is said the wolves instead are ancients, some of the very first."

"Ancients? I thought they were all gone." I had read many accounts of the ancients in the village during my studies with Junnie.

"So it is told. Yet you can see their form is not like our own."

"They're elves?"

He smiled gently. "We cannot know. Legend tells the ancients were more powerful than any of record. It is said that upon their thousandth year, they, being too powerful to pass, merely shifted into the minds of the wolves. Others tell that they share the form with the creatures, each together as one."

I felt a crushing pressure on my chest yet knew it was dulled by the wine. I ran a finger over the grain of the table, looking for some way to ground myself, to stay with the conversation. "How?"

"It is said they were twin." He had misunderstood my question, of course, not knowing that I spoke of sharing the animal mind. But the new information was heady. No twins had been born in the elf nations for generations, yet the power of such a thing was known by all.

"And you believe it? You followed them."

"We do not know, Elfreda. We only accept as truth what can be proven. We are loyal to the wolves because they once did us a great deed. And we are loyal to you because the wolves are."

The conversation had taken such a bizarre turn that I was self-conscious, embarrassed at their declaration. "Why be loyal to me? You don't even know me. *I* don't even know me."

Rhys's smile was reassuring. "We do not pledge ourselves blindly, Elfreda."

I withdrew my hand from the table, my cup forgotten, and I had to resist the urge to flutter my fingers. "Wait, you do know me?"

"We... found out."

"Found out?"

Rider leaned forward, resting a forearm on the scarred wood of the table. "While we are faithful to the wolves, we do not offer our lives without certainty. It was a small matter of research."

My head spun. "What do you know?"

"We know of you, Elfreda. We know of your family."

"My family?"

They nodded, neither apparently worried about my tendency to black out during any kind of stressful situation.

"My mother?" I whispered.

"And the others," Rider said.

The others. "Fannie?"

"Yes."

Sidetracked by the disdain on their faces at the mention of her, I asked, "What about Fannie?"

Rhys's eyes, as dark and overcast as a cloudy night, took on a faraway look. "She had been difficult since birth, we are told, a concern from day one. Though her mother tried to care for her, she was a constant disturbance and grew to be a troublesome child. Rumors flourished that the lord would give up his plan for union with a light one. Upon the birth of the second child, their father merely exacerbated the problem with Francine, showing undoubted preference for Eliza. After a series of regrettable events and a show of your mother's superior power, Francine was passed over, her sister chosen as heir. Certainly, this enflamed her wrath, and after a time, she began to detach from even their mother, Vita."

I was speechless at the easy flow of words describing the horror, though I had read a similar version in my mother's diary.

"Her mother's death was pivotal, though, and it is thought that she meant to resurface and return as a proper lord's daughter. Upon finding her sister's plan to destroy him, she went to their father, exposing the entire plot. At first, he did not trust in Francine, but when confronted with Eliza's journal detailing the plan, he'd no choice but to see it as truth." Rhys straightened, the movement reminding me how still the brothers usually were, and raised one finger. "However, he did not do as she'd expected. Instead of being horrified with his successor's plan to destroy him, he was overjoyed at her power, a matchless power said to be described in her writings. Francine was confounded as he quickly began to form his own plan, which skipped over his only remaining daughter.

"She became incensed. She'd not the power to destroy him and his guard alone, no more than her sister had, but Francine knew Eliza would not accept her now. He'd be expecting Eliza, was aware of her entire design. Francine could only think of one other option. Grand Council."

There was a crushing pressure on my chest as my thoughts ran wild. I'd never even considered why Council had been there. I had merely read that my mother had decided to destroy her father. They'd been circling her, trying to stop her. I'd never realized that Asher wasn't there in those visions.

To think that Fannie, her own sister, had sent them...

I didn't know how long I sat before I saw Chevelle, his face awash with fury. He tried to compose himself when my eyes met his, but as he approached, there was an unmistakable, though unspoken, warning directed at Rhys and Rider. I wondered if that was the reason they were so often separate from the group—not because they were better watchers, but because they would answer whatever I asked. I was fearful for them but also afraid that I had lost their openness and they would tell me no more.

My concern must have been obvious, because when they stood in tandem to excuse themselves, they bowed toward me. "We are here but to serve you, Elfreda." I attempted a smile.

I realized then that Grey and Anvil had grown quiet and that I'd consumed far too much wine. I swayed, resting my head on the table without another glance at them.

Chevelle was silent as he lifted me in his arms and carried me to my bed. He laid me down and brushed the hair from my face.

Then he walked wordlessly from the room.

WHETHER IT WAS the wine or the stories, my dreams were fierce. The fire that surrounded my mother flamed hotter, scorching my skin as I watched her burn. I could see shapes in the flickers, a blaze of deep red curling amongst the orange and amber tongues, and I made out Ruby, the fire fey, dancing in the hideous glow.

The flames blazed in the background of other images, including the screaming, broken bodies as Fannie razed the village, the faces of each council member that she had butchered, the blood spilling from the mouth of the panther as she reaped a terrible revenge, and her knowing eyes finding mine. I saw Junnie, smoldering in the background as she ran, her council colors flowing in the tassels that waved behind her. She wore an unfamiliar dark cloak, and it felt as if she was hiding some threatening mystery. They crackled and popped until, without warning, they were gone, and I was standing in darkness, the chill air stinging my burned skin.

A faint light showed me the face of Rune as he focused on the body before him, the one who writhed in pain and became rigid when the torment redoubled. I stood, helplessly watching, waiting for what I knew was coming, though never quite quickly enough. Finally, I heard the crack, but instead of the strike hitting Rune and gracing him with an eternal scar, the lightning flashed brightly, a painful brilliance that illuminated Chevelle in a way that was not just clear, but lucid. At that moment, I saw him more clearly than I could ever remember, and I knew that he was Rune's son.

THOUGH DRENCHED in sweat and aching everywhere, I awoke with an unexpected calmness—that was, until I realized I was not alone. Chevelle sat on the edge of my bed—trying to wake me or watching me sleep, I wasn't sure. I jerked at the surprise of seeing him, doubled by the shock of the dream, and I was speechless.

He observed me silently for a moment, and when I'd finally retained my bearings, he handed me a drink from the side table. I accepted it gratefully, my hands still trembling.

"You should take better care of yourself," he admonished gently.

He had no way of knowing the cause of my distress, though I couldn't be positive the wine wasn't partially to blame. But I was aware of the reason behind his strong reaction to my other dream, when I'd mentioned his father's name to Anvil, so I wasn't about to tell him. I remembered the color draining from his face that day, and I became paranoid that he would somehow know that I knew, which resulted in a flush. Chevelle stood and swiftly walked from the room, informing me on the way out, without looking back, that I was to meet Ruby in the practice rooms.

Because that's exactly what I need right now.

I crawled out of bed, splashed my face, and attempted to get dressed. I was suffering from the preceding night's festivities, but in truth, that wasn't entirely why I dragged my feet. I wasn't in a hurry to see Ruby, since Anvil had filled me in on my prior issue with the fey, which was apparently causing Ruby problems of her own. I'd been sheltered from the public so they wouldn't recognize that my bonds were still in place, for my own protection, so I hadn't realized she wasn't as free to move about as the others. I wasn't sure how to deal with that, though it wasn't altogether my fault, considering they'd kept so much from me—also ostensibly for my protection—and I was still missing the majority of my memories, such as Rune and Chevelle.

I tried not to let the dream take over my thoughts. Concentrating on lost memories made my head throb and my ears ring, but I couldn't help it—I kept returning to it. Something about it bothered me more than it should have, and it wasn't merely the agony that I'd watched him endure. It was something else, something forgotten.

It felt as though it was right there alongside the anguish of seeing him tormented, the knowledge of his father's identity, and the gratitude toward Anvil for his intervention—a significant truth, just out of reach but adding to my headache. I pushed it away, counting stones in the corridor as I walked to the practice rooms, which to my surprise, I found right away. I had the feeling it was because I'd wanted to avoid Ruby, who stood front and center, impatiently waiting for me.

She saw my state and shook her head, clicking her tongue in disapproval. "Can't you at least *try*?"

I ran my fingers through my hair in an attempt to smooth it, but she wasn't impressed. The way she was looking at me, like it was time for a renovation, actually made me eager for practice. "Ready to get started?" I asked.

She smirked. "Yes, actually. Chevelle asked me to step it up this morning."

My face paled, and Ruby's grin widened. "Prepare yourself, Elfreda."

Before I had a chance to do anything other than cringe, the room lit up in a circle of flames so massive I could not breathe. I struggled for air, wincing as the heat assailed my skin and eyes. I had no notion of where Ruby stood as she taunted me. "React, Frey. Counter."

I had no ideas, no answer to the fire. The circle flared and closed in, advancing at an alarming rate, and still, I stood helpless. Suddenly, the flames disappeared as if they'd never existed.

"Seriously?" Ruby scorned. "What is with you, Frey?"

I was considering telling her when Grey came through the far door. We turned to greet him when, just as he entered, a large, golden mountain lion leapt from the pillars behind him, nearly landing on his back before Grey tossed the beast aside by magic.

"Curse it all, Frey," he complained.

Out of the corner of my eye, I saw Ruby fight a smile as I apologized. "Right. I'll send them away. Sorry."

"Come to watch practice?" Ruby asked him.

"I hear it's going to be a good one," he teased.

"Not so far." Ruby directed an accusing glance my way.

I groaned.

"What happened? I thought you'd been doing well. Heard you'd even bested Red."

Ruby shot him a glare.

"I don't know about that," I said, running a hand over the still-warm sleeve of my shirt. "I just can't think of—" My sentence was cut off. I'd even forgotten I was speaking when the memory came back. I'd been watching Ruby and the affectionate glare she directed at Grey, or maybe it was just being there in the practice rooms, but I remembered. And it had been in the diary. I was nearly positive.

They were both staring at me, waiting on a revelation when I turned from the room. "I have to go lie down," I said in a rush. "I'll come back later."

I ran straight to my room and dug through my pack until I found it, hands shaking as I skimmed the pages for the entry. My fingers ran over my mother's script, the words I had recalled, the words that supported the memory that was calling to me.

FATHER IS ALREADY DISCUSSING arranged marriages, even mentioning Rune's son, of all people.

A FLOOD of heat seemingly ran from the weathered page up my arms as it flushed my neck, my cheeks, overwhelming the thud in my chest. I heard someone behind me. I'd forgotten to close the door in my haste. I threw the book aside and turned, expecting Ruby.

But it wasn't Ruby. The heat drained from my face, surely leaving it colorless, taking my breath and drying my throat as Chevelle stared at the diary on the floor beside me, knowing that he knew that I knew.

He was motionless for an eternity before his eyes made their way to mine. I waited, struck dumb, unsure if I should prevent his explanation, part of me certain I didn't want to know more. As he opened his mouth to speak, I could almost feel the whole memory returning, teasing, as if it would come back if he would only name it.

He closed his eyes as footsteps approached, and the act felt like an apology.

I was unable to look away but regained my breath just before Ruby entered behind him. He took one deep sigh before he opened his eyes and turned to her, giving no explanation, implying that he was waiting on hers.

She faltered, fingers playing over the layers of dyed leather at her waist. "I was just checking on Frey." She was clearly confused, knowing I'd only run from the practice rooms moments before.

It was silent as we waited for his response, my mind running through a thousand scenarios that started with him commanding her to go, allowing us to be alone, him leaving without another word, him turning on me, furious, or the room bursting into flames as Ruby had demonstrated earlier, which seemed like the least painful option.

But none of the visions I'd had prepared me as he faced me and asked, "How are you, Freya?"

My mouth opened to reply but quickly closed again when I realized I'd no idea how to respond. His eyes, as dark as the blackest sapphires, were on mine, waiting, and though I couldn't look away, I knew Ruby's deep-emerald eyes that so resembled mine were as well. Once again, I was lost, fixed on a memory that wouldn't quite develop somewhere within his dark gaze.

Before I could draw it to the surface, Grey was there, summoning Chevelle. At first, Chevelle didn't take his eyes off me, merely raising a hand to dismiss it, but Grey explained, "It is Juniper Fountain."

He dropped his hand, and his face fell slightly in another apology before he reluctantly turned to follow Grey.

10

I might have dreamed of Chevelle, if I'd known what to think or how to feel about the revelations. As it was, he was merely background noise in a strangely calm set of scenes.

I walked from the castle as my former self, draped in a heavy cloak and masked by the darkness of night as I wandered the mountain. And I was me as I walked, still cloaked, through the long corridors of the castle, unable to find my way.

I sat alone in a room, turning a flat stone over and over in my hand, lacing it through my fingers, focusing on it. And then I was outside the castle again in the morning haze, walking from the path just before the great stone that tilted toward the pass like a watchful dragon, curving around between familiar dark-gray patches of rock until I found the entrance.

I bolted upright the moment I awoke, remembering Junnie was there.

I was running from the room and down the corridor before I realized I had no idea where she was. I'd been warned not to leave the safe areas of the castle without escort, so I knew only a section of rooms. I started toward the dining area but turned, heading instead for the room where I'd caught Chevelle with his tall guest before we'd left the castle, briefly thinking it was odd that I'd stored the memory. My footfalls echoed through the stone passageways, their rhythm not slowing until I turned into the doorway. But there was no Junnie, only Ruby, Steed, and Chevelle.

I colored at the sight of him, dropping my head.

Ruby approached. "Feeling better?"

I'd forgotten why I came. I couldn't find my voice.

When I didn't reply, she patted my arm. "Steed, why don't you take Frey to get something to eat. After we're done here, I'll meet you for practice."

I was shuffled from the room, unable to recover until we were walking through the dining room door. I cursed.

"What's that?" Steed asked, laughing as he directed me to a chair at the end of a long rectangular table. He sat across from me, the carved wooden corner between us.

"Junnie," I said. "I wanted to see Junnie."

"She's not here now. She merely stopped in on her way." I clearly wasn't satisfied, so he added, "She passed through only briefly before resuming her course. Grey escorted her from the gates hours ago."

I huffed as a thin, pale servant placed several trays before us. She eyed me in a peculiar way, and I ran my fingers through my hair, convinced I looked frazzled. My hand caught in a tangled braid, remnants of Ruby's handiwork.

"Eat," Steed commanded, sliding a tray toward me.

I should have been hungry, but my stomach was in knots. He was watching me, so I started a conversation that I really didn't have the energy for. "Steed," I began slowly, tracing the lines in the table with the tip of my finger, "Anvil said that I didn't like fey."

He smiled. "It's not that uncommon on the mountain."

"Well, Ruby... she has to hide?"

"Don't worry about Red. She's dealt with it the whole of her life." He had to have seen that the idea didn't console me. "Freya, she had the choice to leave. She enjoys the mountain. And I've never caught sight of an elf she didn't handle for giving her too hard a time." He leaned forward, showing his genuine smile to reassure me.

"But she couldn't ride into the castle with us," I protested.

He hesitated. "That is a different situation, Frey. You see, we are attempting to keep up appearances here to protect you."

Ugh, there it is again.

"It's no secret that once, you would not have befriended one of her kind. It is simply easier this way."

"What would I have done to her before?" I whispered.

He chuckled. "I didn't know you then, but I have known some who did."

I stared blankly as he considered whether to tell me.

When I could see he had decided not to, I stopped him from his planned distraction, stumbling in my hurry to get the words out. "Grey said it was affecting someone besides Ruby."

I saw it had worked. He shook his head and gave a little shrug as he explained, "Anvil was an acquaintance of mine years ago—"

"Anvil?" I interrupted, sure it had been Grey, something to do with his relationship with Ruby.

"He has an impressively wide reaching array of associates. It seems he'd been punished for consorting with the fey."

"I don't get it."

"Do you remember much of Anvil?"

"No," I answered automatically but then corrected myself. "Actually, I remember him more than almost anyone." I shrugged. "But I barely remember anything of anyone, so—"

He held up a hand to stop me. "I'll give you the condensed version." The hand fell to his knee, and he shifted closer. "Anvil had sought the fey for a specific purpose, but before he'd had a chance to explain, you reprimanded him, searing the tongue he'd criticized you with. In your defense, I understand he was quite vulgar."

I was shaking my head, baffled. "I think I remembered that," I said in a rush, "but I didn't know because there was also a hawk and Rune..." I drifted off at the thought of the dark-haired man, but Steed recaptured my attention before I'd gone too far.

"There's that too."

"What?"

"Well, quite honestly, it was a little-believed tale that you'd influence over the hawk of your family's emblem, and in a fit of rage commanded it to attack him. Consequently, though a piece of his tongue was torn out, Anvil proclaimed his fealty to you the moment he'd witnessed your power."

I blushed, remembering that Steed had asked me directly about my ability, and I'd lied. I blurted out another question. "How did it happen *twice*?"

Steed laughed. "That's an interesting one. Apparently, the hawk caught his tongue and tore a piece away. After you settled, he went to the healer and had it stitched up as well as possible. Later, when you'd accepted his allegiance, you were so furious that he'd so blatantly disobeyed you by dealing with the fey that you burnt the exact spot, simply to prove your point."

I felt my brows raise in astonishment. I thought of all the awful stories Ruby had told of the fey and was almost speaking to myself as I asked, "What was he doing with them?" Instantly, I was ashamed that I'd sounded as if I actually did have an aversion to fey.

"Yes, I'd asked the same of him. Odd that someone so faithful would incite such wrath, but he was confident in what he'd done. He believes, still, that had he only the opportunity to explain first, you would have understood."

I waited.

"You see, Frey, it is said that the dust—what is it you called it? Fairy breath?" He smiled. "It is said that the breath of the fey has the ability to grant foresight to some."

I remembered Ruby mentioning foresight, but when *I'd* dreamt under the intense effects of the dust, I knew that wasn't what I'd seen. "He was trying to see the future?"

Steed shrugged. "I believe the elders had led the notion."

I narrowed my eyes.

"But as I said, I was not here then," he explained, closing the subject.

I was reeling. He watched me patiently, letting me assemble my thoughts.

A movement by the doorway caught my attention, and I was annoyed to see the same servant, sure she was watching us. I shook my head—it irritated me unreasonably.

Steed chuckled. "A bit overwrought?"

I shot him a too-severe glance.

"Was that a threat?" he teased.

I was too cross to think he was funny, but when he lunged at me, sweeping me up from the chair, my breath rushed out of me in a huff, and I found myself laughing as he swung me in head-spinning circles around the huge room. Mid-swing, we caught sight of Ruby leaning against the entryway, her arms crossed as she smirked.

Steed set me down, and I tottered three steps before regaining my balance. "Merely training," he said to Ruby as she shook her head.

"Well, since it seems you have things fully under control, you might as well continue her training while I grab a bite to eat," she answered.

"Here?" I asked. They gave me that look, but surely there was a reason we had the practice rooms.

"Why not?" Ruby said. "You should be prepared for anything, after all."

I nervously surveyed the room. There were a lot of knives.

I was sorry I'd noticed as the metal started to rattle against the smooth planks of the table. I took a step back, and Steed laughed. When I realized I'd given him the idea, my mouth screwed into a grimace. Ruby joined his laughter, situating herself to better enjoy the show.

The corner of Steed's mouth pulled up slightly, and I cringed as I realized what was coming. He threw me a quick wink just before the first knife barreled toward me.

My impulse was to close my eyes and duck—I had to force myself to counter the move. I flung my hand palm out toward the blade and turned the knife just before it reached me. I gained confidence after my success, but the blade rebounded from the floor as a second one joined it, both flying directly toward me quickly. I focused on pushing them back, flipping the blades toward him, willing them to strike their target. Steed knocked them aside, losing his playful smile as he focused on the others.

The next thing I knew, an assortment of knives was heading directly for me at an alarming rate. I steadied myself, intending to stop them all with one move, when Chevelle's voice broke my concentration. "Are you throwing *knives* at her?"

The blades clattered to the floor as Steed blanched. Ruby choked on a laugh. I flushed, though I'd not actually been at fault that time.

Ruby, still smiling, stood as she said, "I'll take her to the practice rooms and set her on fire instead."

Chevelle appeared to be in a foul mood. "No. I'll take over."

I didn't understand it had been a dismissal until Ruby winked at me as she turned to go. Steed bumped my side with his elbow on his way past, following her through the door. Throat thick, I forced my gaze to meet Chevelle's, but he wasn't watching me.

He moved to the table, taking a seat opposite our food, and motioned for me to join him. My legs felt like lead, but I obliged.

I sat on his side of the table, leaving a chair between us. It was awkward, but I didn't want him to see my hands tremble or hear how I struggled to breathe. He didn't seem to notice.

The silence built, and as usual, I panicked. "It was kind of my fault. I looked at the knives and—"

My defense of Steed broke off when Chevelle looked up at me. I could see then that he'd not been thinking of my training at all. My mind raced to figure out what could have him so concerned. Too slowly, as always, I recalled seeing him earlier in a tense meeting with Ruby and Steed. I'd been caught so off guard that I'd not noticed the atmosphere. That part of my mind caught up, and before I could stop myself, I asked, "What did Junnie say?"

The question obviously surprised him. After a moment, he nodded and asked in his practiced, careful tone, "You're remembering more?"

Heat bloomed in my cheeks. I could only nod in reply.

"About Council?"

"Oh," I began. "I don't know." I pressed my eyes closed tightly and tried again. "I remembered some of them, mostly just their faces. But the things I'm getting lately"—I blushed—"they are more about... me."

"You?"

"Well, the old me, I guess." His eyes were on me, and I couldn't stop babbling. "And other stuff. I remember Anvil and stones and... and the path." It took all of my strength not to mention Rune, the lightning, and him broken on the floor. Fortunately, no part of me could even consider speaking of the proposed marriage.

He didn't reply as he watched me, but the muscle shifted at his jaw.

"What?" I asked defensively, as if he could somehow read my thoughts.

He shook his head, his tension seeming to ease. "It's just... frustrating."

Automatically, I nodded in agreement. I knew exactly how frustrating it was to have lost the memories, but then what he'd said sank in: *he* was frustrated by it. It was the first time anyone had said such a thing, and I examined the idea, thinking about how my binding had affected him. They'd had to do so much to protect me, all the while taking care of the things that were supposed to be my responsibility and keeping all those secrets. My eyes narrowed briefly, but then I thought of the last of those secrets that had been revealed, the one I'd done my best to avoid thinking about. I wondered if that was the cause of his frustration.

Heat flooded my face before I even had the chance to consider that, before I could think of all those inexplicable looks he'd given me, all the times he'd seemed as if he might reach out to me. I couldn't begin to reclassify all that had passed between us in the months since I'd met—*thought* I'd met him for the first time.

I glanced at Chevelle, sure my flush would have him moving away from me as usual, but he only stared back at me.

That was worse. I swallowed hard, resisting the urge to flutter. "Why are you meeting with Junnie, if she is Grand Council?"

It didn't sound like an accusation, but his brow raised for an instant before he sighed. "It is complicated, Frey."

I gave him a sardonic smirk. *What isn't?*

He reluctantly began, "While Junnie was a leader of Grand Council, she also—"

"What?" I interrupted.

It took him a second to realize what had confused me, and then he was irritated again. "Yes, she was a leader. She does not strictly adhere to their ideas." I shifted, and he held up a hand up to stop me from cutting in again. "She is helping us protect you for many reasons, but you must remember, she is your mother's aunt."

"She's meeting you to protect me?" I'd heard the words so often that they'd begun to have a negative connotation. "So what did she say I needed protection from this time?"

He hesitated, forming an answer. "It is not merely protection. She has her own tasks as well."

"What?" I asked, suddenly brave.

He leaned forward as he answered, and my courage vanished in an instant. "Freya, there is much you do not know."

That much I did know. I swallowed hard. "So Junnie was fighting Council to protect me?" I thought of the battle before I'd regained part of my memories, before I'd learned I'd been intended to rule. She'd fought against her own, but she'd pursued Asher with a vengeance.

"She was protecting you, yes, but she also has issues with the current leaders of Council. I realize that Rhys and Rider have filled you in on Fannie and the events that led to the..." His words trailed off as my face paled.

I collected myself, nodding for him to continue.

"Junnie feels that the event was used as an excuse to rout the leadership and cut the defenses of the Northern rule. While she disagreed with the events that had taken place, she kept with you and Fannie in the village to ensure your safety until those who intended harm were located."

I was astonished even though I knew I'd merely gotten the

briefest of explanations. "So she left the village because we were safe."

"No. She left when I had taken her place." My mind filled in the words he didn't say: *protecting you.*

I struggled to keep breathing normally, but my head was spinning, my stomach in knots. "Why?"

"She contacted me when the first council elder was killed."

"What?"

"Quinn of Loelle was slain. By an animal."

My reply was choked as I tried to force the disturbing information to settle in the disorder of my mind. A flash of something distracted me, and I glanced to the doorway, but there was no one there. When I looked back, Chevelle was gone.

I didn't realize what had happened until he came back into the room. He must have seen something too, and by the look on his face, it wasn't good.

"What is it?" I asked.

He shook his head, advancing toward me to take my arm and lead me from the room. "I shouldn't have expected to be alone with you."

I was confused until we found the others.

11

Chevelle led me to a room I'd never seen, and before I could register that Rhys and Rider were there with Grey, he started spitting out orders. "Grey, take Frey to Ruby and stay with them." He turned to the others. "Storm must be located. She is likely already outside the walls."

When I finally understood, my stomach dropped. Storm was the pale-skinned servant. She had been watching us.

The others were gone, and Grey had hold of my arm, unspeaking as he rushed me through the corridor. His posture left no doubt as to the gravity of the situation, and I struggled to keep pace as we raced through a part of the castle that was new to me. We turned a dark corner, and he glanced behind us before opening the heavy door to push me through. As he closed it after us, I scanned the room, working to steady my breathing. Ruby was waiting there, calm as she looked to Grey for an explanation.

"Storm," was all he replied, his jaw tight. Ruby's eyes flashed with anger. I stared open-mouthed as she composed herself.

"What is going on?" I asked, voice strained.

"Don't worry, Frey. It's fine," Ruby said in an attempt to reassure me.

I might have snorted.

"How much did Chevelle explain to you?" My brows rose, and she sighed. "He was supposed to be conveying some important information to you?"

I thought back to our conversation. "Um, Junnie and Council. And Fannie."

Ruby shook her head and mumbled, "I knew I should have done it myself." Then, louder, "Exactly what did he say of Fannie?"

Chevelle hadn't actually pointed her out as the attacker, but I answered anyway. "Quinn of Loelle. And then we were interrupted."

"All right," she said. "Sit down."

I swallowed hard as I complied, wondering how much more my mind would take before it shut me down.

Ruby ran a hand over the coiled leather at her side, not unlike the way I'd seen Steed pet a horse. "I am aware that you have been through much, Frey. We have tried to shield you as long as possible, but it is time."

I held every part of me taut, determined to stay the panic.

Ruby said, "So you know about Asher—" My puzzled expression stopped her. "He didn't tell you about Asher?"

I shook my head numbly.

She cursed. "Please enlighten me *precisely* on what you do know."

My mind was in disarray, but I gave her the best summary I could manage.

Ruby was confounded for a moment, apparently unable to decide where to begin. "Right," she said. "So the first thing you need to know is who they were protecting you from." She leaned in as if willing me to remain calm as she spoke in a low and steady tone. "Asher."

I stared blankly back at her. "But that doesn't make any sense. He was at your house. Chevelle was meeting him. He was there…"

She squeezed my shoulder. "Stay with me, Frey. There is a great deal you do not yet know." The turmoil must have been apparent. I thought I was nodding, but I lost focus when I realized why they were hunting Storm and that she was watching for Asher. He had spies in the castle. They were protecting me from him.

A vague notion that I was picking up on things much faster than I used to flashed through my thoughts, and then I fell into Ruby's grip.

"Easy," she said, carefully steadying me in my chair. She sighed. "Enough for now, then. We'll talk more after you rest."

I might have protested, but my head throbbed with pain. I let her lead me to bed, where exhaustion dragged me into sleep.

The murkiness of slumber was broken briefly by a conversation that I couldn't quite grasp. A man's voice sounded foggy and far away. "No, that's not why. Ruby didn't even get that far before she…"

Ruby jumped in, closer to me. "I'm afraid to tell her the rest. She can't seem to bear…"

Then a deep voice came from farther out. "I don't know how… It sickens even me. She'll certainly not be able to tolerate the idea…"

Then I was gone, floating in a wordless dream surrounded by dark stone and jagged, misshapen rocks.

I came awake slowly. The room was quiet and dim as I sat up, rubbing my temples. I ran a palm over my face as if it could wipe away everything. But it didn't. The hand dropped to my lap as I sat, staring blankly—thinking I was alone—for a long moment.

When there was a sound in the darkness across the room from me, I reacted automatically. Someone's body hit the block wall behind them with a solid thud. Only then did I process what had happened, that the noise I'd heard was merely someone clearing their throat and that I had slammed them into the opposite wall.

The room lit brightly as Grey regained his footing, giving me a scowl.

I cursed, adding, "I'm so sorry," before standing to help him. He'd been trying politely to let me know he was in the room, and I'd tossed him against the stone. I was halfway across the space when he stopped me, clearly uninjured.

He shook his head, but I could see a smile working its way through. I flushed, tottering the slightest bit before he closed the distance and steadied me. "I think we should both sit down," he suggested, straightening the leather plate that crossed his chest.

He led me to a set of chairs positioned against the wall below a massive tapestry. The panels hung still, no air moving through the windowless room, and I glanced up at the golden edging before looking back at Grey to ask sheepishly, "Are you all right?"

He smiled, his eyes teasing. "You are one dangerous charge, Freya." My cheeks colored. "Regardless, I am glad your instincts have returned. Are *you* well?"

I nodded, and he raised a brow questioningly. Given that I'd nearly blacked out again, it didn't seem that I truly could be well. "Yes. It's just... so much."

"I understand," he said, and I dropped my head into my hands, wanting to wash it all away, to finally have peace in my own mind.

It was scarcely a moment before the door opened and Steed came in, announcing to Grey that he was needed in the inner chamber.

Grey stood, bowing slightly to me before making a swift retreat. Steed took his place, leaning back into the engraved chair beside me. "Elfreda."

I tried to smile but couldn't pull it off.

He touched my shoulder. "It's all right, Frey."

"It's not," I blurted out before I could compose myself. "Everything is wrong and different and so... *ugh.*"

He gave a sympathetic squeeze.

I was suddenly babbling. "I mean, all of a sudden I'm a lord, and I have all these people after me—even my own family—and apparently, I hate fey, and I attacked Anvil, and secrets are everywhere in my dreams, and the one person who I can't even speak to without falling apart is supposed to be my betrothed—"

My hand smacked against my open mouth, cutting off the words. But it was too late. The truth was out.

Steed didn't seem shocked. He was merely watching me with that calm and steady expression.

I lowered my trembling fingers. "You knew?"

Steed shrugged. "It was common knowledge."

I felt the surprise on my face, sure he'd shown far too much interest in me for having been aware that I was betrothed.

He caught my response and leaned forward. A tingle ran up my spine as he explained in a low voice, "You denied him, Freya."

My jaw went slack, and the blood drained from my face. When it all came together, my stomach turned. Steed's hand slid across my back to steady me, and I bit down hard against the torrent in my mind, forcing myself to stay with him.

When I thought I had myself under control, I asked, "Why?" I couldn't fathom why I would deny him. My voice was shaky, and as soon as I'd asked, I wasn't sure I even wanted the answer.

Steed shrugged. "I can't say. I wasn't around then." He grinned with only one side of his mouth and added, "I fancy that he wasn't handsome enough for you."

I felt sick, suddenly wanting nothing more than a subject change. "Where were you?" I asked.

His smile seemed forced. "I don't know exactly when it took place, but I recall hearing about it upon my return." My eyes narrowed and he laughed quietly. "You always have been the best gossip, Elfreda. I was with Grey, I believe."

"Grey?" I asked, sidetracked again.

"Yes." His smile was genuine this time. "I have known Grey for more years than I care to admit. And he has been smitten with Red for nearly as long. It must be so strange for you."

I didn't want to think about it. *Couldn't* think about it. My fingers twisted into the material of my shirt. I wished I had my cloak. "Where were you and Grey?"

"With my father," he answered, fondness plain in his tone. "Grey had shown some interest in the horse trade then."

"He doesn't anymore?" I asked.

"Not since he found Ruby." Steed sighed. "He was lost at his first look into her deep-emerald eyes." He peered into mine as he spoke, and I couldn't be sure whether he was taunting me. "So rare," he said, his voice low.

"Are they?" I asked without meaning to. I'd never seen another besides Ruby's, but I'd just assumed I couldn't remember seeing others. No one in the village had my dark, jeweled eyes, but they hadn't had dark hair, either. Everything about them shone as brightly as their magic. However, the eye color could have been common in the North.

"I've never seen another pair, aside from hers... and yours. But I'd never met your mother."

I nodded automatically, not realizing what we all had in common. We were half-breeds. All the elves I'd seen in the North had brown or black eyes and dark hair. It made me wonder how Fannie had changed, but then I remembered my mother's description of her in the diary, her light features. Thinking out loud, I said, "So, when they bound me, they matched my looks to Fannie's."

"Horrible decision if you ask me," Steed said. I glanced up at him, surprised, and he grinned. "I'm sure I much prefer you raven than hen."

I straightened in my chair. "Steed, the next time Junnie is here, please help me see her. She's all I have."

His expression shifted. He looked as if he wanted to say something.

"Well, except for all of you," I amended, afraid I'd injured his pride.

He began to speak, but the door opened, and both of us turned to see who entered.

"Don't trust me alone with her, then?" Steed teased Ruby.

"You should know by now," she replied, but her humor was only half-hearted.

She pulled up a chair to join us but merely stood beside it, curling her fingers into the ornate railing. The bright scarf tied into her curls seemed out of place in the room. *Ruby* seemed out of place in there. "How do you feel, Frey?"

"Tremendous," I lied.

She glared at me.

"Did you find Storm?"

She hesitated for a moment before shrugging, apparently deciding it was my own fault if I blacked out. "Yes."

"Ruby." I looked her straight in the eye. "Why was she watching us?"

"Maybe she was wondering why you haven't brushed your hair in days."

I rolled my eyes at her then realized what had happened. "Storm was watching me with Steed too, when we talked before we trained."

Ruby cursed under her breath, but her face was smooth again as she looked to Steed. "Anything of consequence?"

Steed shook his head, but I didn't agree. Everything we'd talked about was significant, including my memory loss, my issue with fey, Anvil, the hawk, and Chevelle. I swallowed hard. What I'd discussed with Chevelle was far worse than my conversation with Steed. "Ruby, why was she watching me?" When she didn't answer, I moved to the more important issue. "Who is she reporting to?"

Ruby sighed, probably expecting me to faint when she replied, "Asher."

I knew it. And we'd been speaking of Junnie, her issues with Council, and my concealment in the village, combined with what she'd heard earlier. "Is Junnie in danger?" I asked.

Her expression softened. "No, Freya, be assured that she is not."

"But Asher knows she's protecting me," I argued.

"How would he know that?"

"Because Chevelle and I were—" I stopped because I knew what she'd meant. They had found Storm. I suddenly understood her comment to Steed earlier. She'd been asking if *I* had learned anything of consequence, not Storm. Storm was no longer an issue.

There was a clamor in the corridor, and my gaze found Ruby, but she only stood there as if she didn't hear it.

"Ruby," I said.

"They are simply taking care of a little problem, Frey."

A solid thump that resembled the one I'd heard earlier, when Grey had hit the block wall, sounded outside. I rose, but Ruby put a hand on my shoulder to push me back down. "I promise you, your guard does not need your help."

"They're killing the servants?" I asked.

"Only the ones who warrant it."

My head spun, small spots of bright and dark flashing in my vision. "Maybe I should lie down," I admitted.

They helped me up, leading me to my own room.

DESPITE THE FACT that I'd just napped, I drifted asleep while I waited for my mind to settle. Ruby had stayed with me, sitting beside my bed. I'd been dreaming of Fannie again, destruction and murder, her dark, dangerous cat eyes staring into mine as blood dripped from her muzzle.

The instant I woke, I found the remaining mountain lions inside the castle and snapped their necks where they stood.

My stomach turned, and my breath heaved. Ruby asked if I was well.

"I'm fine," I promised, "only a dream."

"Then sleep, Freya."

But I couldn't. Not anymore. "Ruby, what's going to happen to Fannie?"

"I can't say. She's got her share of tails." Ruby giggled at the remark and amended, "Pursuers."

"What will Junnie do?" I asked.

"Junnie is hard to predict, though I suppose she's got Fannie on the top of her list."

"Why?"

Ruby seemed to be considering whether to tell me. "Well, I guess you're already lying down," she muttered. She crossed her arms. "For taking out Council."

"But why would she care? Chevelle said that she didn't agree with Council's ideas."

"She doesn't agree with them *on certain points*," Ruby stressed. "Chiefly, that they manipulated events to control the rise of the North. But that doesn't mean she'd see them slain."

"I saw her fighting against them before we got to the castle."

"Only those who attacked you. Some did it for their own reasons, not Council's desire." She moved closer. "I can see you're not grasping the full scope here, Frey. Junnie's *entire* family is on Council."

I drew in a sharp breath. I couldn't understand how I had been so oblivious. I'd known even before I'd left the village that her family had received the calling. "And Fannie's killing them."

"Yes," Ruby answered, "and it is only worse that Junnie is responsible for saving her from your mother's fate, having protected her for those years in the village, though Fannie considers it punishment and entrapment and hungers for revenge."

Her reply had the tone of her fey tales, and I was confident once again that there was truth in all of them. I remembered what Steed had said, that Junnie had merely stopped on her way to warn us. "So is that what Junnie's doing here, searching for Fannie?"

"Not exclusively," Ruby said. "She has many arrows in her quiver."

I recalled the battle again and couldn't help but ask, "Why is she after Asher? If she doesn't agree with Council about suppressing the North's rule, I mean."

"That is an entirely different issue. Junnie is fine with leaving you in charge."

"But not Asher? Why?"

"Freya, there is much you do not know. Sleep now. Tomorrow will turn up soon."

12

———

I had wanted to argue with Ruby about sleep, but I was exhausted again, and she'd given me plenty to think about. My thoughts were swimming in the eddy of my mind, and it took a while to sort things out. But before long, they had slowed, and I was in a deep sleep.

My limbs felt heavy as I dreamt, each step a monumental undertaking. I walked forever through the corridors and from the castle, never certain where I should be until finally, I recognized the stones, the distinctive marker on the path, and turned to find the passageway. It was dark and cold inside—it felt abandoned, forsaken. I heard the cry of a prey bird but could not see the sky, merely blackness. The bird called again, screeching more loudly, and it pierced my ears. I tried to find it with my mind to silence it but instead found something foreign. Pain seared my mind, and the shriek became metallic and unbearable.

I drew my hands to my temples, pressing uselessly against them, and suddenly, I wasn't alone. I could feel a presence and heard my name.

"Frey!" Ruby commanded.

My eyes twitched open as a shudder tore through me. *A dream.* Ruby pulled my fists from my head and ordered me to calm down.

When I'd finally relaxed, she asked what was wrong.

"Just a dream," I answered.

"What about, a dragon's lair?"

I knew she'd meant to be sarcastic, but something about it seemed right. "No, only rocks," I said.

"Rocks." She shook her head. "You nearly scared the fire out of me."

I laughed at the odd expression, and my throat was raw. I must have been screaming.

After cleaning up to Ruby's standards, we went down to the dining area for breakfast. Chevelle was waiting for us. His voice was demanding. "Elfreda."

I cringed. "Yes?"

"Why are there dead cats scattered throughout the castle?"

I instantly felt sick again. "Sorry, I forgot."

"Forgot what?" Ruby asked.

"I forgot that I'd left dead cats scattered—"

Chevelle cut me off, taking a step forward. "*Why* are they dead, Frey?"

"Um, no reason, really." They stared at me incredulously, and I said, "A bad dream." It sounded almost like a question.

"Fannie?" Ruby asked in a low voice, probably remembering my inquiry when I'd woken in the night.

I nodded, and they dropped the subject. I doubted Fannie could reach the cats from outside the castle, but the others had no idea it could be done from a distance or that I had done it from farther still.

Grey came in, and Chevelle excused himself not long afterward. Ruby was discussing imaginative training ideas with him when Rhys and Rider found us.

"Good morning, Elfreda." They bowed in tandem, both of them wearing nondescript black cloth draped over the dark leather of their new garb.

They had once made me uneasy, but not anymore. I smiled.

"Good morning." Inspiration struck, and I turned to Ruby excitedly. "Why don't Rhys and Rider train me today?"

It was plain she didn't want to agree, but they spoke up before she had the chance to deny me. "It would be our pleasure, Elfreda."

She threw a glance at Grey, who excused himself from the table and hurried from the room. I knew I didn't have much time.

"Can we start now?" They were standing already, not having touched their food, so I amended, "Do you mind?"

"Of course not. It is our honor," Rhys said.

My grin widened, and I rushed from the room, hoping Ruby didn't follow.

"No need to run, Elfreda," Rider laughed when we were clear of the dining area. "You may query us on the way."

"Was it that obvious?" I asked.

He merely smiled. "What is it you wish to know?"

Unprepared, I blurted out the first thing that came to mind. "Tell me about Junnie."

"Juniper Fountain, I presume."

"Yes. Please."

"You are aware of her ties with your mother. What else are you curious about?"

"What she's doing now. I know of her pursuits, but why else, aside from searching, is she here?"

"Ah, I see. You are interested in the new Council."

"Yes," I lied.

Rider tucked a thumb beneath the thick leather vest that covered his chest, keeping pace beside me. "Since the conflict with Grand Council over the issue of northern rule, Juniper—Junnie, as you call her—has detached herself from the group. I assume that you are already aware of her surrender of leadership in order to safeguard you and Francine in the village?"

"Mm-hm."

"Then you know of the sacrifices and hardships she's faced. With the death of her sister, her decision was made, her path sealed."

Rider, who was walking several paces behind us, interrupted. "Elfreda, would you not have Chevelle know of our discourse?"

"No," I answered automatically.

"Then we shall train," he said, directing me into the practice rooms.

I hadn't thought this plan through. I was standing in the open space of the stone-walled room where I'd oft been tortured by fire and whip, facing two powerful silver-haired elves who towered over me. To make matters worse, before we'd even begun, Chevelle rounded the corner to join us. Ruby, smug in her triumph, popped through the second door only moments later.

Rhys, holding a carved wooden staff, announced, "It begins."

I barely had time to let his tone concern me before the staff tilted toward me. I stepped back, stumbling when the stones at my feet shifted. I glanced down, struggling to keep my footing. A crack echoed through the room, the only warning of the flash of light headed for my chest. It would have struck me, but before I had a moment to react, the blow was knocked aside by Chevelle, suddenly between me and the pair of opponents.

Every part of me tingled in warning, even though his fury was not directed at me. "Stop," he said.

Rhys smiled faintly, and for the first time, he looked almost menacing. "You overreact, Vattier. We know her capacity."

"She is bound," Chevelle replied icily.

"You shield her," Rider interjected. "She will not find her potential without cause."

"We have observed her with the others," Rhys said. "She has the faculty when you are absent."

Chevelle took two steps toward him, but before he could react in the way I feared he would, Grey spoke up from the door. "It's true."

I glanced at the others. Though their eyes were on Rhys and Chevelle, it seemed everything hung on Grey's words. To my surprise, Steed had also joined us, standing quietly by the second doorway. He stepped forward as Grey continued, "Her instincts have returned."

I cringed at the memory of flinging him across the room.

The tension in Chevelle's shoulders eased just a fraction, and I breathed again, the worst of this confrontation appearing to be over. "Since the temple," Grey added. Where I had caught his fist during our last practice.

"Why did you keep it from us?" Ruby asked, plainly irritated with him.

The group had gathered closer, and I let myself relax as Grey answered, only in trouble with Ruby at that point. "You knew she was improving. She'd bested you without aim."

Her eyes narrowed on him.

"Besides," he said, "you seem to make her uneasy."

Though Ruby was prepared to argue, Grey persisted, indicating Chevelle with a tip of his head. "But mostly, it's him."

My cheeks went hot, and I wished not for the first time that I had some control over the blushing.

Chevelle watched Grey, and we waited. It felt like an eternity before he finally reacted, glancing briefly at me then walking from the room.

A silence lingered until Grey spoke up. "I mean not to offend you, Elfreda."

"Um, no, not at all," I stammered.

He glanced at Ruby as if to extend his apology, and she sneered back at him. "Then we should carry on," he suggested to Rhys and Rider.

"Wait," I interrupted, not so anxious to resume. "What happened to the floor?" I gestured toward it, no more than the dark, polished stone it had always been. It had been writhing and swelling beneath my feet moments before.

"Merely an illusion," Rider explained.

"And the ball of light?"

He smiled at my term. "Not an illusion. And quite painful, I might add."

I raised a brow at Rhys. "So what's with the staff?" I heard a snicker and turned to glare at Steed, but he was gone. Grey tried to flatten his smile.

"It is merely an instrument to control my focus," Rhys explained.

"Even so," Rider said, "never hurts to have a big stick."

The painfully familiar sound of Ruby's whip unfurling brought me around to face her as she spoke. "Earlier, Grey and I were discussing how helpful it would be to give Frey the experience of a more complete battle."

Understanding her intention, Rider stepped a pace back to open the group, and Grey fell in beside Rhys, making a circle of sorts.

"I mean, even if we make her uneasy," she taunted, "it is not as if we will not be in battle beside her." I ignored the implication, knowing full well I would be no help in a fight. I backed away, concentrating on not getting hurt despite it being next to impossible any time a whip was involved. I thought I might settle for not getting hurt badly.

"Do not think of us, Frey," Grey instructed. "Better still, do not think."

His words were not comforting, but I was, in fact, not thinking when the first strike fired. Ruby's whip cracked not at me but precisely at Grey's face. The split-leather tip would have kissed his cheek had he not vanished a fraction of a second before it made contact.

Before I could draw in a breath, Rhys's staff reached forward and twisted Ruby's whip from her hand. She spun to plant a kick in Rider's chest, but he threw his own strike before she connected. She was flung backward, landing low on her hands and feet like a cat set to pounce. Grey appeared suddenly, hurling his fists forward. I could almost see the force that flew from his hands as it impacted Rhys and Rider's chests, tossing them backward and nearly off their feet.

Someone was behind me, and without the intent to do so, I spun, opening my arms wide to heave the energy to block the assailant. Ruby pitched back, smiling, and only then did I realize I had anticipated her attack. She landed softly, but before I had a chance to speak, I felt it again, coming from behind me. I spun, my hand thrusting beneath the opposite arm just in time. The energy hit Grey's chest and pushed him away as Rhys approached from the side.

The ground came from under my feet.

Heart in my chest, I pushed against the floor with that same force, straightening a hair's breadth before smacking the stone. I was very near regaining my footing when I was struck again. I was unprepared and fell backward only to be shoved by some unseen force to standing.

I could feel the tempo of the fight building, boiling in my blood. I was facing Rider across a narrow strip of space, and he launched his fist forward with a blast that sizzled across my senses. I knew what was coming for me, and unable to make time to find the others and a safe escape, I threw my own energy out in response. The two collided, and a mere breath in front of me, the air exploded.

"Very nice, Elfreda," Rhys said.

Then my legs collapsed. There were a few snickers as Ruby came to my aid, pulling over a stool for me to sit.

That was when Rhys helped Rider to his feet. "What happened?" I asked, confused.

"You defeated him," Grey explained.

"How?"

"You overpowered him," Ruby said.

I couldn't tell if she was still annoyed or merely stunned. My mind tried to catch up with the mêlée.

"How could I?" I almost whispered.

"What do you mean?" Grey asked.

"I mean, how could I have? I don't have near what anyone else has."

Though my voice was hushed, Rhys answered from where he stood. "Elfreda, you are of the most powerful line in the North."

I stared blankly at him, but Ruby seemed to understand. *Probably because she read the diary*, I thought sourly. "Freya, though you are merely half elf, your mother was of the strongest line of light and dark. The magic that allows their rule may be lesser in you than your kin, but it remains stronger than most"—she glanced at Rider with an apology in her gaze—"others."

I sat silently as her words sank in. My mother's diary had said

Asher had taken Vita for her strength and rumor of a unique power. My mother had been chosen as his heir over Fannie, not merely because of her features, but because Fannie had hidden her gift from him. He'd had Rune train me, even if I couldn't really remember it.

I considered what I'd learned of the events that brought Council to my mother on that unspeakable day, examining the differences in the accounts that hadn't come from Chevelle. Ruby had said the "*rise of the North*," not the rule. And Rhys had called it "the issue of Northern rule." They'd made it sound as if the North had been poised to take over everything before the conflict.

I stopped, chiding myself for having an overactive imagination. But there was also what I'd learned just that morning, when I'd asked Rhys about Junnie. There was a new Council.

"Frey," Ruby said, placing a hand on my shoulder. "Are you all right?"

I didn't think I was. All the training, all that "we're trying to protect you" rubbish, was because people were trying to kill me, and it suddenly made sense.

"Frey?" Ruby questioned again.

"Yeah," I said, forcing a smile. "I think I overdid it. I'm going to go to my room."

"Of course," she replied, moving to come with me.

"No," I assured her. "I'm all right on my own." She didn't look like she agreed, so I said, "Ruby, I just defeated my *guard*."

She was irritated, which made Grey laugh, but when I realized that it was true, my stomach turned. I hurried out before they could see me go pale.

I wandered down the corridors, not fully aware that I was getting lost again until the stone beneath my fingers became too cold, the fires in that part of the castle unlit. Heaving a sigh, I vowed to pay more attention to my surroundings as soon as I found my way back.

After making a few turns this way and that, I eventually recognized a hallway. I wasn't sure exactly where I was, but I knew I'd seen it before. Heading farther to a narrow, unadorned door, I found it was stuck shut. I glanced down the corridor in both directions, but I didn't have a better idea of where I should go, and it felt right. I pushed against it with magic, and it finally gave, opening into a damp, dark cellar. I flicked a flame over my palm to light the room.

It didn't figure how I'd been so certain a storage cellar was the right door. As I decided to give up and keep walking through the maze of corridors, a thick metal plate caught my eye, leaning against the back wall. I crossed damp stone floor to examine the design embossed in the steel. I reached out to run my fingers over the snake where it seemed to writhe in the beak of a hawk but was suddenly gripping the entire shield, pulling it loose from the gear that lay at its base.

I tossed it aside to stare directly into the mouth of a hidden tunnel.

13

Before I could stop myself, I was moving through the passageway and down the steps. Even with the flame, I couldn't see more than a few paces ahead, but that didn't slow me. I was confident—it was as if my feet knew the way, and I followed them without doubt, stepping faster and faster as I approached whatever lay ahead.

The question of exactly what was there slowed me just before I broke through to sunlight. As I stepped from the passageway, which was shrouded in a dark mass of stones, I grew cautious, surveying the land below. No one was in sight. I glanced behind me in the direction of the outermost castle walls. The entry to the tunnel couldn't even be seen—the boulder masked it. But I knew where it was.

I jumped down to the flat rocks, crouched, and ran toward the path, where I'd be able to pick up speed. I was close. I could feel it.

Then I heard the barely perceptible pad of paws hitting stone, their pace gaining on me, and I stopped. I turned to find a silver wolf with his sharp black eyes on me as he leapt from stone to stone in a full run, showing off his agility. In only a few strong strides, he was to me, his great paws landing with a muffled thump on the rock over the trail. He stared down at me, and though I wasn't precisely afraid, I knew I'd been caught.

I simply stood and looked back at him, both of us as unmoving as the stone surrounding us. Then I heard the others.

Caught. I smirked at the wolf as Chevelle, faster than I would have believed possible, closed the distance between us. He grabbed my arm, spinning me to face him. He began with a few choice expletives and ended with a gravelly, "What were you *thinking*?"

I had no idea how to answer, because I *hadn't* been thinking. I'd only been following some out-of-reach part of me, some forgotten memory. But as I looked into Chevelle's eyes, I didn't even attempt an explanation, because just below the anger, I could see something else: relief. Rhys, Rider, and Grey were watching us, and I couldn't help but glance at them. It caused Chevelle to ease his grasp, though he didn't let go as he turned to escort me back up the path.

I hadn't the slightest notion of how far I'd gone we were walking back to the castle. I was exhausted, though I was unsure whether it was because of the intense practice session or being discovered. Chevelle still had hold of my arm when we accessed the castle through a concealed entryway, and while it wasn't a tunnel, I wondered just how many hidden openings there were.

Ruby was waiting at the door. "Well, no wonder she's uneasy around us," she chided as she spotted his grip on me. His gaze narrowed on her. It was hard to tell if his mood was compounded by her reminder of Grey's comment, or if it was merely because he'd left me alone with my guard and they hadn't guarded me.

I was disappointed when they led me to the dining area because I only wanted to go to bed, but I didn't complain. I sat quietly as a member of the kitchen staff brought out trays full of meat, and when I realized it was a servant I'd never seen before, a replacement for Storm, my stomach twisted. *What* had *I been thinking?*

Ruby asked, "What is it?"

I became aware that I was shaking my head in disbelief at myself. "I don't know what I was doing. I'm sorry." I swallowed hard.

They stared back at me, mystified, and I kept talking.

"I was just walking and got lost. The next thing I knew, I was outside, and… I'm sorry."

No one spoke.

"I won't do it again," I promised.

Steed chuckled, and Grey shook his head, but they both went back to eating. Ruby stared at me for a minute before grabbing an apple from the tray in front of her, disregarding everything else to examine its smooth red skin. I turned to Chevelle, my gaze restating the apology.

He stared back at me.

I had the feeling that he was about to reach out to me or confess something, but he didn't. When he didn't take his eyes off of me, I flushed and had to turn away. Rhys was pouring wine, and I snatched a glass and downed it before I could think better of it.

It wasn't long before the flow of spirits and food loosened up the atmosphere, and everyone began private conversations. I still felt ill at all that had happened, so I only picked at the food. Drained as I was, I didn't know how much longer I could hang on, but I wasn't about to ask to go to my room, considering that was how it had started in the first place. So I sat quietly beside Chevelle and sipped my wine.

Ruby had moved to converse with Grey and Steed, and the others had started to mill around the room when Chevelle finally stood. Relief washed through me at the thought that I would finally be able to sleep, but when I followed him from the table, he stopped just a few yards away. I ran into him.

"Oh," I said, realizing my tongue was thick.

He steadied me. "Don't you learn?"

He was probably teasing, but I colored at the memory of my last episode with too much wine. "Sorry."

He put his hand under my chin, tilting my face up to meet his gaze. "So you said." My answering smile was quick, and he winced, his words coming out as if he couldn't stop them. "I've missed you, Freya." His voice was low and husky, and I found myself leaning into him, brazen with drink.

I stepped forward, wanting to push him toward the door, but I was off balance. When he tried to secure me, we simply ended up turning enough that I could see the others in the room. I'd forgotten we weren't alone, so I rose up on my toes, putting us in a tangle that was too close as I whispered, "I'm right here."

That was all it took. With a compulsion that seemed so strong that it might have been driven by addiction, he found my lips and drew me against him without regard for anything else. It was hungry and unrelenting, and all I could feel was the warmth of him, the nearness, and a fierce tingle over every surface of my skin. My legs gave way, and though he didn't free his grip in the slightest, he pulled back from the kiss to check my wellbeing.

It sobered me. "Why would I ever have denied you?" I was surprised when I realized I'd spoken aloud and that I hadn't sobered at all.

His face went colorless and expressionless as he dropped me from the embrace.

When my feet hit the floor, I kept a hand on his chest to stabilize myself.

"Who told you that?" he asked.

My eyes inadvertently flicked across the room to Steed before I even realized what I'd done. Chevelle's hand shot backward, and I stared in disbelief as Steed was lifted from the ground and hurled into the far wall. His body crunched.

I stared at Steed as without as much as a glance backward, Chevelle pushed by me and out of the room. Steed was stunned, but judging by everyone else's reaction, not going to die. I spun before good sense could prevent it.

Chevelle was halfway down the corridor, but I caught him easily, seizing his arm when he didn't acknowledge me. He didn't turn and only looked down at me as he waited for me to speak. His face was his stern mask, but his chest rose and fell as if it was an effort to breathe.

"How do you even know someone told me, that it wasn't just something I remembered?" I snapped.

He leaned toward me then, his face painfully close as he answered, "Because that is a memory you would never have."

My grip went limp at the intensity of his response, and the moment I'd released him, he resumed walking. I stared after him. When he reached the end of the corridor and disappeared from view, I finally turned to go back to the dining area. Ruby was watching me from the doorway. I sighed.

"It wasn't intentional, Freya." Ruby patted my shoulder as we returned to the room.

Though Chevelle had never looked away from me when he tossed Steed into the air, I was pretty sure he'd hit his mark. "It looked like it to me," I said.

She laughed. "Not that. That was intentional. And a very nice strike, if I do say so. I meant that Steed didn't intentionally mislead you. He simply did not know."

I moaned.

Even though I was certain I'd heard bones breaking, everyone including Steed assured me that he would be fine. He didn't seem terribly irritated as he dusted himself off and straightened his clothes. However, finding out that everyone had heard the comment that caused it was about all the humiliation I could stand. "Ruby, will you conduct me to my room, please?"

She laughed. "But you are so much fun when you're crocked, Freya."

I let her have that one, but only because she agreed to let me go.

As we made our way to my room, Ruby asked, "So where exactly *were* you going today?"

"I don't know," I answered honestly. "I just started walking, and the next thing I knew—"

"But why did you go outside?" she persisted.

"I'm not sure," I hedged.

"You mean you were standing in a doorway and didn't think, 'hmm, maybe I shouldn't be doing this. Maybe I shouldn't walk out this sealed door—'"

I cut her off. "Sealed?"

"That's the other thing. How did you break—" She stopped short. "You didn't know the doors were sealed?"

My mouth went dry, and she came to a standstill to narrow her gaze on me. "How did you get out, Frey?"

"I really don't know. There was just this passage, and—"

"Passage?" Her pitch rose. "Where?"

I shrugged. "I was lost when I found it. I was searching for the way back to my room or anything I recognized when I saw the door to the storage room."

She leaned toward me, and I actually felt a spike of fear.

"There was a storage room in the hallway, and I felt like it was right, so I looked under the plate with the bird and the snake. Then I went in. I won't do it again."

I was relieved when her intensity came down a few notches. "A bird and a snake?"

"Yes, a big metal plate with a hawk on it and the snake in its mouth. You've seen it?"

"Yes, I've seen it. It's your crest, Elfreda," she answered caustically. "Plague strike me, did you not think this was important?"

"How was I supposed to know? You don't tell me anything."

"Because you go out like a lame waterbird every time I try."

I wanted to be offended, but she wasn't wrong, so I only glared at her, feeling my jaw tighten. She bit down on her words, as well, but still shook her head as she whirled around and continued toward my room. I managed to stomp behind her a few paces, but my head began to throb. A couple of steps later, I felt my shoulders droop, suddenly too heavy to carry myself through who knew how many more corridors.

"Frey." Ruby was impatient as she stood in my doorway, waiting on me.

I had no idea we'd been so close.

I DIDN'T REMEMBER GOING to sleep, but I couldn't forget my dreams. They were so unreal—not at all like my usual dreams but just as uncomfortable. Ruby and I were arguing. "You didn't tell me," she'd said.

"Yes, well, apparently, I've had some trust issues!" I'd yelled back. The room was spinning around us, filled with anger and bitterness.

Suddenly, Fannie was there, joining in the quarrel, but it wasn't the new Fannie who was set on revenge. It was the old Fannie, the one from our house in the village, cursing me for the mundane and insignificant. When Ruby faded, Fannie attempted to persuade me of her theories of High Council's conspiracies. She was vehement and ferocious as she started to distort, her shape deforming until it resembled a great dog then shifting into a cat. It was not the frightening lion, but a slighter, less menacing version that melted away into the carcass of a snake that curled and writhed as if it lived.

Her words echoed through my mind, disgust evident above all else. "*It must be brought to an end. It is a perversion, brought on by lust for power.*" It struck me that although I knew it was her, it didn't sound like the Fannie I'd known, didn't carry her unadorned style. Nor did it sound as if she was speaking of Council.

When Ruby woke me before I was ready, I was a little testy. "What?" I complained. She didn't answer, and when I opened my eyes, ready to convey my grievance, I was surprised to see Chevelle standing beside her. She smiled archly. I sat up too fast, and my head spun. Neither of them reached out to steady me.

When it cleared, I peered up to give at least one of them a dirty look, but something was wrong.

"What is it?" I asked, unease waking me fully.

Chevelle's gaze was level. "We need to know where the storage room is."

"I don't know. I already told Ruby. I was lost when it happened."

"It didn't simply happen, Frey. I need you to tell me everything you can remember about it."

"There was nothing. It was only a plain door in the middle of nowhere. I can't find it again." But then I hesitated because although I didn't know how to find it from inside the castle, I knew where the exit was. I started to stand, and Chevelle pitched back, though I couldn't understand why.

"What are you doing?" Ruby asked right before I toppled forward.

Chevelle caught me, and I groaned. When the dizziness passed, I looked up at him and sighed. "I know how to find it."

"Then tell us," he said.

"I can't. I don't know how to explain it. I just know where it is. From the outside."

Chevelle's hold contracted in the strangest way. "What do you mean, Freya?"

My chest tightened at the endearment, and it took a moment to find my voice. "I mean, I don't know where the storage room is, but I know where the tunnel comes out."

An exceptionally nasty word escaped Ruby's mouth before she pressed it into a thin line.

Chevelle said, "You took a *tunnel* out of the castle?"

"Not on purpose." I wanted to defend myself, but the set of his jaw betrayed his anger, and I started to babble. "It's not like I can remember anything. I thought I was going the right way when I found the storage room. I saw the tunnel, and I don't know what happened. I was just running through it, and once I came outside, I knew where to find the path, and I was almost there when—" My words broke off as I reached the part about being caught.

"Almost where?" Chevelle demanded.

"I don't know. I can't explain it."

Chevelle gave us all a moment before starting again. "We need to know where you were going. Can you tell us where to go from where we found you?"

"No. I'll have to show you."

He shook his head. "No."

"There's no other way," Ruby interjected.

He glared at her. "We don't even know what she's going toward."

"We will all be with her," she argued. "It's got to be sooner or later—"

He cut her off. "Later. It will be later."

As he looked at me, an awareness seemed to dawn that the hold he'd employed to steady me was nearly an embrace. His arms dropped. "Rest, Elfreda." He stepped away but glanced back to add, "Let us know if you recall any other details."

I nodded, sliding my hands behind my back to keep from wringing them. Once he was gone, I slumped onto the bed.

Ruby was fidgeting and restless, a rarity for her.

"What?" I said.

"Nothing, Frey. Rest."

It wasn't long before Grey was at the door, and she practically bolted past him before he stopped her. "What's going on, Ruby?" When she feigned ignorance, he said, "Then I guess I'll be going. I was merely checking on you, since Chevelle informed me not to relieve you of your charge."

She gritted her teeth. "He did, did he?"

He laughed. "That's what I thought."

She'd disappeared before he'd even turned to greet me. "So, Elfreda, what have you done this time?"

I grimaced before confessing, "I got lost and took a hidden passageway outside the castle."

The smile dropped from his face.

"Yeah," I continued, "and I don't really know where I was going. Ruby wants me to show them the way—"

"And Chevelle knows better," he finished.

I nodded, conceding his point. Ruby really did enjoy trouble. It reminded me of her laughter the previous night. "How's Steed?" I asked.

"Fine." His brow shifted. "How are you?"

I answered with a vague gesture.

"You are much improved, aside from the wine, of course. We were all relieved to see your response during training yesterday."

"If only I could get to my mind that way," I groused.

"It won't be long, Frey." I looked at him, confused, and he explained, "You are so close now—only one more to release your bindings."

I straightened. *"What?"*

Before he could answer, we heard bickering in the hall, rapidly approaching our door. Ruby filed into the room, followed by Chevelle, Rhys, and Rider.

"Let's go, Frey," Ruby directed. "It's decided. You will show us the way."

Chevelle's posture was rigid, but he didn't argue. Ruby tossed my shoes at me, so I hastily put them on while she barked out orders. "Grey, go get Steed. Anvil is waiting at the south gate. We leave now."

I didn't understand how Ruby had taken charge of the group until I saw Rhys and Rider's expressions. They had agreed with her. I was certain Grey would go along with her as well, even if he thought it foolish. And if Anvil was already waiting for us, Chevelle must have been the only dissenter.

That was how we found ourselves standing in the middle of the path, waiting for my murky brain to tell me the right direction to take.

Chevelle was so near me that I could barely concentrate, and everyone stood either staring at me while they waited or watching the surrounding rocks as if they might come to life and crush us. It was making me anxious.

I was watching the vulture circling above, about to give up, when the wolves signaled from farther down the path. We started toward them as a group, and then I saw the misshapen boulder that leaned just so over the pass. Everyone but Chevelle kept going as I stopped to examine it.

"What is it?" he asked in a low tone.

"Here," I said, heading off the trail, around a tall rock, and down the hidden path before he could stop me.

"How far?" he asked, glancing back for the others, whom we could only hear from our spot off the path.

"I'm not sure," I said, "but it feels close."

He put a hand on my shoulder. "Wait." Anvil was suddenly behind us, returned from the others on the path ahead. Chevelle turned to him to find the cause of the wolves' call.

"Carrion," Anvil said, but his tone was so off that I almost looked back to see what was wrong. I didn't, though, because I could see the way in.

It took only two more steps to reach it, and Chevelle was in such a solemn discussion with Anvil that he didn't notice me move until I cried out.

I fell back, crashing into Chevelle just as his arms wrapped about me. Then I retched into the rocks at my feet.

The cavern I'd been so familiar with, so eager to find, held nothing more than a pair of ruined corpses. The withered hands of the two bodies curled over their sunken chests, as if they'd died in the midst of some horrible torment

14

I sat in my own bed with Ruby, Chevelle, and Grey anxiously watching me. There hadn't been much discussion once I'd stopped heaving into the stones that surrounded the cavern. They'd simply brought me back and waited for me to regain some semblance of wellbeing. I took a very small sip of water, proud that I could place the cup back on the side table without knocking it to the floor.

"Thanks, Ruby," I said, gesturing at my fresh change of clothes as I leaned onto the pillows. I was certain I had it under control, but then the idea of why she'd had to replace them was back, and—

I sat up suddenly, heaving over the edge of the bed, but there was nothing left to give. They moved closer despite my retching, and I waved them away. *I can do this.* I swallowed hard. "What was that place?"

"I was unaware of it," Chevelle said, his gaze shifting to one of the carved bedposts. "It must have been a site shared with you by Asher."

I knew my features contorted at his reply. I'd not exactly examined the room, but what I had seen was no mere cave. There had been a well-built chamber just inside and wood-plank doors leading to at least two separate quarters. It was dim, but the stones were smoothed and turned, the space clean except for the blood.

The image of the carcasses rose to the surface, and I couldn't stop myself from seeing the hands again. I didn't know why they were so important, unless it was simply that my subconscious didn't want to see the rest of the of the mangled, torn, destroyed bodies. However, the hands had been intact, the fingers discolored but pale, and caked with dark, dried blood. It had been apparent that one pair was male and the other set was clearly a woman's—they were petite, and I could still see the delicate beaded bracelet that hung undamaged around her tiny wrist.

"Who were they?" I asked.

"Deimos," Chevelle replied tentatively. My chest tightened at the name, but I couldn't understand why. He could see the question in my eyes. "He was a member of Asher's guard."

I steeled myself against the wave of unease. "And the girl?" I asked.

He seemed surprised by my observation. "We do not know."

I was certain there was more to his answer but kept on. "What happened to them?"

He hesitated, and though I was confident I knew, I had to hear him say it. A cool prickle ran over my skin before he said, "It seems to be an animal attack."

A movement at the door made me jump, but it was only Anvil. He gave Chevelle a pointed look, but when Chevelle's gaze returned to me, Anvil stepped closer. His shadow fell over both of us as he placed a hand on Chevelle's shoulder. "I will sit with Freya."

I was sure I'd missed something but couldn't bring myself to question it at the moment. Chevelle eyed me hesitantly but stood, gesturing for Ruby to follow him from the room. Grey gave me a parting nod as he joined them.

I glanced up at Anvil, who seemed distracted. When he finally settled in and saw my curiosity, he only shook his head. "You're driving him crazy."

I blushed.

"Yet it is much improved," he said. "It was exceptionally strange before. You were akin to a child."

I bristled. "Well, it's not exactly easy on my end, either."

He barked a laugh. "I would reason not. You expected naught and found it nonetheless. We expected Lord Freya and got—" He held his hand out toward me in a gesture that he cut short, along with his intended description, at my expression. "Now, now," he explained with a grin, "I mean no offense. It is merely unsettling to meet someone you have known and find they are not at hand."

The word unexpectedly produced the image of the remains, and I shuddered. Anvil leaned closer, but when he reached out to me, his massive hands only revealed what had been so disturbing about the frail, petite fingers in the secret chamber. They had belonged to a woman, a human. Heat rushed up my neck and cheeks, my fists clenched involuntarily, and it took all of my will not to rise from the bed.

Anvil backed up slightly.

"There was a human in the cave," I started, surprised by how composed I sounded in comparison to the way I felt. He didn't respond, but his posture straightened as I continued. "A human was in Asher's secret burrow." My words ended in something like a hiss. I was caught off guard by the course my thoughts had taken. "Why is there a dead human in Asher's hidden chambers?"

"Well now, that's a loaded question."

I forced the flames to remain in my fists, waiting.

He cleared his throat and crossed his arms over his broad chest. "Do you prefer to know why there was a human present, or why she no longer lives? I assume you will only make it through one narrative or the other." When the flames bit at my forearms, he was speaking again. "Then I choose before you receive neither. Asher persists in his design to strengthen his line. A disgrace it is, an abomination."

I watched the disgust on his face with confusion. He wasn't making any sense. *Where were all of these humans coming from? Why would anyone want them? What—*

Suddenly, Anvil's words sank in. They swirled through my mind as the familiar, biting pain returned, along with the ringing background noise behind the repulsive concept. *Strengthen his line.* I felt faint, so I forced myself to focus. "Asher means to breed with the humans."

Anvil nodded once.

Just as my mind formed the notion *because he knows*, the revelations became too much. My head spun, and I had to close my eyes against the flashes of light and dark. I wanted to fight it, to finish the conversation, but it was too hard.

Anvil's voice came soft and low, his fingers brushing my arm. "Rest, girl. You're only fighting yourself now."

I slept, regardless of whether I'd meant to or not. But even in my dreams, my mind refused to accept the idea that Asher knew I could reach inside the mind of a human. So my dreams focused on other minor details.

~

WHEN I FINALLY OPENED MY eyes, I was staring into Chevelle's deep-blue eyes. I smiled sleepily at him and spoke my first thought aloud. "Your eyes are like your mother's."

The expression on his face clued me in that my dreams had not been insignificant at all. I remembered his mother's eyes. I tried to recall more of her but couldn't see her image through the haze.

"Frey?" Chevelle's words brought me back. He was so close, and he was asking if it was me or her, the old me.

I didn't speak. I merely leaned forward, knowing what would happen if he thought it was her. But I'd been wrong. I'd underestimated him.

He grabbed me roughly and pulled me onto his lap, his face only inches from mine. I could feel his breath on me, coming faster as his eyes rose up to meet my own. My name slipped through his lips in a low moan as they joined with mine, his hands tightening around me. Somehow, we had gotten even closer, and I straddled him on the bed. His touch was overwhelming and consuming.

When I finally recognized the sound of the others approaching the door, my breath caught, and I was surprised to find that I was lying on my back with Chevelle over me, his dark eyes nearly black. He didn't take them off me as his hand flew toward the door, barring them from entry before his mouth returned to my lips and urgently traced the line of my jaw past my ear and down, his kiss opening on the skin of my neck and—

"Frey!" the voice at the door called, but I couldn't find enough interest to take in whose it was. They were insistent, trying to enter the room while my hands frantically searched for the skin beneath Chevelle's shirt. Suddenly, he was pulling me from the bed, and I protested, but something they'd said must have convinced him that it was important enough. I stared at him breathlessly as he composed himself and released the hold on the door. It flew open.

Ruby and Grey rushed in but stopped short. They must have thought something had been wrong, though I couldn't bring myself to imagine what at that precise moment. Their eyes went from Chevelle to me and lingered just a moment before Chevelle barked, "What is it?"

Ruby was apparently speechless, as Grey was the one who explained, "We have word that Brahn has been located."

Chevelle released a long breath and nodded. "We leave at dawn."

"How do we split?" Ruby asked, evidently recovered.

Chevelle turned to me expectantly, and I stared back at him blankly. "Frey?" he demanded.

"What?" I asked, baffled.

The look of sheer disbelief on his face clued me in. He had thought I was her, thought my memories had returned—because I had led him to believe so—and I'd just revealed my deception with one word. My face flushed, and he watched me for only a moment before turning back to Ruby and Grey.

"We should meet with the others," Chevelle said brusquely. He walked from the room without glancing back at me.

I deflated and crumpled onto the bed. Ruby approached, and I sat back up just in time to see Grey stop her. "Go ahead. I'll walk with

Frey," he said. Her eyes met his in a silent challenge, but I was on my feet, stepping between them with the intention of speaking up.

When I'd gotten close enough to Ruby to feel the heat radiating off of her, I stepped right past them and through the door in no less of a hurry. Grey laughed quietly as he followed behind me. I didn't look back to see Ruby.

I fell behind Grey as we walked into the room, not especially eager to meet Chevelle again so soon after what I had done. I stared at Grey's feet, keeping as close to him as possible so that Ruby could not grab me for an inquiry, but my head jerked up when I heard Junnie's voice.

She'd been in the midst of a conversation with Chevelle when we entered, and they broke off, turning to greet us. She gave a slight nod and nearly smiled. "Freya, you look well." She glanced at Chevelle and asked, "Have her faculties returned?"

His eyes met mine as he answered, "Her memories are fractured, but her powers are much improved." I found my feet again.

I could feel the questions linger, so I swallowed hard and raised my head as if I wasn't mortified by what I'd just done. It was harder to pull off than I'd expected, and I was suddenly talking without cause. "Have you found Fannie?"

Junnie seemed surprised at the directness of my question but only hesitated a moment before shaking her head. "Merely signs of her."

Signs. "Animal attacks?" I asked.

She nodded, and Chevelle seemed to become uneasy beside her. "I understand you have seen such evidence yourself," she said.

A vision of the human carcass returned, and I had to look away from Junnie. I scanned the room for something else to focus on. Anvil and Rider were staring at me with concern. I was still nodding.

Ruby wound an arm around my waist, and I concentrated on that while they resumed their conversation.

"I have since located only carnage and two stillborn," Junnie explained. "Other than your most recent find, have there been any other indicators?"

"Three servants for certain," Chevelle said, "and four others who could not be verified."

"We have removed those threats," Rider added. "No others remain within the walls."

I floated away from the exchange, scanning the gilded patterns on the edge of a wall hanging. From there, I traced the lines of stone as they spoke, their words merely background noise as I discovered an interesting design on the floor and followed it through the room. I tracked it until it ran under someone's boot, and I trailed up the leather to where it met the dark cloth of pants, upward over a leather weapon belt and fitted shirt, then reaching a strong chin before lingering on lips that I knew. Then I moved upward still, finally reaching his sapphire eyes.

Sapphire. Suddenly, it was right there, the name I'd tried so hard to recall, Chevelle's mother. All that struggle, and there it was. I barked out a laugh.

They turned to stare at me. I attempted a sheepish grin, but that only seemed to make it worse. A minute gesture from Chevelle had Ruby pulling me from the room. I hadn't realized how heavily I'd been leaning on her.

When we were nearly to my room, she asked, "Are you going to pieces, Freya?"

"No," I answered, but I didn't recognize my own voice.

We turned through the door, and she led me to the bed, sliding a chair over to sit beside me. "No need to worry. You are in good hands."

Ugh, hands again. I forced myself to concentrate on something else, but my mind didn't get far from the scene before my mouth opened. "Ruby, why would Fannie do such a terrible thing?"

She somehow knew what I meant, but her reply surprised me. "Is it so terrible?"

I stared at her, stunned.

"I cannot say that I'm not satisfied that it is done. Fannie is merely removing the foul... *things* that Asher is producing."

I considered that. I couldn't argue that it didn't make some sense, to Ruby at least, but it was so hard to think of without seeing the bloody mess in the hidden chamber and knowing those had been living beings. I felt my eyes flutter, so I moved forward, or at least sideways, with the conversation. "Why did Fannie go to Council when she discovered my mother's plans?"

Ruby looked puzzled. "I thought that was explained to you?"

I nodded. "But why Council?" I thought of how much I loathed them and how part of them had hunted me down. "Why would she think they would help her?"

She answered in a careful tone, "Grand Council is a birthright." I stared at her. "Oh, you are missing so much." She sighed. "Fannie didn't trust that Council would help her, but she knew that by rule they *must* defend her. The laws of Council have been in place for centuries. Your Vita was a member of Grand Council, as was her family before her. Therefore, by default, Fannie and your mother were also components."

"So Fannie was a member of Grand Council?" I asked.

"Yes." She sounded exasperated.

I gave her an incredulous look.

"Well, she didn't attend meetings or anything," Ruby snapped, "but she had the right to request protection."

"I don't understand," I said. "If they had to protect Fannie, why didn't they protect my mother?"

Ruby nodded. "You see why Junnie took issue with the outcome."

It was getting too complicated. "So Junnie is starting a new Council?"

"Yes, quite skillfully, as a matter of fact."

I wasn't sure about her tone. Chevelle came in and motioned to Ruby, and she leapt from her seat and dashed out of the room, probably to meet with the others to see what she'd missed. I sat up as Chevelle took the chair beside me.

"Are you well?" he asked.

A moment passed before I remembered I'd been escorted from the conference. "Oh, yes. Where's Junnie?"

"She's just departing."

"No," I complained.

He didn't comment, only glanced at the window. I was on my feet and to it in a heartbeat. I scanned the grounds below and finally found her, already too far from the castle. I squinted to see her better. She was being escorted by someone. Grey, I thought. And there was a low, dark mass beside her... A large, black dog.

My chest tightened as she carried on, the animal running contentedly beside her as Grey slowed to turn back toward the castle.

I slid away from the window, resting on the edge of the bed. I knew that dog.

"Freya?" Chevelle leaned close to me.

I looked into his eyes, not even thinking before I spoke. "I remembered your mother's name. Sapphire." His expression was unreadable, until I added, "Like Ruby."

His face changed, as did his entire posture, and his answer came out harsh. "No, not like Ruby."

I drew back, caught off guard by both his reaction and the idea that I'd spoken it aloud. He settled, smoothing his expression with purpose, and I cursed myself, wondering why I couldn't faint when it was convenient. "I can't remember," I defended in a voice near a whisper.

His hand lifted, but he caught himself. "I should tell you," he started.

I waited, my chest constricting as my wide eyes gazed into his.

He took a deep breath of his own. "You said that you recalled Rune, my father."

I nodded, not missing the strain in his last words.

"And you know that Asher was Lord of the North," he continued slowly. "So, you understand that, as such, I—*we* were under his rule."

The tension in my chest sharpened, as if a blade had been forced in, and I clutched it as I absorbed his words. I was backing away from him but couldn't stop myself. My suspicions had been correct—he was working for them. They all were. He reached out and, though I flinched away, caught my wrist to hold me in place. For one terrible moment, I felt as if he would hurt me, but I caught myself because he'd saved me for Asher. My frayed thoughts ran in a thousand directions, wrenching me into pieces.

But he did hurt me. Not how I'd expected, not physically—he hurt me with his final words, spurning in me a fear so deep I didn't truly understand. "Not us, Freya, not my father and myself. We"—he gestured between us—"you and me."

Everyone.

We were slaves to Asher and his will, loyal to the man who tortured my mother, the man who was responsible for this all.

15

I had wanted to deny it, but the truth was there, and it was a painful, all-consuming knowledge. I had no idea how I'd been so blind. Of course we would all have been under his rule, especially me. Asher had acted as my father and had been the Lord of the North. I was his second.

Chevelle's father, Rune, trained my mother and me, ordered by my grandfather. Though I had more blank spots than memories, I knew Rune was a close ally to Asher, so obviously, Chevelle would have been loyal to Asher.

No, not loyal. I couldn't be sure where the thought had come from, but I knew it was true. Chevelle had been under his rule, yes, but not loyally. I didn't know why I couldn't remember the same of myself or how I could be sure of his allegiance but not my own. I recalled the dreams, my memories of his tormented body on the ground as his own father, wearing that malevolent smile, tortured him. Maybe that was why.

Ruby cleared her throat.

I groaned, still raw. She leaned closer, and my eyes flicked open.

"Good, you're awake," she cooed.

I glared at her. "What, Ruby?"

"Tell me what you did to Chevelle last night. He has pushed back our plans and refuses quite sourly to explain why."

I thought past the raw ache of his closing words. "Something about his mother," I muttered.

She eyed me suspiciously. "Yes, well, he is likely sensitive about that, if all the stories are true. And they generally are."

I sat up. "What stories?"

She smiled wickedly. Then her expression grew serious, and her tone was so low I had to strain to hear. "These stories, though widespread, are not told boldly. It is said that Lord Asher was involved, so to flaunt them would assure death."

I felt the slackness of astonishment on my face.

Ruby leaned closer. "Sapphire, Chevelle's mother, was much loved by him, though she was not acknowledged by leadership. She was forced to live outside the kingdom, just as he was required to reside inside the castle with his father. Rune was a hard man, and Chevelle was equally stubborn. Reports of strife began even at a youthful age, and the discord only increased with time. Their distaste for each other did not arrive from one particular incident, but one achieved the breaking point."

My hand rested on my throat as I listened, riveted.

"From that moment, Chevelle declared his division from his father by claiming his mother. He intended to go to her and leave the life that had been set before him."

I was shocked, but Ruby wasn't finished. "Asher was informed and did not interfere, which was highly suspect. But on the day that Chevelle was to depart, he was summoned to the gates." Her expression went cold. "What he found there was the body of his mother, draped in a royal gown, a lifeless beauty, intact but for her eyes. Those striking deep-blue eyes that so mirrored his own"—her voice dropped lower, almost a growl—"had been cleaved from their sockets."

I could feel horror and disgust distort my features, and Ruby nodded in silent agreement. I considered the awfulness of it for a long moment before questions flooded in. I chose one of the less appalling ones. "Why would Asher be involved in something so horrible?"

I saw in her expression that I'd hit the heart of it. She seemed as if she wanted to find a way not to explain, but she'd gone that far already, and when she finally spoke, it was in her careful tone. "Freya," she said, "in all fairness, it is not known that Asher was to blame."

"But—"

She cut me off, holding up a hand. "It is thought so because of several factors, among them Rune's strong reaction. He was openly devastated by the loss, something that would have been an embarrassment to one of his position. Furthermore, he was angered by the display."

"Rune didn't do it? He didn't even know?" I asked, baffled.

"It appeared he did not."

"So what did he do?"

She shook her head. "He held Chevelle responsible."

I was mystified. "Ruby, I don't understand. Why would Asher care if Chevelle left?"

She clenched her jaw, looking as if she would refuse to answer.

"Ruby," I begged.

"It was not Chevelle's leaving that he took issue with, Freya." She leaned forward and placed her hands on my shoulders to steady me. "It was that his second intended to join in the departure."

It took longer than it should have to connect her words with their meanings. When they finally did, I was only able to whisper, "Then we ran?" For a moment, I couldn't help but remember my first real memories of Chevelle, how I'd run from Fannie, from the village, how Council had come after us...

Ruby was shaking her head. "No," she said. "You chose to stay."

"He left me?" I asked, with an unfair hint of resentment.

"No, Freya, he stayed for you."

I saw his crumpled body again, a mass of pain on the floor, and felt the agony of his mother's lifeless body being brought to him as a threat or punishment by those that he had to give allegiance to. *He stayed through that. For me.*

It was quiet for a long while. A torrent of emotion washed through me while my mind tried to sort itself once more. When Ruby finally moved, it was to glance up at Chevelle, who'd been standing near the doorway, watching us. I couldn't say how long he'd been there, but I was sure by his expression that he wasn't aware of our conversation.

I stood, walking to him. Maybe it was simply that my mind was overwhelmed, and maybe it was that I'd been wanting to for so long now, but when I reached him, my arms slid beneath his and around his chest in an embrace that seemed to shock him. He was probably wondering if I had regained the old Elfreda, but I didn't speak a word, only held him until his arms finally relaxed around me in return.

My eyes were shut tightly, but I heard Ruby slip by and close the door behind her.

Chevelle's arms lowered to my waist as he asked in an uneven voice, "What is it, Freya?"

I raised my head from his chest to look into his eyes and had to stop myself from thinking of how blue they were. Leaning in, I pressed my lips lightly to his throat. He pulled me closer, and I lifted to my toes to find his lips for a soft, slow kiss. He let the kiss deepen, but it felt as if he was reserved, uncertain. He had wanted me, I was sure of it. But he was trying so hard to protect me. I pressed harder against him, desperate for his response.

There was no question the moment his restraint broke. My body was overcome with such force that I lost track of my surroundings, aware of only him. Tremors washed through me, and I could not seem to get close enough to him. I was filled with a bottomless, compelling need, and pleasure at each touch, thought, and breath besieged me.

I was lost in him, but not as I had been all the months before. It felt true. There was no doubt it was what I wanted, something every part of me demanded.

The coupling was so intense and consuming that I had no idea whether it had been moments, hours, or days. I lay sleepily in his arms as he placed gentle kisses on my cheek, my neck, my ear...

It must have been the kiss, which brought my full and complete concentration to the place his lips were touching, that caused my dreams to slip back to the deepest depths of my memories. My ears, rounded like my father's, figured prominently as several of my childhood memories played out in my dreams. They were not unpleasant, though that, too, could have been influenced by my mood as I'd drifted to sleep. Even those of Asher were calm and lacked any form of fear. I recalled him at the battle, his mouth moving silently as he stood by, watching. And he was other places, too, whispering chants, focused on the fallen, focused on me. He seemed to grow bigger in each new setting, and I nearly laughed at the vision. The dreams progressed to include Chevelle, and even in my unconscious state, I was interested in seeing the new details that had previously been unknown to me.

So I was irritated when Ruby's sharp voice woke me, stealing the images away. "Wake up, Freya," she urged as she jerked the blankets down.

I sat up, mortified at what she'd see, but I was dressed. And Chevelle was gone.

Ruby was oblivious to my horror. "The boys are meeting downstairs. With any luck, we'll be leaving shortly after."

She smiled, delighted. She had no idea. Chevelle must have prepared things before his meeting, thank decency.

Ruby chose clothes from my wardrobe, cheerily packing them in the case, happy we would finally depart as she'd been hoping. I was still overwhelmed with contented satisfaction from the previous night and couldn't help but feel grateful that she'd shared the story of our past with me. I didn't exactly owe her, but I wanted to help her somehow.

"Ruby?" I asked tentatively.

She turned to me, smiling. I hesitated, and she stepped closer, stopping near the edge of the bed.

I steeled myself. "Don't you want to... to be with Grey?"

She looked startled then laughed. I didn't see what was funny. "You were so serious, Frey. I thought you had some significant dilemma."

"Is it not significant?" I replied, defensive.

She was still smiling as she sat on the bed. "Do you mean is Grey significant? Of course."

I waited.

"Frey, we have been together for ages."

"But not *together*."

She nodded. "There are many reasons for that, none of which are so solemn as you imply. I do enjoy his company and nearly always have. But I do not enter into a union lightly."

"But Ruby, what happened to you before..." It made me uneasy to speak about her poisoning her own mother. "It won't happen now. You know how to prevent it."

She shook her head. "Silly Freya, I know that. He is as safe from my venom as my whip."

I didn't think anyone was entirely safe from Ruby's whip, but I resisted pointing it out. "Then why?"

"The bond is not so simple among us, Frey. If I were wholly fey, a union would be uncomplicated. The fey joining is easy. Many find themselves with more partners than adversaries at the end of the day." She laughed, folding a gauzy patch of material into the pack. "It is different with the elf blood. Coupling among us would create a strong, enduring bond."

"So?"

"It is not something casual, Frey. It is an attachment that could persist a lifetime. Even if you wanted it broken."

My stomach twisted. I'd known that those who coupled were together for centuries, but I'd never considered that it wasn't by choice.

"I guess you must have lost the memory of those lessons as well." She patted my hand. "Your Vita was a victim of that bond."

Vita had died of grief.

Ruby stared at the tapestries above my bed as she made a thinking face. "Though her bond was weightier. Union with a lord and all." Unexpectedly, she perked up and grinned. "Not to worry. There's plenty of time to decide."

I thought for an instant that I might be sick.

Grey appeared in the doorway and gave a sharp nod to Ruby before he disappeared again. She grasped my arm and pulled me out of the trance to face her.

"Now, Frey," she demanded, "let's go."

Her tone spoke of the seriousness of the situation, so I followed her as she jumped up to throw boots at me and snatch a cloak from the wardrobe. My pack was over her shoulder when she grabbed my wrist and yanked me from the room, and I began running behind her. We hurried down the corridors to a hidden entrance, and as soon as we stepped outside, I could see that the others, each in their own dark cloaks, were mounted, waiting on us.

When Rhys and Rider saw us, they kicked up their horses and sped from the group to ride ahead with the wolves. I found Chevelle, and he acknowledged me with his eyes, but his face was severe. Ruby threw me onto my horse, and as soon as I'd mounted, all of the horses were moving. Chevelle was to my right, Ruby to my left. Anvil was slightly ahead, and the hooves of Steed and Grey's horses followed closely behind.

We rode hard without interruption across the craggy rocks and away from the safety of the castle walls. The group was silent and alert. I was terrified.

Chevelle stayed near me, and when we finally did stop, he stepped from his horse. In one fluid movement, he pulled me from my own to stand beside him. His face was hard, and I didn't ask the questions that were swimming through my mind. I was sure I didn't want the answers, anyway.

I'd thought it was merely a respite for the horses, but when I realized Steed was directing them back the way we had just come, my optimism sank. Chevelle led me to the cover of a few short, spiky trees, giving me no more than a reassuring nod before Ruby took his place. I watched him with Anvil and the others, the wolves pacing restlessly around their group. I could not hear a word of their discussion.

"What's going on, Ruby?" I whispered.

She responded in kind. "We had received word of Brahn's whereabouts, but the delay in our departure will mean some searching for him. The guard will split on short excursions to hunt without losing the group, while keeping you center."

My stomach tightened. "Won't they need the horses?" I asked as quietly as I could manage.

She shook her head. "From here, we keep on foot for stealth."

I pressed my thoughts into the deepest depths of my mind, silently watching two sets of two rotate searching while the remaining three stayed near me. *The center.*

We had finally reached what we'd been working toward.

Occasionally, the core of the group would move as well, allowing new territory to be scanned, and after a while with no encounters, signs, or anything to speak of, my muscles began to relax, and I settled into a long, uncomfortable resignation.

Once, Chevelle was with me, with Ruby and Grey nearby but watching outward. I leaned into him, finally calm enough to rest. As we sat on the cool stone with my back against the side of his chest and his arm around me, the tightness in my chest released. I almost dozed off, my mind wandering.

I felt the familiar sensation of a bird and fell easily into it, pleased to find it was a hawk. I soared lazily across the sky, the current so mild it barely ruffled a feather. It was so peaceful, so relaxing, to be with the hawk in my mind while my body was safe with Chevelle. I was contemplating how my tension had eased in relation to his proximity when the hawk spotted movement on the ground. It started to turn, but I urged it to stay, focus more clearly on what we were seeing.

Chevelle's hand covered my mouth when I gasped. My eyes flew open, and we stood, his palm pressed against my lips, his other arm wrapped tightly around my waist as Ruby and Grey rushed toward us. I was panting through my nose, and Ruby gave Chevelle a hard glare until he released me.

He spun me around, his eyes commanding an answer.

I tried to steady my breathing as the words rushed from me in the softest voice I could muster. "Fannie. She was running. I didn't know at first, didn't understand. But I saw Brahn behind her. He was after her."

"Where?" Chevelle demanded.

I closed my eyes and concentrated on remembering where I'd been so leisurely flying. They waited, but when my eyes opened and I gave them the best directions I could, they were in motion before I took another breath. The others appeared as we headed toward Fannie and her pursuer.

Chevelle's grip on me was tight as we ran, but he was too fast, and I couldn't keep up with him. Steed came to my other side, grasping my free arm, and they ran in tandem, my feet pulling from the ground to skip steps as I struggled between them. When I started to recognize the area I'd seen from above, one of the wolves called ahead of us. They did not slow, but Chevelle released my arm and moved forward even faster.

Steed kept his hold, and Rhys fell in to Chevelle's place as the others flew past us. They approached a structure of sorts, and suddenly, the field ignited into flame.

I stopped running. Steed and Rhys did not, and my feet began to drag, catching among the rocks and dirt. My legs responded a moment later, but neither Steed nor Rhys seemed to notice. They were focused solely on the battle we were approaching with frightening speed.

I could see Ruby amongst the flames. She was burning several large elves, two of whom I recognized from my nameless memories. Grey was fighting near her, seeming to flick in and out of vision with his swift movements. I searched for Chevelle and found him alongside Anvil, both fighting for entrance to the structure. It had all happened so fast, I'd not had time to even consider fear. When we reached the group, their opposition had been reduced to unresponsive piles scattering the ground.

Chevelle looked back to me before his eyes scanned to find each of the others. Then he visibly braced himself and walked with Anvil through the door, his sword drawn.

16

We didn't hesitate as we followed them in, but I froze at the scene inside.

The one-room structure was entirely open space, filled with large, lethal elves, Asher's guard. Steed and Rhys still had hold of me, and the others were lined up in front of us. Chevelle and Anvil had their backs directly to me, Rider and Grey were angled slightly away, and Ruby paced impatiently. Her whip was loose at her side, her hand wrapped around the base as she swayed like a snake. Her eyes were flicking to each of the figures in the room and repeatedly to the floor. I followed her gaze and found that a body had already been downed. It was Fannie.

My legs crumpled beneath me, but Steed pulled me to him, securing an arm around my waist as Rhys released his hold and readied his staff. I stared at Fannie's lifeless form on the floor, unable to comprehend what had happened to her. Trembling, I looked up at Steed, but he was not watching me. His eyes were intently directed to the center of the room with such heat that I couldn't help but follow. My legs gave way again when I saw it was Asher, but Steed kept me from collapsing.

I wasn't sure how long we had been standing there, but I didn't think anyone had spoken or moved since our entrance, aside from Ruby's agitated rocking. Tearing my eyes from Asher, I scanned the room again, purposefully avoiding Fannie on the floor, and the pieces started to fall together. We were outnumbered. Both sides were waiting for the first move. I began to size each of them up, wishing I could remember their strengths, and found Brahn, who'd been chasing Fannie. My eyes shot to her body—her corpse—and back to him. He was smug, his sneer a kind of boast.

Before I knew what was happening, I was stepping forward. Steed, caught off guard, struggled to stop me, but I was determined, and I was the first to speak.

"You," I growled to the beast, who seemed for a fraction of a second as shocked as the rest of the room. He quickly recovered, straightening his shoulders, but did not respond. He might have been twice my size.

Chevelle and Steed tried to pull me back, but I stood fast. I saw the symbol of the guard on his chest and wanted to burn him. "You killed Fannie?" I demanded, not recognizing my own voice.

He did not answer, and my hand came up to punish him. The others moved to stop me, my own guard protecting me from my ignorance. I couldn't feel ashamed for my impudence toward someone of his station, someone under the command of my powerful grandfather.

Asher's barking laugh caught everyone's attention. I glared at him, and his hand tightened on his staff. "You forget your place, Elfreda."

"She was your daughter," I hissed.

He shook his head calmly. "No longer. She had turned against me." It was a warning.

Chevelle's voice was low in my ear as he pulled me back once more to plead, "No, Freya."

Asher's gaze flicked to Chevelle then. "Ah, still whispering in her ear, Vattier." He spoke with such disdain I couldn't stop myself from looking back to gauge Chevelle's response. It was cold and hostile.

"She will learn," Asher continued, and I noticed something behind him, a movement of his cloak. I glanced down to see that it was not his own, but a second cloak of the same material, a small figure huddled on the floor behind him. With horror, I recognized what it was by the feel of its mind.

My eyes met Asher's in a moment of disgust, and he smiled as if he had just received the greatest of pleasures. "So it is true," he whispered.

The wind was knocked out of me at my own stupidity. He knew I could enter the minds of humans. How long I had spent fearing him knowing, and I had just given him, without a scrap of resistance, my last secret.

I felt all eyes in the room on me as Asher watched me with open delight. He must have been eager to share with them his new awareness, because he stepped slightly to the side to allow a partial view of the woman behind him. There was an intake of breath as they all registered what I had already seen: a human. Then they looked back at me appraisingly, finally understanding the exchange.

"You'll not have her," Chevelle warned, stirring the entire room back to readiness.

Asher laughed again. "You'll not stop me."

He raised his staff a fraction of an inch, and the whole room went still.

I had no idea what he was doing, but I couldn't take my eyes off the human behind him. Her eyes were on me, too, wide and terrified, and I saw that they were nearly the same soft brown as her hair, which could be seen beneath the oversized hood of her cloak. Her skin was pale, and she was unquestionably weary, but there was something else, something that didn't seem right. I just couldn't place exactly what. Humans were odd, but this one seemed wrong.

I felt Asher's eyes on me and glanced up to see that he was still smiling as the room remained motionless. It was as if, for once, the world was working at the same pace as my mind. I was trying to understand what was happening around me, how it would turn out, what I should do, if I would scream when they burned me. Suddenly, my eyes were back on the woman. She was clutching her stomach, holding herself protectively. She was swollen with child.

Flames flew from my hands before I could stop them. My eyes bored into Asher's, focused on my strike, and he remained smiling a confident, unpleasant smile.

The fire I'd thrown at him might have been the strongest I'd ever produced, but it fell short. He had barely twitched to deflect it, and I could already feel the drain it had caused me. The anger waned, and I suddenly understood the gravity of the situation. I understood everything.

I knew why Fannie's body lay on the ground before us. She'd been the animal that had mutilated the bodies of the human and the elf they had named Deimos. He'd been Asher's guard, and he'd been minding the human, who was essentially a broodmare, just as the unfortunate woman who was now cowering behind Asher was. Her beseeching eyes were still on me.

Asher had killed his own daughter for slaughtering his children, his half-bred offspring that she'd thought a perversion. I couldn't place my feelings for Fannie now. She'd had a cruel life, and though she'd been instrumental in my mother's death, I couldn't say it was truly her fault. She'd tried then to prevent the horror she knew was coming, and in the end, she'd stood alone against her father to stop what all of us abhorred. But she was gone, at his hand.

I knew then that he'd planned it, the slaughter of Council by my guard. He'd wanted it not merely because they intended to stop him —he'd had another agenda. I could see him there at the battle, the spellcaster whispering chants at the edge of notice until Junnie pursued him. I recognized why Ruby had owned a book on magic and remembered how she had spoken of stealing someone's power by taking their life, releasing their energy to use as one's own. *All of this in his quest for power.*

But that wasn't all, and I knew that too. I recalled Grey's words, and it further sickened me that they had all known that there would only be one outcome. They had known that every move they made would bring us all to this one moment, and that I would never be whole without it. Asher was the final remaining captor of my mind, and he had no intention of freeing me. *One more to release my bonds.*

Maybe it was the anticipation of battle that had sharpened my mind. Maybe it was Asher's presence. Maybe I'd been so blind to it all along because I'd not wanted to face it, but it was all suddenly there. We were defeated. My guard stood frozen because they too knew that they could not defeat Asher. He was too powerful for any of us, possibly too powerful for all of us, and his guard stood before him.

I glanced at each of Asher's guard again. Separately, they could have been overcome. Their confidence came not from an assurance that they could top any of us, but that they didn't need to. As illustrated by the brief encounter outside, my guard was not easily conquered. If not for Asher, they would overwhelm this impressive group nearly as quickly. But there *was* Asher, and he watched me as I considered, knowing he had me and that I would find no way out.

He would take me in and use me to regain his rule. He would succeed. Many of the Council were already dead, and he would finish it. I could feel the memories tugging at me, and I knew he would be a cruel leader. He would exploit my ability, continuing to make new offspring in hopes of gaining a more unique power. He would slowly steal those who were dear to me. Chevelle. Ruby. All of them.

He was quicker and more powerful than any of us. A move against him would be instant death—I knew that. We all did. And yet my guard stood with me, as if there was a chance. It was sad that they had so much faith in me. I was no more than a pawn in Asher's game. What could I do except—

I stopped cold, feeling the smile crawl from one side of my lips to the other.

I had the pleasure of seeing confusion cross Asher's face before I closed my eyes and sank, deeply and swiftly, into the mind of the small, brown-eyed girl at his feet. He had protected himself from us, but not from her. *Not from the piteous human.*

Her hand sped to the sheath at his waist then plunged his dagger into his heart.

The woman's scream threw me back to my own mind, and my eyes flickered open to see chaos. I was standing in the middle of a war, staring at Asher's body, which had landed in the trembling, bloodied hands of the fragile woman. She stared at him, her mouth still open but silent. I gazed into his eyes and knew that he was proud. Somehow, he was in awe of me, that I had defeated him. He'd been foolish to forget the human—he'd thought her as insignificant as a witless animal, and he hadn't protected himself from her. He smiled at me, and then his mouth moved in a silent chant.

As the life slipped from his body, I felt sudden, intense pain in my own. It became excruciating, and I nearly lost the capacity to breathe, but it crested as the icy heat of power rushed through me. It wasn't solely my energy coursing through me—I could feel Asher, the strength of his line, the depth of his magic, and the power that allowed his rule. I was overwhelmed, a torrent of violence and pleasure sweeping through me, almost knocking me from my feet. A deluge of memories, thoughts, and emotions followed, flowing together and joining with the agony and bliss.

And then the storm was over.

I had my mind back.

Although my inner conflict remained, it was not the painful tumult it had been. It was two sets of ideas, as if I was merely undecided. I looked around, disoriented.

Bodies were strewn on the ground around me. The circle of clear floor where I stood seemed to be the only area not destroyed. The downed bodies were my guard—no, Asher's guard. The blank, dead eyes of Eris, whom I had liked, looked back at me from the ground as blood leaked slowly from the corner of his mouth. A few feet beside him, in what might have been two separate pieces, was Domnal. Three of the bodies were burned beyond identification. Near the back wall, I saw Cleve, his form intact but lifeless nonetheless. I wondered if Dunn was among them, and Aren.

I saw Anvil, kneeling in what I feared was injury, but it was not. He was silently saluting me. I found a smile for him. I continued scanning the room and bristled for a moment when I saw a fey, but it was Ruby. *My Ruby.* She seemed to be smoldering. I nearly shook my head in disbelief but resisted. Rhys and Rider watched me from behind her, their robes in tatters, and I nodded my respect. Sitting proudly in front of them were my old friends, Finn and Keaton. I smiled at their knowing eyes, trimmed in a beautiful silver fur. Nearby was the handsome Steed, clearly staggered as he stared back at me. I gave him a quick wink before I searched for who else had been left standing. Grey was undamaged. And beside me, though a few paces back, I found Chevelle's eyes scrutinizing me.

My Chevelle. I knew him in both sets of memories. He'd been there for it all, and I was irrevocably tied to him.

I looked away. Asher still lay in the arms of the human. I took a step forward, and she gave a little whimper as she jerked a hand to protect her stomach. I sighed. Through all the time I had spent wishing to get my memory back, I had known. Somewhere in the mess of my mind, I'd understood that acquiring the magic and memories would not release me from the difficulties of my life. That was the third and final thing I'd always been certain of.

But I wasn't Freya anymore.

I was Elfreda, Lord of the North.

THE FREY SAGA: MOLLY

THE
FREY SAGA
BOOK 2.5

MOLLY

MELISSA WRIGHT

MOLLY

Small lines of text curled deliciously around the page, leading through a decadent city, a torturous romance, a wicked betrayal. Molly's hand traced the intricate pattern of runes that interlaced and surrounded the illustration of the temptress, Floret Shade, and she became distracted from her reading, studying the fairy's long golden hair, which seemed to float on the wind and mingle with the folds of her gown. Such a rich gown, beaded in an impossibly complex design that one would likely never even notice, considering how the bodice, cinched unfeasibly tightly, presented her bosom. And as if the display were not enough, her pale skin was dappled with droplets of jewels that glistened in the twilight, ensuring her prey would be ensnared. Molly sighed as she rolled over, hopelessly yearning for that sort of strength and beauty.

She felt the cool grass beneath her skin and became aware once more of the passage of time. It was nearing dark, and if she didn't return quickly, her father would skin her. She tucked the book into her satchel and hiked up her skirt to run through the tall grass.

"Molly Mayanne!" Her father's sharp tone cut through her daydreams of fairies, and she froze, forgetting for a good half minute to drop her skirt back down. He stared at her.

"Father." She struggled for a moment, deciding whether to come up with some sort of explanation. But she couldn't know if he was angry about the late hour or something else she'd done—or forgotten to do. She settled on a brief, "Hi," and a smile.

It was the wrong choice. He grabbed her arm and began to haul her back toward the village, chastising her the entire way about wasting time on foolish tales of fairies and magic when there was work to be done. She hoped he didn't see her roll her eyes, but after a few more steps, her temper got the best of her. She jerked her arm free and glared at him. "I am certain you don't intend to let the neighbors see you treat me this way," she spat as she stomped the remainder of the way back.

He followed her and shut the door behind them before starting up again. "Molly, a young woman cannot be traipsing around the forest. A lady must protect her virtue."

She snickered. Her virtue had been lost long ago, when she was but six and ten, to handsome John Black under the shade of the heart tree.

Her apparent lightheartedness clearly infuriated her father. "Molly, it is time to choose a husband."

She bit down hard against the words that would come.

He saw her defiance. "*Past* time."

The insult stung, and she stewed for a long while after he left her alone in the cabin. And then, eventually, she began to prepare their dinner. Her mind wandered from the resentment at her situation to the options available to her. Joseph Black, John's older brother, was a farmer, and she imagined herself in a muck-smeared apron, carrying slop to the pigs or tending the crops on her hands and knees. There was James Black, their cousin, who earned his living hunting and trapping and might expect her to skin and tan hides. She'd missed her chance with John—he'd long since married another, as he seemed unable to forgive her for kissing one of the Baker boys. She couldn't even consider the preacher, who'd made his interest in her quite plain, without giggling. No, she couldn't see herself with any of them. And that was how she'd ended up without a husband so late in her years. She wanted more.

When her father returned late, he seemed in unusually high spirits, especially given that Molly had allowed his dinner to get cold. As he sat at the table, she eyed him suspiciously from her chair in the corner of the room. She would have dismissed herself to her room, but she was in the middle of the tale of Bonnie Bell, and no matter how often she'd read it, the story made her skin crawl. Her father finished his meal and stood, humming a cheery tune as he carried his dish to the basin, dipped it in, wiped it dry, and returned it to its place on the shelf. Molly sat up.

When he spun, a grin sneaked across his face.

"No," she declared immediately.

He threw up his hands, and all mirth dropped from his features. "Molly, there is no reason—"

"No." She crossed her arms as defiantly as she could manage.

"Are you not even curious—"

"Fine." She stopped him again. "Who?"

He sighed and settled back into a chair, bracing himself with a forearm on the table. "Jackson Redding."

Her gasp of horror shut him down a third time. Jackson was more than ten years her senior, and those years had not been kind. She knew her father would not allow her dismissal on such vain grounds, so she chose another argument. "He's married thrice."

"He is widowed," her father insisted, "and you would be his third wife."

"The third to die and make him a widower again," she shot back. "Is that how you would see me?"

He stood to face her. "I would see you married before my years are over and no one remains to care for my only daughter." His declaration deflated her and she stared at the floor as he continued,

"Jackson has made an outstanding offer, and I urge you to consider it."

She didn't respond and, after a moment, he went to his room. She felt guilty and relieved the conversation was over and distraught about the entire matter until she heard him stop just outside his door. She froze.

"And if you refuse the offer," he said, "you will inform him yourself."

~

The next morning, her conscience had her up early. She hated spending long days inside, sewing and mending and such, so she pulled down a basket and headed out to pick berries.

As often happened when she set out with good intentions, she ended up lying on the creek bank, perusing the collection of fairy tales, empty basket at hand. Her father had advised her that by simply leaving the book at home, she could avoid such issues, but she'd thought him ridiculous. She would never abandon something of such importance—she carried it with her everywhere and had even sewn a hidden pocket in the back of her gown. The book had been aged when she'd found it, and though she endeavored to keep it well, the pages were tattered and worn.

She had drifted from those pages, imagining a life among the magic and dreams told within when a sharp sound pulled her from her reverie.

She glanced around but couldn't determine what it was because of the babble of the creek. She stood, narrowing her eyes at a motion a short distance away, and followed the sound, leaving her basket and book in the grass. As she approached the dark mass, its movement increased, and she could see that it was a small animal growing frantic at her advance. It seemed to be caught among some weeds and abandoned fishing lines near a shallow on the other side of the creek. She stepped closer to the bank and leaned forward, trying to judge the depth. There was no way she could cross at that point, but she was fairly certain there was a rocky area a little farther down. She'd never crossed there. She wasn't even allowed to be so far out.

The ball of fur whined, and she realized it was a pup.

She ran excitedly down the bank, searching for the rocks, worrying the entire way whether the pup had been abandoned by his mother, if there were more, and whether her father would allow a mutt to run in the village.

When she saw the rocks, she leapt in, not bothering with searching for the best path. She splashed across and nearly fell but managed to only soak the hem of her skirt. When she reached the far bank, the pup called out again, and she was off.

He shuddered and yowled as she came close, and Molly put her hands up in a calming gesture as she slowly stepped forward. It was too much. He struggled free of the tangle. She went after him, aiming to grab his body from behind, but he was fast, and her boots were slick. She slipped twice and muddied her skirt and apron before righting herself and starting again.

They ran and ran. The poor little fur ball was exhausted, and he finally gave, dropping onto the fallen leaves with an exaggerated sigh. Molly approached in a lowered stance, crawling the last few feet. She crouched and watched him for a long while. When his breathing finally slowed, she leaned forward to her knees and then her belly as she lay on the forest floor beside him and reached out tentatively to touch him.

He was so soft. She was amazed by the feel of him and took to petting the silky fluff, cringing at the few bald spots he'd created by tearing free. She cooed, and it only took a moment before he warmed to her, nuzzling his little black nose against her arm and inching closer.

They lay in the shadow of the trees for some time, until the pup became restless again and began to whine. Even covered as he was in fluff, she could feel the bones of his ribs, the narrowness of his stomach. Slowly, she stood, taking him in her arms to carry him home, regardless of her father's likely reaction.

It only took three steps to realize she didn't know which way was home. She hadn't noticed how far they'd come in the chase, but it had been far enough that she'd lost the sound of the creek. She glanced around and, clutching the pup to her chest, headed toward what appeared to be an opening in the canopy of trees. If she could get out of the forest, she could find the creek and her path.

But when she reached the clearing, she was encircled by trees. She narrowed her eyes in a challenge to the dark forest and headed back in, determined to find her way home.

Nearly an hour later, she realized someone was following her.

It had crept up on her, that feeling of being watched, that sensitivity to the softest noises at her every turn. She slowed, forcing herself to only glance back momentarily and not to run. There was nothing there but trees and shadows. She breathed deep as she turned to continue—and then she froze.

Standing casually in her path was the most terrifying, beautiful... *creature* in existence. He could not but be a creature, for he was no man.

Riven stood before the human girl, waiting for the instinct of flight to kick in. He looked her over as she stared back at him. Her skirts were caked with mud, her hair a tangled mess. *Filthy humans*, he thought as he tried to estimate her age. No more than one and twenty, he was fairly certain—old enough for breeding stock, at any rate. She was thin, but her hips appeared adequate, her bosom sufficient. *Good enough*, he decided. As his eyes returned to her face, he took in her expression and saw the coy smile, the flush of her skin. She was flirting with him.

She lowered the animal she held to her waist, presenting herself more fully. He closed the distance, grabbed her arm, and yanked her toward him. Her face contorted only a moment before smoothing as she pressed into him. He recoiled, moving her back by her upper arm.

She glared at him, finally understanding her advance was unwanted. "Well, you're the one gaping at me," she huffed, indicating her chest with a glance.

He stared at her, baffled, as she struggled to release his grip. He had never understood the creatures, but that one might have been the oddest of the lot.

"Remove. Your. Hand," she demanded firmly.

"Calm yourself," he instructed in as even a tone as he could manage. She did just that, crossing her arms and slanting a hip. It seemed surprising she had accomplished the posture, given that one arm was solidly in his grip and the other held a young cur.

She raised her brow, questioning and challenging.

He allowed himself a small nod. She would do just fine. There was no doubt Lord Asher would be pleased.

And Asher had been pleased. The girl had not even required persuasion. It seemed she took in everything, understood the whole of it, and accepted her place in the matter. The only emotion appeared to be pride as she gladly received the honor a king offered to bestow on her.

It was effected quickly, and before the next moon, they were crossing the hidden passages again—Riven, the blissful human girl, her unborn child, and a ravenous pup. They rode for days, stopping often in consideration of the fragile condition of the girl.

Riven nearly smirked at the thought, knowing full well that her condition wasn't the concern. His lord had wanted the child above all others, certain the girl's stubbornness and bizarre bearing were somehow a sign of what she would produce. Had Riven any question about the idea, it was quashed by his orders to hide her in their most secure location.

He was a faithful warrior. He had never challenged his king. But this commission was testing him.

"And he will be strong," Molly carried on, her posture so different from that of the girl he'd found in the southern forests. Her tone was haughty, as if she'd been born crowned. "I'm certain his eyes will be hazel, as my father's are."

Riven scanned the clearing, using all of his senses in the search.

"Ah, my father," she continued, "has no idea of my good fortune. I have often wondered what transpired there after I left. Had the villagers searched far enough, they would have found the muddy prints on the far bank." She paused, likely reconsidering their reaction. She'd maintained they would be convinced she had run off after her father's demand that she marry. She didn't seem to relish the thought of him in pain. She forced a laugh. "No, I'm certain they found my book of tales and decided the fairies spirited me away."

Her hand fluttered in the air, and Riven resisted the urge to break her fingers.

They stopped, and Riven dismounted his horse, pulling his pack with him. Molly stared at him until he assisted her from her own. When he pulled her pack down as well, he snapped a command at the horses, and they crossed the clearing in a trot then disappeared into the trees.

"Why did you do that?" she demanded.

"We continue from here on foot."

Molly's mouth fell open in shock, but she quickly schooled her features. *Not long*, she thought, *not long and I will be treated as a queen.* She unwrapped the shoulder sling at her side and helped the puppy down for some exercise. She'd not given him much attention over the last weeks, though he'd been her only real companion. The elves seemed pleased to have her, but they weren't exactly sociable. The pup was her only source of true loyalty thus far.

When she looked up, Riven threw her a hunk of dried meat. The pup bounced excitedly, so she slid the food into a waist pocket to eat later, when she could discreetly share with him.

Without a word, Riven began walking. Molly picked up the pup, wrestled him back into his carrier, and pressed her forearm against the bag to settle him as she hurried to catch up. Riven had a long stride.

They walked for nearly an hour before the exertion began to be too much for Molly. She pushed the hood of her cloak back, and the chill breeze prickled the damp skin of her neck. She tilted her head back and fanned the material of her blouse to let the wind reach more skin.

The sky was beautiful, blue, and endless. A hawk circled lazily far above them. Molly stumbled on a rock and brought her eyes back to the ground to watch her footing. Riven hadn't seemed to notice, but the pup at her side groaned at the disturbance of his nap.

A dull thump sounded a short distance to her right, but before she had a chance to look, she walked into Riven's back. He'd stopped in his tracks, looking toward the noise. Molly's eyes followed his, her head cocked to one side as she realized it was the hawk. It had fallen out of the sky.

Suddenly, she was jerked off her feet as Riven began to run. He had a death grip on her, and she wasn't able to look behind them. When she looked forward, there was nothing but a tree line in the distance. She had no idea where they were going or what was happening, but Riven's reaction spiked unadulterated fear in her.

And then he stopped running. His chest heaved as he dropped Molly to her feet beside him. He released his grip on her, but she stood frozen. Riven stared on as they were descended upon, his arms and shoulders braced.

The first to approach were ethereal, tall and thin and wearing silvery robes beneath their cloaks. Molly stared at them in awe. They stopped several feet away and spoke to Riven, but Molly couldn't focus on their words because she'd seen two wolves, great beasts, in the distance.

There was a commotion in front of her as the three exchanged low, angry words, and she turned back to find more elves confronting Riven. The newest arrivals were warrior-like, with the same otherworldly beauty as Riven, with dark hair and eyes and strong, muscular builds. She might have mistaken them for more of Asher's guard, except she'd seen no other address Riven as they did.

Two cold words escaped one particularly large elf, and she meant to focus on him, but Riven had dropped beside her. Her eyes fell to him, but there was nothing but a lumpy pile of material where he'd stood.

His cloak.

Face ashen, mouth agape, she looked back to the gathered mob, suddenly certain of her doom. Their grim expressions reinforced that theory, and she swallowed hard, her eyes wide. She felt the breeze hit her skin one last time.

"Stop!"

For a moment, Molly thought the voice was her own, but it wasn't. She found the source of the command, staring back at her with the same shocked, fearful expression she wore herself.

She was a small, striking woman who mirrored Molly only in age and stature. Her hair was dark, her eyes lush green. There was something about her that wasn't quite human, Molly thought. And then Molly realized the force with which the very large, very strong elf was holding the woman back. He stared down at the dark beauty, his jaw tight. He nearly seemed to be in pain. He nodded, and Molly recognized it as a command to one of the other elves. She steadied herself for her fate. The breeze picked up again, a gust of wind hitting her square in the face, stealing her last breath.

She thought she heard a whispered, "No," as she closed her eyes.

Nothing happened. It might have only been moments—she'd lost all track of time since Riven had started running—but she opened her eyes to find the pair again. His eyes searched the woman's face, and she seemed to be asking him for something, begging.

After a long instant, he turned from the woman, his expression hard, and gestured to one of the others, calling off the order.

Molly gasped in air, her knees weak, her hands trembling. Her frantic gaze fell back to the woman just in time to see her flushed skin go pale and her eyes roll back into her head. Dimly, she recognized that the woman was having a seizure or maybe fainting, and thought the same might come of her shortly. She lowered herself to the ground, shaking, but couldn't keep her eyes off the band of elves. They surrounded the woman. A wild redhead and the elf who had held her back earlier were holding her, easing her quaking body to the ground. *No, definitely not fainting*, Molly thought. The redhead looked worried, but the elf whose expression had been so severe before had changed—his face melted into pain as he stared at the woman. He pulled her from the redhead, cradling her trembling body in his arms to calm her. It was a restraint. It was an embrace.

Molly's breath hitched. She realized she was sobbing.

She realized she was alive.

It was some time before Molly's brain began to operate properly again. She knew she had been moved and was aware of the goings-on around her, but the passage of time had become fuzzy.

When she'd rested, been settled onto a blanket, and been given a canteen, things started to clear up again. She couldn't say it was a sense of security. After weeks with Asher's guard, she wasn't that naive. But she didn't think the group planned to kill her. Not immediately, anyway.

The elves had assembled a camp, built a fire, and paced around a lot. Molly had been watching them without realizing she'd been doing so, slowly grasping what was happening around her. The tall, white-haired elves were no longer in the camp. The rest, including the large, frightening one, the wiry one who seemed to be always moving, and the handsome, cheerful one, appeared to be doing what Molly's father had called "busy work." The other handsome, definitely not-cheerful one and the redhead were sitting by the dark-haired woman, who had yet to recover. Those two had barely spared Molly a glance, except when the redhead occasionally shot her an accusatory stare, though Molly couldn't understand exactly what she was being accused of.

She knew they'd killed one of Asher's head guards. She hadn't dared to let on her purpose, why she'd been with Riven, or that it had been voluntary. But they hadn't asked, either. In fact, they had barely spoken to her at all.

A grumbled complaint came from the bundle at Molly's side. She pulled the last of the dried meat from her pocket and slid it toward the pouch. The pup's head poked out, and he anxiously sniffed until he located the source in Molly's hand.

She started when someone approached her. She looked up from her spot on the blanket to see a tall, handsome elf, the cheerful one.

As he stared down at her, or rather at her pup, Molly realized maybe cheerful had been a stretch. He was indeed smiling, but it was a slow, sexy smile. She glanced quickly to the other handsome one, the one watching the dark-haired woman, and decided she'd have to stick with Cheerful and Not Cheerful, as both were exceedingly and unnaturally attractive. The group spoke little and had yet to call each other by name. She wasn't about to ask.

A low laugh escaped the elf beside her, and her eyes automatically returned to him. She would have to try to quit gawking.

He lowered himself to squat and reached out to run a hand over the pup's head. This caused the young dog to sit back then bounce excitedly. He was playing with her pup. A nervous laugh bubbled up from Molly's chest, and she nearly choked on it.

"What do you call him?" The elf's eyes connected with her own as he spoke, and she lost her voice, her breath, for a moment.

"I... Uh, I don't have... Haven't named him yet." There, she'd gotten it out. She'd been in the company of elves for weeks and had grown accustomed to at least those of Asher's guard who didn't outwardly show their distaste toward her, but she'd been certain the new group would cut her down as they had Riven. It had taken a toll on her confidence.

Cheerful was watching her. His smile had the slightest twist to it, just on one side, and she wondered if he was amused. "Well, it seems he should have a name. Don't you think?"

Molly nodded, still not quite able to return a grin.

"We shall work on that," he said.

She decided that did not sound like something someone would say if they were planning to kill her, and the tension in her chest released with a long sigh.

He obviously noticed. But before he had a chance to comment, Molly's attention was drawn once more across the camp to the other woman.

Molly realized then that she'd heard Not Cheerful and the redhead talking to the dark-haired woman in low tones since Cheerful had settled beside her, since the others had stationed themselves closer to her. The woman had woken and apparently wasn't very happy about something. There was a bit of commotion, and then the redhead suddenly had hold of the woman's wrists as she and Not Cheerful glared at each other. At that point, Molly considered renaming Not Cheerful "Murderous Rage."

Cheerful cleared his throat in a decidedly un-elf-like noise, from what Molly had gathered, and spoke again as if to distract her. "He will be quite large," he said, raising one of the puppy's heavy paws. Molly had noticed that before, as well as the dog's insatiable appetite. When his paw was released, the pup lifted both again in an attempt to regain the elf's attention. Cheerful rolled easily to his hip, kicking a bent leg out and leaning over to an elbow beside the pup, who took this action as a great victory and leapt toward the elf's outstretched hand for more play.

Molly laughed, familiar with the pup's antics.

"How does Rollo fit?" Cheerful asked, almost to himself. "No, no. Fredrik."

Molly scrunched her nose.

Cheerful laughed. "Not Fredrik, then. Dranson?"

The pup snuffed as if he held great disdain for the name.

He tried again. "Flufferby?"

"That's ridiculous," Molly giggled.

He smiled. "You should call him Giggles. He seems to have that effect on you."

She shook her head, deciding to play his game. "Snickers."

The elf smirked, and she suddenly had the oddest suspicion. None of the elves she'd met had been so casual, and there he sat, creating silly names for her pet, not even asking her name and not giving his own or any of theirs.

She looked toward the others. Something about each of them seemed to push Molly's gaze to fall on the woman with constant protectors. It reminded her of Asher and his guard.

The next day, the group was quiet as they departed camp. The horse Molly had been given was calm and steady, so though she hadn't spent much time ahorse, she was able to relax and take in her surroundings. She didn't recognize anything. The ground was damp but too peppered with rock to be muddy. The air was chill, and the mountain loomed behind them, black and ominous. A heavy fog hung near its top, clouding the sun and adding to the air of threat. Molly pulled her cloak tighter around her and shifted the pouch to cradle the pup in front of her.

She realized that the wiry elf was watching her. Being watched wasn't unusual for her as of late, but it was generally Cheerful, not the others, none of whom seemed to like her. At all. She looked back at the elf for a moment. He was lean and handsome, with an inexplicable quickness about him, even in stillness. His skin was flawless, his eyes as dark and rich as the bark of the roca pine. He wore a wary expression, saturated with distaste, and Molly averted her gaze. She knew he had an easy smile—she'd seen it. But it was only for the redhead.

Cheerful rode up beside Molly just then, acknowledging her with a nod. She beamed back at him. She couldn't help it.

He appeared to bite back a smirk. "Are you faring well with the mount?"

"Oh yes," Molly gushed. "He is a handsome steed. My father would pay a pretty coin for such a stud."

Abruptly, Wiry choked on a laugh and kicked his horse to a faster pace. Molly looked to Cheerful, who seemed to be openly laughing at her. She didn't appreciate being made fun of, though she had no idea what she'd said wrong. And the memory of her father caused a stab of guilt, so with her feathers ruffled, she purposely guided her horse away from Cheerful, impatiently willing Asher to finally come for her and for his child.

It was the one thing she clung to. He would come for her. He had to come for her.

And then, early one evening, things changed. They had stopped well before nightfall, as they often did, to make camp. Molly had a suspicion the group was worried about the dark-haired woman. She seemed to need so much rest. She seemed... unwell. Not that she looked it. Truth be told, Molly was quite envious of her unnatural beauty. But there was something not quite right about her, and the others hovered around her as if they expected a catastrophe at any moment. The woman didn't appear exactly graceless to Molly, but in comparison to the agility of their company, she might understand their concern.

The woman sat across the fire from them, and as usual, Cheerful settled in beside Molly, angled between her and the others. As a general rule, Molly tried to avoid looking directly at the woman, but every now and again, she caught sight of her face and recognized some of her own emotion there, a fierce determination, a confidence that belied her size. Only the woman carried even more. Behind her eyes was chaos and fury.

The redhead noticed that Molly's attention had fallen on the woman and intervened. She stepped before the fire, circling the rising flame as she spoke. She told of fairies and great tales of wondrous places, and Molly was mesmerized.

Every eye was on the redhead, and she clearly relished the attention. Her gaze fell in succession to each in her audience as she moved, a clink of metal and a wisp of material accenting every passage. The fire licked the air behind her, as if dancing to the melody of her words, as if even the flames were entranced by her story.

Molly was enchanted, the yarn a dull thrum as her gaze fixed on the blaze. Sudden raucous laughter broke her trance, and she blinked, her eyes dry. Coming back to herself, she glanced around again at the elves.

Cheerful was watching her. He smiled, and Molly believed it was genuine. "She has a way with words," he said.

"Yes." Molly sighed. Her eyes roamed the camp again in wonder at the world she had stepped into, a world right out of her books to which she had only dreamed of belonging. Her gaze fell on the dark-haired woman, and she considered what her role could be in everything. She clearly mattered to the group. Molly wondered if there could be some reason for another human to be among these beings.

"And where's your pup, Sunshine?"

Molly smiled at Cheerful before turning back to her contemplation of the woman. She jumped when he reached for her.

He leaned in as he tucked a strand of hair behind her ear, whispering conspiratorially, "Don't see much blond around here."

For the first time in years, Molly blushed.

And then the fire exploded. For a moment, Molly thought the dark-haired woman was burning, that the explosion had thrown flames onto her. But as everyone in the camp stared at the woman, waiting, Molly realized it was nothing of the sort.

Molly's mouth opened for a moment, then closed, then opened again as she struggled for words. The woman... Flames had burst from her hands, but she was unharmed by them. The woman had magic.

She was no mere woman, Molly realized, staring after the dark beauty as she and her male companion walked from the camp. When they were nearly out of sight, Molly turned to Cheerful, who was still watching the couple. She couldn't quite make out the emotion on his face, but he seemed to snap out of it, suddenly turning to Molly. She knew the questions were clear in her expression, and she saw the same signs of displeasure appear on Cheerful's face that her father had worn in all the years since she'd turned eight. It made her smile.

Something in his eyes gave her the courage to ask her questions. "She isn't human, is she?"

He stiffened slightly, which was answer enough for Molly.

"You protect her," she continued.

Without warning, the largest of the elves was standing in front of them, the abrupt halt of his boots throwing chunks of dirt onto Molly's blanket and skirt. She looked up uneasily to find he was staring not at her, but at Cheerful. He stood, and Molly found herself staring up at them, Cheerful's frame dwarfed by the other's massive one. She felt a tingle run up her arms.

And then the wiry one was there. "We should discuss this elsewhere, I believe."

Molly was momentarily lost. She'd not seen a discussion. The giant didn't spare a look at her before turning from Cheerful and leaving the camp with Wiry.

Molly watched them. They were heading in the direction of the dark-haired woman and the one who, no matter where he stood, watched the woman, the one who wore the tortured expression each time she slept. He was her watcher, her protector.

Yes, Molly thought, *this will be what awaits my son. He will be powerful. He will be protected. He will rule.*

The idea that they were protecting the woman stopped Molly cold. Asher was the ruler of the North. He had told her so himself. These elves had killed Riven, Asher's guard, and they surrounded her as if she were a treasure of highest consequence.

At first sight, Molly had thought the woman human. But she wasn't. She had magic. She had a guard.

Molly started when Cheerful spoke beside her, and she had to tuck away the implications for later. "Pardon?"

"Dinner," he repeated, gesturing with a small hunk of meat.

The pup launched himself toward it, quick as a whip but too slow for the reflexes of an elf. Molly laughed, not only at the attempt but at the absurdity of her situation.

"Yes," Cheerful said, "Snickers is an apt name for the tiny beast."

They sat in companionable silence as they ate, and the others returned. The woman was rubbing circles on her temples, her gaze trailing the ground. Molly stole the opportunity to examine her face.

Molly would have said her features were sharp, if she'd never seen an elf. She was unearthly, her beauty dreamlike, even in obvious pain. Molly categorized this as well—she hadn't seen any sign of ache from any other elf in all her time with them. *With the exception of torture,* she amended, but she didn't like to think of those incidents. And then there was the look the woman's watcher wore. It looked very much as if he was being tortured.

Her gaze automatically flicked to him, and her chest clenched as she realized he was staring at her and not at the woman. *Not Cheerful, indeed.* Molly immediately bowed her head, eyes on her lap as her fingers curled tightly into the blanket beneath her. *Not today,* she thought. *Don't kill me today.*

Asher would come for her, for his child. He had to.

She heard the dark-haired woman's fitful sleep that night, but Molly did not think of her. She gave the fire her back and stared into the trees, watching the flames throw shadows like demons. She would live. Her son would live.

By dawn, Molly had slept little. The others were nearly always awake, obviously waiting for the woman. Molly didn't miss that the massive elf and the wiry elf had positioned themselves near her and remained there.

They rode farther, the portentous darkness of the mountain a constant backdrop. She was never allowed to be alone, but the redhead did escort her from the group each day for some privacy.

It was on one of these occasions that she knew for certain what their intent was.

The redhead stayed near her, and though she gave Molly a few lengths' retreat, there was no question that Molly would be caught if she attempted to escape. She gathered her skirts as she walked through tangled brush. The redhead became slightly distracted, staring into a copse. Molly might have been more interested in what she saw next if they hadn't made her wait so long for the break. The redhead deftly scaled one of the trees, disappearing into the foliage.

Molly had known the elves were fast, nimble, and not human, but she was always surprised to see it demonstrated. She shook her head as she raised her skirts higher and lowered herself behind the brush. She heard voices and froze, afraid of someone walking up on her.

But they didn't know she was there. If they did, they didn't care.

"The human is dead weight," said was a strong, deep voice.

"It won't matter once she's back. None of this will matter."

Molly couldn't be sure who was speaking—maybe Massive and Wiry. It couldn't be Cheerful. He'd never spoken with such loathing.

"He gives her too much. She does not have the capacity for this decision now."

There was a muffled, almost imperceptible, thump. It caused their conversation to halt.

Then came a long silence.

Molly nearly stood, but she heard one more comment: "It is right. You know that well."

She heard the clink of metal and straightened, hastily smoothing her skirts, to find the redhead walking in her direction. Behind her were the shadows of three large figures moving toward the horses. Molly looked up, speculating whether she was crazy for thinking the redhead had dropped from the trees into their conversation about dead weight.

"Come." The redhead gestured for her to follow.

Molly nodded, her mouth dry. She swallowed hard and stepped through the brush. Asher would come for her, for his child. He would.

They rode on. When they stopped for the day, she numbly took a seat on her blanket.

Some time passed before Cheerful spoke. "You are quiet this evening." He made a comment about her wicked pup and grinned.

She tried a smile but faltered. She felt a little ill.

"Are you well?" Cheerful asked, reaching up to lightly stroke her cheek with the back of his hand, in the way her father used to check for the heat of a fever.

In spite of her best intentions, there was heat, a flush that tore through her at his touch.

He grinned wickedly at her response.

Suddenly, she lost all sense of balance. Her eyes floated for a moment before coming back to Steed. She swayed. *Wait, who's Steed?* Her eyes closed tightly against the dizziness, and then she blacked out.

When Molly awoke, they surrounded her. They helped her up to sitting, seeming to care whether she was sound. It would have made her feel better, except they seemed exceedingly and unnaturally concerned with her condition. But Molly didn't know what to do with that. She didn't know what to do with any of it.

Something is wrong. The feeling stuck with her. They left her be for some time, and then, later, Cheerful returned to his place beside her. He'd been toying with the pup but came nearer without warning.

His proximity brought Molly from her daze. "Feeling well, sunshine?" She heard a new, odd distress in his tone.

Her mouth was dry. She licked her lips while searching for words. "Something to drink, then?"

Unintentionally, Molly's eyes found the dark-haired woman's across the camp, meeting those dark emeralds and catching in their violent depths. Cheerful murmured something as he leaned forward to reach for the canteen on the blanket behind her.

Molly knew it wasn't an advance. But, for some reason, she swung her arm full force and slapped him across the face in a flash of anger before she was reeling again. Her vision fluttered, and she squeezed her eyes shut, determined to control it. When she was certain she'd regained herself, she opened them again. She found him staring at her. She didn't think she was going to be calling him Cheerful any longer. He didn't *look* like he was going to kill her. *Not that they ever do,* she reminded herself.

She quickly opened her mouth to apologize then saw the puffy red welt, and the offending hand flew up to cover her mouth. *Had I hit him that hard?* Molly was no maid—she had slapped men before, but playfully. She had never struck with such force, had never followed through as boys did when they came to blows. Her palm still tingled, even stung, from the contact.

"Are you well?" her victim asked in a level tone.

Her hand fell from her mouth, but she was unable to find words.

He waited, staring into her eyes as if examining her.

Once, Molly had slipped from her room to walk in the moonlight after a fine spring storm and found a field of freshly turned soil, dark with dampness. She thought his eyes were richer than that brown. She thought she might get lost in them. They narrowed on her.

She cleared her throat. "Yes," she croaked. "Yes, I think I am well." She tried to appear remorseful.

He nodded then stood to join Wiry.

Molly was quiet after that. They all were. They rode for several more days, and she silently prayed for Asher. *Come for me*, she thought. *Come for me now. Something is wrong.*

She had been sick twice. The first day, without inquiry, the redhead had offered her a preparation, but Molly only slid the powder into her pocket. She was wearing down, though, and when they passed a pond late one afternoon, Molly's stomach revolted against the scents.

The redhead appeared to notice her discomfort and gestured to Wiry, who suggested they stop for camp. Cheerful helped her from her horse, and she leaned heavily on him for a moment, breathing deeply against his chest. He felt sorry for her, she thought, for no real reason. She steadied herself and nodded, determined to overcome it.

But her resolve could only get her so far. It wasn't long after that she was on hands and knees in the cool grass as the redhead stood over her, watching her retch. She must have seen it coming, for she had practically dragged Molly from the camp just before the convulsive heaving began.

After some time, there was nothing left. Molly cautiously raised to her knees, wiping her mouth with the back of her trembling hand. The redhead waited as Molly ran her fingers through her hair and smoothed her bodice and then helped her to her feet, not releasing her arm until Molly could stand.

Molly took a deep breath and nodded, shaking out her skirts but not daring to bend over to straighten them properly. The redhead offered her a tonic, but she waved it away, taking another breath as she indicated she was ready.

The redhead looked skeptical. But before she had a chance to say anything, her head cocked a fraction, and she went still. The action reminded Molly oddly of a dog. Then the redhead's posture changed suddenly, and it only added to the effect.

It caused Molly to recall her pup, and she glanced down to find him at her skirts, sniffing what she sincerely hoped was only earth smeared across the hem.

She didn't feel like carrying him, but the redhead had scooped him up, pushed him into the pouch, and slung it over Molly's shoulder before she had any opportunity to protest. Shortly, she was being pressed out of the trees and into the clearing where they had camped.

Molly instantly knew something was wrong. The clearing was silent as Cheerful and Wiry stood near the center, their backs to her. They were in front of the dark-haired woman, protecting her. The woman stared between them, and Molly's gaze followed.

Her heart skipped as she saw a cloaked figure in the distance with Not Cheerful. *Asher*, she thought, *come for me*. Her knees gave a fraction, but she caught herself. The redhead didn't seem to notice, only firming her grip on Molly's arm.

And then the cloaked figure turned, and Molly could see golden curls from under the hood. It was a woman. It was not Asher.

She felt sick. Her hand automatically fell to her stomach. He had not come for her, for his child.

The newcomer's head flicked toward Molly then, her eyes hard. The dark-haired woman turned to see what had the newcomer's attention with confusion in her gaze. And then there was a low voice —a muttered curse, Molly thought—before the dark-haired woman's eyes lost focus and rolled back into her head.

Molly watched as the woman collapsed into the arms of her protectors, only half aware as the cloaked figure appeared before her, speaking two more words that sent Molly into blackness.

She was confident she'd been out for days when she finally came to. Her limbs were weak, her mouth parched, her stomach hollow... Molly jerked upright despite the fatigue, her hand finding her stomach.

"There, there," a soothing voice purred from beside her. She jumped and cursed, curving her arm around her middle. "No harm will come to you, child," the woman assured her.

Molly stared, working to clear the muddle of her mind. The woman waited patiently as Molly took in her surroundings, a small room with makeshift cot, blankets, supplies, food, all doing their part to calm her. She took a deep breath and continued to scan, her eyes finally focusing on the woman, falling over her light cloth pants and her deep-brown shirt, narrowing on the golden wisps that fell around her face.

"What did you do to me?" Molly seethed when she recognized the woman as the cloaked figure from the camp.

"I have not harmed you," the woman replied coolly.

Molly's eyebrows rose.

The woman remained composed, merely shaking her head, and Molly took stock. She guessed she wasn't hurt, only ill, as she had been before the incident. But she was outraged. Her mouth opened to hurl accusations at her captor, but before she could speak, a sharp pain sliced through her side.

She cried out, clutching the source. The woman reached toward her, and Molly wrenched away.

"It is not I who cause you this pain," she said, indicating Molly's stomach.

Molly could not respond, only breathe through clenched teeth as she waited for it to pass. When the woman tried again, Molly didn't fight her.

"How long?" she asked as she slid a warm hand against the curve of Molly's waist.

Molly didn't answer.

"You are only hurting yourself, child." She pressed two fingers below Molly's ribs, and the pain dulled then subsided.

Molly's panting quieted, and she lay back against the pillows. She would not trust the woman. She lay still, settling her breathing, and all the while the woman sat wordlessly beside her. "Why did you take me?" Molly eventually asked.

"Many reasons, child."

Molly sat up, angry again. "Stop calling me 'child.'"

The woman looked doubtful. There was a slight twist to the corner of her mouth, but Molly couldn't tell if she was mocking her. She had a gorgeous smirk, if that was what it was. Her lips were the same flushed pink as her cheeks, and her eyes sparkled like shattered glass in the sun, like light catching ripples in water...

Molly shook herself, unsettled.

The woman smiled then, and the change in her face took Molly's breath. She was a vision, ethereal and strong.

"Who are you?" Molly whispered.

"Juniper Fountain, daughter of Elerias."

"Are you"—Molly swallowed—"a fairy?"

Juniper snorted.

Molly was suddenly embarrassed. "You're just how they described them is all. And you're so different than the others. And, well, I've never met one, so how would I know?"

Juniper's smile faded. "Yes." She was silent for a moment, and then recalled herself. At the woman's mild smile, Molly had the errant thought that she needed something from her. "Ah, but dear, I saw you with the fire fairy."

Molly stared at her blankly. *A fire fairy?* She recalled the illustrations from her books, remembered the descriptions of the wicked red ones and the flicker of the flames. *The redhead. How could I have been so oblivious?* "Curses," she snapped, startling the woman as she smacked her palm to her face in disbelief. All her life, she'd wanted to meet a fairy, and that one had watched her pee. Molly realized she'd gotten sidetracked. "So you're an elf?"

Juniper nodded. "I am of the light elves."

"And the others?" Molly asked timidly.

"Dark, of the North." She paused, searching Molly's eyes. "You should be glad I have taken you. They would have disposed of you."

Molly nodded. She'd expected as much. But she was further from Asher, for he was Lord of the North. "And what will you do with me?" she asked.

"Help you," Juniper answered.

The days turned to weeks, and Juniper did help her. But there was only so much that could be done, and Molly's condition deteriorated quickly. Molly had seen women ill while carrying before. She had helped with some of the villagers when needed. She knew hers was not such an illness. It was something else. Something was wrong.

She had been suffering from tremors and was plagued with strange sensations—once as if she were floating, and occasionally as if she were afire. Juniper had eased the pains for the most part, but the odd impressions were unsettling, and they were getting worse.

Juniper had stopped leaving her alone, though. At first, she would depart for one or two days, leaving Molly with supplies and powders, tonics and instructions. It had taken Molly a few weeks to realize the trips came after questions of her travels, when she'd given details of her captors and particulars of surroundings she'd remembered.

But Juniper hadn't gone lately. Molly couldn't be sure whether it was because of Molly's state or because Juniper had accepted that Molly had no idea where to find Asher. It couldn't be called trust, the bond she had developed with Juniper, but she had no other option but to rely on the woman. Molly knew there was more, so much that she did not understand, but she had to stay alive for Asher. For her son.

"Drink," Juniper insisted. "The fevers are burning your fluids off."

"I'm not being stubborn," Molly maintained, "you know I can't keep it down."

"Drink," she repeated.

Molly scowled.

Juniper laughed, a sound that had been noticeably absent of late.

"What's so funny?" Molly asked.

"Nothing, child. You simply remind me of someone."

"Who?"

"Only someone I used to care for. Someone of your age." A shadow passed over Juniper's face.

"Where is she now?"

Something similar to a hum escaped as Juniper considered her answer. "She is in between."

Molly assumed that must have been an elf term.

"My Freya," Juniper murmured as she refilled her own glass.

Molly froze.

The action caught Juniper's eye, and her gaze narrowed on Molly.

"I know of her," Molly whispered. The words came of their own accord. "She is *his.*"

Juniper's jaw went tight, her eyes turning to ice. "You know nothing."

Molly jerked up, ready to fight, but the action caused a tremor. It was a bad one. Her throat constricted for a moment, and then her skin began to burn.

Juniper grabbed her arms. "Calm yourself. Breathe. Remain still."

Molly felt her head shaking. *No, no, no. This is wrong. It shouldn't be like this. Something is wrong.* Fire and razors tore through her midsection, and her hands went numb. Panic-stricken, she looked to Juniper.

"I cannot help you, child. There is nothing to be done." Every word was sincere.

Molly only had one question, and it was clear.

"The child will live," Juniper answered.

But you will not.

Pain ripped through Molly, her body convulsed, and then she was granted one moment of reprieve to gasp for air. She was suddenly soaked with sweat, shuddering violently before the cold turned back to fire. Every inch of her skin was ablaze, every hair a needle, every breath an ache so severe that to not breathe would have been relief. But she could not give in. She forced each breath, thankful for the pain. The pain meant she had not surrendered.

Her chest rose from the cot in a spasm, and then she fell back, grinding and twisting uncontrollably against the torture. Tears flowed from her eyes, and her mouth tasted of copper. Her fingers clutched at the blanket beneath her, searching for purchase, something to help her pull herself up.

Juniper pressed her back. "Be still, child. Be still," she murmured.

Molly convulsed again, gagged, then bore down as the knife pain cut through her once more.

He's not coming, she thought. *He's not coming, and it will be too late.* Her hands found her midsection, and she pulled air through her nose, biting down on the agony to force words through clenched teeth. "You have to find him."

Juniper brushed the damp strands of hair off Molly's face without responding.

"You have to find him," Molly repeated. "Take my son to him."

Juniper did not answer, but Molly could see her doubt through the haze of tears.

"He will not come in time," Molly explained. "I am his favorite. His chosen. My son will be king."

Juniper stared down at the girl who was dying to bring Asher a child.

His favorite. She wondered how long had this been going on and how many more there were.

The girl bucked convulsively against the magic rending her from within, and Junnie sighed, readying herself for what was to come. Not simply the next hours in camp, but the deadly months ahead for everyone.

Mother save you, Freya, she thought. *There will be an army of them.*

BOOK III: RISE OF THE SEVEN

THE
FREY SAGA
BOOK
3

RISE
of the
SEVEN

MELISSA WRIGHT

1

I couldn't say I wasn't disappointed when I got my memory back. Somehow, I'd expected to be smoother. I'd thought the old me was exceptionally clever, sharp, and sure-footed. She had been in line for the throne, after all. I'd nearly convinced myself that my ineptness was all because of the bonds, because they'd messed with my brain. But that wasn't it, and not only had I retained a good deal of awkwardness, but it seemed worse because everyone was watching me all the time.

I held back a sigh as my gaze again traveled through the room full of elves. All eyes were on me, their Lord of the North. I straightened my shoulders, which were heavy with thickly armored plates, my new decoration for formal gatherings. A lean, raven-haired elf whom I recognized as once being a leader in the eastern range seemed to make the decision to approach, but before he'd moved more than three steps, Rider was in front of him, matching his height. I glanced at Rhys, who appeared to be scanning the room for others who would attempt approach, and decided I'd had enough.

I stood, my hand sliding to rest on the hilt of the sword at my waist as I addressed the crowd: "Your attendance is greatly appreciated. Please enjoy the feast and the wine. Good evening."

As I stepped down, the room was silent. I could see the smirk on Anvil's broad face but didn't care. I turned from the gathering and slipped out of the room. I knew I needed to keep up appearances, but I really hated castle politics. My guard had been doing what they could, keeping the most troublesome leaders from private conferences with me, and they had handled the stream of subjects who'd lined up at the season change for an audience with me—me, Lord of the North.

I snorted, shaking my head, and someone laughed. I looked up to find Grey leaning against a corridor wall, watching me. His expression held a thousand secrets.

"What?" I demanded defensively.

He simply smiled, pushing off the wall to join me. "And where are we headed?"

I didn't have the slightest idea. "The library."

He laughed again, clearly seeing through the fib with ease. "To see Ruby, I presume?"

Agh. I hadn't known she was there. Ruby, though I considered her invaluable in my guard, still felt the need to hide because before I'd been bound, Northern rule hadn't exactly tolerated fairies. It was something I would have to work on changing. "I'd like to see if she's made any progress," I lied. The moment I saw her, she would spill whatever she'd been researching, so it was a safe lie.

Grey only smiled. His devotion to Ruby was boundless, but he knew her character even better than I did. We both knew she was going to be in a state.

Her head popped up the moment we entered the room, her red curls bouncing with the movement. "Well, that was fast," she chided. She glanced out the window as if checking the height of the sun, though it was dark with night. "You'll not establish yourself as Lord of the North by running out on guests after a matter of minutes."

We all knew I'd made it at least an hour, but I didn't argue the point. "I mean to make a reputation as a mysterious captain."

"Mysterious and all-powerful," she replied, then changed the subject as my jaw tightened.

It was no secret that I was uncomfortable with my new strength. It would have been enough merely to have regained my own power, but I'd been inundated with that of Asher and all those before him. I could still see his lips move in a silent stream of the words that would release me, the recital that would drive the forces of the many he had taken into my very soul.

"I found several stories regarding the wolves," she announced, pulling me from my trance.

I grinned. She'd been obsessed with Finn and Keaton since the moment she'd found that I'd known them before and I'd not been willing to give up their secrets. Truth be told, I didn't entirely know the whole story, but it was fun to mess with Ruby.

She grimaced. The secret annoyed the fire out of her. Occasionally, I felt a little guilty about it—after all, she had helped deliver me from the evils of Grand Council, but it was too entertaining not to keep it up, and it wasn't as though she didn't have it coming after what she'd put me through when I was bound.

She snapped the book she'd been reading shut. My cheeks tightened, fighting to pull back into a smile, and her expression nearly caused my laughter to boil over.

Grey intervened. "Well, since Freya has left us without the benefit of the feast, I say we head to the kitchen."

Ruby took a deep breath, leveled her shoulders, and walked right past us.

"I think she preferred the old me." I laughed as Grey and I followed.

Her head poked back through the door as we were nearly to it, and she started to speak, made a face that suggested she'd thought better of it, and turned to continue on her way.

I saw Grey's smile out of the corner of my eye.

Ruby's posture changed the instant she stepped through the kitchen door. "Steed!" she exclaimed, bouncing forward to greet her brother.

I felt like the wind had been knocked out of me. I glanced

nervously around the room. My eye caught Steed's, and he grinned in that sly and sexy way of his. "He wasn't hungry."

I forced my expression into confusion, though I knew exactly who he meant. Every one of us did.

Steed stepped toward me. "You look well, Sunshine."

I laughed. He'd been such a charmer when I was bound, but his banter was only for play. There was someone else for me. My stomach turned, and I had to bite my lip before I asked where he was.

What I had done to Chevelle had been underhanded, and I knew it. But as we'd stood among the remains of battle, after all was settled and my memories returned, I had panicked. I had been overwhelmed with the power I held, the emotions that threatened to run feral, and the realization of all that had happened and what would follow. I'd been a coward, plain and simple.

I'd been aware of his eyes on me the entire time, and as we finalized affairs, I'd ordered him and Steed away. I could still see the look on his face, the set of his jaw, the strain of muscles at his neck and shoulders. I'd directed them to finish off Asher's guard, to find and eliminate his supporters. "Make a show of it," I'd said. "The kingdom will know I've returned."

It was the last thing I'd said to him. I had been certain that I would figure out what to do and how to deal with it, that I would get a handle on my emotions. That had been nearly two weeks before. My palms felt clammy, but I couldn't decide whether the anxiety was because I wanted—*needed* to see him, or because I was still a coward.

"No," Ruby said, "I didn't like the old you better."

My gaze snapped to her.

"You were fun, yes, but you got that vacant stare." She narrowed her eyes on me. "And I could never tell where you were. And you slept all the time." Ruby smiled, making it clear that she knew exactly where my mind was.

I brushed past her to where Grey and Steed leaned against the table. They'd apparently been watching my daze as well. Grey offered me something to eat, but I had absolutely no interest. I badly needed to get out of there. "I'm glad you're back," I said as I turned to Steed.

He looked doubtful, but he gave me a smile anyway. "I am too. Can't wait to see what you've done with the place."

I nodded and excused myself. When I hit the hall, I had to force myself to remain standing and not to bend over, brace myself on my knees, and hyperventilate. I had myself under control—the fear was back in check, I hoped. I was ashamed of it, and I'd been determined to overcome it. I hadn't been able to just yet, and the realization scared me even worse.

It felt out of control, the wave of need that accompanied any thought of him. And I had a lot of thoughts about him. A lot. Most of them centered around the one night I'd spent in his arms. But that wasn't what scared me—that had been incredible. What scared me was what that night stood for and what I had—or had nearly—sacrificed for it. I had—no, we *all* had—gone through so much to restore myself from the bonds forced upon me by Council, only to fall into a new set that was just as dangerous.

The problem was, I couldn't decide whether the new bonds had taken. I felt a need, yes. I felt the yearning, the pull. I knew the connection was in place, but I couldn't know if it was a full bond. It didn't feel secure enough—it wasn't as I'd been warned it would be. I couldn't be sure whether that was due to the fact that I'd been bound already, my magic not fully in place, or because I was not wholly elf. I was half human, and there was no way to know how that type of bond would affect me.

But I knew that when his eyes were on me, I would run right back into his arms. If the bond wasn't set already, it would be the instant I got close enough to touch him. It was why I'd sent him away, though I could never admit it. There was too much at stake.

I reached out and traced the cool stone of the wall as I walked, a longtime habit of mine that reminded me of my childhood years spent running carefree through the corridors, my arms outstretched as if in flight. My laughter had echoed through the halls, whether I was alone or being chased by Chevelle.

The touch centered me. My fingers trailed lazily around the

corner as I walked through the door to my room. I froze when I found Chevelle there.

2

———

Chevelle casually leaned back in the chair, though the set of his mouth proved he was anything but. He still wore his dark leather traveling clothes and an assortment of blades. I forced myself to move, walking my fingers along the last few inches of doorframe before lowering them to my sides in artificial nonchalance.

He didn't speak.

I felt the hand I'd lowered slide up my leg, and before I had a chance to fiddle nervously with it, raised it to tuck the hair behind my ear. The gesture seemed to unnerve him, and that made me want to smile.

I watched him watch me for a moment, but it wasn't going anywhere good. *Right, then.* "Were you able to locate the remainder of the guard?" I asked, forcing any emotion from my tone.

"Mostly. Axe, Frost, Steele, and Waters proved difficult. It appears they were warned."

"Anyone of note unfound?"

"Only Rowan, but he has a knack for such."

I nodded. Knowing Rowan, he might not resurface for a century.

He was one of Asher's best guards, and his talent for stealthiness was legendary. "And you made a show of them?"

"Oh, yes," he answered grimly. "We made quite a spectacle of it."

"News has not traveled back to us. Have you received any word of reaction?"

I could tell that he really didn't want to answer.

I waited.

"Not all were convinced. I would suggest a gathering."

It was not what I wanted to hear, and Chevelle saw my hesitation. I'd developed some bad habits during the time I'd spent bound. I'd been working to regain the control I'd spent my childhood forming, the ability to mask emotion that seemed to come so easily to the others. I nearly had it mastered, but Chevelle knew me well.

"This isn't simply your distaste for exhibition."

"No," I answered. His patience astounded me. I glanced down at my hands then faced him, chin up. "I am having some trouble controlling the magic."

He stood and crossed to me, the slightest hint of worry in his gaze. "The bindings?"

"No, no," I assured him. "Not my magic. His." I meant the magic Asher had given me.

"Should we try to undo the casting?"

"No!" It might have been overemphatic, but I hated spells. There was no way to be sure of Asher's methods, and so much could go wrong. It wasn't worth it.

"Then there is nothing left but to practice."

I bit my cheek to keep from commenting.

Silence hung between us for a moment, and then in a soft voice, he asked, "Are you well, Freya?"

My heart clenched. I could only nod.

"I know this is far from over," he said, "but I feel you are safer now than in the village."

I knew it wasn't his fault. What had happened had been beyond all of our control. I could see his guilt, just as I felt my own, but none of us were entirely blameless, either.

After my family began the massacre, I'd been imprisoned in the village by Council. They'd not wanted me, but they would not end me because of my connection to the animals, something they revered, and my ties to one of their own. We had all made our choices, and we had gotten to that end with those choices, even if others had a hand in them. The time following the destruction must have been hard for everyone, but I had been bound and unaware during so much of it that I remembered little. I shook off a chill. "It was a long time." I let it sit there, not exactly an accusation, but close enough.

"Yes, it was," Chevelle answered, and it sounded like regret.

There was nothing to do but move on. "A banquet, then," I supplied.

He nodded. "I will arrange it."

"And practice." I grimaced for old times' sake.

He smiled genuinely then, and I ached, seeing the contrast to the pain he'd worn only moments before. He started to reach for me then caught himself, and the gesture made me want his touch so badly that I wondered if I *had* been truly bound to him.

That question was the only thing that kept me from closing the distance between us.

"You should rest," he said. "I will meet you for practice in the morning. Our usual time?"

I laughed. It hadn't been usual for a long time, and there hadn't been much practice involved.

He moved a breath closer and whispered, "Sleep well, Freya," before walking past me out the door.

I had to pinch myself to keep from following him. I loosened the straps on my armor and shrugged it off, tossing it toward the narrow wooden table by the door, where I saw a box, centered and alone. I wasn't sure how long I regarded it before I moved, but when I finally reached for it, my hands shook. I had to sit down. I set the box on the bed and curled my legs in front of it, terrified to open it, knowing it was a gift from Chevelle and remembering it from times before.

Asher had taken everything from me: my mother, my freedom, my safety. But given the enormity of those things, it was often the small treasures that I'd thought of most. They were naught but tiny remembrances that had given me comfort. In his attempt to control me, he had taken even those.

Those last bloody days of my fighting to be free, to be out from under Asher's cruel tactics, had been the tipping point for my mother, I was certain. Had I known what the outcome would be, I might have let the tokens go and yielded to Asher. They meant little compared to her life. But I had fought him harder then, as if his taking of those mementos was the worst of it, when he had done so much more. I didn't have the temperament of the others. The elves were stoic but chanced being overcome when pushed too far, unable to return to themselves. I had to fight to hide my emotion, but it could come and go as the winds, leaving me no worse for the storm.

There was no wind as I opened the carved stone lid. On top was a letter, a small note folded in half. I laid it aside and pulled a strip of silk from the box. My fingers ran across the soft fabric, a piece of my mother's favorite dress. When Asher had confined her, the scraps had accompanied her messages so I would know them truly hers. I held it to my nose, breathed in the scent of her. She was rain and honeysuckle, a cool winter night. Her scent was a contradiction, as was she —she was both light and dark, as was I, but I also had my father's blood, and I had often wondered what that made me. When we were young, I had asked Chevelle what I smelled like. Without hesitation, he'd answered, "Wet elk."

With a smile, I returned the scrap to the box and touched the smooth stones, gold ring, and leather strap that lay inside. The amulet was there. I wondered if Chevelle had known its origin. The inky blue had reminded me so much of its owner, Sapphire.

We both blamed Asher for Sapphire's death, though I shared some blame. I had been a fool to think we could escape him. After all he had done, I had known there was no true escape. Somewhere deep down, I had to have understood what I was risking by trying to escape. There was no doubt that such blatant defiance had to be answered. I had not cared about the cost until we'd found her.

I could still see her lifeless body cradled in Chevelle's arms. I could feel the anger, taste the bile, recall the first flavor of hatred. Nothing else could have driven me to seek such a final revenge. She had been innocent, but they had cleaved her eyes from their sockets because I'd intended to walk away from all of it, to leave with him. They had never acknowledged her in life, but in death, they had dressed her in a royal gown and adorned her with jewels.

The blue of her eyes, the same depthless sapphire as Chevelle's, was a message to me.

Chevelle had returned those items to me, including the stone that had been his mother's. Though they meant little anymore, they had once been precious, the only way I'd known to hold on to the things I cared about and defy the man who'd been trying to take everything from me. I'd no doubt the box had been a trial to recover. I didn't know if I had the courage to read his note, but my hand moved numbly toward it.

I took a deep breath and opened the fold. Two small words changed everything: *my love.*

Chevelle knew me. He'd given me all that he could and left me to decide.

My head fell, and I put the note in the box, closed the lid, and slid it into the hiding spot beneath the third stone under the floor of my bed. I walked out of the room without looking back, turned down the corridor, and ran.

Six doors, two stairways, and one window later, I was scaling the last ten feet to a roof of the castle. I'd stolen a cloak on my way, and when I reached the top, the wind caught and flipped it behind me with a snap. My hair whipped my face as I made my way across to perch on the only point that was blocked from wind by the tower but still allowed a full view of the mountain below and sky ahead. I wrapped the cloak tightly around me and felt settled for the first time in days.

It was silent for two hours, and then the quick, light padding of paws approached. Keaton and Finn settled in beside me. Their silvery fur caught the moonlight in an ethereal glow.

Even aside from the warnings of the elders, the cautionary tales we'd heard since birth said that the bond could be dangerous even in stable beings, even in full-blooded elves. But I wasn't just a half-breed, and it wasn't just Chevelle and me.

I was Lord of the North, and a bond with him would weaken my position. It would give those who wanted to remove me from power reason to do just that. It would make me vulnerable to their threats and let them turn my connection to him into leverage. Worse, it would make Chevelle a target.

"I can't leave him," I said.

The wolves did not respond.

"I may not be able to be with him, but I cannot leave."

3

I awoke on the perch as the sun broke the clouds. My first thoughts were curses—I should have met Chevelle at dawn. I hurried down, running until I reached the corridor and saw the servants. I didn't recognize them, but that was no surprise, considering that so many of them had to be removed after they'd been found out as Asher's spies. The castle was finally fully staffed again, and each of them, uniformed and well mannered, prepared for the banquet. Chevelle had been busy. Remembering my own station, I straightened my shoulders and slowed my pace.

When I reached the practice room, I thought he'd given up on me. I walked into the empty space for the first time since I'd regained myself fully. It held an echo of memory and emotion. I walked farther, glancing up to see the morning sun stream in through the filigreed windows, catching dust motes in its rays. I sighed, thinking of how it must have looked to him when I hadn't shown up after the gift he'd left me.

Then I saw him. He stepped forward. He'd been on the ledge, probably watching out a window while he waited. He stopped, the sun at his back, throwing his features into further shade, and I had a flash of nervousness. I didn't know if I could pull it off.

I straightened. "I fell asleep."

I thought I saw the corner of his mouth pull up, but I couldn't be positive. He jumped down and crossed to me. "Good," he said. "You'll need your rest."

Sleep had once been a sore subject with me. I'd required about twice as much as the others, and I used to fight it, trying to keep up with them. Chevelle knew that. He'd seen what I'd done to myself, how I'd run myself so ragged that I'd been on the edge of breaking.

I'd been different in so many ways, and he knew them all. Things didn't work the same with me. I wasn't born with the natural instinct for magic. I'd always had to work at it, to find the power and force the control. I had overcome it, but I had a new problem.

"So," I started, "practice."

"Show me what you've got," he answered.

I really didn't want to do it, but I closed my eyes, centered my breathing, and released. The stones beneath our feet started to vibrate and shift, the walls shook, and the iron in the window let loose an ear-piercing metallic creak. Tiny sprinkles of rock fell onto my face, and I stopped, sealing the stones back in place before opening my eyes once more.

He looked dubious.

"Yep," I said. "And that's not even angry."

"You've been angry?" he asked.

"Ruby's been here."

It was clearly a joke, but he didn't laugh, not even a little.

I smiled as I realized how he'd been forced to deal with her antics while I'd been bound. I wondered what she'd put him through. "You chose her," I reminded him.

"I used to think so," he said.

I chuckled. "Things do tend to have a way of working out for her."

"Cursed fairies," he grumbled.

"Cursed fairies," I agreed.

"Do you have a plan for tomorrow's demonstration?" he asked, clearly determined to change the subject.

"I think I'll wing it."

"Brilliant."

We were silent for a moment. Finally, he asked, "Fire?"

"All right," I answered with little confidence.

He stepped beside me so we were both facing the long, empty space and used his magic to chuck a rock from the box in the corner. As it flew across the room, I raised my arm and pointed at it in an attempt to focus solely on striking it with a fireball. Not one flame lit, but the rock exploded.

"What was that?" Chevelle asked.

I shrugged. "Did I mention sometimes it doesn't work properly?"

He nodded, expressionless. "This time, try to shatter the stone."

Another rock launched from the box, flying straight into the expanse. I focused on splitting it, and it burst into dust. I looked to Chevelle.

He tore a small piece of fabric from the hem of his shirt and held it before me. "Burn this." I started to glance down, but the first finger of his other hand stopped me. "Not my palm."

Right. I concentrated on the fabric for a moment before the idea of burning his palm made me recall one of those odd, not-quite-me memories. The lines of a map had been burnt into my palms, an old trick we'd used on Fannie. It was only a fraction of a second before I realized I'd gotten angry.

I gasped at Chevelle's intake of breath and raised my hands in a helpless gesture as the flames died down.

"I see what you mean," Chevelle said through clenched teeth.

"Ah, I'm sorry. I just... I got irritated for a second. Let's just call it even."

"Aye."

"And," I continued, "in case you've forgotten, we are in agreement that you'll not use spells near me unless absolutely necessary."

He stared me straight in the eye. "We are even from here."

My jaw rolled involuntarily. Come to think of it, there'd been a lot of catching up on his end while I'd been bound. "Fine," I answered, taking a step toward him.

We stared at each other for one long moment, and then the

unburned hand clenched into a fist. When I'd been bound, I had thought him constantly angry with me. But I knew him again, and I understood that his was a different kind of restraint. He wouldn't touch me. He would let me decide.

When I didn't respond, he stepped back. "The others will be waiting."

With a promise to continue practice in the morning, we made our way to Anvil's study. Asher had always met with his guard in the throne room, keeping it a formal matter, but I didn't care for the echo of the high ceilings or sitting elevated among those who protected me. And it wasn't as if Anvil ever used his library.

It was a small room compared to the other meeting places in the castle. A long oval table was centered at one end, and a few plush chairs sat at the other. High windows cast odd shadows in the corners, but the natural light focused on the flat of the table. Scattered about the room were my guard.

They came together, each taking their place around the oval, Chevelle at my right. It was then, as I stood before them, that I realized it was my first meeting of the guard as Elfreda, Lord of the North. I resisted the urge to run a hand over my face. It was something I had never wanted. I forced myself to stand tall and meet the eyes of each of the seven before me, the seven who would enforce my rule, the seven who would give their lives to defend me.

I spoke their names as my gaze connected with each, a tradition that outdated this castle. "Chevelle Vattier." He was no stranger to the formalities, and he stood at his post with confidence. I could almost see the promise in his eyes.

Grey waited to Chevelle's right. He was quick and loyal, and I was lucky to have him. "Grey of Camber." He gave a small nod in answer.

My eyes followed to Rhys and Rider. I knew little of the brothers, but I trusted Finn and Keaton, and as I spoke their names, they pledged themselves as well.

"Steed Summit." Steed had gotten involved by chance, or so Ruby would have us believe. But he had proven himself.

"Ruby Summit." I nearly smiled at the heat radiating from her. I would never know if it was pride at her new station or the idea of all the trouble she could get into here, but it didn't matter, not after what we'd been through.

"Reed of Keithar Peak." Anvil inclined his head, his shoulders straight. He, like Chevelle, understood his place at the table and held his duty above all else.

I took a slow, steadying breath then began as if it was not a monstrous undertaking. "Chevelle tells me he and Steed were successful in eradicating Asher's remaining supporters. However, it seems we have some convincing left to do." Only two of my guard were familiar with castle politics. I had a feeling Ruby would fit right in, but she presented a whole new problem. We were going to have to play it out as Asher would have, and that left a bitter taste in my mouth. "Chevelle has suggested a banquet."

Anvil nodded. The rest of the table sat silent.

"A show of power," I explained.

Then I deferred to Chevelle, who outlined the details and responsibilities of each of them: who should watch which clan leader, who should cover which areas, which signals meant what or whom. Everyone had a task, everyone had their role. Except Ruby.

When Chevelle finished, he glanced at me, a question in his eyes. I nodded grimly, giving him permission.

"Frey has an issue with control."

A snigger escaped from Ruby's side of the table, but my glare cut it short.

Chevelle continued, "We will meet each morning to assist in her recovery."

"Why do we not simply cast—" Anvil's words were cut short as an intensified version of the glare narrowed on him.

"Again," I stated as clearly and loudly as possible, "there will be no use of spells on or near me without absolute necessity."

Steed raised his hand. It wouldn't have been funny if I hadn't spent time in the village and seen the schoolchildren, but I had, and it was a struggle not to laugh. Ruby smacked him.

"If you are planning to inquire as to why, don't," I warned. So far, this was nothing like Asher's meeting of the guards. I moved on. "The banquet is settled. Is there any news to table?"

Grey spoke up. "There is word of the new Council. Whispers of Juniper's plans have flooded Camber."

"We have heard such as well," Rider put in. "It is said she has gathered a following, not only among the villagers, but some of the rogue Southern clans too."

"There is no evidence," I said.

"You've seen her cloak," Anvil offered in a decidedly nonconfrontational tone.

"She is no longer of Grand Council. What else would she wear?"

They were silent for a moment.

I couldn't help but defend her. Junnie was all the family I had left. She'd given up leadership in Grand Council to protect me, had stayed near me in the village. Sure, she had disagreed with what they were doing. They had killed my mother when by right she was owed their protection. Junnie had taken umbrage with their attack on the North. She had suspicions about their plans, but she'd given up everything. Besides, the villages and forests were none of my business. I wasn't Asher.

I dismissed the subject and the meeting, with a reminder of practice at dawn. As the others left the room, Ruby stopped to examine a book on the wall shelves. I sat at the head of the table, thinking of all to come. My demonstration at the banquet would have to be severe. Not only did my mere existence as a half human cause issue, but rumors of a new Council, one stronger than the one that had nearly destroyed the North, were running rampant. Even I had seen Junnie's sigil. I could not deny the possibility. I would have to assert my rule without doubt at the banquet.

I felt the corner of my mouth pull up into a half smile. "Ruby," I asked, "how would you like to start some trouble?"

4

———————

We met in the largest practice room. The sight of the others there reminded me so much of the group practice session when I'd been bound that I had to laugh. I had been so certain then that one wrong move could have destroyed me. But Chevelle had chosen those men, and I had grown to understand that he'd trusted them all with my life. He'd had to, when an errant thought or moment of temper could have cost him his sparring partner. I was restored, though, and knew they could not hurt me—their magic would never have touched me in more than the annoyingly painful way they had used it to teach me. They'd only been doing it to protect me.

"Me first," Ruby said right away. Apparently, my promise of trouble for the evening had not sated her.

I smiled. "Ready when you are."

A tingle ran up my back, and I knew she'd attempted a sneak attack. I squelched her flame and raised my hands to the side and ran my own flame down my arms to light in my palms, as if I'd stolen hers. If she wanted to play dirty, I had my own tricks. The floor lit behind her as she readied her next attack. I flung my outstretched arms forward and released the fire. Ruby didn't even flinch until it turned to icy-blue mist that showered against her.

She cursed and pulled the whip from her side. *Oh, yes*, I thought, *I do owe her.*

The tongue lit as it curled around, and she began to shift her weight from foot to foot, priming herself for another attempt. She cracked the whip at the right side of my face, missing it by a hair's breadth, while simultaneously throwing a fireball at my left thigh from the side. A burst of white stopped the flame from touching me, and another headed toward her stomach. She leapt quickly out of the way then set the room ablaze.

Flames surrounded us, engulfing our section of the practice room. It was impressive.

I had planned to smother the fire, but something went wrong. The floor beneath Ruby fell. She caught herself, and the conflagration died.

"Not okay, Frey," Ruby complained.

I stepped forward to help her. "It wasn't my intention."

When she was on her feet, we stared into the hole in the floor. "Where are the stones?" Ruby asked.

I shrugged.

"Are you sure this is safe?" Grey asked from beside her.

I looked up, catching the concern in Chevelle's eyes. "Maybe I'll just practice on my own from now on," I suggested.

Rhys shook his head. "I believe it will be safest if we assist you."

All eyes fell on the two tall, slender elves.

Rider explained, "Though we are not twins, we are brothers and share a connection. We have the ability to combine our powers."

Stunned silence followed. Finally, Steed spoke up. "How does that work?"

"Usually, only one of us has control. Clearly, we cannot both command it. We essentially borrow the other's energy while directing our own," Rhys explained.

A quick glance at Chevelle confirmed that he had not been aware of their rare talent. Certainly the wolves had been.

"Is it possible, then," Grey asked, "that the same technique could be used to direct Frey's power?"

"You mean to displace it?" Ruby asked.

"No, I was thinking of it not being entirely of her, and therefore Asher's power could possibly be split from her own. But displacement may be a better option."

"Would I be able to do that?" I asked Rider. "Can you send one another your power, or would I have to allow someone to borrow from me?"

"It is impossible to guess." Rider contemplated the idea for a moment. "When we borrow, it is with a shared will. I am unsure whether it can be done otherwise, without that connection."

I thought again of the wolves. It was no coincidence.

Rhys spoke up. "There is a danger in trying without the connection." No one wanted to ask how he knew, but I was sure he could see our interest. "We discovered the link as children, quite by accident. I was under attack and would undoubtedly have fallen. My assailant was toying with me, enjoying the torment as he forced my brother to watch."

My stomach turned as his words made me recall the memory of Chevelle's prone form writhing in agony.

"As I lay on the floor, listening to Rider's shouts of protest over the sound of my own horrified screams, all I could think was that if I were as strong as him, if I had his power, I would crush this terror standing over me. And he could think of nothing but saving me, giving me his own life in order to keep me alive, to defeat the elves attacking us."

Anvil was generally not the meddlesome type, so his question surprised me: "Why were you attacked?"

Rider nodded. "It was some time before we understood that ourselves. At that point, we were very young, too inexperienced to grasp the extent of the situation. We were unaware that the entire kingdom was fearful of us. Some spoke of prophecy, and others dared not speak of us at all. The pair of us were blamed for each calamity that came upon the realm and each misfortune of the king, though we were merely boys. The mob that came for us had no reason but fear and superstition and possibly clandestine orders from their ruler."

I started to speak but faltered. Their tale was too reminiscent of raw memories.

Rhys finished Rider's explanation: "The irony is their attack gave us the ability they feared. Forced it upon us. Our response to that action not only revealed to us our full strength, but turned it against them."

The room was silent for a long moment.

"What about the danger?" Chevelle finally asked.

"Yes," Rhys answered, coming back from what was plainly an emotional memory. "I doubt there would be issue with an attempt to borrow from Frey. But we have found it is impossible to give the power to others without injuring them."

"They take it as a strike," Rider explained. With a hint of chagrin, he added, "We also learned such by accident. As children."

"Didn't help our cause," Rhys said.

I had my doubts, but I was positive the wolves had not brought these men from the ice lands without good reason. "I will try." Several of the others immediately bristled at the idea, but before they had a chance to voice their arguments, I held up a hand. "Not today. I have a few things to check on first."

"I will research the archives for the twins," Ruby said.

"Thank you," I replied, though I was fairly certain she would have no luck there. When I had a free moment, I would have to find the wolves and hope they would give me some indication if we were on the right track. "I think we should break for now," I suggested. "I don't feel I can overcome this in one day, and I'm confident you all have other tasks before this evening's event."

The group split into small sets, obviously agitated by the new plan. I glanced at Chevelle, unable to remove the painful image Rhys's story brought to mind. His eyes met mine, and I could see that he understood. As he stood speaking with Anvil, his hand rose to his collar, and he slid the material between his thumb and forefinger. I smiled and did the same. Funny how the small gesture meant more with Asher gone than when we'd conceived it to subvert him.

Ruby grabbed my elbow and pulled me from the room, chattering about her ideas on the new theory. I let her without really paying attention.

When we reached the hall, Grey and Steed were standing together, deep in conversation. Ruby released her grip on me and immediately started a new discussion with Grey, drawing him down the hall with her.

Steed shrugged and laughed, apparently resigned to finishing his exchange with Grey later. "Hungry?" he asked.

"Ravenous." I smiled and walked with him toward the dining room.

When we were alone in the corridor, he slowed his pace. "I've been meaning to apologize."

I glanced at him curiously.

"If I had known... Frey, I never would have..."

"Oh." I stopped him when I realized he was referring to his interest in me. "No, I cannot blame you for that."

He smirked.

I smacked his arm. "What I mean is, I can't charge you for what neither of us knew."

"Still," he said, "I do express my regret." And then he smiled. "To you, anyway."

I tried to bite down on my grin. I couldn't expect him to be sorry for the irritation he'd caused Chevelle with his advances on me. Besides, Chevelle had thrown him across the room and into a wall. I was pretty sure they were even.

"It was Asher," I said. Our slow pace came to a halt as Steed turned to me. I wasn't sure why I'd said it—probably because of the fresh memories brought up earlier and all that had come back to me the last few weeks. But once I'd started, I couldn't seem to stop. "He found out."

Steed placed his hands on my arms in a comforting gesture.

"I'd hidden it from him. I knew I must. But he figured it out." I drew a quick breath. "He used it against me. He decided to take Chevelle for his own purposes. It would keep me in line." A harsh laugh escaped. If he'd only known. "I hadn't realized he'd caught on. I thought it was a banquet, a show of power, just like any other. But the room was crowded, and he had me in a gown, not in the clothes of a warrior. I stood beside him, his second." I could still see Asher as he moved to silence the crowd. I shook my head. "When he announced the arranged marriage, all my training vanished, and I couldn't stop myself from finding Chevelle across the room. You should have seen his face."

I looked into Steed's dark eyes. "I couldn't let him. I stepped forward and refused." I took another shallow breath. "I denied him. For everyone."

Steed was speechless. I had meant for him to be released of guilt. There was no one who knew the truth of it but us. Steed couldn't have but believed it to be fact. But I could see my explanation had only made it worse.

"Later," Steed asked, "when Sapphire was taken?"

"Yes, I decided to run with him. And they killed his mother." I tried to keep the shame from my voice.

Steed pulled me against him, and we stood in silence. My cheek pressed to his chest, I finally breathed deeply. I had never spoken of it —I couldn't have. But Asher was gone and could no longer hurt us.

I was so wrapped up in thought that I didn't realize footsteps were advancing until Chevelle stepped around the corner. And then, when Steed shifted, I was struck by the fact that we were locked in an embrace.

Apparently, Steed had shifted to see who was approaching, because his arms dropped from my back, and his chest slid away. I hung there for a moment, watching Chevelle's frozen form at the end of the corridor.

Steed cleared his throat. I straightened. Both of us resisted the urge to explain it was not what it looked like.

I wasn't positive how long the three of us stood so, but it seemed like an incredibly long moment before Steed's mouth quirked.

"Well," he said, "I'll see you in a bit, Sunshine."

I turned just in time to catch him wink at me and casually continue down the corridor in the direction we'd been heading. He began whistling a tune, and I could only be thankful he was moving in the opposite direction from Chevelle.

We stayed frozen for an eternity, and then I picked up Steed's cue and smiled at Chevelle as if everything were completely normal. "Hungry?"

He finally opened his mouth to answer, but the clatter of metal on stone caused us both to pause. When no other sound followed, I waited for Chevelle to respond, as his hearing was superior to mine. I held my breath until he rushed toward me, and then I spun to catch him on his way past. He was heading for the noise, and he didn't look happy.

As we ran, it occurred to me that Chevelle was holding back. I was far from able to keep up with him when he was at full speed. What I didn't know was whether he was setting the pace to stay with me as my guard, or if whatever he'd heard wasn't such an immediate threat. We met Rhys and Rider in the corridor, and the four of us turned into the dining area to find Steed with his sword to the neck of a small male elf on the stones before him.

The scene made me pause, as I'd not seen Steed use a sword, and then I realized that the clanking metal had been the elf's sword hitting the stone floor where he now lay, his arms bent behind him as if he planned to crawl backward and away from the very intimidating dark elf. I was a little proud of my guard. Steed looked impressive.

Steed didn't take his glare off his captive when he said, "Bind him."

"Done," Chevelle answered.

Without turning, Steed tossed the sword to Chevelle, who caught it by the base of the blade and did a cursory examination of the handle. Steed grabbed the prisoner by his arm and hefted him up to walk beside us as we crossed to a more secure location.

Two doors down, Rhys and Rider were posted outside as Steed

tossed the elf into a chair and bound him to it. Chevelle sealed the room. They did quick work, and I simply stood in the center of the room to stare at this strange character. He wore nondescript clothing with no markers of any kind. His hair was a muted brown. He definitely did not have the look of a light elf—no inner glow or glistening eyes—but he didn't appear to be of the Northern clans either. He was young. And he looked scared.

"What's this?" Chevelle asked from beside me.

"I am not exactly clear on that," Steed answered. "But it seems he has some business with our lord."

Chevelle threw the sword at the elf's feet. I could feel the anger roll off of him, but his tone was smooth. "Business?"

The prisoner lifted his chin defiantly. Both Steed and Chevelle took a step forward. He swallowed as he appeared to gather his courage. "Bring me to her," he demanded. Neither of the other men glanced back at me.

If he didn't know who I was, I wondered what he was doing there.

"What do you want with her?" Chevelle's voice was deadly, and I could only imagine the glare that accompanied it.

"I will see the pretender," he hissed.

Well, that was telling. I elbowed past my guard and leaned toward him, showing him my eyes.

The green was pretty effective. He was speechless. I was confident we would break him, so the small silver blade that materialized in an instant and shot toward me caught me completely off guard. Instinct caused me to turn, but as I rolled away from the dagger, it sliced the meat of my shoulder.

I spun, landing in a defensive crouch just in time to see the fatal blow Chevelle landed on the young man. Danger thwarted, both men turned to me.

"What was that?" I yelled. They stared at me. "Did he just pull silver out of the air?"

They reacted to my words then, their eyes landing first on my arm, which was wet with blood, and then on the floor behind them.

A flat shard of metal lay on the stone. Chevelle's gaze returned to me, but Steed's went back to the chair. Rhys and Rider were suddenly there, struggling to take in whatever had happened.

Chevelle moved toward me, and I became aware I was nearly panting. I straightened and slowed my breathing, my hands and thighs still tingling with adrenaline. He examined my arm as Steed picked up the sword at the feet of the corpse. Steed appeared thoroughly confused as his gaze returned to the blade on the floor behind him.

Feeling returned to my arm, and I jerked, but Chevelle kept a tight grip. "It is a clean wound," he informed me. He bound a strip of fabric around it to stop the bleeding and instructed Rhys to find Ruby.

Chevelle turned. "Rider, this was an attempt on Elfreda." No one missed that he'd used my official name, and everyone in the room tensed, including me. "We know nothing but can assume he did not travel alone." His tone deepened to something resembling an animal's growl. "Find them."

Rider disappeared from the room without another word, and then Ruby was in the doorway. She had some choice words for the scene but attended to my injury.

Steed was standing over the offending blade, and with my shoulder taken care of, Chevelle joined him. They didn't seem to want to touch it. Ruby was pestering me with questions and poking at the gash in my arm, so I didn't catch what they were saying. I stood to join them. My head spun a little, and Ruby protested wildly, but she followed me, working as we went.

Steed glanced at me. "It doesn't seem to be the same metal."

"What does that mean?" I asked.

"He didn't pull the element from anything on him. I checked him myself. If it wasn't the sword…" He trailed off.

"How is that possible?" Ruby asked.

No one answered. There was no answer.

Chevelle straightened to face me. "What did it look like?"

I was confused for a moment but realized that neither he nor Steed would have been able to see it from their vantage points. I had a feeling neither was happy that I'd pushed past them and stuck my nose in the attacker's face. "It was quick. Smooth but not liquid. His eyes were connected with mine, and he never lost focus. There was nothing, and then silver." I sighed. "I'm not even sure I realized it was a blade until I was moving."

Ruby glanced at the chair. "Who bashed his skull?"

Steed and I gave Chevelle matching accusatory glares. He didn't budge.

"Well, we'll never find anything out now," she complained. "What do you suppose he wanted?" Her gaze flicked to my shoulder. "Aside from Frey."

Chevelle really didn't like fairies. I answered to save her. "He must have been put up to it."

"He had to have snuck through the kitchens," Steed put in. "There's no way anyone with knowledge of the castle would have sent him that route."

"Did he say anything else?" I asked. "When you found him, what did we miss?"

Steed shrugged. "He immediately demanded to see you, sword drawn." He met my gaze with a kind of apology. "I had no idea he was a threat. He seemed so weak."

I waved it off and looked back at his lifeless form. It didn't seem possible. "He's just a boy."

"No one of note helped him," Chevelle said. "They would have waited."

I thought about the banquet and wondered why he hadn't waited to attack then, when I would have been vulnerable. He could have walked right up to me and done it in front of every clan leader. "Was he a warning?" Unease filtered through the group. "Maybe he was never meant to succeed?"

"But the silver," Steed said, shaking his head.

"Maybe he thought he was strong enough to do it. The talent made him special where he was from, so he decided he would just raid the castle," Ruby suggested. "Where *is* he from, by the way? He doesn't look right."

"We didn't find out," I answered, and we all looked at Chevelle again.

Still nothing.

Grey came in, a wild energy lighting his face. I'd seen him move quickly before, but never on task as he was. It made a difference. "Witnesses saw a similar youth matching the description come in with the deliveries. He seems to have been working alone, as he was unaware of a few customs and didn't appear to have a purpose. No one accosted him—they presumed it was merely due to inexperience. We would like to confirm his identity with the witnesses."

Chevelle nodded. "Very well, but keep him from anyone else's sight. Resume the search within the castle and surrounding the gates, but only until the guests begin to arrive. I want no one to know what has happened here."

6

———————

As I lay back in the tub, letting the warm water ease the strain caused by the morning's events, my mind kept returning to the dull eyes of the boy who'd nearly killed me.

It had been so close. I'd been exceptionally stupid. In a matter of hours, I would be facing every figurehead in the North. I could not make the same mistake again. I would have to make my position clear, leave no doubt, and the banquet could be my last chance to do that.

I sank lower into the tub, allowing the water to soak my patched-up wound. It burned horribly, and I closed my eyes, letting the pain sear my memory, keeping it as a reminder of what my slip could have cost me.

A muffled click came from the door, but I didn't bother looking. "Ruby, get out of my washroom."

She huffed. "How do you always know it's me?"

I turned to glare at her over the rim of the tub. "Because no one else would hassle me here."

"Hmm." She dropped something on the counter and turned to go.

"I was simply bringing some things you'll need for this evening. I have to prepare myself as it is."

When the door shut behind her, I tilted my head back again, contemplating a display of power that would cement my place. I recalled a few of Asher's triumphs, but most of those disgusted me. He considered his banquets a success if each of his guests left in fear. He used his power as a threat, constantly reminding those around him of the damage he could do. He'd explained to me privately that he had to because it was the only way to secure our rule. But I knew better because he'd used it against me, and I'd had no desire to reign.

Asher had known me better than I'd known myself. No matter how I'd played along with his games, he'd kept me under his power and showed me what he could do. When I'd strayed, he'd found ways to remind me. Even after so much time, I could see Chevelle's tortured form writhing in pain at the hand of his own father. No matter his end or that he too was gone, I still hated Rune. He had smiled as Chevelle lay before him. Chevelle had refused to cry out in pain, but his body had reacted against his will, his jaw clamped tight, his muscles bucking against the stone floor.

Anvil had stepped in to save us that day, but I'd vowed it would happen no more. I'd made a demonstration of my own.

But Asher had always been one step ahead of me. Sapphire's death hadn't been punishment for my defiance—it had been a device to keep me, and it had worked. When I'd seen her lifeless body, getting out had no longer been an option. I had to stay and overcome Asher. I could not have done otherwise. I could not let him do the same to anyone else.

My mother had known that. She had seen, even from her prison, that my struggle with Asher was reaching a boiling point. She had thought to save me, and she had burned for it.

I sighed and rose from the tub. A trail of water ran from my feet, tracing the seams of the stone floor. I pushed it with magic, testing my new powers once more. It moved as if a gentle wind blew. I was pleased but not quite confident enough to dry myself using magic alone, so I used a towel.

I'd moved into one of the suites in the castle. From the washroom, there was a wardrobe closet through the first door and a bedchamber beyond the second. As I walked through, I picked up the small bag of items Ruby had left me and glanced inside at an array of greasepaint and rouges, lip balms, and kohl. She was incorrigible. I set it aside and sifted through the various costumes hung along the back wall. I pushed aside a dark cloak and faltered when the long white gown came into view: my mother's wedding dress. I ran a hand over the beading, exploring the fabric, the detail.

But, no, it wasn't that dress, which had burned when she had burned. The gown I touched had been created by Junnie. It was a symbol, a warning to Council.

Because of my mother, that white dress had become legend among the light elves. It had given the stories that indefinable something, making them appealing enough for the fairies to repeat, not that I'd ever heard them. Bound as I had been, the villagers would never have dared to reveal anything of my past. But I had heard since I'd been back, and I understood.

Junnie had left me that dress when Council had decided to try me. They'd intended to imprison me, and Junnie had sent them a grave reminder of who I truly was.

The crystal necklace had no real power, but it had frightened the council leaders unreasonably. I guessed that was a kind of power of its own, just a token. That was all it took.

An idea for the banquet was finally forming. I nodded as I slid into a pair of black leather pants, adjusted my top to cover the wound on my arm, and laced up my boots. I would not wear armor over my injured shoulder, so I opted for wrist cuffs and seated a light cape into the shoulder clasps that had been fashioned after hawks. I would be a warrior that evening, and I would look the part.

I began to step into the next chamber but stopped. I hadn't wanted most of what Ruby had left for me, but there was one thing that might prove useful. I slid a small canister from the bag, lining my eyes with gloss black, nearly the exact shade as my hair and lashes. It highlighted my green eyes perfectly. *One of a kind*, I thought, and then

I smirked—Ruby sported her own set of green eyes as well. Let them think of that, of the color we half-bloods shared.

I strapped on my sword and headed for the study to meet the others. Two guards were positioned at my door, with four more at the end of the hallway. My path was lined with waiting soldiers who held their gazes steady as I walked past. It didn't matter. I knew they were there to watch me. Annoyed, I turned the final corridor to the study.

Grey, Anvil, and Steed were waiting for me, each decked out in their castle finery. Steed and Grey had yet to get used to the formal gatherings, but they definitely looked the part. Leather and silver adorned their upper bodies, and they wore their weapons at hip and back. They were strong, and though Grey appeared especially slender next to Anvil's mass, the group somehow felt unified. Steed wiggled his eyebrows at my appearance.

I ignored him. "What news?"

"The witnesses have confirmed the identity of the intruder," Grey reported. "Due to the banquet, we have been unable to gather more information regarding his route to the castle, but once here, he wasn't linked to anyone."

"Has anyone of note refused the invitation?"

"No," Anvil answered. "All are anxious to bear witness to the new power they have heard of... or to see you fall." He smiled.

"I would imagine," I said. "No change, then. We will proceed as planned."

Steed and Grey did a little salute of sorts at my command, the shuffle of their boots on stone bringing my attention to their straightened posture.

I shook my head at their dutifulness. "To the hall."

As with the throne room, there was a private entrance to the hall, designed to allow direct access to the designated position without having to navigate the crowds. Asher hadn't liked to be touched. Still, it was a good idea and also handy for making a grand entrance.

Chevelle was waiting for me there. I had the pleasure of seeing his jaw go tight at my arrival but was quickly distracted by his own getup. He wore the garb of a warrior, and it fit him well. It had been a very long time since I had seen him so, and I'd forgotten exactly how well he wore it. I cleared my throat.

"Elfreda." He nodded formally.

"Vattier," I threw back, and irritation took over as his chief emotion. I could deal with that. The other was too distracting.

He recounted the arrangements for the evening once more before asking, "Have you made your decision about the demonstration, or are you still planning to... wing it?"

I didn't bite. "I have a fully choreographed performance. Not to worry."

He looked dubious.

We stood there for a moment, knowing a full hall awaited us but neither eager to proceed. He would not be at my side through the evening, as Asher had spent many years planting seeds of distrust and prejudice against Chevelle to prevent any alliance on my part. My public denial of him had done nothing to help matters, either. As it was, the position he held as my guard was generating plenty of whispers.

Chevelle stepped forward, his hand on my waist, and my pulse stuttered for an instant. But he spun me around, speaking quietly. "Checking your wound. No one must see this." He adjusted the material, verifying everything was still in place, and spun me once more to face the door as he stood behind me. His hands ran along the edge of my cape to settle on the bare skin of my upper arms, and he leaned in to murmur, "Show them who you are."

His breath on my ear caused a shiver, and then his hand found my lower back and gave a little push toward the door. I didn't look back when I heard a low chuckle.

And I was so glad we'd called "even" earlier, because I was about to tip the scales.

The hall fell silent the moment I entered. They had been waiting on my arrival, but no doubt it didn't hurt that all the servers stopped what they were doing and turned to the dais. I stopped for a moment to find each of my guard—excepting Ruby—scattered about the room, purposefully not acknowledging the presence of any leaders.

I'd had a gathering before, but not of that magnitude, and many were left out intentionally, so I continued as if no other event had ever occurred.

"As the former guard is disbanded"—it was a reminder that we'd killed them—"I have invited the clans to gather"—a reminder they were here upon invitation—"to honor the seven of my new guard."

The men were no fools—they had watched my eyes fall upon only six men. There would be a building curiosity to the identity of the seventh. I nodded toward the steward, and service began. It was a brief speech, but there was more to come.

I stepped from the dais and took my seat at the head of the table to feast among the leaders of the North. The room was furnished not like the dining area, with its long, narrow tables, but with many short ones, arranged so that my slightly elevated position became the focus of the room, along with the dais behind me.

Anvil had positioned the attendees in order of preference: two elderly men who had supported me throughout sat on either side, progressively moving to people less supportive and more trouble-some, all the way to downright dangerous. That meant most of the rogue clan leaders were across the room, and I avoided their stares as I was served. I raised my glass to the air and toasted, "the Seven," before bringing the wine to my lips, the scent of oak and spiceberry hanging in wait. Rhys's and Rider's gazes took in those who did not join in.

A feast was served, and as instructed, the wine flowed at an increasing rate. Soon, the hall was loud with conversation, banter, and debate. Those near me, thanks to Anvil's design, did not speak of much, so I was able to catch bits of various discussions throughout the room. In an attempt to disguise my focus, I let my eyes fall on the immense tapestries insulating the cool stone walls, most adorned with images of my crest and a variety of innocuous scenes, as Ruby had removed any in tribute to Asher—she'd had any evidence of him that could feasibly be removed taken from the grounds and burned. The castle was pretty bare at the moment, but torches, candles, ridiculous centerpieces, and elaborate dishes seemed to be more than adequate cover, at least in that room.

The clansmen were more at ease, loosing their armor, shedding cloaks, and leaning back in their chairs, sated with food, wine, and talk.

Sudden warmth against my palm stole my focus—it was a signal from Ruby. I looked down to find that the napkin under my hand had caught fire, but I was able to snuff it out before anyone noticed. I made a mental note to be more specific with the details next time.

I straightened in my chair just in time to see her enter. I gasped, but the slip went unnoticed in the noise. It was fortunate—an instant later, the hall fell silent. I'd not expected her to follow through so absolutely.

I gave them a moment to take in what I'd seen: a petite fairy, covered from chest to toe in slim black leather, her arms bare but for wrist cuffs, belted with short, shiny knives, and donning the crest of the guard at her collar. The brown leather whip at her hip had been exchanged for polished black, with what appeared to be silver spikes at the tip. Her heeled boots were gone, as she'd laced into the flat guard-issue footwear. Her face was unpainted and impassive. All that remained of the familiar Ruby was the blazing-red hair that curled ferally around her, proclaiming her fey.

Before anyone had a chance to regain themselves, I stood, raising my glass to Ruby. "Now that we are all present, let the festivities begin."

One more breath of stunned silence was all that remained before the hall erupted into protest. I drank the toast but didn't see whether any of my guard partook because my eyes were still on the fairy guard. She watched only me, not the crowd, and I smiled at her. I couldn't help it.

So far, I thought I was off to a pretty good start.

7

—————

The room was in near chaos, which probably meant that Ruby was happy.

I wasn't sure how long to give the disorder before proceeding to the next step, but the display received a stronger reaction than I'd planned, and it was gaining momentum. Maybe we'd served too much wine. I sat, contemplating my next move, and the crowd settled a bit. One of the guests stood, and I realized they'd only quieted to hear his confrontation with me.

I leaned forward in waiting, not surprised to find that it was Rothus.

He was tall and broad, nearly as large as Anvil. His black hair was long, slicked back into a braid. He wore a cape of fur, and a pegged mallet hung at his waist. He had plenty of magic, but he preferred blunt force. I nearly winced at the thought of what he'd likely done to the animal whose pelt covered his shoulders.

"You dishonor these grounds with a fey whore."

Oh, that would do it. I stood to meet his gaze. "You challenge my decision?"

All sound ceased but the flickering of torchlight.

Rothus was a prideful man who held grudges. He hated fey as

they hated iron. What I didn't know was whether he thought that hatred more important than his current existence. The silence keyed him in on his mistake, and he pushed his chair back to take a knee, but he didn't exactly recant. "They have no place among us."

"As you have no place to dispute the pronouncement of your lord." I paused for a heartbeat and then added, "Guard, acquire your price." Then I sat, my obligation resolved.

From my periphery, I saw Grey flinch and feared he would intervene. I'd not thought to gauge his response to Ruby's appearance or the risk she was taking. It was a mistake on my part, and I added it to the list, but Steed caught him with a gesture so minute, I was confident no one else saw it. Besides, they were all watching the fire fairy in guard's garb cross the room to her target.

Wearing a blank expression, Ruby walked coolly through the crowd to stand behind Rothus. On bended knee, he was nearly as tall as she, and I was grateful he'd shown at least that respect. She pulled a dagger from her waist and grabbed hold of his braid. The whole of the hall tensed until a swift move sliced the braid, and a crop of black hair fell forward around his face. It was insulting, but far from what the other guests had expected. Without a word, she walked back to her place, a firm grip on her dagger in one hand and the braid in the other.

I'd given none cause to dispute the action, and the fact that Ruby hadn't used fire in her revenge might have kept her heritage from the topic when the story was repeated.

Another round of wine was served, and the crowd eventually settled into the din of conversation.

I had decided to give them a bit longer before the display of power when an exchange caught my attention. Dagan of Camber was a little too far into his drink, speaking noisily of "before." Dagan had clout. He held dominance over many there, and some believed that fear of his power had kept the region from going completely lawless in my absence. I wanted no conflict with him, but his words were irritating me. I resolved to go ahead with the next step to shut him up, and that was when it all went out the window.

Looking back, it was hard to recall exactly what he said that caused my anger to explode, but something about Chevelle went right through me, and what happened next would likely be repeated through history.

I'd only intended to shatter the cup in front of him to get his attention. Instead, a deafening blast sounded as every cup on every table in the entire hall burst into pieces at once, sending shards of pewter and glassware flying to clink against walls, splinter into tables, and shower down on everything, excepting myself. The fact that I was staring at Dagan clued everyone who'd not heard his comments in on the cause.

The room fell silent once again, and the drip of wine from table and stone seemed amplified by it. Red splattered my guests as if they had attended a massacre and not a feast. The final few who were still taking in the scene came to join the others in their gawking at me.

I realized I was standing, which I didn't remember doing. My own wineglass sat undisturbed, my person and all that surrounded me in an arm's-length radius untouched by the destruction that blanketed the rest of the hall.

There was no question that I had instilled fear in them, in spite of my wishes not to be like Asher. My task was complete, and I didn't have much taste left for festivities. I leaned down, lifted the glass in salute to my guard, and turned to walk from the room.

When I reached the corridor, I allowed myself to breathe again. I walked toward the study, thinking of the faces of my guard, sprayed with red and numb with shock. I kept walking past my chambers, past the commonly used rooms, up the stairs, and out the window to my perch on the roof. The wind was cutting, but I stood to face it.

"Tell me that wasn't your plan," Chevelle said from behind me.

I choked on a laugh. I'd been standing in the wind so long that my eyes watered and my nose and cheeks burned. I turned to look at him, relieved to find him clean and out of uniform. He untied his cloak and stepped up behind me on the small platform. When he reached around to blanket me with the cloak, the warmth felt so good that I held his arm to wrap around me. I felt him relax into the embrace, and I snuggled my face into the cloak to thaw. I breathed in his scent then straightened, hoping he hadn't noticed.

"I had a good plan," I said as we stared out into the night.

An agreeable rumble vibrated in his chest. It reminded me of a purring cat, and I smiled. "I don't suppose it matters now."

"They were convinced," he assured me.

Chevelle wasn't like me. He possessed a nearly unshakable calm and considerable patience. After all we'd been through, there was no question that he would have taken revenge on Asher. Everyone knew that. What they couldn't guess was the backlash it would cause, what traps Asher had set for him, or if he was to have failed, what that would have meant for me, or if he had succeeded, what that would have meant for the realm. Chevelle had understood that. He'd kept me from acting rashly out of a reckless vengeance that would have likely gotten me killed. I would have retaliated with passion. He could wait.

He was right—there was a difference between courage and suicide. Honor wasn't much good to the dead.

"Chevelle?"

"Hmm?" he purred.

I shivered. He could think it was from cold. "How did you know I'd kill Asher?"

He stiffened. "We didn't."

I felt my face contort but couldn't decipher what they'd actually planned when we'd confronted him among his guard.

Chevelle sighed. "When we found that he'd set bindings on you, we had to allow him to live."

They'd made a deal.

"He'd been collecting new powers. He'd learned to create a binding that would not release upon his death."

That explained why Chevelle had been studying bindings instead of just hunting Council.

"When Council attacked your mother, it set so much more into motion. Francine was to be taken, and you, but Junnie stepped in. She forced their hand with an arrangement no one could refuse by council law. Council bound you both, for their safety, and permitted you to live under their watch."

"I can't remember," I said. "I remember everything but the bindings. Was it long?"

"No, the entire process was very quick. When Council descended, Asher set his spell and ran. And then you were gone." He faltered, then corrected: "In the village."

I had been gone for what had seemed a very long time.

"He watched you to be certain you weren't affected by the castings. Apparently, he saw enough of your old self there to approve. Once Council was disposed of, we expected him to release you. He wanted you back as his second, under his control."

"So, when I stabbed him..."

"Not exactly the plan."

"Wow."

A short, strangled laugh, the kind that was a cross between relief and disbelief, escaped him. We sat in silence for a few moments, recalling Asher's last words, the words that released the bindings and directed his power to me. If it hadn't been for some messed-up sense of pride on his part, I would still have been bound, trapped in my own mind, or dead.

"There is something you should know, Frey."

I waited.

"Junnie saved your life. She protected you. She fought for you."

"But?"

"We are not certain she meant to keep Asher alive long enough to unbind you."

I nodded, forcing myself to ignore the tightness in my chest. "All right." I took a deep breath. "But she's still done nothing to warrant my enmity." There was no way to prove she had intended to keep me bound any longer, though it was possible. If nothing else, she might have only been trying to keep her family alive. I couldn't help but wonder how many of the council members who were slaughtered had been her blood.

Fannie had been responsible for many of those deaths. Junnie had saved Fannie, but as Fannie escaped her bonds and regained pieces of her old self, she slipped into madness, reaping revenge on those who had trapped her. She had cut down her own family, Junnie's family, my family. A small voice whispered that as a result, Council's resistance to Junnie had shrunk by half, but I choked it off. Fannie was dead. Asher was dead. Junnie was all that was left.

I sighed and turned from Chevelle's embrace to face him, handing his cloak back. "I'd like to meet with the guard in the morning."

He stepped back and gave a curt nod, and it made me feel as horrid as I was being.

8

———

They were scattered about the study, patiently waiting for me. It still annoyed me I was the only one who needed so much rest. Ruby's hair was pulled back, exposing the points of her ears—not entirely fey, but close enough.

"What news?" I asked before they had a chance to take their places at the table.

Anvil reported. "Word has already flooded the valleys. There were but a few minor protests south of Camber. No news of the reaction of the rogues."

"We will ride out today and silence the dissidents," I said.

A few eyebrows rose.

"Grey, Chevelle, Rhys, with me." I glanced at Steed. "Ruby will need to lie low for at least three days. Please attend her." I wasn't finished, but Ruby was bloodying her lip waiting to respond. I let her.

"Three days?" she asked.

"One for word to reach the outlying camps. One for them to form a plan. One to implement it. If they do not strike by then, they will not bother. At which point, and only then, will you be allowed free rein." Her eyes narrowed on me, and I decided to nip the rest of my fairy problems in the bud.

I turned to Grey. "Until the fourth day, she will be Steed's charge." He looked as if I'd slapped him. "You put us all at risk last night, but none more than Ruby. Had you stepped in to protect her, she would have no power. When we return, you will lead a scouting mission for information on the boy. Someone will have seen him or his silver." I knew I would need to find the wolves.

Mention of the assassin had brought a stillness to the room. I struggled for a way to express my thanks to the group that meant so much to me. They had brought me back from nothing, risking their lives for me. Everything seemed inadequate, but the silence was growing too loud.

"You have done the North proud," I said.

GREY AND RHYS were mounted and waiting at the gate when I reached the stable. Chevelle stood outside, holding the reins of both horses. It seemed as if people were always waiting on me. I picked up my pace.

Chevelle handed my reins over with a wry smile. "Your Steed."

I bit my cheek at the name I'd given my horse and swung up into the saddle as quickly as Chevelle. As we rode side by side, I replied in a hushed tone, "I am surprised you've let me keep him."

The smile dropped from his face. "Yes. Well, I considered replacing him. But in truth, he is one of the nicest mounts in the land." He winced at his own words and kicked his horse up to gallop.

I swallowed a laugh and joined him.

We were quiet as we made our way from the castle. Once we'd cleared any foot traffic, Grey and Rhys rode ahead as sentries.

I still felt guilty about berating Grey so publicly.

Chevelle saw me watching. "You wounded his honor."

"It was right."

He eyed me knowingly before returning his gaze to the mountain. "I heard what Dagan said."

I flinched. "That doesn't mean I wasn't right."

He didn't respond. Leave it to Chevelle to stand up for him. It was hardly the same thing.

It was my first outing since our return from Asher's lair. Any of the guard could have made the demonstration, but I wanted to see the mountain myself. The dark rock had been my home, the pathways there, my playground. I wanted to see what had changed, what had been lost. I needed to know how I would be received by them all, not just the clan leaders.

After the massacre, there had been no one in control. We all knew that Asher had lived, and though he had been in hiding, I supposed that fear of his return had been heavy in the minds of those who might have taken advantage. I, as his second, would have been regent if not in hiding myself. As it was, with neither of us ruling but neither confirmed dead, the goings-on had continued day by day. The staff had cared for the castle and the grounds, completing their tasks as usual. No one wanted to lose their positions, let alone their lives, if Asher were to reappear.

He might have been a harsh ruler, leading by fear and control, but he was lord. He was respected. He was obeyed, and since he was gone, his half-breed granddaughter who had never wanted to rule didn't quite strike fear in the hearts of her people. There was only one thing they hated more than fey: humans.

Over the last few weeks, I'd realized it was fortunate, the way things had worked out. We could have died a thousand ways, Chevelle and I, as we went for revenge in the grasp of rage. Nothing short of losing every memory I had could have kept me from settling scores, and nothing short of recovering me could have kept him from doing the same. I had taken care of Asher. Chevelle had seen me returned. One objective remained, and I would stay alive long enough to see it through if it was the last thing I did.

"You look like you're trying to memorize something," Chevelle said.

"You look like a member of the royal guard," I retorted.

His eyes narrowed on me.

I shrugged.

And suddenly, we were flying through the air. For half a second, I thought Chevelle had retaliated, but there was nothing playful about the hit I'd taken. I hadn't even seen him come off his horse, but he'd slammed into me at full speed. We came to an abrupt stop as we smashed into the rock beside the path. Chevelle rolled into a crouch as I lay there, staring at the sky. The impact had knocked the wind out of me. A screaming pain in my side accompanied the return of my breath, but then instinct kicked in and I was on my feet again, crouched beside Chevelle.

Our horses were gone, the clatter of their hooves fading as I listened. Rhys and Grey were across the path, a few lengths ahead, scanning the mountain. It was obvious I'd missed something, and it didn't look good. Beside me, Chevelle was searching as well. I sank to my knees and closed my eyes.

A falcon nested in the branches of a thorn tree not far from where we hunkered. I set it to flight, ignoring the metallic tang of blood in my mouth.

Nothing was different. Everything looked right, normal. Nothing was out of place. There was no danger. I released the bird and opened my eyes. I glanced over to find Grey and Chevelle in the middle of an exchange of silent gestures in the distance. I'd clearly missed most of it, but I could tell that they had lost my attacker.

My head snapped up to find Chevelle. His grim expression confirmed what I'd thought I'd seen pass between them. I'd been attacked again.

His head tilted toward the ground behind us. Several yards away lay what looked to be a shard of glass.

"No," I hissed.

Chevelle nodded. There was only one thing that created weapons like that: an ice fairy.

We both stepped closer to the offending splinter of ice. It was solid, nearly unbreakable, and almost impossible to see coming. I shook my head. I hadn't even seen a fairy. I reached to pick up the icicle, disturbed by how much it reminded me of the silver dagger that had all but stabbed me, and Chevelle put a hand on my arm to stop me.

"It's not right," he whispered.

Obviously, I thought, and then I realized what he'd meant. It didn't smell right. There was a nasty, acidic tang to it. Poison.

Rhys and Grey were suddenly behind us. "Are you well?" Rhys asked.

They all waited while I took stock. "Yes."

Chevelle eyed my side—I hadn't been aware that I was keeping pressure against it. I dropped my hand, daring him to question it. He didn't, instead dealing with the most pressing issue. "We should return to the castle."

For a moment, I considered going ahead with our agenda, but that would have been foolish. I nodded.

He stared at me for a moment.

I stared back.

He raised his eyebrows.

Mine met the challenge.

He sighed. "Frey, would you like to *ride* back?"

Oh. I bit my lip as I called the horses to us.

I STOOD SILENTLY, watching my guard. Angry words flew through the study, including curses and violent threats. No one had seen my attacker—a whisper of sound had been the only warning. No evidence remained but the sliver of ice. It lay on the table in a sealed container, still frozen—we hoped that Ruby could discern the toxin. I couldn't breathe. I pulled shallow puffs through my nose. Anything deeper was a knife to my side. The ride back had nearly killed me. I was fairly positive something was broken.

Unexpectedly, the group separated and headed for the door. Chevelle lingered, and I guessed he must have dismissed them. As the last noises faded in the corridor, he approached me. "You've gone pale."

I nodded.

He smiled a little, obviously glad I'd finally given in. "Come, then." He walked me to my room and sat on the bed beside me, pulling my shirt aside to examine the injury. I raised my head to see, but as he pressed the skin over where it hurt, I fell back against the pillow with a gasp.

"Fractured rib, I think." He restored my shirt and patted my leg. "Hurts like a beast."

"The good news," I wheezed, "is I've barely thought about being assaulted again."

He looked as if he might be sick.

Someone cleared their throat at the open door, and Chevelle's hand on my leg tightened. "I've asked Ruby to tend to you."

I glared at him.

He smiled and stood, leaving me to a special kind of torture.

RUBY HAD TALKED while she worked, trying to distract me to ease the pain. I'd refused her concoctions, and she'd eventually left me to rest, but sleep wasn't coming. I lay staring at the canopy of the bed, building more and more anger as time passed.

Council had killed my mother, murdered her in an attempt to suppress Northern rule. Protection had been her blood right—my blood right. They had intended to take me and had only settled for my mind because of their own fear. No other threat would have been strong enough. Junnie had stepped in and used their superstition and their regard for the beast to quell their desire for domination. They had trapped me and held me prisoner, and when I'd finally been returned, I had been attacked again in my own castle, the one place I should have been safe.

I was Lord of the North, and I couldn't hold my own home.

I couldn't know if Council was behind that attack as well, but the silver boy's hair had been too light, his eyes too dull. He wasn't of the North. And if Council had never displaced us, none of it would have happened. I wouldn't have been riding out to control uprisings, and I wouldn't have been attacked yet again. By fey. I bit down a growl.

"I've brought you some tea," Ruby announced from the door. I sighed, and the movement brought pain again.

She set the cup on my table and took a chair beside the bed. I continued staring at the ceiling because it hurt less to lie still.

She didn't ask how I felt. "While you were gone, I arranged some of your things," she said.

I didn't take time to speculate whether she'd been trying to annoy me, teach me a lesson for shutting her in the castle with a babysitter, or simply distract me.

"I've been wondering about something I found. The scroll."

I could see the words as plainly as if they were before me now: *Fellon Strago Dreg.*

"I've looked everywhere. They are in no book that I have discovered."

My mother's script had been a warning.

"I thought that maybe—" She cut herself off as I stood, holding my breath to control the pain. She stared at me.

"Ruby, gather the guard. We are going on a trip."

Her face was blank for a moment, but as I moved toward the closet, she walked from the room. I bit down hard as I pulled the shirt over my head then replaced it with another, lacing a vest tightly against my rib cage. I struggled into my boots and grabbed a cloak before heading out the open door. The corridor was empty, and I wondered if Chevelle had lost his trust in even the castle guard.

Ruby was fast. When I strode inelegantly through the study door, they were all there, waiting for me. By the way they watched me, I thought she might have told them I'd lost it.

"Prepare the horses," I said.

They stared at me.

"We ride out for Junnie."

The stillness of the room erupted into disorder. I raised a hand, and they settled again.

"This is no coincidence," I said.

"You think she would employ the fey?" Chevelle asked incredulously.

I shook my head. "I cannot be certain any of this is her doing, but we will find out."

"She has the most to gain," Ruby said.

"Junnie has done nothing but assist in Frey's return," Grey replied.

"As such, she would have aided herself," Rhys said.

"She wouldn't be able to raise a new Council with a lord who stood against her," Rider agreed.

I couldn't dispute that. Junnie might merely have seen me as the lesser of two evils, but I couldn't say I didn't feel the same way about her and the supposed new Council compared with the old.

"Did she not risk all when she saved Frey from the massacre?" Steed asked. "Was she not honoring her family? Defending their birthright? Why else would she have rescued Francine from the same fate?"

"Fannie could never have been truly saved," Chevelle answered.

It was true. Fannie had approached Council for protection—they were the only place left for her to turn. It had started something that she could not have anticipated, but none of that would have changed her outcome.

She had reaped her revenge on Council, but she had gone back to Asher, and she had paid for that with her life.

They continued the exchange, but it was nothing but useless speculation. The only one who hadn't voiced an opinion was Anvil. When the conversation died down, I looked to him.

He sighed, his large chest rising before falling in a defeated gesture. Anvil had been around for as long as I could remember, strong and solid. But as I watched him, I could see the first signs of age on his face, the smallest creases around his eyes and mouth. He didn't want to tell me the last of my family could be my greatest adversary, but he was loyal. "Power can turn any," he said.

It was the only answer I needed. "Mount up."

We rode through Camber on our way, making no secret of our travels. The guard took formation, which would have been intimidation enough, but as we went through the Southern encampments, we took the time to enforce our rule and make a show of our presence.

By nightfall, the ache in my side had become agonizing. When the vague outline of a structure came into view, I realized I'd stopped paying attention to my surroundings, simply riding along with the others. I was grateful to see the fort, and it felt downright rapturous when the horses came to rest. Chevelle was at my side, gingerly lifting me down, and the sense of relief was overwhelming.

We settled inside the walls, under an open sky, and Ruby lit a nice fire. The warmth eased my muscles, tired from working to hold myself still against the jostling of the ride, and having a purpose improved my mood.

I finally glanced around the camp. Rhys and Rider had taken watch outside. They had informed me the wolves would remain at the castle, though I was unsure whether they'd not wanted to confront Junnie or whether they'd had some other purpose. The others relaxed around the fire. I was finally able to grasp the peculiar feeling that had been plaguing me all day. It was so like those odd memories from when I was bound, given the days of riding, the nights by the fire, and the same faces watching me warily.

Chevelle saw the smile playing at the corner of my mouth from where he sat beside me. "Are we amusing?"

I laughed with a shallow huff. "Just remembering."

My eyes met his, and he understood but he didn't appear to find it humorous.

Ruby, however, picked up the conversation. "You were so funny, Frey." She tilted her head as if making a decision. "But I still like you better now."

Grey snorted.

"I don't know," Steed said, "I think she was remarkably entertaining." He winked, and I glanced down to hide my smile. He wasn't genuinely flirting anymore, but only being Steed. I was still fairly positive that his mere presence irritated the devil out of Chevelle.

"That was probably the abundance of fairy dust," I said pointedly to Ruby.

Her eyes narrowed on me. "I was trying to help you. I thought it would make it easier to find your memories or at least give you some relief."

I felt almost guilty for a moment until she smiled and added, "But it was fun to watch."

Grey made a comment about some ruckus she'd created by dusting an imp, but I wasn't listening. My gaze had fallen onto Chevelle. He and Anvil were the only ones who had known me before, who had understood how truly lost I was, and who had felt the full impact. "Gone," Chevelle had said.

He saw my expression and met it with a sad sort of smile. "There were so many times we thought you were back." He shook his head. "I knew it wasn't possible, but still..." His brows pulled together as if he was still trying to work it out. "It was you."

I thought of the first day I'd seen him outside Junnie's door. "I'm surprised you even recognized me under the blur of glamor."

He chuckled. "I heard you stealing around the back of the house.

You were about as stealthy as a bull elk in a boar's nest. Junnie tried to stop me. I wasn't supposed to be seen." But he'd been there, still and solid as a statue, and I'd nearly tumbled into him. "I suppose it was fortunate you were masked."

I remembered his face, the tightness in his muscles, the restraint apparent in every part of him. He'd turned from me with fisted hands and disappeared.

"And then you broke it," he continued. I glanced up at him, pulled from my reverie. "You stood before Council and transformed." He glanced at my hair. "Dark seemed to seep out, drowning the pale like oil over straw." His gaze moved to meet mine. "And your eyes shone as green as a fey flame."

I remembered. I'd unwittingly summoned the wind and crushed the council speaker's windpipe.

Chevelle laughed humorlessly. "I thought you were going to kill him right there. And then you just left."

I'd run.

I was unaware of how low our conversation had become—it was nearly a whisper—until rowdy laughter brought our attention back to the others. The banter between Steed, Anvil, and Grey had taken a fevered pitch, and they appeared ready to roll around the rock like tiger cubs.

Ruby was egging it on. "Yes," she taunted Anvil, "but you are more of a one-strike wonder." Grey and Steed were in an uproar, but she carried on. "Steed can outlast any man."

A snicker escaped me, and she turned to us.

"Would you not agree?"

I bit my lip.

"Cursed fairies," Grey quipped, and suddenly, a bolt of fire headed for his chest. He rolled and twisted and was abruptly standing behind her, hands at her hips. Her face was near the color of her hair, and I laughed full out. She was going to slaughter him.

"He's quick," Chevelle said, shaking his head.

"You'd have to be." I smiled, indicating Ruby.

The exchange had evolved into a full-on brawl, and Chevelle gave me a look that clearly implied it was my responsibility to manage it. Each day, I had more sympathy for what he must have endured on our previous journeys.

Steed tumbled over Grey, and their boots landed in the fire, kicking up smoke and embers.

"Children," I commanded, reasonably certain they'd not even heard me. I tried again, standing for the order. "Cease."

Steed looked up from his place on the ground, his cheeks smeared with dirt and ash, and he quirked his brow. That sly grin was the only indicator that he was about to launch himself at me. I could have said I had no intention of joining in the melee, but that would have been dishonest. I was going to have a little fun with him.

I dropped into a defensive stance, my arms out at the ready despite the ache in my side, just to give him permission. When he moved, I straightened back to my casual posture and waited. I let him get about halfway.

He was off his feet, airborne in his leap for me, when I flicked my wrist to leave no doubt where the blast had come from. I felt the percussion as it collided with his power, but it barely affected the strike. It threw him back with considerable force, which I expected, and into a very large boulder some distance from the camp, which I did not expect. The previously boisterous onlookers fell silent, not even laughing at Steed's shocked expression.

I might have overestimated the amount of power required for the move.

I hadn't meant to end our playtime so abruptly, but it was no time to admit it. I tilted my head slightly in acknowledgement, as if I'd not just humbled him in one motion, and turned back to my seat.

The smile I found on Chevelle's face could be called nothing but satisfied.

No one challenged me over the following days, but they didn't really spar, either. I wasn't sure if the upcoming meeting was weighing down their moods, or if they were saving their energy. Either way, I didn't plan on practicing until I'd figured out control. I pledged to myself that I would find the wolves when we returned and work out how to share or store my extra energy before I hurt someone. And then I had to bite my lip not to smile at the memory of Steed's face when I'd sent him flying through the air.

"All right," Chevelle said as he brought his horse to a stop. "This is the nearest we can get you. We can wait for her to find us or search for some clue of where she's hiding."

I smiled. "You make it sound as if she's—" My words cut off at a sound from the trees behind us.

I turned to find Rhys and Rider entering the clearing. They'd been following at a distance because I'd been attacked on our own lands. No one had expected the trip, so if there had been any other plotters, they would have been on the mountain, and that was not to mention that we didn't want any of the rogue clans pursuing us there, in the First Forests. Words forgotten, I scanned the surrounding trees.

I'd been surprised when Anvil had told me where Junnie would be. I wasn't exactly shocked that she'd gone into hiding, considering she'd turned on her own council and lost most of her family, but I hadn't expected her to stray so far north of the villages and forests that had been her constants. The trees were thin and wiry, more needled than broadleaf. The forest floor was moss and ink-bristle. It was a palette of night blossoms and jade flower, not the sunny rainbow of her home. She would have felt out of place there, cold.

I realized the others were watching me and waiting. "Set camp here. I'll have a look around. I should be able to tell where she's been." Surely, I thought, there would be some mark of her, some sign of growth or garden or change.

Ruby went straight to forming a large fire. I doubted we'd need to make a spectacle—it wasn't as if we would be hard to spot, but I didn't spoil her fun. Rhys and Rider stayed close. I knelt, splaying my hands on my legs and closing my eyes. I didn't expect to find Junnie so easily, but it was early afternoon, and I could at least get a feel for the land before she came to us.

I found a harrier and sank deep into its mind so I could cover a greater distance. It was easier with my own hawk and took less focus once I'd gotten familiar with its mind, but that was why I hadn't brought it. That familiarity allowed me to find it even back in the castle. It meant I could still keep an eye on things.

The forests were a striking green with dark patches among the clearings. The harrier took long, lazy circles, and I could see the patches grow larger, taking over the clearings farther south. We weren't terribly far from the base of the mountain—we were closer to it than to any of Junnie's own people. It was a disturbing sign.

For a long time, I saw nothing out of the ordinary, no indication that she'd touched the land. But there was no hint of anyone else, either. It was simply wilderness, far from anything.

Then I saw a dog. It wasn't mangy—in fact, its coat was clean and shiny, a fluffy black that appeared to float about it as it ran. It didn't look as if it'd missed a meal, either. I touched its mind briefly and knew that it was the dog that had belonged to the human girl who had died.

I came back to myself, shaking my head. They were watching me. "She's there, a league or more from us, in a copse of blood oak."

Anvil glanced at the sky.

I nodded. If Junnie was behind the attacks, I didn't want to sit in wait.

"Do we go in mounted?" Steed asked.

I nodded. "Yes. It's not as if we'll be able to sneak up on her." We could have been stealthier on foot, but I was confident that by then, she knew we were coming.

On Steed's command, the horses gathered, and in moments, the packs were secure and ready. The dog was still running the field when we approached.

"Is that..." Grey trailed off as the animal spotted us and advanced, immediately picking up speed.

I answered with a flat "yes," but the question on their faces was plain: *how could he have grown so quickly?* He was a giant, some terrifying mix of a mastiff and a wolfhound. I tried to work out his age in my head, but no amount of arithmetic could reconcile the massive beast with that puppy. I tore my eyes away long enough to glance at Chevelle, whose expression was wary.

"Does he plan to eat us?" Anvil asked.

I managed a laugh. "No, but there will be slobber."

Ruby made some sort of disgusted noise, and I turned to smile at her. The fey didn't like dogs, and that one was bigger than she was.

We continued riding, though we could see the trees that framed Junnie's lodge. She'd formed the structure within the copse of blood oak, using the trees as column and canopy. Native ferns and mosses camouflaged it further, and with the smattering of rock by the entrance, no one would have easily found her.

As we neared, she stepped from the trees in all her blond glory. We stopped as a group and dismounted, and the hound tested each of us, his cold nose snuffling for our scent. Once finished, he chuffed and went to stand beside Junnie.

"He's grown quickly," I commented, though all of us knew it was unnatural.

Junnie smiled, and I was struck, as I was each time I saw her, by how different we were. There was a lightness about her shimmery golden hair, her bright sky-blue eyes—everything about her seemed to glow. It was made all more perceptible by the new colors of her robes. "I am glad you are returned, my Freya."

"Thank you, Juniper. I am grateful for all that you have done to help us."

Her gaze fell on the others. "Word of the Seven has traveled far. Even here, I have heard of their imposing presence."

I wanted to trust Junnie. I wanted to take her endearment, hold it in my heart, and keep the last of my family, but I couldn't stop myself from questioning her words. I couldn't keep from wondering who had told her of the guard or what she'd meant by "imposing presence."

A silence hung in the air. Anvil stepped forward, bowing slightly in greeting. "Juniper."

"Ah, Reed. Forgive me, but it is simply such a shock to see Freya restored." She tilted her head to return his salutation then smiled. "Alone for mere weeks, and I've lost all trace of civilization." She still didn't invite us in.

"I am certain Frey has been eager to see you," Anvil said, clearly struggling with the dictates of etiquette himself. "But that is not the reason we have come."

Junnie straightened.

"She has been attacked."

Junnie's eyes flicked to mine, and I could tell she was concerned, but that ugly voice in the back of my mind wondered if she was worried for me or for herself.

I took a deep breath against the tight lacings of my vest and moved closer. "Twice, actually."

She stared at me, waiting for more information or maybe an accusation.

"A boy entered the castle through the kitchens. Pulled silver from the air and formed a blade." I purposefully left out the fact that he'd managed to slice my arm and the details of his coloring. "And then a second, outside the castle. It was in the form of an ice shard."

"Fey?" she asked incredulously.

Ruby spoke up: "There was a toxin within the crystal. I have been unable to identify its makeup, but it doesn't appear to be plant based."

I started to turn back to Junnie, but Steed caught my eye. With the smallest glance, he conveyed his suspicion. By the time my eyes fell again on Junnie, I was just as wary. She was troubled—there was no doubt about that. But that wasn't what was bothering me. I wondered why she hadn't invited us in.

As they continued to discuss the attempts, I let my mind wander, trying to figure out what she could possibly have been hiding. She should have wanted the meeting to be under cover.

That was when I felt it: a human.

10

Before I could stop myself, I was past Junnie, pushing through the door. I could hear them all on my heels, but I didn't look back. I followed that strange feeling, that connection, through her house. Just before I threw open the last door, Junnie spoke my name. It was a cross between a plea and a command, and I ignored it.

On the back wall of a small, clean room was a crib.

I did look at her then. Her face held a hint of an apology but not regret. I opened my mouth, a thousand thoughts fighting for issue, but all that came out was, "Why?"

Junnie shook her head, but I couldn't figure out what else was playing in her eyes—sadness, perhaps. "I could do nothing else," she said.

"You could do nothing else?" Anger and incredulity warred for my tone.

She sighed. "Asher chose this one above all others."

I stared at her for a long moment, her words repeating in my head. Then understanding came, and a burst of power escaped in my fury as I turned back for the child.

"Hold!"

The word brought me up short. Rhys had never spoken anything but gently to me, but that word had been nothing short of an order. He stepped forward and tilted his staff past me. Where the grip touched, mere inches from us, the air rippled. There was a ward protecting the crib.

My teeth gritted as I glared at Junnie.

She appeared unrepentant. "I did not create this child, Freya. But she will not be destroyed."

My hand came forward, but Junnie was too fast. She stepped through the ward, cradled the babe against her chest, and burst out the back wall of the lodge.

Rage tore through me, and the other walls surrounding us exploded into bits of kindling. My guard flinched, though most of the shards had flown outward. I took a breath. We could have gone after her, but we would have had to have killed her to stop her.

I glanced at the others and saw something like guilt on a few faces. I stepped forward, narrowing my gaze on Chevelle.

"We did not think it an issue," he said.

I waited.

"The girl, Molly. It was clear she wouldn't survive to term."

I stood stock-still, certain if I moved at all that it would be to keel over and expel the contents of my stomach. I remembered Molly and the days she'd spent with us. She had irritated me inexplicably, though I could see that it was likely because of my childhood and the constant conviction of my people that humans were detestable. And we were the same, she and I, as alike as I was to the elves who surrounded me. She hadn't appeared with child to me. But she had been a human girl, and we had found her with the head of Asher's guard. "You knew?"

Chevelle shook his head. "Ruby. The girl had gotten exceedingly ill."

I glanced at Ruby. She looked a little sheepish. I was finding it hard to breathe. My vest was too tight.

"No one expected her to make it," Chevelle continued, "and when Junnie showed up..."

"You didn't want us to kill her," Steed said.

"Junnie took the girl without asking," Chevelle added, not sparing a glance for Steed, "but it did seem like an acceptable outcome." He shook his head. "I never thought she'd allow this."

"It was the child," Anvil said. "She said Asher chose this one. She will not destroy one who can connect with beasts. She will wait and see."

So Junnie thought the child might carry our ability. And those of the light were morally against destroying it. But there was no way to know. She was risking it merely because Asher had believed her special.

No. My stomach twisted at the thought. "She said 'above all others.'"

An image of the small bloodied hands of a human girl came unbidden, along with the ruined bodies of her and the guard in Asher's secret grotto near the castle.

"We believed them all destroyed," Chevelle assured me.

No one moved, and I had a sudden flash of memory from when I'd been bound, when they'd all thought at any moment, I could lose it. "How many?" I asked.

"It is not known. Council, Junnie, and your guard have each dealt with their own." His voice was gentle, and the "your guard" held a quiet assurance.

I didn't stop to ponder the details or to wonder if he and Steed had found more when searching for Asher's guard. There was something else more pressing. "How long has he been doing this?" I searched the faces of my guard, but I found my own answer. He had taken Vita and had created Fannie and my mother. He had stolen me. "They're his."

My voice met stony silence.

"The others, the attacks. They are his."

"They are children," Anvil said. "They are not working alone."

He was right. But I had to wonder who had put them up to it.

∽

WE RODE STRAIGHT through the night and barely rested for the remainder of the journey. When we finally reached the castle, I fell into bed, exhausted, but sleep still wouldn't come.

The attacks had been too odd, with the silver and ice. Though we'd not seen the source of the ice, I was certain it wasn't fey, as we had seen the boy. His features were too light and his eyes too dull. He had pulled silver from the air. He might have been old enough and might have believed he could defeat me, but I couldn't figure out why or what he would gain from it. It was easier to believe that the boy didn't hate me enough to want to kill me but that he'd been after the throne.

Maybe he'd been abandoned. Maybe Asher had made promises and never returned. Maybe the boy had merely come for revenge or because he had nothing left. And maybe not. The more likely scenario was that someone was still out there. Someone had told him he was the rightful heir. Someone had told him that I'd killed Asher and that all he needed to do was kill me.

I wondered whether it was Junnie and if she could do that to me.

Of course she could—she'd turned against Council and slaughtered however many of them. She'd had years of experience in underground maneuvers. By all accounts, she had plans to create a new Council. She had followers, but that didn't mean she would hurt me.

I found it hard to believe because I wanted to think that it wasn't emotion driving the conviction. But I had to look at the facts: Council had nearly destroyed the North, and they had used my mother as a pretense in their bid for control. They'd been losing to Asher, and they'd dealt with him. Junnie might have split from Council, but she still aimed for control. She might have preferred me to Asher on the throne, but there was no guarantee she didn't want to rule all. Junnie was a match for me in power, but I had gained Asher's along with my own. It was my only edge, aside from my guard, but I knew she could amass a council larger than any of my forces. If one received the calling, they served. It wasn't a matter of free will or loyalty.

And then there was the child. I wondered whether Junnie was

truly keeping Asher's daughter because she felt it was wrong to do otherwise or because it would be her ally, her key to the North.

I rolled over, kicking the bedsheets away. It could have been the rogues. It could have been the fey. It could have been anyone. But I really didn't want it to be Junnie.

My thoughts turned to Fannie then, who had been betrayed by her own father. He had essentially disowned her, choosing my mother over her as his second, and then me after he'd all but driven her insane. Fannie had turned to Council to protect them as their birthright, and Council had betrayed them as well. She hadn't had someone to protect her as I had. When her bonds had begun to break, she'd thought Junnie and Council had entrapped her, and she'd gone for revenge. It had cost her her life.

My thoughts floated in and out of those images of Fannie razing the village that had been our prison, of the fires that had burned my mother. It was hard to say when they morphed into dreams, but I could see my mother in a gown of azure and lilac, leaning forward to whisper secrets.

"It was the bond," she said softly. "That was why my mother couldn't leave him."

"But—" I started, and her finger came up to silence me.

"It isn't right, my Freya. I cannot let him destroy her family so he might lay claim to more land."

And then she was burning. The flames licked at her white gown, beaded and lacy. Screams surrounded us, but I could hear her whispering, "Others will come. Others will come." The flames engulfed her, and I was suddenly underwater, struggling for air. *Others will come.*

I jerked awake, damp with sweat and panting. I lay staring at the ceiling, one thought circling through my mind like a bird over prey: *others will come.*

I cursed Asher. He had made an army of his children, and they were going to come for me, one by one.

11

———

Eventually, I accepted the fact that sleep would not be returning anytime soon and dragged myself out of bed. I took a long bath before getting dressed and let myself wince as I laced a corset around my rib cage. It was getting better, though, and I was able to take a few deep breaths before heading down to find the others.

I stepped into the hall and found Anvil leaning against the wall beside my room. I raised a brow.

"Only until we are certain," he answered.

I nodded. "It won't be long, I assure you."

He smiled a fiendish grin, and I reached up to clap him on the back as we made our way down the corridor.

We found Ruby, Steed, and Grey in the dining area. When we sat to join them, I realized they were eating lunch and wondered exactly how long I'd slept.

After two servings of braised elk and cornmeal, I decided I could face what I was going to have to do. "Find Rhys and Rider. We'll have a meeting as soon as everyone is gathered."

I excused myself and headed for Chevelle's study. He was

standing near the back wall, staring out the window. The silver dagger lay on his desk.

He turned and obviously saw my focus. "It is an alloy."

I lost all awareness of my intention. "Alloy?"

He nodded grimly. "Yes."

"So..."

"So we have no idea the kind of threats we'll be dealing with. This and the ice"—he stopped when a note of anger slipped into his voice. "We will be fighting blind."

If I'd had any notion he'd forgiven Asher, it was gone. I was beginning to build on my own resentments as well. Even after Asher's death, I wasn't free from him.

Chevelle stared at me for a long moment, and I realized I'd forgotten my purpose. "Oh. I've called a meeting."

He nodded and began to walk toward the door, but as he neared me, he saw there was more.

"I wanted to see you first," I explained.

His gaze fell to the hand fisted at my side, lingered, and then returned to meet mine.

"You trust me."

It wasn't a question, so he didn't answer. He simply waited for me to go on.

I didn't.

He came closer, reached down to take my fist in his hand, and loosened the fingers. I understood the gesture was meant to ease me, to let me know I could relax and just tell him, but it didn't have that effect. I fought the flush but forgot to mask my expression.

He moved even closer and released my hand so nothing stood between us but a few inches of air. I dropped all emotion from my face.

Chevelle's jaw tightened in response. "Do you know the one thing I enjoyed?" he asked, reaching up to cup my cheek.

I could only manage a quiet, "What?"

His thumb brushed my lip, and the flush returned despite my best efforts. "You couldn't hide it," he whispered.

I took a deep breath, reining it in as memories of every look, every touch rolled over me. "Well," I said, working for a steady tone, "you weren't doing so well yourself."

A sexy smile took over his face. "Still, it was"—his eyes fell to my lips, slowly tracing their line—"satisfying."

That was it. I'd finally made a good decision, and I was going to cave after one touch from him, one word.

Ruby cleared her throat from the doorway.

I turned to her, stepping away from Chevelle, and couldn't decide whether to be angry or relieved at the interruption.

She looked a bit concerned for her safety. "The others." She pointed vaguely in the direction of Anvil's study.

Chevelle walked past me and out of the room without another word, but Ruby jumped aside as he neared the door. I raised a brow.

She leaned out the doorway to peer after him, only looking back to me when he'd cleared the corridor.

I smirked.

"What?" she said. "I thought he was going to pluck my ears off."

We entered the study, and Ruby took her place among the others, purposefully walking a wide path around Chevelle.

I really should have discussed what I was about to do with him first.

"Call another gathering," I said. "No pomp—this will be a congress." I glanced at Anvil. "Bring in the clan leaders singly and anyone else of note." My eyes traveled down the circle. "Steed, you and Grey flank Ruby all evening. Rhys and Rider, post by the south entrance. All others will be sealed." I didn't look at Chevelle or Anvil when I directed them. "Anvil at my left. Chevelle at the opposite end of the long table. I want you in my line of sight at all times." This brought a few peculiar stares, but I kept on. "Tomorrow."

They had their orders, and they clearly knew it was serious. Then came the part I'd been dreading. The others deserved to know my motivations. I would have to make them understand. Chevelle and Anvil would get it—if not my choice, then at least my reasoning. It was why Asher had wanted me. It had been a constant battle to stay on the throne. He had needed a powerful second to rule without challenge.

I would have to do the same. It was my only option. I opened my mouth to speak, but they all froze, tilting their heads as if they'd heard something I hadn't... or maybe something I'd ignored. The pat of boots against stone grew louder.

My guard were on their feet. Grey was at the door first. At the sight of him, the watchman yelled, "Rogues, south gate!"

I gritted my teeth and ran. I wasn't as fast as the others, but I'd been running those corridors since I was a child.

We burst from the castle as one, and the seven formed up around me as if they'd been doing it for years. The yard was bloody. The rogues had worked fast. There were twenty of them, a ragtag band of thugs with greased hair and spiked armor. I scanned the faces and found Vandrell, son of Stryder.

He was huge, with fists as large as my head, and he was ugly. His jaw was misshapen and scarred from fighting, his cheeks stained with animal blood—war paint. They used it when raiding the villages. His hair was tied back too high on his head, and the front of it stood in pointy tufts.

He was staring at Ruby.

"Re-form!" I yelled, and they followed without question.

Steed and Grey stood before Ruby, with Rhys and Rider at her sides. Anvil and Chevelle had stayed in position, but I stepped through them to the front of the line.

The rogues came to rest, waiting for my reaction. They were obviously enjoying their little outing and wanted to drag it out, reveling in their triumph. They were fools. I let my eyes roam the line, falling on each of them. Their leather was worn black, their armor dented from battle. A few wore mail. All carried hammers.

"You raid my castle as if it were a village," I accused.

"You will fall, half-breed," Vandrell answered, "and the fey whore will decorate my pike." With that, he raised the weapon in the air, hammer still at the ready in the other hand.

"Save the pike," I said levelly to the seven behind me.

Vandrell roared, and the twenty rushed forward, joining in the battle cry.

I didn't take time to wonder how many of our people they had killed, to worry whose blood covered their hammers or splattered the yard. It didn't matter anymore. There was only one way, only one justice. I raised my hand and silenced Vandrell first. Power shot from my palm and shattered his heart. Fire erupted beside him, and lightning burst from behind. There was a flash as two more collapsed, all before I'd focused a second attack. A crunch of bone sounded along with the thick wetness of exploding flesh.

Twenty men—twenty *warriors*—fell on the stone without so much as a weapon being raised by my guard.

I walked among the bodies of the fallen and reached for the pike. When I turned, my guard remained motionless in their formation. I moved to Ruby and placed the pike in her hand.

"Tomorrow," I said, looking over my shoulder to Anvil. "Congress."

I WASN'T sure how I'd gotten blood on myself. I couldn't remember being close enough. I scrubbed at it, thinking of the stares I'd received on the way back to my room. Everyone had been watching. It had happened so quickly, and I wasn't sure exactly how I'd done it, but they had all found a window to lean out, a doorway to peek around, some way to watch. I hadn't wanted to leave the others to clean up the mess, but I couldn't stay once I'd realized the size of our audience.

I knew they would take care of it. They would honor those of our people who'd been killed before we arrived. They would report who had been taken to me, and I would pay tribute to them, show my respect to their families. Ruby would spike Vandrell's head.

I stopped scrubbing. My skin was raw.

I dressed in clean pants and a loose tunic and returned to my room. There was shuffling outside, but I didn't go to check to see who was on duty. I stared out the window into the empty darkness of night then closed my eyes, searching for the wolves. I hadn't felt them since I'd returned from our journey. They must have left while I slept.

I wondered where they were, if they knew about Junnie, and what I was supposed to do with all of my power. I wondered why they'd brought Rhys and Rider, whether they'd known about Asher, why the rogues chose today to attack, and who else wanted me dead. I wondered when I'd get some sleep.

LATE THE NEXT MORNING, a light knock sounded at my door. I was already awake, but my voice was still hoarse when I answered. "Yes?"

Ruby poked her head in.

"You're knocking now?" I asked.

She pushed the door open and shrugged. "I brought you some bread."

She set it on the table by the door—whether she could tell I wasn't interested or because it had only been an excuse to see me, I wasn't sure.

"I stood the pike by the gate," she said. "For our guests."

A flicker of concern that I'd given Ruby too much authority edged out my other worries for a moment, but when I looked up at her, it appeared she'd simply done what she thought I wanted. I nodded. "I suppose that's for the best. I'm sure they've all heard by now."

"The others are still hunting down the clan leaders for tonight," she offered.

"So you are my guard."

She nodded. "And Grey." She paused, looked a little guilty, and added, "And Rhys."

"When Chevelle returns, please let him know I'd like to speak with him." I really needed to tell him my plans before the congress.

Ruby rolled her jaw but kept her lips tight.

"What?"

"I..."

"Ruby," I demanded.

Her face twisted into a grimace. "I don't know," she began, "but I think he's looking for Stryder."

"Alone?"

She lifted a shoulder. "It isn't as if he can't handle it."

And he'd left me with no fewer than three guards. I swung my legs off the bed to stand. "How long has he been gone?"

"Too long for you to stop him."

"Then that's how it will be," I said. I could tell she was burning to ask, but I ignored her. "Let's get dressed, shall we?"

12

The rest of the day was a blur. I'd chosen a formfitting black leather costume. A short cape, which would allow freedom of movement, was clasped at the shoulders with a pewter crest of my line. I wore a cuff on my left wrist, but my right was bare. Ruby had painted the hawk and intricate runes there, just above the base of my palm. I was outfitted for a special kind of battle, and my opponent awaited.

I stepped forward, leaving the two watchmen at my private entrance to the hall. The room was silent as I took my place before them. Anvil stood at my left in all his regalia. The walls had been covered with dark silks and standards, all bearing the crest. The room was windowless and smaller than the banquet hall, and I couldn't help but feel closed in with so many in attendance. The torches and candles flared brighter, and I wondered if Ruby could tell what I was feeling. It was hard to say, as she had a flair for the dramatic. I scanned the room. It appeared that they'd been able to locate representatives for most of the clans. My guard was in place, but I couldn't bring myself to look at Chevelle. What I was about to do—

No, it has to be done. There is no other I will name.

"I have called this congress..." I heard myself droning the words, but I could focus only on the crowd. They had already formed opinions of Chevelle—they had heard the rumors. Some of them had even been there when I had publicly denied him as Asher sought to arrange a marriage, and what I was going to do would be like denying him again, permanently.

A second was backup, there to step in when the lord fell. They could never be in a union, because one who was bound would likely die if they lost that connection. If I chose Chevelle, if I named him my second, it would be like announcing that we would never be bound. Otherwise, it would only be for appearances, for he would not live long after my death.

"... and call you to order as I name my second."

As I made it through the lengthy speech, my eyes finally fell on Chevelle across the long table. It was as we would always stand at such ludicrous functions from then on, at opposite ends, never side by side.

I felt wretched.

"Chevelle Vattier. Born of North Camber, Guard of the Seven, Second to the Lord." I held his eyes, skipping over the part that listed his mother and father, though it was secret to none. I'd already all but slapped him in the face.

Aside from the intake of breath, which might have come from Ruby, silence smothered the room. I gave it a heartbeat, two, three. It crossed my mind that I should have prepared my guard further, but I couldn't be sure what the clans' response would be. They could oppose it, but to question my order so blatantly would mean execution. They could fight, but they would lose. They might have had a chance, if they had all agreed and had prepared before coming, but they hadn't known. I had the support of at least a few. I hoped the rest simply accepted it. Far too many had died only the night before. I didn't want to go through that again.

After several more moments of quiet, I glanced around the room. For the most part, everyone in attendance seemed confused and eager to escape with their lives. No one wanted to be caught up in bloodshed in the castle.

Chevelle stood completely motionless, expressionless, as if a statue in the costume of a guard.

"I call you forward to bear this token," I announced.

He seemed hesitant to move, and I drew in several long breaths through my nose. The token was nearly meaningless to all others. Mine had been the amulet that Asher had previously given my mother. I hadn't wanted it and had returned it to her, and she had worn it on the day she burned. It was all that had survived the fire, and they'd left it with me when they took me to the village.

Chevelle finally made his way across the room, coming to stand at my right. I turned to him, nodding to his arm as I pulled the thin leather strip from my belt. I had retrieved it from the box of things he'd returned to me, and when he saw it, I knew he recognized it. The slightest twitch at the corner of his mouth was the only indication he might someday forgive me.

My hands were trembling, but there was nothing to be done for it. I tied the strip around his wrist, knotting it over his cuff to complete the ceremony.

I turned back to face the room. "As the High Guard bears witness, so bear the agents of the North. It is decreed this day, until the hour of our death, by none disputed."

"Hear, hear," the Seven chorused.

"Hear, hear," repeated the crowd.

I quickly dismissed the meeting and exited the hall, deciding to head to my perch on top of the castle, where I watched tiny little bands of the leaders scurrying from the grounds. Even from that height, I could spot Rhys and Rider's shocks of silvery-white hair in the moonlight. It was cold, it was late, and I couldn't decide if I wanted Chevelle to show or if I was petrified that he would find me.

He didn't come.

I fell asleep there, waiting for something to happen or hiding from just that. When I woke, it was fully dark, the moon covered by vaporous clouds. I'd been having an odd dream featuring Steed and Ruby. They were flying through the air, drunk on the effects of dust, and she was giggling uncontrollably. It might have been funny, seeing

Ruby race through the air, laughing riotously as her red curls flowed, if I hadn't witnessed the fey raids as a child.

They would sneak in, hundreds of them, flitting through the castle at incredible speeds. Some of them were nearly too quick to see, except that they never went unnoticed. Chaos and madness were left in their wake. They destroyed, pillaged, ransacked. They set fires, loosed floods, poisoned. They were tiny, sparkling furies, bent on destruction. Asher had nearly declared war but was finally able to quell the attacks.

I stood, ready to make my way back for warmth and maybe some food, and was thrown forward, almost knocked from my perch. I grabbed a stone pillar and fell into a squat, looking behind me before jumping down to the roof. It might have been a strong gust of wind, if it hadn't giggled.

As soon as I saw the sky was clear, I leapt from the roof and into the window, then ran through the corridors full speed. It hadn't been a dream. That meant they'd been here too long already.

A dull thump and a scrape echoed through the halls from far off. The torches came alive, flaring at full heat. After half a dozen more steps, I rounded a corner to find Grey, who was heading for me at what had to be his own top speed. *Where are they?*

"East wing," he said, answering my thought.

They'd probably sent Grey because he was the fastest. At the atrium outside of the east wing, Chevelle and Steed joined us. Chevelle's right side was splattered with blood and glitter. Steed looked as if he might be sick.

"Where is Ruby?" I asked frantically.

Steed glanced toward the clamor.

"They will take her!" I shouted. It appeared that they hadn't even considered the danger.

Chevelle nodded, but I could see that his concern lay elsewhere.

I stared down Steed and Grey. "Do not leave her side."

Grey was gone before I'd finished speaking, but we were right behind him. We followed the clatter of metal and chirping laughter to the great hall.

It appeared to have exploded. The furniture was in splinters, and pieces of wall and ceiling lay in piles of rubble. Several small gray fey lobbed the stones about. Their feathers were wet, as was about half the room, which was scattered with patches of ice and puddles of water.

The tapestries were set to a slow burn, though no one seemed to think them significant enough to put out. Given that there were at least a dozen other fey who could set even the stone ablaze, I could understand the decision. Anvil had taken to electrocuting a couple of water sprites, which the lilac-skinned Flora and Virtue considered uproarious. They floated above the scene, rolling in the air with laughter.

Rider was cornered by a waiflike winter sprite, and two frost monsters were hovering above Rhys, trying to get a hand on his staff. The room hummed with the beat of so many wings and stank of sulfur and spring violets.

"I hate fairies." My voice was surprisingly even.

"Hear, hear," Ruby whispered, catching my eye as she stood behind Steed and Grey midway across the hall.

I drew my sword, grateful I'd stayed in my fighting attire from the evening's meeting. I would have to be careful bandying around magic in a room full of fey. They had a bad habit of affecting energy in unusual ways, and I was barely in control of it myself. I sincerely hoped, once again, that the ancients Finn and Keaton had a plan to help me channel it, even if it would be difficult to communicate with them in their wolf forms.

"Pretty, pretty," a frost monster murmured to Rhys's staff.

"Anvil," I said with as much calm as I could muster.

He ceased transmitting the current toward the water sprites, and they shuddered, jerked, and dropped to the floor. They were trembling and muttering incoherently, but their audience became bored.

I stepped in before they found another attraction. "Flora, why have you come?"

Twin amethyst jewels gleamed at me, and I had to focus not to get lost there. Her smile was stunning, though I knew she mocked me.

The heliotropes had hypnotic powers. Her lips were thin, a muted pink against the pale lilac of the rest of her. She wore but a scrap of clothing, revealing the tiny feather-like strokes of mauve covering her body.

Her only response was to purr.

I looked at Virtue. She raised a violet brow.

"Why?"

"You will see, lov-el-y," she taunted, dragging her words out. "You. Will. See."

I stepped forward, sword at the ready. Virtue was more of a soft lavender with the markings of a cheetah. I'd always heard her belly faded to white. As I looked at her, I doubted that anyone had actually gotten close enough to find out. She wore the full armor of a warrior fey and a smile that promised to devour.

"He comes," whispered a soft voice from behind the walls.

"He comes," repeated the gray-feathered fiends, forgetting their game of stone-throwing to watch the large hole where the window used to be.

We stood motionless, dreading the "he" who was coming.

No sound accompanied his arrival, but as his form appeared in the opening, the sun broke over the horizon, silhouetting the figure of a winged god in the golden light of dawn.

If I hadn't been so angry, I might have rolled my eyes.

13

Veil, the lord of all fey and protector of their lands, hovered there for a moment, allowing all to glory in the display. Anvil spat, Grey shook his head, and Rhys struggled to keep his staff from the pale, wiry fingers of the frost monsters.

Finally, Veil spread his arms and drifted into the great hall.

"Nearly through with your presentation?" I asked, not bothering to hide the bitterness in my tone.

He smiled as if I'd applauded him. He tilted his head to the side, perusing my attire. He took his time, and when his gaze finally came back to meet my glare, I could practically feel the anger radiating off of Chevelle from his position behind me.

"You look well, my Freya," Veil purred.

Something similar to a growl escaped my second, who was, at least for the time being, faithfully guarding my back.

"You look ridiculous," I shot back. "And your insects are swarming the castle."

His smile turned sexy, and I tried not to notice that he was indeed worthy of the hero status he had among the fey. "They are not like your little birdies, are they?"

I glared at him. In that moment, there wasn't much else I could do.

Fey had a knack for knowing absolutely everything. They held secrets that were impossible to learn. It didn't do much good to anyone else, because one could never get information from them, and any sort of trade ended with being in worse shape than before. But they knew, and Veil had a special talent for it, so I wasn't surprised that he'd hit me with a very personal endearment and a reference to my ability within the first minute of conversation. But there were only two reasons he would be there: because I knew something he didn't or because he knew something I didn't.

"Why are you here?" I asked, slowly enunciating each word.

He flew closer, stilling his wings as his soft-soled boots touched the floor. "My dear," he said as he stepped nearer, "you are the talk of the realm. Where else would I be?"

I tightened the grip on my sword.

His gaze flowed over me before he turned his palms up and glanced around the room. "And your Seven. My, my, what a glorious mob." His eyes met Ruby's, and she held his stare defiantly. I glanced at Grey, but he seemed to be controlling himself, though he wore a murderous glare.

Veil continued to survey the room, pacing in a narrow circle in front of me like a preening peacock displaying his wares. I wanted to look away, but I didn't trust him that much. So instead, I watched his effort to impress me with as much disgusted indifference as I could manage.

It was difficult, given that he was shirtless and wore low-slung pants, but I hated fairies. He showed off his lean, muscled torso and his gorgeous amber wings dappled with a mesmerizing pattern of swirls and circles, somehow reminiscent of eyes. His eyes were striking amber gems that complemented his bronzed body, set in a handsome face adorned with a charismatic smile. He was no less than captivating. But I hated fairies.

I realized he'd stopped moving and simply stood there with a satisfied smile, watching me take him in. "Are you quite done?" I snapped.

He replied in a low, seductive voice, "May we speak alone?"

"No," I answered too quickly, nearly flushing before I caught it. Chevelle was still behind me. "Anything you have to say can be spoken in front of my guard."

Veil's eyes were roaming my body again. "I understand you've chosen a second." There were a thousand implications in his statement, chiefly that I would not be getting bound to Chevelle.

A crash sounded in the corridor, followed by a high-pitched, "Oopsie!" and a giggle.

"Get on with it, Veil, before I slaughter your minions."

He appeared oblivious not only to my comment, but to all of the destruction surrounding us. "An unexpected choice: your blue-eyed guardian."

I stepped forward. "Spit it out, or I'll remove your tongue."

He laughed and glanced at Anvil, who had lost a bit of his at my command long ago.

I *hated* fairies.

"And especially so soon. You seem concerned for your safety," he said, his eyes falling back to mine.

How he knew within a matter of hours not only that I had chosen a second, but why, was a problem. "It seems you are concerned with my affairs as well," I said.

His face became serious but retained the sexy. "I am very interested."

I leaned back.

Veil leaned forward. "Perhaps we can make an arrangement."

I was momentarily speechless and not entirely certain what he was offering.

"I can protect you," he murmured.

My mouth dropped open, and a few choice words emerged.

"You are very appealing when you're angry, beautiful Freya."

I was tempted to hurt him, but I couldn't afford a war. Not yet.

"No?"

"Never."

"Ah, well." He stepped back, resuming his pacing. "So then, a gift."

I felt a sudden but light pull on the cord that held my mother's pendant at precisely the same moment Veil winked at me.

"Let me know if you change your mind," he hummed in a remarkably alluring voice.

I glanced down just as his boots lifted from the floor and then I found the gift attached to my necklace. I didn't waste time unlacing it, instead yanking the entire cord free and away from my skin. When I looked up again, the others were watching a few dozen fey disappear from sight.

Unfortunately, that left far too many still within the hall. The pair of gray-feathered fiends looked at me and smiled. I flinched, not only at their promise, but at what appeared to be blood on their prickly little teeth. I secured the necklace behind my belt and readied my sword. "Leave now, and we will remain at peace."

It was a useless warning. All who'd traveled with Veil had only come to unearth trouble, with the possible exception of Flora and Virtue, who followed him everywhere. But they were gone, along with the ones who didn't care to risk death. Then again, I really wanted them to just go.

The winter sprite who had been harassing Rider moved to the center of the room and joined another of its kind. They were nearly as tall as Ruby, but incredibly thin and pale. Their hair was long, a silvery gray that fell down in waves and complemented their paper-thin silver-and-white wings. They were very dangerous despite their frail appearance. They had the ability to create shards of ice that pierced like glass and broke like steel.

"We have come for the girl," the one farthest from me replied.

I knew exactly who she meant, but I didn't dare take my eyes off them to confirm Ruby's safety. I trusted my guard. They would protect her. *Please, let them protect her.* "She will not leave here," I pledged.

As if they had been waiting for the challenge, for my denial, the rest of the fey gathered in a very large half-moon behind them, except for the frost monsters, who still hovered above Rhys, yelling, "Mine, mine," for his staff. I wasn't sure they were even aware of the impending battle, let alone Veil's departure. At least they hadn't tried freezing him yet.

I hated fairies. "Don't do this." I tried again.

The gray fairy on the right raised a slender hand to ready her troops.

In typical fey fashion, a small male broke the charge early, heading straight for Ruby. Steed's sword came up to meet him and sliced through his thin frame from hip to shoulder, crosswise. It was fortunate he'd flown in low. That was rarely the case.

"Idiot," the second gray fairy muttered.

As the first lowered her hand, Anvil took a knee to steady his shot and threw lightning at the water sprites. He'd been battle-trained to fight the fey. I hoped the rest of my guard knew better than to use much magic. Rhys and Rider moved to cover our backs, and Chevelle shifted to my left. The fey split into approximately three lines, hovering high over our heads, just above us, and at ground level.

It was a brilliant tactic. The largest were on foot, coming at us with magic and weapons. While we were busy chopping them down, the airborne line came at us in formation, while the highest fey took turns swooping in to dive-bomb unexpectedly. Swords flashed, dust flew, wings sang. It was complete and utter chaos.

A robust ginger-skinned male with auburn hair and orange-brown wings came at me with a half-sword, and I parried then cut through his chest on the back swing. As he fell, a gorgeous, lithe female, who might have passed for an elf if not for the thin cerulean wings, shrieked a battle cry and leapt in a kick at my face. I dodged and spun, knowing better than to grab her as she turned to face me. Over her shoulder, I could see Rhys still struggling with dual frost monsters, who had hold of his staff.

Chevelle had closed ranks behind me, covering the attack. The fairy flung two knives at me, which I dared not dodge for Chevelle's sake, and spun into another kick. I deflected one of the knives with my sword and held the other with the smallest amount of magic I could release, which happened to be far too much, and shattered the blade. The distraction caused me to neglect the kick, and it landed directly over my healing rib. By then, I was just mad.

I punched her square in the nose and brought the knife from my hip up to plant in her chest. When I moved to return to the line, I saw the strangest thing. Standing in the center of a triangle formed by Grey, Steed, and Rider stood a glorious red-headed fury. True and steady, she swung her whip in circles around the lot of them. There was no particular pattern—she moved it up and over, around, back, down, sometimes swirling it above them several times before returning to cover the others. Each time a fairy came in for attack, it met with a sword or risked being tangled by the whip, which brought the fliers down neatly for a knife to the gut.

It was inspired, as the rest of us were vulnerable to the air strikes. It made me wonder if that was the reason she'd chosen the weapon. I inhaled, which made me wonder if Veil had known about my broken rib.

I edged in between Chevelle, who had amassed an impressive pile of fey corpses, and Anvil, who had efficiently removed the threat of the water sprites before they'd had a chance to flood the hall. Two large shadow stalkers rushed forward, and I raised my blade to strike. I caught one in the side, but they were fast, and the other dodged the blow completely. As I pulled back, Chevelle sliced through the second with deadly accuracy before turning to deflect a jade fairy's blade. I finished off the shadow stalker just as the advance fell.

The handful of fey that remained were airborne, alternately lunging toward Ruby and then feigning back at her strike.

"Bring them down," I commanded, surprised at my own vehemence. "I want this over with."

My guard responded by surrounding Ruby in a large, loose circle. They watched the air as two russet fey dove simultaneously. Grey struck one with a miniscule amount of energy, causing it to bounce into the flight path of the second. Ruby caught the second off guard with her whip and slung it to the ground by an ankle. Steed sliced its throat. Recovered, the first tried to rebound, but Rider speared it through the chest.

One of the remaining watchers screeched, and three others flew wide in a sudden attack on me. I blasted them from the air, hoping they wouldn't have time to feed off my power, and Chevelle leapt over one and slammed into another, who had already been rising. The few that were left had apparently been driven to madness by their defeat, because they were frantically darting around the room, high-pitched birdlike screams and hisses trailing behind.

Steed began to drop stones from the ceiling, which finally brought them low enough to be caught. Spitting and cursing, they resembled cats, claws and all.

At last, the room was silent. I glanced around, incredulous at the destruction. Water and blood pooled on the dismantled stone floor, and the furnishings were scattered shards of wood and metal. Bits of wing littered the ground like confetti. My gaze caught as it came across the strange pale scraps covering the floor near the back wall where Rhys had stood. It appeared he'd found a way to deal with the frost monsters. I felt a shiver and turned to the others, who also seemed to be in various stages of shock and post-combat unrest.

"Steed, take Ruby to her room. Bar the door."

He snapped out of his stupor quickly enough.

"Grey, Rhys, Rider, search the castle. I don't want to find any strays later by accident."

They didn't waste any time, either, which left three of us alone.

I turned to Anvil. "How did they get here so fast?"

He shook his head. "It isn't impossible, but they likely discovered your decision on the way."

"So, why were they coming?"

"To celebrate your return?" he offered.

I scoffed.

"It is possible Veil has heard of the attempts."

"I agree." I bit my lip. "See what you can find out."

"Indeed," Anvil said, touching his fist to his chest.

Chevelle and I stared after him. I remembered the bloody battle and the proposal by Veil.

"When this is over," he growled.

"I know," I answered. *War*.

14

———

For as long as I could remember and even during those times when I couldn't, I'd had one thought, one obsession: if I could just overcome that one insurmountable obstacle, then things would be bearable.

But my whole life had been a series of those hurdles, and each time I crossed one, there was nothing but another on the other side: a chasm, a mountain, one more impossible challenge. As I stood there with Chevelle, wanting only to right Council's wrong, to avenge my mother and my kingdom and be done with it, I could see nothing but more problems on the horizon.

I pulled the necklace from my belt and stared at the pendant beside my mother's. It was a long spike formed by four smaller strands twisting together. Two of the strands were cold, those of ice and silver, the other two—one of bone and the other the color of blood—warm in my hand, but I didn't think the pendant was charmed, as I'd feared at first. I wondered what Veil had meant by it. There was no question the fey were tricksters, but they were clever as well. It was no simple gift, but I couldn't figure out if he'd intended it to be a warning or a promise. He'd seemed sincere in his proposal, though he hadn't given me the pendant until I declined his offer.

I couldn't blame Veil for all that had happened, but I couldn't entirely trust him, either. Between the lot of them, they'd invaded my home, insulted my second, and attempted to steal my guard, and that didn't even account for the ones we hadn't seen.

I glanced at Chevelle, who seemed to have his anger under control. "We should probably help the others," I said.

He moved to place his hand at my lower back as we started for the corridor but stopped just short of touching me. I pretended not to notice.

The halls were a quiet mess. The staff tended to stay in their rooms during a fey raid, so the corridors were empty aside from the fabric, beads, broken furnishings, and occasional foodstuffs scattering the floors. We came across a door covered in ivies, another painted with profanities, and a third that had been busted through. Oddly enough, the libraries were intact.

"Wouldn't want to destroy those. They might need to borrow a book," I muttered.

At the end of another hall, right before the entrance to the kitchens, was a large T-wall. I stood staring for a long moment at what appeared to be a portrait of the new lord of the North, naked. It was plainly a hurried job, but all the important parts were there. I turned to Chevelle but couldn't decide whether he was trying to conceal a grimace or grin. I took the time to glare at him before moving on, just in case.

Hurried footsteps caught up with me shortly, but they were delayed enough that I knew he'd taken care of the graffiti.

The fey had managed a considerable amount of damage to the castle in the short time they'd been liberated, but no one had been badly injured. The kitchen staff had had it the worst—there were plenty of utensils to clang around and batter with—though I'd not checked the stables. They always had fun in the stables. I kicked a broken crate from my path.

"We've got one," Grey announced from the doorway, and I turned to find him ragged, his clothes torn and his face scratched.

"A lion?" I asked.

He had no sense of humor, not that I could blame him. His answer was flat. "A fairy."

We met him at the door. "Thank you, Grey. Go see Ruby before she tears Steed apart."

THEY HELD the tiny female in an unused room, empty of all but a wrought-iron chair and two visibly irritated guards. Rhys and Rider weren't scraped and tattered as Grey had been, but they didn't get agitated much, so I figured she must have been a difficult one. They had tied her to the chair at the wrists, ankles, elbows, knees, thighs, waist, and chest, and the chair had been bound to the stone. I didn't ask what they'd done to the chains to keep her from working free, because I was afraid the answer was a spell.

I walked closer—not too close, as I'd learned my lesson from coming too near our last prisoner—and nodded toward the gag. Rider reached in and yanked it free. A stream of curses followed, I assumed picking back up directly where she'd left off when he'd shoved the rags in her mouth in the first place. It was quite impressive, and I let her run with it for a few moments to wear herself down.

"... son of an imp, and your mother was an unbonded flaxen *wench!*" she finished.

Rhys had gone pale. Apparently, neither he nor his brother had dealt with many fairies before. Once she ended her rant, she turned her gaze to me, and her natural beauty returned, smoothing her face into ethereal magnificence beneath sun-kissed chestnut curls.

The light streaming in through the small, slitted windows behind her reminded me that it wasn't even midday. I suddenly felt exhausted. "Why are you here?" I asked, skipping the introductions.

Her gaze flicked to Rider. "Because this ignorant ram's ass tied me to a chair."

"Indeed." I cleared my throat. "But why were you here, in the castle, before you were tied to a chair?"

She smiled. "Surely you would know, Lord Freya." She added

enough sweetness to my name to make it perfectly clear that she meant the endearment to be satire.

"Veil is gone. The others are dead."

Only the slightest flicker of emotion flashed, too briefly for me to tell whether it was worry or anger, but long enough that I was certain she hadn't meant to be left behind.

"I know you are not a spy, but it is too dangerous to keep you here."

For a fraction of a second, she appeared relieved to hear of her coming release, at least until she realized she'd mistaken my meaning completely. "What will it take?" she asked.

"The truth."

"Each holds his own truth. What will it take?"

"Why are you here?"

"Because I was bored," she answered. "That is my truth."

"And the others? What was their purpose?"

"I cannot know."

"Then you cannot live. I will not waste the lives of my guards watching you, nor risk them for the same." I turned to leave.

"I could guess," she offered nonchalantly as I reached for the door.

"What do you suppose, then?" I turned back to face her.

She shrugged. "Might have been the girl. The grays seemed very interested in bringing her back."

"For whom?"

She shook her head. "I am guessing, remember?"

"You've heard."

"I hear a lot of things. It doesn't make them true."

"And Veil's truth?" I asked. "What is that?"

Her eyes peered into mine. It was more than a little disturbing, but not as disturbing as her statement. "He does want you."

"Why was he here?" I asked, forcing my tone to remain steady.

She glanced at my neck, seemed confused, then shrugged it off. I waited. "There was some sort of gift," she said finally.

I nodded. "And what do you know of this offering?"

She shook her head. "Gift. And I know nothing."

"Release her," I said to Rhys and Rider. "She's of no use to us."

It was essentially true, but mostly I wanted her to stir a few things up on her way back to the fey lands so Anvil's contacts might be able to gather the information we needed.

Chevelle followed me to the hall, ready to resolve the disasters left behind by the fey.

"When Anvil returns, we will meet," I said, drained.

When I finally made it to my room, I unlaced my shirt and took a long, deep breath. I was fairly certain the kick I'd taken had set my recovery back a few more days, but the rib wasn't as painful as it had been the first time, and I was grateful for that. Leaving my boots on, I stretched out on the bed to close my eyes.

The lightest whisper of footsteps outside my door let me know my guard was once again on duty. I sighed.

Lying down intensified the fatigue tenfold, but I didn't sleep. I searched the mountains, reaching for the minds of Finn and Keaton. I wasn't able to find them, so I moved ahead to my next task and located my hawk. He had fled the castle in the raid but was perched nearby one of the gates. I set him to flight and circled the grounds.

Apparently, the fey had been warned to come in stealth, because nothing outside of the yards was damaged. I could see the staff, who appeared to be annoyed at the mess but relieved to be unharmed as they tried to set things to rights. I had a feeling it was going to take them a while. Continuing my inspection, I checked the roofs and crevices, anywhere the fey might be hiding or might have left a snare.

Eventually, I came to the stables, saving my most dreaded chore for last. I really didn't want to see what they'd done in there. The hawk alighted to a post outside the stable, and I was surprised to see Steed walking a mare into the yard. He must have come to check on his stock as soon as Grey had relieved him of his charge. I hopped to a nearer post.

The poor beast was covered in a shimmering violet dust, and Steed stood beside her, humming while he gently brushed it away. I bounced to the post closest to them and saw that the ground was littered with various shades of the stuff. He must have brought each one out and swept them clean by hand. The way he looked, I was curious if he'd done so for the animals or himself. Surely, he could have used magic, which would have been much quicker. His hum to calm them—the way Ruby had hummed me to sleep so many times before my recovery—changed into a full song, and the corners of my mouth drew up.

Steed was so engrossed in his work that he had only glanced at the bird when it landed near him. It wouldn't have seemed unusual, after all, because it lived in the castle. But as I watched him, he began to glance more frequently at the hawk. Apparently, it didn't normally stalk him.

The mare nickered, and Steed answered in a low tone, "Yes, darling." She rolled a shudder down her back, shaking out more dust. "There's a girl," he murmured.

I cocked the head of my host sideways just as Steed flicked another glance at it. His eyes narrowed infinitesimally. I wasn't certain it was his audience that had him unnerved, but it sure seemed that way. I thought I'd check. As he moved to work the dust from the mane of the mare, rubbing between her ears, he glanced over again. I raised one clawed foot from the post and held it forward in salute.

It was definitely the bird. His face twisted into an unease I'd never before seen on him. He stopped singing and stared straight ahead, over the mare's back.

I sprang to the mare's rump, landing lightly about a foot from his face. He jumped.

I felt myself chuckle back in my bed and then was startled out of the hawk by a familiar voice.

"Freya."

I didn't know why I felt guilty, but I bolted upright, wincing at the pain in my side from the sudden move. Chevelle handed me a cup, and I took it without thinking. It was warm against my hand and smelled wonderful. One sip, and I was choking and spitting uncontrollably.

"Ruby prepared a blend for your rib."

I wheezed.

"She mentioned it might be strong."

I looked up at him, completely unable to form a response.

He smiled. "Rest, Freya."

IT MUST HAVE WORKED, because the next thing I knew, Ruby was waking me for our meeting. She seemed well, considering the fey had apparently placed a bounty on her. I took a breath before questioning her, realized it didn't hurt, and inhaled and exhaled deeply several times. "Ruby, what did you give me?"

She shrugged. "Tea. Now, come on." She threw clothes at me, impatiently moving about the room while I put myself in order.

"You're unusually twitchy," I mentioned as I walked toward the door.

"Maybe I just don't like waiting," she snapped. She walked two paces in front of me all the way to the study, clearly not wanting to discuss whatever had her so on edge. It definitely wasn't fear, though.

When we entered, she pointedly did not look at Grey, which of course caused me to. He was staring at her with an intensity that would have caught a normal woman on fire. Ruby, however, had been born of fire.

I shook my head. *This is just what we need.*

All eyes fell on me as I stepped to the head of the table. I threw the pendant down, the twisted strands landing with a clanging thump on the wood surface. "Ice, silver, blood, and bone. Our gift."

They stared at the pendant, the spike formed from four intertwined strands. There was no question in my mind that the ice and silver were related to my attacks, especially since Veil had mentioned my safety. How they were related was another matter entirely. They were cold to the touch, while the blood and bone were warm. A gift, our prisoner had insisted. Leave it to the fey to offer a puzzle instead of a clear message.

"It's the same," Ruby said, wide-eyed. She hadn't had a chance to examine the pendant yet, to see the thin thread of ice, which was still frozen solid.

"I suspected as much." I glanced at Chevelle. "And the silver?"

"It appears so," he answered, clearly displeased with the revelation.

"The question remains: is this admission of their involvement, a threat of further attacks? Or is this truly a gift, an answer to our search?"

Rider leaned forward. "Why would they admit their own involvement? Why not just fight with full force if that was what they wanted?"

"For that matter, why would they help you by handing you the enemy?" Ruby asked.

Chevelle tensed beside me. Both questions could be answered by Veil's interest in me.

"I don't understand," Rhys said, "why they would risk it at all."

I waved a hand dismissively. "They've been doing it for ages. Never mind that half of them were killed. They don't consider the risk—they just want a good night out."

"There's something else," Grey said. We all took notice of his tone. "They didn't offer a trade." It was obvious what he meant. They had wanted Ruby.

The room was silent for a long moment before Anvil finally spoke up. "It means nothing. Veil would not soil his hands so publicly in such an arrangement. By coming, he has already placed himself on unstable ground."

"About that," I interjected. "This was the largest force I've seen for a very long time. There were no fire fey."

Anvil nodded. "Hard to say at this point, but I am hoping they support your choice." He paused. "That's not to say they would not welcome her return, unwilling as it would be."

Steed changed the subject. "As for the pendant, is the blood meant for death or lineage?"

"That, as well as the bone, can be interpreted in many ways," Anvil answered. "The fey are not easy to read. And they like it so."

Rhys looked disgusted. "Then this token is worthless."

I shook my head. "No. Even if we don't understand their motives, even if we never decipher their clues, it tells us one thing for certain. The two attacks were connected, and the fey know how."

"If this is a threat"—Steed shifted uncomfortably—"then no response is an act of battle in itself."

Ruby nodded. "And Veil's going to work up a good lather over your refusal."

"And then they'll be back," Steed added. "In force."

"No." Chevelle's voice was cutting. I wasn't positive he'd meant to speak at all.

I sighed, not wanting to voice the problem but needing to explain it to the others. The fey loved a good war, and if they could manage it, they would be back soon enough. The group we'd dealt with had been nothing, merely along for the ride, toying with us over Ruby. A true raid would have left us with more damage than a few scrapes and bruises.

"Some fey have the ability to manipulate the magic of others. A strike against them can be turned, distorted..." I shook my head. "Let's just say it's ugly. The problem is, with my magic in such a volatile state, I would be risking not only myself but the release of these powers to the fey."

"To Veil," Chevelle said.

There was a collective silence. I imagined the flying amber god with the combined energy of himself, myself, and all that Asher had amassed.

Ruby had gone pale. I decided to throw her a bone. "Finn and Keaton may be able to assist with this. They have brought us Rhys and Rider for a reason, and I believe their connection plays a part. When the wolves return, we may have one less problem to worry about."

Ruby immediately appeared to lose all concern for our crisis. "The legends are true? The wolves are the ancients?" She stared at me a moment before her scarlet curls whipped around to find Rhys and Rider, both of whom smirked. I would have to remember to thank them for that later.

The meeting ended with nothing at all resolved. Anvil hadn't been able to discover anything useful in his first attempts at tracking information from the locals, but he intended to try again since we had released our captive fairy back into the wild. Grey and Steed were planning a trip to Camber under the guise of guard duties to see if they could learn anything useful. Ruby had flatly refused their offer to go along, which I attributed to the sparks that were flying between her and Grey and to the possibility of her missing Finn and Keaton's return.

She followed Rhys and Rider from the room, but they were tight-lipped. They seemed to be thoroughly enjoying themselves, and I wondered what she'd done to them to merit the torment.

Chevelle and I were alone in the study. He stood staring at the pendant on the table.

I watched him. "You think Veil made the offer because he knows of my uncooperative powers."

Chevelle let out a breath before raising his gaze. The emotion in it was crippling. "No. He has always wanted you." His eyes fell to my lips, and my throat went dry.

"You think we should trust him?" I rasped.

A sardonic smile answered my disbelief. "I think he wants you safe." Chevelle's hand slid across the table, moving closer. "For him."

I purposefully directed my gaze to the pendant. "Then it's a warning. But a warning against a fey campaign, or someone else?" The twisted strands of silver and ice caught the flicker of the torchlight, shimmering like the ornament of a fairy, not an elven lord. "If it is someone else, we need to decipher it. And if it is the fey, then there is no way to stop them from coming for me." I contemplated the devious, underhanded war tactics of the fey, thought through what would happen, and remembered what Chevelle had said. "And he wouldn't let them have me, would he? If they come, he can't stop them. But he won't... *can't* allow them to have my power. He would take me."

I felt the change in Chevelle beside me, but I dared not look up. There would be nothing I could do to fight Veil without risking the release of my power, but I had no doubt of Chevelle's intent.

"I will find control," I promised. "And we will solve the pendant's riddle."

REGARDLESS OF WHO was trying to kill me, I still had a kingdom to run, so as I worked to catch up and set right all that had gone undone in my absence and awry since my return, I puzzled out the clues. I knew one thing for certain: the attackers were Asher's offspring. The boy's coloring was likely due to a mixed birth. And the fact that the fey were involved made me wonder if the ice attacks were from a half-fey child. Ruby, after all, had turned out strong and dangerous. Fortunately, she was on my side.

I had mentally crossed the rogues off the list, as the massacre in the yard would have never come to be if they had control of anyone in line for the throne. They were brutal, but they had enough sense to use a tool like that in the most effective way: they would have gathered a following. If it was the fey who had control over an heir, then they were either just playing with me until they could place him or her, or they had more than one and they were trying to thin out the stock, neither of which was highly likely. Still, I couldn't stop the shiver that ran through me at the thought of a fey-influenced lord on the Northern throne. But even if they didn't have a child or children, then they knew who did, and at the very least were tracking the situation. I had the strands of silver and ice to prove that.

That left two options that I could think of: Asher and Junnie. Asher had not been gone long. He could have spent years training and molding his children, he could have told each they were his rightful heir, and they could be coming for me because I stood in his place. The attacks had not come together. The silver boy had been alone, and he had called me "the pretender." But if Asher was the cause, there was nothing to be done but wait for the others to decide it was time. There was no way to find them, to flush them out.

There was a way to find Junnie, however. And Junnie was raising a child of Asher's, a half-human child whose mind she could possess. Junnie had been with me in the village, so she couldn't have raised the other children. But she could have taken them when Asher was on the run. They hadn't been with her when we had found her, but she had a following by all accounts, and there could be someone supporting her, someone who wanted the new Council, who wanted control of the entire realm. Maybe there was an army of them. Maybe a new Council had already formed. I shook my head, silently praying once more that it wasn't Junnie.

I didn't even consider Grand Council on my list, even though they too had wanted reign over all. It wasn't because their key players had been removed and they were regrouping or because they wouldn't do it if they could. I didn't consider them because in a matter of days, there would be no more Council.

I would finally avenge the wrong done to my mother. I would repay the debt owed to my people. In a matter of days, there would be one less barrier before me, one less burden to carry.

"Frey?"

"Oh, sorry, Ruby. Please continue."

She glanced at the scrolls, a large pile of messages from across the realm, and I could tell she was calculating how much longer it would take to finish.

"It comes with the uniform, Ruby. The guard has never claimed one who was merely a fighter. If you want to choose the dead, you have to manage the living. It keeps us from turning murderous."

She cocked a brow at me. She knew full well that Asher's guard had been more deadly than productive, but they had all been given other chores—not decent, moral duties, I thought, remembering Riven and his charge, but duties nonetheless.

Ruby picked up another scroll. "Alianna Denae of Camber is with child. The child's father, Klave, was killed by the rogues outside our gates. She is grieving badly, and it is feared she'll not make it to full term."

Manage the living. "Send her an invitation to the castle. Note that she is to come when the child is well and they will be safe to travel. Maybe we can give her something to look forward to."

Ruby nodded, appearing pleased that she might yet have something enjoyable to oversee.

"If she takes a turn for the worse," I added in a hushed tone, "assure her that the child will have a place here."

Ruby's eyes held mine for one long moment before returning to the scrolls. She had been an orphan, abandoned by all but her half brother, Steed. With that single task, I had given her reason enough to serve others. With that one thing, she had to understand. She was of the guard.

Her shoulders straight, she relayed the next message.

16

———

I sat on the edge of my bed, twirling the fey spike of ice, silver, blood, and bone in my hand. *A gift.* The words had begun to circle, as twisted in my mind as the strands that formed the pendant. I tried to force them away, to see the puzzle from a different angle, but they were only replaced with new chants and the dream of my mother, her warning that others would come and the other warning. The words were not of a vision, but a living nightmare: *Fellon Strago Dreg.*

I dropped the pendant on the side table and lay back to focus on something that was actually productive. I found my hawk and scanned the grounds, covering the mountain as best I could. No sentry was out of place, and there were no strangers with light hair, ice-wielding half-breeds, or a winged, shimmering fey army. I checked for smaller inconsistencies, anything that would indicate a problem. But I found nothing, and after a long while, the search became more of an easy glide, and I felt my body back in bed, relaxing with the task.

Chore accomplished, I thought I might be able to finally get some sleep. But just before I pulled from the hawk's mind, I spotted Steed in the yard. I drifted down, landing on the parapet to watch him prepare for the trip to Camber. His humming stopped the moment my talons touched stone. I smiled, though he would never see it. Wings stretched, I glided past him, not missing the way his shoulders tensed as the bird passed behind his back. He latched the pack tightly against his horse, resolutely not looking my way. I swung around to settle on a post opposite him. Stone-faced, he cinched Grey's pack to the second horse.

I waited him out, certain he couldn't keep his gaze from finding mine for long. When he at last broke, I held utterly still and winked. His expression was priceless. With a much-needed laugh, I returned to myself and kicked off my boots to finally get some rest.

It was the last I would have, because when I woke by the light of dawn, there was someone in my room.

Instinct tore at me to move, but I was trapped. Some unseen force had turned my limbs to lead, and I could do nothing but stare up into the face of a fey idol.

Veil held himself above me, his bare torso inches from mine and his fisted hands on either side of my immobile shoulders. I opened my mouth to curse, but my chest had the same heaviness as the rest of me, and my lungs seemed empty of air.

"You should have heeded my warning," he whispered so quietly I had to strain to hear. "You have disregarded the gift in your eagerness for vengeance."

I stared up at him, contemplating whether to hear him out or risk using magic. My chest rose and fell unbearably slowly beneath him. He glanced down.

Suddenly, as if he realized too late what my reaction to such a gesture would be, he was closer, peering into my eyes as he whispered, "No. Do not tempt me by using your power." He was so near that I could see his pulse hammering, but I didn't know whether it was fear or excitement. Sometimes with the fey, they were one and the same.

He shook his head. "Revenge tastes sweeter with time, my Freya." His gaze roamed my face, the dark strands of hair across my pillow, the bare flesh of my neck.

I narrowed my eyes at him and felt the thickness in my throat giving. It wouldn't be long before I was free of the dust. A few more minutes, and I would strangle him. Veil could see the change in me, and his mouth turned down in what I would have called a grimace on a less attractive man. His wings flicked once in frustration.

He had to have known he was out of time. I wondered who stood guard behind my closed door, unable to hear his words, no louder than a breath.

Veil's warm eyes, usually the color of honeyed tea in the morning light, met mine. But they were darker so close to my own, like maple sap over stone. I mentally shook myself, trying to work through the drug. It wasn't the same as Ruby's blend, but it wasn't right, either.

He waited for me to focus on him again. He wanted my attention. "If you do this," he warned, "you will leave me no choice."

He'd obviously found out about my plan to end Council. As far as warnings went, it was pretty clear. I wondered briefly why he'd taken such an un-fey-like action. And then I wondered how he could possibly smell so good. And then I remembered I hated fairies and wondered if I could drive the spiked pendant on the table through his side without risking my magic. The last thought made me smile, which clued both of us in on the fact that I'd regained muscle control.

We reacted at the same time, my head snapping forward to slam into his chin just as he moved back and off the bed. I flipped myself up to land beside the bed, but I wasn't fully recovered, and my legs crumpled beneath me. From nowhere, Veil grabbed my upper arm to steady me. My right fist swung across to strike him in the side. The scuffle lasted only a fraction of a second, but it was enough. Rhys burst through the door, and Veil was gone.

"Find Ruby!" I yelled. My voice was weak, but anger propelled the command with sufficient force. Rhys didn't stop to question it.

I stared at the floor, panting, struggling to manage the effects of dust and adrenaline. It seemed like only seconds later when Chevelle showed up, but it must have been longer, because my breathing was steady, and I could feel the tingle of my legs and the cold of the stone floor where I sat.

He surveyed the room, searching for any lingering threats, and I knew the instant his gaze found the glitter on the bed.

My head fell into my hands, a very unlordly gesture, and my shoulders shook with silent, frustrated cries.

Chevelle was staring at me. "What did he want?"

"To warn me." I took a deep breath before attempting to stand. "The fey don't want us to take out Council."

"Since when do the fey care about elven politics?"

I shrugged. "I don't know, but if they know we're coming, then Council does."

"It doesn't matter," Chevelle said. He stepped closer. "Tell me what he said."

I took another deep breath.

He waited.

"'If you do this'"—I sighed—"'you leave me no choice.'"

Chevelle's fist slammed into the bedpost, splintering the wood to pieces.

"It has to mean they have always cared about our affairs," I said. "But the power was shared before, split between the North and the villages."

He didn't respond, staring blankly across the room through the empty space where the bedpost had been.

"So if we remove the remaining leaders of Council," I continued, "then I alone control the realm."

Chevelle turned his gaze to me.

"And if I control the realm"—I paused to swallow, my throat still thick from dust—"then they will call war. And Veil will take me. If I don't find a way to manage this power, then I can't fight him."

I could see the anger building through Chevelle's entire body, but I couldn't prevent myself from finishing.

"I will avenge my mother. I will right the wrong done to all of the north. The fey will not cow me into submission. We will leave at dawn as planned."

It felt a little like a speech, and I should have been ashamed for making it. Chevelle knew exactly what Council had done to the

North. He knew every single person who'd been slaughtered in the massacre, and he knew how it had affected the ones who lived. He didn't need to be lectured on honor or principle.

His shoulders rose very slowly in an effort to remain steady with each breath. "Vengeance can wait."

His words tasted far too much like Veil's warning, and the fury of his attack, as I lay helplessly in my own bed, went through me. "No," I hissed. "I will not be controlled."

I had meant by the fey. I had meant by Asher. But it hadn't come across as such.

"Curse you, Frey." Chevelle's voice was pure rage, and I almost stepped back from him. As if he sensed it, he moved forward, daring me.

We stood inches apart, both of us furious, both struggling to retain control, when suddenly Ruby was beside us, frantic.

"Are you hurt? What happened? What did Veil do to you?"

I shook myself as my mind caught up with events. I stared down at our bare feet on the stone floor.

"Ruby," I said, "you have webbed toes."

She shoved me back into a chair with unnecessary force. "She's been dusted," she announced with more than a little irritation, and I laughed. It might have been dust or madness, but it didn't much matter.

At the exchange, Chevelle seemed to deflate a bit. And then, as if realizing he had work to do, he walked from the room, leaving me with Rhys and Ruby. That only left Rider to help him search the grounds, so I leaned back in the chair as Ruby fluttered about me, making what I hoped was a remedy, and found my hawk. I doubted we would see anything. Veil had likely come alone, and he had a talent for hiding.

It was no accident that he'd come when the others were gone. He'd taken his best chance, and he'd beaten my guard and bested all of us by sneaking into my bedchamber.

The hawk dove through the castle window and rose above the

yard, searching. I had an irrational thought that it hated fairies too and wished the dust would let go already.

Ruby was mumbling as she worked, complaining about the fey and their gifts, and I came back, opening my eyes to stare at her. Her gaze was narrowed on the pendant—the gift—atop the side table.

"That's it," I said.

She jerked, curls bouncing, then shrugged my outburst off as an effect of the dust.

"No," I defended. "The gift. She kept saying 'gift,' not offering. It isn't about the pendant. It's about the boy. The silver boy."

Ruby stared blankly at me as if deciding whether I was babbling or if she should be attempting to decipher my words.

I pointed to the pendant. "Four strands. The fey call them 'gifts,' not talents or abilities. Silver and ice. That leaves two more. Blood and bone. He's got four children remaining." I shook my head. "No, three now. We killed the boy."

Her mouth came open, her brows raised, then her face fell. Once she understood, she was speechless.

"Ruby," I snapped, "give me that tea and go figure out what the devil blood and bone means."

She barked a laugh. "It isn't tea." She shrugged at the question in my expression. "Veil doesn't work that way. It's more of a… skin rinse."

I opened my mouth to reply just as Ruby closed one eye in a wince and turned her cheek to me. Warm, cloudy liquid splashed into my face. Instantly, the effects of the drug cleared but were replaced with utter shock at her action. She dropped the cup, putting both hands up in surrender as she backed out of the room.

"It had to be done," she promised.

I was still staring at the open door when Rhys finally laughed.

17

Finn and Keaton had still not returned. Ruby and I sat in the study with Rhys and Rider, poring over fey scrolls and books. I'd been able to find a few notes hidden in Asher's private study, but it didn't look as if we were going to find anything useful. Anvil was due back by evening, as were Steed and Grey, so we held a sliver of hope that they would be able to offer some help. I hadn't seen Chevelle all day.

Ruby slammed a book shut in frustration. "Even if we find the answer, even if we know this kid's 'gift,' it still doesn't solve the problem."

We all stopped working to give her our full attention, though I had a feeling we were just looking for an excuse to take a break.

"If we don't know who's pushing them to attack Frey, then we don't know how to find them. If we find one, or even two, we still have to find the others. We still have to discover who's plotting against us."

I had to fight a smile at her use of "us."

Rider held up a finger. "I believe it is a mistake to consider them children. I understand Asher may have been fostering this strategy before even Francine or Eliza were born. Simply because the one who created silver was a boy does not mean we should expect the same of the others."

Rhys nodded. "If I were the influencer of these heirs, I would send the weakest first."

Ruby's eyes went wide. Apparently, she'd underestimated the cunning of the brothers.

"You are right, though." Rider twirled a quill in his hand as he thought. "We do need to find the source."

"I feel like we're beating our heads against the same rock," I complained.

"At least we know it isn't the fey," Ruby said with mock cheer.

No, I thought, *they want either to keep us balanced or to own us all.* With a sigh, I returned to the passage I'd been reading on rare fey talents.

The fey liked to keep records of other people but preferred no written history of themselves. I had always assumed that was why so many fey tales were spoken. And they surely considered the embellishments that came along with stories passed by word of mouth a bonus. But I supposed it was safer that way as well. *How much had Ruby learned from her mother's diary?*

As I scanned the pages, I recalled the fey visits when I'd been bound in the village. They'd caused no ruckus among the light elves, but they'd only been allowed to come one at a time, occasionally in pairs, to study in the libraries. And if I really thought about it, I had no idea whether they'd caused trouble in the village. For all I knew, they'd been the ones messing with the council documents, not Fannie—Fannie, who had burned that village to the ground.

I hadn't dreamed much of Fannie since regaining myself. My new nightmares were of my mother. But the flames had been real, a memory instead of a vision, and they were so much more disturbing with added details like the taste of smoke and the scent of blood. Every night, the screams of the slaughter tore through me, along with the sound of my mother's crazed laughter as they burned her, the pain ripping my own chest as I stood helplessly and was dragged away, and the icy water pulling me under, stealing my breath.

Chevelle had held me back, the only thing that had saved me that day. He'd pulled me into the water, and I had wanted to scream. Liquid filled my lungs, choking me, and I might have wanted to be swallowed by that darkness, except for the fire of vengeance that boiled in my blood.

Ruby had been reading through one of the books from Asher's private study, and she went still as she flipped a page. I glanced up at her.

"Frey," she started but didn't continue when she saw my face. She wordlessly slid the open book to me. On the yellowed pages lay a tiny scrap of paper with three words: *Fellon Strago Dreg.* A ribbon of blue silk was attached to the corner.

I stared at it for a long moment before sliding the silk between my fingers. Nothing on the pages of the book was relevant to the message. Someone must have intercepted the note and simply tucked it away as if it hadn't mattered.

"What does it mean?" Ruby whispered.

I glanced at the table covered in documents and ancient tomes. "Nothing." I shook my head, coming out of the stupor. "Nothing, Ruby. Let's take a break." The light through the windows said it was late afternoon. "We've missed lunch. I'm sure we could all do with something to eat."

I spared one last look at the note before sliding it into my pocket. *Fellon Strago Dreg.* It was as if the words were following me, warning me.

By evening, I'd done all I could to prepare for our departure. Anvil had returned, but he hadn't been able to find anything useful in regard to either the fey plans or the attacks. When I'd told him about Veil's visit, he'd been so angry that the hair on my head tingled with electricity before he left me to "go over some final details with the patrols." The sky lit two shades brighter not long after that.

Steed and Grey had also returned, convinced that no one from us to Camber had seen anything out of the ordinary. We went over the final details for the morning, and when Steed and Ruby got into a heated argument about some traps she'd left set in her Camber house, Grey took the opportunity to discuss our purpose.

"They are all still mourning," he said. "The shock of your return and the stir over your recent actions... Those have only been a distraction." He absently ran a hand over his jaw. "They need this as desperately as you. We have all lost so much."

I glanced at Steed, whose own mother had been killed in the massacre. It had driven his father so mad that he'd fallen under the thrall of a fire fairy.

Grey sighed. "You are doing right, Frey. And when it's done, they will follow you."

I bit my cheek to stop myself from pointing out that the entire venture would be wasted if one of Asher's progeny found me.

"Thank you, Grey." I squeezed his arm, grateful for his words, and knew that Chevelle had not chosen him merely for his connection with Ruby.

"Have it your way, then." Steed seethed as he strode from the room with less than his usual cool.

"I will!" Ruby yelled at his back.

When she realized Grey and I were staring at her, she threw her hands up in disgust. "I don't know what's with him lately." She shook her head as she glanced back at the empty doorway. "He's so jumpy, always looking over his shoulder. You'd swear someone was stalking him or something."

A choked cough escaped me, but neither seemed to know why. I simply kept watching Ruby.

Grey tilted his head. "You did leave traps for him, Ruby."

She let out a disgusted sound. "Not for *him*." Her hands moved to her hips. "Besides, he should have known I would have set them."

Grey shrugged. "Well, he found them, regardless."

The corner of her mouth raised in a snarl, and I was suddenly laughing. Grey turned to stare at me, and I shook my head. "I think I need some sleep."

I excused myself and walked the corridor at an easy pace while I considered the coming event. We had given Council time to regroup. It would be a fair fight. I had confidence in my guard, but I couldn't bear the idea of losing any of them. The thought crossed my mind that I could leave and live out my years running with the wolves, but I wouldn't leave—not my guard, and not the North. Grey was right. They needed it as much as I did. I would never really rest until I'd quenched the flames of my nightmares.

I hadn't been back to my perch since the fey had nearly knocked me from the roof, so I found myself standing in the throne room, staring across the empty space. Mine had been an ugly childhood, with Chevelle the only bright spot. Asher had done all that he could to take that from me, to force me into something I'd never wanted, to secure my place as his second. And there I stood, alone on the throne and separated from Chevelle. Even in death, Asher had succeeded.

I took a deep breath as I sat, curling my fingers into the ornate carvings on the arms of the chair. My eyes fell closed, and I found my hawk to take flight, gliding over the mountain one last time before morning. Darkness had begun to fall, and torches lit the grounds like fireflies in a Southern meadow. Nightfall brought the revelers out in the towns and rogue camps, but the sentries were still on duty.

The circles became smaller as I scanned the castle then finally dropped through a window and into the east wing. I opened my eyes as we came to the corridor outside the throne room and watched the hawk fly in under its own authority to land on the stand beside me.

I smiled at the sizeable bird, and it cocked its head with a quick twist.

"Someday, I will name you," I said, gently stroking the feathers along the back of its neck. It shuffled closer, its talons claiming the soft wood of the perch. We sat so for a long while, not counting time as we relaxed together, I as unthinking as the bird.

Finally, it stretched its wings before bringing them back together, shaking as it settled into a solid form, its neck disappearing into the mass of feathers, its eyes winking shut. "I agree," I murmured, knowing I needed sleep even though the time with the bird had been more restful than any night of the past weeks. I stepped down from the chair, aware once again that it was a throne, and headed to my room.

I walked through the door, tossed my scabbard and sword on a side table, and kicked off my boots. When I rose back to standing, I found Chevelle across from me against the far wall. For a fraction of a second, my heart quit. When it started back up again, I knew I was flushed.

Embarrassment at being caught off guard and frightened made me irritated. "What are you doing?"

His face didn't change, though I knew what he was thinking. Not a day ago, I'd been confronted with a fey idol there. "I will be placing protections on the room."

My anger grew. "What?"

Chevelle remained as he was, but I saw for the first time that his posture was set for a fight. "It is the only way—"

My glare cut him off. "You will not cast on or near me."

"I will protect your room," he answered levelly.

"Then put a guard outside."

"A guard outside does no good. He's proven that."

"No spells," I repeated.

"You'll not sleep unprotected."

"Then I'll not sleep alone," I shot back.

I had answered without thinking, but once the words were out, they hung between us, taking on a new meaning. And the longer they hovered there, the stronger that meaning became. He stared at me, his gaze unflinching as I stood motionless, afraid even to breathe.

I knew we shouldn't. There was good reason not to. I was sure of it, even if I'd forgotten exactly what that reason was. A flash of memory hit me: the taste of him, his bare skin beneath my hands, the unbearable feeling of being so near him and still wanting him closer. I forced myself to stop, but the hunger in his eyes intensified, as if he knew what I was thinking. He was beginning to look as if he might lose control. I swallowed hard, trying to find a way out, certain that I needed to.

It wasn't clear to me what caused him to break, but he was suddenly moving, and the room seemed to shudder with magic. Power slammed into me the instant before he reached me, and I almost managed a word. But when he finally touched me, when his hands came around me and his lips crushed mine, even the notion of speaking was gone.

18

Hours later, I couldn't say I regretted it. My head lay on his chest as his hand slid slowly up the skin of my arm and across my shoulder. He gently drew my hair away to bare my neck, and then his fingers retraced the line.

"Do you feel any different?" I asked.

His chest rumbled beneath my cheek with a sort of chuckle, and I turned to examine his face. He stared at me for a long moment as if finally understanding something important. "You don't know, do you?"

"What?"

Eyes never leaving mine, he let out a slow breath. "We have always been bound, Freya."

I stared at him, unable to process his words.

The corner of his mouth turned up in a gentle, sympathetic smile, the kind one gives a small child when they couldn't possibly understand something larger than their world. But it wasn't offensive. It was beautiful and filled with affection.

"The bond," he explained. "We created it without intent, very long ago."

I was pretty sure my expression fell somewhere between shock and confusion.

His fingers continued to trail the line of my back. "I think it is usually created while coupling"—he smiled a slow, sexy smile and tilted his head up to place a kiss on my forehead—"because that is when two are the closest. Their magic, their bodies, their... love." He kissed me again more passionately, and I had to focus hard on what he was saying.

I sat up, which did nothing to discourage him. "But that can't be right," I said numbly, searching for an argument.

His gaze drifted up to meet mine. The hand that had been tracing lazy circles on my skin stilled.

"The elders," I explained, "they all said it would change us, keep us from being true to anything but ourselves. We would hold our union above all others."

He raised my hand for a kiss. "Do you mean abandoning the throne to run away with me?" he asked, as if inquiring whether I'd like a glass of wine. He leaned forward and kissed my forearm. "Or waiting for you when you were trapped... searching for a way to release you... risking all for your return?" His lips trailed farther up my arm, pausing only as he glanced at me once more. "Keeping me close to you, all the while knowing it could cost you your life?"

We were already bound.

For as long as I could remember, I had always wanted him.

He was tied to me.

We were bound.

The idea was overwhelming, but suddenly I couldn't spare it another thought, because his lips had reached my own, and I was once again lost to the outside world.

TIME WAS nonexistent until the shuffle of boots in the corridor pulled me from my contented trance. I sat up suddenly, recalling our plan. "What time is it?"

Chevelle dragged me back against him, tilting his head to place slow kisses on my neck.

It almost worked.

A noise farther down the corridor reminded me that we were late. I pressed back far enough to kiss him thoroughly then freed myself of the bed. His face fell. I smiled.

I was dressed well before he was, securing my scabbard as he laced his shirt. He was in no hurry, but I knew he wouldn't ask me to postpone again—not after our argument, and not after last night. We would see vengeance. That at least would be done.

He sat to fasten his boots, and I watched him as I thought again of his promise. *We have always been bound.* My mind had been fighting for some way to dispute the idea but could only come up with evidence to corroborate it.

Something had always called me to Chevelle. I knew, but I'd simply never understood. I couldn't have. No one could have.

He raised his head, and suddenly I was staring into his depthless sapphire eyes. My stomach tightened, and I hurriedly turned to open the door. A hand on my shoulder stopped me, and he pulled my hair to the side to place one last kiss on my neck. Wordlessly, we walked from the room, with Chevelle settling his leather breastplate as we went.

We found the others in the study, the light spilling through the windows making obvious that it wasn't exactly dawn. *Close enough*, I thought, glancing around to be certain everyone was accounted for.

"Steed is readying the horses," Ruby supplied.

I nodded. How she or any of the others managed not to comment or at least betray some emotion about Chevelle and I was beyond me.

"We are set to go," Anvil agreed.

I supposed that was how they'd managed, knowing what we were about to set out to do. "Then let us go," I said. "For the North."

A harmony of agreement met my oath, and we made our way to the yard as one, a small army by all outward appearances. Ruby's curls were smoothed back, a braid from each temple meeting at the base of her neck to form a knot. She had forgone the silver—she and each of the guard had donned black uniforms, our insignias marking the shoulder clasps of their dark cloaks. Only the shine of Rhys's and Rider's hair stood out among us.

As we walked from the castle, my eyes met Steed's as he waited with the horses. I'd barely had time to process his expression before the sentry called out.

All eyes fell on Edan as he sprinted across the yard. "The fey are attacking Camber, as many as seventy, no structure"—he paused to take a breath as he reached us—"just rioting."

We stood in shocked silence for one moment before the lot of us swung into motion. Chevelle clapped the sentry on the shoulder before he mounted, and without another word, all eight of us ran our horses through the gates. Steed took the lead, setting a fierce pace and keeping to the path.

I couldn't believe I'd neglected to sweep the skies that morning, knowing that the fey were aware of our plans. I fell in behind Grey and dropped quickly into my horse's mind, urging him to keep pace before finding the hawk. It was perched on a castle wall, tearing meat from a rodent beneath its claw, and I had to force it to flight.

I had intended to make a broad sweep of Camber, but when it took wing, everything fell apart. I froze at what I saw then heard the clatter of rocks the instant before I opened my own eyes to find that Chevelle and Rider had been forced from the path, nearly tumbling into my horse when we went from a full run to an abrupt stop without warning.

I swallowed hard, unsure what to do as they stared at me, waiting. I knew we shouldn't split up. It could have been another trick. The elves at Camber could handle the fey and would likely have done so before we arrived. But it wasn't right to leave them to it, either. I cursed myself for not having more animals at the castle. It would have been all I needed to resolve the issue in a matter of minutes. But recruiting the cats had ended badly, and I'd not wanted a repeat.

"Frey," Chevelle called, and I grimaced, knowing I could wait no longer.

"Council trackers are stealing up the mountain. They are almost to the castle." I glanced at the others, who had backtracked when they'd heard the commotion of the sudden stop. "Anvil, Chevelle, with me. The rest of you, go on. We will join you as soon as the castle is secure."

No one looked happy with the idea, but they nodded their assent.

"Rhys," I added, surprised at the intensity of my own voice, "save one for me."

They turned back to the path, resuming the run with a new drive. I dropped from my horse and ran, knowing Chevelle and Anvil would follow. They were faster, but I knew the secret paths and tunnels. We hadn't ridden far before I'd found the intruders, but I hoped that any spotters thought we were well gone.

I cut from the path and through a narrow pass between boulders, climbed a rock wall, and slid behind a tattered group of thorn bushes before stopping to check the trackers' progress.

"There are four," I whispered. "One is scaling the north wall. Two outside the east wing—they appear to be waiting for a signal. The fourth is farther down, hiding among the rocks."

The instant my eyes opened, I was running again, darting through crevices and climbing over stone. I would lose the tracker once he was inside the castle walls, but I couldn't stay with him and keep moving. I had to figure out where he was going, what he wanted within. They knew we were gone, surely. They had waited for the opportunity. But I couldn't figure out why.

I slipped on a loose rock and narrowly caught myself before falling. Cool moss beneath my palm signaled we were nearly there, and I glanced up, searching the wall for the entrance. I nodded confidently, and Chevelle pulled a dagger from his belt as we began again. We were through the entry and sprinting down the dark corridor when I realized where the tracker was headed.

"The vault," I said, breathless from running.

Anvil cursed. "I'll take the two on the east wing. We'll catch the fourth before he swings back around. There's nowhere for him to go."

I nodded. "Here." It was the only warning I gave before throwing myself through the end wall, where the corridor turned. I felt Chevelle and Anvil falter at my use of magic, but they recovered quickly, Anvil splitting from us toward the east wing as we kept on for Asher's vault.

The hallway was too quiet. The pad of our boots seemed to thunder in the silence. But that didn't matter as soon as Chevelle busted open the door to the vault. The seal had been broken, so he must have expected the tracker to replace it with a new one.

I couldn't worry about who the tracker had killed to get there or where the fallen might be, because once the door was open, flames burst into the hallway. They died down after a moment, and I could see Chevelle again, forced to the opposite side of the opening.

He gave me a look that said, "I thought you said they were trackers."

I turned my palms up. They had been dressed like trackers, and they had moved like trackers. Someone with such power shouldn't have bothered learning stealth.

The wall beside Chevelle blew out, large chunks of stone flying into the corridor, and he jumped back, pressed even farther from me. *Had Council been cross-training their strongest fighters all along, or had we given them too much time to regroup?* The next blast opened the wall beside me, and I leapt out of the way, flinching as pieces of rock pelted my side.

I glanced back at Chevelle, whose expression left no doubt that he was about to pummel the nasty interloper. But just as he shifted to move on the entrance, a cyclone of paper, Asher's precious documents, swirled into the corridor. I bit down hard. It was just one man. We were wasting time.

I stepped in front of the opening in one swift move, just as Chevelle did the same. The documents parted—Chevelle's magic—and the tracker's arms and legs broke at the biceps and thighs—mine. He fell back against a shelf, gritted his teeth, and threw a vicious strike toward me, which met my power and dissolved to nothing. He threw another and then another, to no avail. I stepped forward, ready to question him, and recognized his face: Archer Lake.

He smiled at my recognition. It was an ugly, hate-filled flash of teeth, and I wanted to destroy it.

Flames returned with the memory. I felt the heat surround us as I watched my mother burn. He had been the one who'd finally overtaken her. They had all killed her, but Archer Lake had possessed the strength to overwhelm her, a legendary energy. He had burned her.

And he had taken pleasure in it.

I vowed to make him suffer—*he will blister and burn in agony*. My dark hair whipped my face as I drew air into the room to feed the flame. *He will boil. He will suffer.* He threw another blast of power toward me, but I couldn't even feel it anymore. The collision was nothing. *He* was nothing.

"Frey!" Chevelle's voice cut through the anger, and I was startled by the inferno. We were surrounded by flame.

Had he been yelling? I glanced at him beside me, unburned but clearly in pain, and shook myself. The fire extinguished while I let out a long breath, as if blowing out a flickering candle, and I released the magic. My eyes connected with Chevelle's, and we stood for a moment, understanding passing between us. He was right. We had to get to Anvil.

I looked one last time at the man who had killed my mother. He was badly burned but seemed relieved, as if he had been saved.

I shook my head in disbelief then severed the large vessels of his heart. He wouldn't die slowly enough, but he would die.

19

We found Anvil among a pile of rubble that used to be the east wall. He was winded, and between that and the chaos of the stone, I knew the two there had been no mere trackers, either.

"What happened?" I asked, glancing at the destruction surrounding us.

He shook his head. "Not trackers. They were waiting for whoever was inside to return." He took a deep breath. "They were going to ruin what they could of the castle and grounds."

I eyed the remaining section of wall. They hadn't done a bad job of it.

A few sentries were running toward us, finally aware of the attack. I couldn't fault them, as it had all happened rather quickly. Chevelle gave them a brief explanation and instructed them where to search for the fallen and what to repair first. I took the opportunity to find my hawk.

When I opened my eyes again, Anvil had recovered. "Where is the other one?"

"Hunkered down on the northeast crag. No doubt he heard

this"—I gestured toward the wall—"so he must have known better than to run."

"Or he has some agenda," Chevelle said.

I shrugged. "We can find them here or at the temple. It will end the same."

From the east tower, a sentry called out that he'd found a fallen comrade. The three of us looked toward the sound.

Chevelle's voice cut through the silence that followed. "Then let us end it."

We moved swiftly across the yard and down the jagged black rock to where I'd seen the Council member.

As we neared the target, Anvil shouted, "Show yourself."

There was no response, so we stepped carefully closer, the three of us spread out along the mountainside. I could barely see the colors of his robe where he'd concealed himself, and a surge of apprehension prickled my skin. It felt like a trap.

"Hold," Chevelle said from across the rock.

I glanced at him then heard the chanting. It wasn't fear prickling my skin—it was the edge of a spell. I stepped back involuntarily.

"You cannot protect yourself," Anvil called to the mass of rock. "Will you go out like a coward?"

The chanting grew louder, and I had to fight not to move back again.

Anvil's gaze fell on Chevelle, who appeared to be silently questioning whether he recognized the words. Chevelle grimaced, the gesture conveying that we would not be able to cross the bounds of the protection spell. He glanced at me, and I immediately shook my head. There was no way I was going to let him battle a Council member with spellcasting.

I sat on the rock behind me, careful to secure my foothold among the looser pieces below my feet, and closed my eyes. It took longer than I would have liked, but I tried to focus solely on bringing the animal in with as much speed as possible instead of thinking about the attack on Camber or that I should be with my guard, not there in the broken shards of the crag with a single council member.

The cat had been hunting at the base of the cliffs, so it came from below us, its agile form moving swiftly up the treacherous granite to the saw-toothed rock where we waited.

From that vantage point, I could see the man—it was Clay of Rothegarr. He had not bothered protecting the back side of his enclosure.

His face changed into some mixture of wonder and dread when he saw the golden fur of the mountain lion rushing toward him. He hurried to defend himself, drawing a thorn bush toward him and heaving as much energy as he could into expanding its size. The cat struck, clamping its strong jaw around his leg, and I could feel the muscles of his thigh tearing under the biting grip as he struggled against it. The cat hadn't been able to reach his neck in time, but instinct would kick in, and it would wait for him to die, never easing its grip until it was over.

I felt my own body jerk as the thorns pierced the cat's hide. Through its eyes, I hadn't seen the vines growing, only the blood as it poured from the councilman's wound and bubbled up beneath our muzzle. We bit harder, twisting and tearing, and lost our footing as the vines pushed us from the ground. A thorn ran through the pad of our paw and broke through the top, and we yowled before striking again, but we missed, our jaw snapping shut against air as the vines caught our neck and held us in place. We struggled, furious and desperate, but the tree only tightened around us.

A hand on my shoulder, a word in my ear brought me back to my own body, gasping for air. Right—it was the cat, not me.

"Can you get my lion out?" I whispered to Chevelle.

He knelt beside me. "Not without casting."

I swallowed hard, my throat dry, then shook my head. It was too risky.

A high-pitched cry escaped the cat, which was wounded and trapped within the thorn tree, and I acted without thought, placing my hands to the ground in front of me and cursing the council member to death.

"Frey," Chevelle warned from beside me, moving to stand as the ground shook beneath us.

Rock crashed into rock as it tumbled down the steep mountainside, and I could hear Anvil swear as he and Chevelle worked to protect us from the avalanche. But I couldn't stop. It was all wrong. We shouldn't have been there, trying to drive out one remaining nuisance instead of fighting against Council in a proper clash. We had given them time to regroup, and they were fighting as dirty as the fey, who were, as we sat there, attacking Camber. We were being assailed from all sides when we should have been avenging the massacre, setting the wrong to right.

"Frey!" Chevelle's voice was commanding as he grabbed me by the shoulders and hoisted me to standing. But I didn't fight him. I was done.

The mountain fell quiet as the final rock settled, and Chevelle spun me to face him. He was angry, and I knew he intended to ask me what I thought I was doing, but whatever he saw in my expression stopped him.

"Is the casting broken?" I asked in a lifeless voice.

He nodded. We'd not been able to use magic within the boundaries of the spell, but the rock had made it through. Clay of Rothegarr was dead.

"Will you get my cat? We need to go."

He released my arms, and I closed my eyes to call our horses to the castle. Rock clattered as Chevelle cleared the debris surrounding the thorn tree. I dropped quickly to the mind of the cat, willing it not to hurt Chevelle as he freed it.

We needed to get to Camber. We needed to end it. All of it.

I GLANCED at the sky as we rode for Camber. The sun was low on the horizon, though we'd been running since we left the castle. Chevelle had carried the mountain lion to the yard, where he'd left instructions to build an enclosure for the animal and tend to it as well as possible until Ruby had returned. We'd barely spoken since, the rhythmic thump of horses' hooves on the path the only sound until we neared the bounds of Camber.

"Is it safe?" Chevelle asked from his place behind me.

The heavens were empty, likely due to the fighting, so I drew a red-tail from its perch in the safety of a black spruce. There was nothing in the outlying crevices and copses and nothing on the paths into town. There was nothing at all until my circles brought me closer to the epicenter, where smoke and dust rose in caustic clouds above Camber.

"It's over," I said, opening my eyes again to clear skies and order. "And I don't see anything lying in wait for us."

When we finally reached town, most of the major damage was restored. The ground was littered with fairy dust and bits of wing, pebbles, and ash. A dozen busted wine casks were scattered in front of the Kraig residence, and the deep-purple fluid splashed beneath our horses' hooves, where it ran in rivulets over the dark stone path, trickling halfway through town before waning to nothing. Troughs were overturned, crowns of houses were lying in rubble on front porches, and horses were painted with berry juice and shimmer. But the fires were no longer burning, and the floods had been diverted. No bodies lay in the street.

Rider met us near the center of town. I could tell by his appearance that what we encountered had not been the case when they'd arrived.

"I suggest making your way to Ruby's house," he said. "It appears her protections worked quite nicely to deter the fey." He glanced around, clearly not wanting to voice the real reason in front of a crowd. "Rhys waits for you there."

I nodded, understanding his hesitation. They'd saved one, and by the looks of the elves here, they wanted no part of it.

"Is anyone hurt?" I asked.

"Ruby is tending them," he said. "Seems they've taken to her, here at least."

I didn't conceal my uncertainty.

"We have everything else under control."

He was right, but it wasn't easy to walk away.

Rider glanced past me to Anvil. "What did you get into?"

I followed his gaze to find Anvil's forearm caked with blood. I hadn't even noticed.

Anvil waved it off. "They weren't trackers. Sent some muscle to tear up things while we were down there looking for them."

I wondered briefly if there was more truth to his words than he realized. Council might not have been at the temple at all, but I didn't mention it, for it was no time for supposition. Chevelle and I left Anvil and Rider to exchange stories and assist the others. As we rode through Camber, the passing elves stopped to watch, a mixture of emotions meeting our presence.

Ruby's home stood out among the rest, clean of assault, and I had to wonder if it had been her protections, as Rider had suggested, or if the fey had done it intentionally.

We stopped in front of the house, where another horse stood, drinking from the only unmolested water trough in town. I stepped down, staring at the poor beast as it puffed into the water. A smattering of small handprints painted its rib cage, while its mane stood in thick, gooey spikes. I shook my head—I would never understand their fixation with horses.

Chevelle waited for me at the door, where I took one deep breath before nodding for him to go on. We slipped in quickly, and I dreaded what we would find on the other side.

Ruby's living area seemed smaller, though I couldn't say whether it was owing to my memory or the pale-blue fairy that hovered above the couch, flittering nervously from side to side.

"Myst," I sighed, undecided if I was relieved.

"Lord Freya," she crooned, "so good to have a friend here." Her expression was hopeful until she saw that mine did not change, and then her shoulders fell.

I moved forward, taking a seat across from her as she dropped gracefully onto the couch. Her feet never touched the floor as her slender legs curled up beneath the wispy fabric of her skirts. The material would have been too fragile for most fey, but Myst was more than a few decades old, not that anyone could tell by looking. The fey were ageless, growing to full maturity within a couple of years and remaining as such until death, which more often than not came by some means other than old age.

I glanced briefly at Rhys, who appeared to be in fair condition. Myst was exceedingly well behaved, given her current predicament. Compared to what she would have found outside, escape would have been far worse than anything we could do to her.

She waited for me to speak, though anyone could see it pained her to stay still. One corner of her pale bottom lip was tucked under her teeth, and she picked at the poppy seeds detailing her skirt, but her colorless eyes remained on me.

"Tell me you're not in league with Grand Council," I said.

She laughed, but it took on an uneasy stutter when she realized I was serious.

I leaned forward. "Why are you here? All of you?"

"We were supposed to have free rein once Council was removed." Her gaze flicked to Chevelle then back to me. "You know, before someone called war."

I glared at her. We'd not even left the castle before they'd attacked, let alone given them reason to declare war.

She shrugged. "We got a little excited."

I stood, suddenly no longer able to bear being in the room.

She stood as well, her slender, silk-covered feet landing noiselessly on stone. "What about me?"

I smiled. "You are free to go."

20

She wouldn't leave, I knew that, but I had to get away from her. So I was standing in Ruby's tiny guest room, staring blankly at my reflection in the large, ornate mirror when Chevelle came in.

"You were right," I said numbly, unable to look at him as he approached to stand behind me.

He didn't speak.

"I was about to cause a war. A war we couldn't win." I looked down at my hands, feeling helpless at my lack of control. "I nearly set into motion a conflict that would all but hand our world to the fey."

His fingers slipped against my waist, and the simple touch brought if not relief, reassurance. I turned to him, sliding my own hand up his arm, but when I finally looked into the deep sapphire-blue of his eyes, all I could think was, *What now*?

"Freya," he started.

I cut him off. "What is it?"

He held up a scroll with his other hand. "A messenger was here."

I took two sideways steps to sit on the bed, not positive I could remain standing when he told me who'd been lost. "Who?"

"Two watchmen, a sentry, and the keep guard. The sentry was of Camber, and the second messenger is with his family now."

They had killed four, masquerading as trackers, sneaking onto the grounds and taking down anyone who'd seen them. Archer had attempted to steal the casting ledgers from the vault while the rest lay in wait to burn and raze the castle, I suddenly knew.

I was abruptly standing again. Chevelle saw my fury, but he didn't attempt to calm it. We would have to answer for it—if not now, then soon. The realization eased my temper enough that I could at least consider our options.

I began pacing. Asher had never allowed me to pace. It was a weakness, he'd said. But he was dead.

"I should see the family," I said, an amorphous plan forming that was based purely on faith—but it was a plan, and it was the only one I had.

Chevelle nodded. "As will I. Burne has a grown son. His wife is Camren. She's known for her talent with wind."

I came to a standstill, straightening my scabbard before gripping the hilt of my sword. "Yes, we will see her first." My eyes met Chevelle's but before I could decide whether to tell him my plan, there was a crash from the front room.

I bit down a growl, muttering, "I hate fairies," for what was almost certainly not the last time as I opened the door to the living area.

A pale-blue fairy was perched on the arm of the sofa by the tips of her toes. Her hands were behind her back, and she wore an all-too-innocent smile as she greeted me in singsong: "Frey-a."

I grimaced at her as I asked Rider, "What did she break?"

He nodded toward the corner, where a gooey mess oozed from broken chunks of what I assumed was once a clay pot. "Not sure, exactly, but it smells like the back end of a goat."

Myst grinned wider, as if her perfect teeth could charm me into friendship.

"Clean it up, and I will let you live."

She started to laugh but caught herself, clearly unsure whether

I'd been joking. Her wings flicked, shaking silvery dust onto the couch, and then she moved to pick up the mess.

I headed to Ruby's room to locate a scroll then stood frozen in the doorway. The entire room was covered in a thick white powder. "What happened?" I managed, choking on fumes even though the dust had long since settled.

"Oh," Rider said, "that was Ruby."

I turned to stare at him.

"One of the traps she'd laid before leaving."

I pointed a thumb over my shoulder, my face blank as his words sank in.

"Yep, that's the one that got Steed."

The laugh that escaped morphed into a cough from the vapor, and I closed the door without having stepped a foot inside. My eyes were tearing up. No wonder he'd been so angry. "Any chance either of you have a scroll and a quill?"

"Here," Myst called from the corner, "there are some in this side table."

I glanced at Chevelle, who had the same irritated expression I imagined I was wearing, and headed toward the table.

Myst stood. "And a jar of ink there." She pointed toward a row of shelves built into the south wall, where it appeared she had been meddling when she'd knocked down the clay pot. "It's the blue one." Nose scrunched, she bent back to her task.

When I pulled a scroll from the drawer, she glanced up at me, her eyebrows dancing up and down. "Writing a missive?"

I narrowed my eyes on her, and she smiled sweetly before wiping the remaining goo from the floor.

Sitting in the chair opposite the couch, I slid a small table to me and laid out the scroll. Myst set the jar of ink beside it without a word and moved across from me, curling her feet under and resting her elbows on a couch pillow in her lap while she watched. It wouldn't matter—she would read it as soon as she was out of my sight, but I took the time to glare at her anyway, blowing the bangs out of my eyes as I looked up from the table at her. She didn't seem to mind, bringing her tiny fists up to rest under her chin as she waited. Her soft blue-gray locks fell forward in loose waves, and the color reminded me of the sky just before rain. It seemed apt, considering the storm I was about to unleash.

I had the first line down when Ruby came in. Her face was smudged with dust and blood, and fuzzy tendrils of red curled around it where they'd escaped her braid. She stared blankly at the blue fairy roosting on her couch, and then at me.

"Is everything well, Ruby?" I asked.

"I've done all I can." She sighed. "I'm going to clean up."

I nodded, hoping she remembered the explosion of powder waiting in her room.

I was on the last line when Grey came in. I glanced up just in time to see his eyes meet Myst's. She let out a cat like "reouw" sound and sat straight up, looking at him intently. Grey, along with the rest of us, simply stared in open shock at her display.

When Ruby appeared from nowhere and leapt at her, Myst only had time to half turn toward her as she collided into the fairy, and both rolled across the floor beside me. I heard an oath, recognized it as Grey, and realized he'd joined the fracas, struggling unsuccessfully to pull Ruby from her victim. Another curse flew out as Myst scratched his cheek in an attempt to gouge his eye, and I slowly became aware that I and the remaining members of the guard were simply watching as a bizarre scuffle ensued. Before I was able to react, Ruby drove her forehead into Myst's petite nose and flipped her face-first onto the ground. My mouth popped open as Ruby pinned her, pulled Myst's wrists together behind her back, and leaned forward to whisper into a long, pointed ear.

Whatever she said made Grey flush as red as one of Ruby's silk scarves, and I flashed a look to Chevelle to see if he'd heard. His eyes were on Grey, his jaw tight with restraint as he held back laughter.

"Ruby," I said, staring down at her, "I need this one."

She nodded, pushing roughly off Myst's back to stand.

I leaned over the scroll to sign my name, not as Veil and the fey called me, but as Elfreda, Lord of the North. Myst sat up, wiping blood from her busted nose, and handed me a ribbon and seal as if nothing was out of the ordinary.

I rolled the parchment slowly, considering my words, which were part bluff, part bravado, and part outright deceit. I could only hope it worked. Veil was no fool, but I had to believe he didn't want war. There was no other reason to warn me. Well, there was one other reason, but I refused to think of that. I knew I was tied to Chevelle. *It has to work*, I thought. I wrapped the ribbon once around the document, attached the seal, and pressed the clasp of my cloak, the molded form of a hawk imprinted as my seal, into the clay putty.

Myst leaned forward, blew gently on the putty, and smiled as it hardened to ceramic. She rolled to her knees, eagerly awaiting her instructions.

"Deliver this to Veil."

She nodded. "And you'll get me out of here alive?"

I knew what she meant and wondered if I'd get her safely out of Camber and if the men would heed my orders. I didn't have the slightest idea, but at least she had enough respect not to say it.

I rubbed my face. "You'll leave with us. It's the best I can do."

She pursed her lips in another unspoken question: *Where are we going?*

"We will keep the balance, and that is all that matters. Tell him we planned to return to the castle."

For the first time, a truly sincere smile crossed her lips, and I knew we were in more trouble than we could handle.

I stood to address the guard. "We leave at daybreak. Please let Steed and Anvil know. We won't have much time to wrap things up." I indicated Chevelle. "We are going to pay our respects to Camren. When we return"—I glanced at Myst—"we will discuss strategy."

As we made our way to the door, I realized I hadn't known Burne. I wondered briefly where we would find his wife and what condition she would be in. But as soon as Chevelle drew the door open, where she was became quite apparent, if not her condition.

Marching toward Ruby's small home was a band of angry townspeople. They were dressed in battle gear, with their armor and swords, knives and shields. Their faces were smeared with the blood of the fey, their hands clenched upon hammers and axes. And leading the pack was a stout woman in her fourth century, dark eyes rimmed in red, her mouth taut with determination and pain.

"Camren?" I whispered.

"Yes," Chevelle answered behind me.

I took a deep breath, watching as the woman's raven hair whipped around her.

The group came to a staggered stop as they reached the street in front of the house. There were about thirty—a few knelt to show respect, and a few rocked impatiently from foot to foot, but most stood in wait as Camren approached. I stepped onto the porch, and Chevelle followed, coming to stand beside me. Rhys and Grey came to my right, and I heard the door shut behind them, locking the fairy away from view.

"You go to take your vengeance?" Camren asked in a raw voice.

Her question left no room for the indecision I was feeling. "The fey attacked this town because of our plan to confront Council."

Camren's jaw went tight. "Do you go to take your vengeance?"

"Retaliation could mean war," I said.

Three of the large elves behind her spat at my answer, and several others muttered unintelligibly. They clearly had no fear of the fey, and Council had taken one more of their own that day—one too many, it appeared.

I sighed. "Many of you will die."

No one in the line so much as flinched at my words. From the corner of my eye, I saw Steed and Anvil approaching to join us. Not an hour before, I'd been questioning my actions, convinced I'd made a poor choice and that I had started a war that not only the North, but the whole of elvenkind would lose. Now, I could see no other way.

I glanced at Chevelle and knew he felt the same. It was right. We would have to do it, regardless of the cost.

When I gave the order, I stared solely into Camren's eyes with a promise: "Then we go. Recompense for the fallen." I looked past her then, into the eyes of the men and women behind her. "Not just for today, but for all days. These men will answer for their actions."

A clatter of sword against shield met my words, the applause of battle, and I looked to my guard. We were ready.

The fey attack and the trackers had thrown our plans into chaos, but the gathering outside Ruby's door added urgency. We had no time to revise our strategy, or we would risk giving Council notice, not to mention a return of the fey. So I decided to tell the mob of townspeople of my messenger and to trust them to allow her departure.

But when I opened the door to the living area and her gaze skipped over the crowd to land directly on the horses with a giddy, "Oooh, do I get one?" I considered letting them rip her apart. Unfortunately, I couldn't chance sending anyone else into fey territory under those conditions.

"Go now or not at all, fairy," I hissed below earshot, biting my cheek as she curtseyed for the spectators.

Myst beamed at me before dipping and shoving off the porch to disappear about as quickly as I'd ever seen a fey disappear—excepting Veil, of course.

Straightening my shoulders, I took one more look around before calling the order to mount. We had split the group into five. I would ride with the guard as we had intended, as if we were alone. Two sets of Camber's best horsemen would ride slightly eastern and western routes, and the last two, the strongest and fastest, would come in on foot. It wasn't the most honest formation, but they'd played dirty first, and I didn't aim to lose any more men than necessary.

We rode swiftly and silently. I spent most of the ride falling into the minds of various birds, in an effort to keep us safe. There had been a fair share of attempts on me, the guard, and the North of late, so I couldn't be sure of what exactly I was looking for, but nothing seemed amiss. It was maybe too calm. It reminded me of the ice attack. There was nothing to be seen, nothing out of place.

That train of thought distracted me as I scanned the grounds below. I didn't need to be distracted, so I forced myself to stop worrying about Veil and how I could control those powers. I needed to focus on our current task and to overcome one obstacle at a time.

I glanced left and right to find Steed and Chevelle. Chevelle's eyes were scanning the trees, and Steed's moved from the landscape, over the horses, and back again. Rhys and Rider rode ahead, with Ruby, Grey, and Anvil behind. I checked on the horses, wondering how much farther they could run, but it seemed we might not have to continue on foot. Chevelle had been right: they were fine stock.

We didn't slow through the darkness of night. The cool air seemed to recharge the horses, and their excitement recalled old memories to me.

I could hear the purr of breath and see the black coat glistening over straining muscle through the blur of ash and tears. The stench of burning flesh still remained in my nose and throat, and the screams of so many still echoed through my mind. My ears roared with some unknown resonance. All I could do was hold on to Chevelle's back, though I wanted nothing more than to tear everything apart.

My mother's words sang softly to me in a warning just before I was attacked. A deep-green vine rose to strike, curling like a viper, and shot out, its thorns piercing my arms like fangs as its rapidly growing body wrapped around my wrist in a choking hold.

"Frey."

I jerked awake, so suddenly pulled from the dream that I struggled against Chevelle's grip on my arm.

"Frey," he repeated.

I sputtered, yanked my arm once more, and finally breathed. He watched me, only releasing his hold when it was clear to both of us that I had my bearings.

"Thank you," I whispered in a hoarse voice, at last realizing that I'd fallen asleep as we rode.

His head tilted forward, and I followed it to find familiar rocks marking the way to the temple. It was time.

We dismounted, and as Steed turned the horses to graze, I took one last trip to the sky to be certain everyone was in place.

I opened my eyes to find seven soldiers watching me. I gave them a nod that I hoped conveyed everything and took my first step toward River Temple.

Two hundred steps later, the trees took on a new appearance. Great oaks and maples grew vigorously, limbs overlapping as their massive trunks stood too close together. The excess of leaves created a low canopy of dappled green that was out of season with the cool air. We continued through the maze wordlessly, treading lightly and on watch. We had no guarantee they weren't lying in wait.

When the forest border began to clear, my guard took up lines. Rhys and Rider led as Chevelle and Anvil flanked me. Ruby, Steed, and Grey walked behind, rotating to watch our backs and the sky. After their attack on the castle, I was sure Council—the men and women who had murdered my mother and so many of our people— would try again, but they weren't waiting for us in the surrounding forest. They were waiting for us in the temple.

Seventy white robes lined the temple floor. Twenty more were staggered between the sandstone columns. Three and thirty stood along the balcony railing. Bright eyes and golden hair were all that set them apart at that instant. Gone was their jovial mood. No one smiled anymore.

My eyes scanned the room, searching. The floor was nothing but fodder. Single tassels adorned most robes—none wore more than three. These were fresh recruits, brought in to wear us down. A few among the columns might be able to contest the townspeople, but held no threat to my guard.

The balcony was where our targets waited. They watched us with no hint of wariness, only pure hatred. They thought us evil. They wanted to take our lands, destroy our people. They had bound me. They had burned my mother.

The ground shook. It was only when Chevelle's hand touched the small of my back that I realized the tremor came from me. I had to control Asher's magic. It was too much to release it in overwhelming anger. It would consume us.

"Elfreda of Camber," the council speaker called from the balcony.

I stopped him before he could finish his speech. "It is *Lord* Freya."

He set his jaw. "We of the Council of the Order of the Light Elves…"

I glanced at Chevelle, knowing that they would proclaim their innocence, their rightfulness, and play out their display in front of the new members, in front of those who didn't know the truth.

They intended to win.

They didn't expect those on the floor to live, but they were covering their tracks in case a few survived before wearing us down, the seven of my guard and me.

I stepped forward. "Your words waste your final breath. We come to avenge the lives of the lady Eliza"—I let my gaze trail the balcony—"of Rosalee of Camber"—Steed stiffened beside me at the mention of his mother, but I carried on—"of all the mothers of the North."

I lost their attention for a moment and knew that the warriors of Camber had arrived to our right and that Camren would be among them. I continued, "We come to avenge the lives of Burne and all the husbands of the North."

The thrum of beating hooves followed, and all eyes fell to the approaching horses behind us. "We come to avenge the honor of our lands, of our people. We come to avenge our lives."

At this, three council members on the upper level stepped back, but I only smiled. The fourth band of Camber warriors waited behind the temple.

"What say you, Speaker?" I said.

I had anticipated some hesitation at the sight of the additional fighters, but there was none. What was left of Council had decided to end the North, and they apparently had no notion that they might lose.

Their first strike was swift and severe. Some unseen signal unleashed a hail of fire, exploding light, and countless bursts of energy. There would be no weapons—it was all magic. The council members on the floor would be instructed to kill or die. They would have no second chance.

There was a thundering response from our line, and nearly a third of the seventy council members on the floor went down. In a matter of minutes, the ones who remained pushed back behind the columns, where their second line of attack waited. The two groups worked together to bring a deluge, to crush and drown our line. The resounding roar of water was accompanied by a vibration that quickly grew to shake dust from the columns of the temple.

When the wave crashed onto the floor beneath the balcony, the Camber lines stepped back. They had called the river on us, and it was moving forward with no sign of restraint. A wall of water rolled toward us with the force of two dozen elves' magic. I raised my hands, wondering if I could release enough power to stop it without harm to myself or my guard.

Chevelle shouted an order to the lines beside me, but the sound was lost as a violent wind struck the wave with a boom that reverberated through the room. The water fought against the barrier, stopping in its advance mid-crash as it hung before us. It happened so quickly that it took my mind a moment to catch up.

"Push back!" I yelled, releasing only a portion of the strike I had planned to unleash. As soon as the wave fell back into a flood, I searched the line for Camren, but it was too late. Her body lay motionless on the ground. She'd given her last breath to our retaliation. Two villagers moved to kneel beside her, and I looked back just in time to see the water wash over the temple floor, flushing at least a handful of council members with it as it crossed between the columns and out of the structure.

We surged forward, taking the last of those council members to leave only thirty remaining above: the leaders of Grand Council.

"*Dratva Sprego Drangia Rema.*"

The words fell from the balcony, heavy with a vow of devastation, and I looked up to find their source. It was Elden of Longarten, the man who'd set fire to the gates of the castle during the massacre. They'd not wanted anyone to escape. They'd wanted all of us to burn like my mother had.

As the spell took hold of the others, fury spread like that fire so long ago through my veins. Hot, burning anger devoured every part of me until it seemed to burst, snapping any connection I had to calm, rational thoughts. If the ground shook again, I did not feel it. If the spell attempted to harm me, I did not know. The only thing there was rage.

I stared into the eyes of my mother's killers as the stone cracked and split.

I saw Nyle, who had drowned the young sentry in his own blood.

I saw Sandon, who had slowly choked the serving girls with bay vine while chaos reigned around them.

I saw Fawn, who had opened the chests of the watchmen, a smile playing at the corner of her honey-rose lips as their insides spilled onto the castle floor.

I watched as the balcony gave way.

I watched as they fell with the floor beneath them.

A cloud of dust rose as the heart of the temple crumbled onto the ground in front of us. Lightning flashed, and thunder boomed. The wind whipped as though the edge of a hurricane flew among the columns. Fire and screams tore through the air in a battle so reminiscent of the massacre that it made my chest hurt. But the knowledge of my final revenge didn't ease the pain. Even as those who were guilty took their dying breaths, the ache only grew.

Body after body fell. What remained of the fourth line advanced, and we surrounded the last of the council leaders. A flash of light shot out, intense enough to bring me from the trance of the anger that had destroyed the temple. I was moving, but Rider was faster. He threw himself forward to let loose an explosion of power so violent it seemed to burn my skin.

Wincing against the flare, I turned back to see it strike its target and issued an attack of my own. The remaining council leaders were few, but they were strong. Twin blows punched my chest, but I pushed them back before they could tear me apart. Anvil stepped in front of me just in time to catch a third, and I felt a jolt as it collided with his shoulder.

Chevelle moved forward as we all advanced on them and deflected two more before Rhys and Rider moved to the front. Their skill was incredible as they pooled their energy to defend and attack. I shifted to throw another strike but faltered when Ruby fell beside me.

I had to force myself not to reach for her. Her red curls had slipped loose of their binding and dropped onto the temple floor, muddy with dust and blood, as she'd collapsed. I could not reach for her. I had to keep fighting.

My feet were frozen as if afraid to disturb what lay beneath me as my eyes fell again on the enemy. The ache in my chest had intensi-fied, risen to choke me. I could not bear to think of the possibilities. I could only attempt to channel the hurt and anger.

I swayed, the power roiling through me as it searched for escape, and the others turned as if sensing the change.

Energy cracked through me, and I nearly lost the capacity for control. I felt myself begin to lurch forward but somehow held fast just long enough to discharge the shattering force. With my eyes narrowed, willing myself to focus, I watched as something inside them seemed to burst.

There were suddenly no more. They had all fallen.

The realization found me keeled over, braced against my wavering knees. For one long moment, I closed my eyes, and for that moment, I felt as if my world might fragment, as if my being might dissolve, as if my insides might find their way out.

I managed a shallow breath inside my tight chest and let it out without gagging. I opened my eyes to find Ruby staring up at me from the ground at my feet.

"Huh." She coughed.

I didn't know if the sound was impressed or stunned, but I choked out something like a laugh as I fell to my knees with relief.

22

I watched numbly as Grey carried Ruby away. They'd assured me she wasn't terribly hurt, but it was obvious that she wasn't terribly all right, either. Blood had smeared her face, and she'd wheezed in shallow breaths.

My hands were still wet from lifting her matted curls from the muddy floor, and I knew there would be blood on them if I looked closely. Not hers. It was the lifeblood of the men and women of Camber.

When something brushed my arm, I started but quickly relaxed when the warmth of a familiar hand settled onto the small of my back. I gave Ruby one more moment before turning my gaze to Chevelle beside me.

His deep-blue eyes were intense, questioning and comforting me at the same time. We had done it—we had crushed one obstacle. We had avenged my mother and the North, but it had cost us. I stared back at him, hoping to convey my answers and to offer him some comfort in return, and he reached up to place his palm against my cheek. I closed my eyes, breathed deeply for the first time since the battle, and felt the last of the trembling in my limbs subside.

When I opened my eyes again, Chevelle slid his hand free and brushed the dampness from my cheek. We turned to survey the damage.

River Temple lay in ruin. Half of the columns were rubble. The rest were covered in ivies—the council members had tried to use the plants to elevate themselves above the flood waters. Patches of floor had dried from the winds, dust and blood leaving rust-colored stains. In a matter of weeks, the damage would look centuries old.

Several men were climbing over the remains of the balcony where it lay on the ground, searching the dead. I didn't need to check—their faces were seared into my memory. I was concerned most about our men. From our position at the front of the line, we hadn't been able to see who'd been injured.

I scanned the area, surprised to find that most of the wounded were already being tended. A few of the Camber warriors were limping or bloodied, but the majority of them appeared well. They had taken their place among the front, but Council had targeted the townspeople anyway. I tried not to count as I watched them being carried away, but I couldn't help it. Fourteen were dead, Camren among them.

We approached the marble tablet, where Bayrd and Emeline were cleaning up the injured.

Bayrd looked up from his work. "Lord Freya." He dipped his head respectfully, causing his patient to flinch as he pulled against the stitches. He smirked before deference fell back in place to address Chevelle: "Excellent battle."

I glanced at Chevelle, but he didn't seem as surprised as I was to find them in such good spirits.

The large leather-clad elf beside him called out as Emeline set his shoulder into place. "There you are. Good as new," she promised. He didn't appear to believe her, but he stood, shrugged his shoulder twice as if testing it, and dipped his head toward Chevelle and me before leaving.

Emeline turned to us. "That about finishes things up here." She glanced toward the clearing the warriors had made. "Except for the ceremony."

Bayrd tightened his last stitch.

"I'd like a messenger to notify the villagers. Some of them will have family here," I said.

Emeline nodded. "Merek will go. He's a fast rider." She eyed the afternoon sky. "Likely he could make the rounds before dawn."

"Thank you," I said.

She smiled. "Lord Freya."

Emeline brushed past me, and by the time I'd turned around, Merek was mounted and kicking a slender black stallion up to running.

All evidently taken care of, we went to find Ruby. The task was easier than expected, because we could hear her fighting with Grey before we took the first step into the forest.

"I *said* I was fine," she argued in a raspy voice. The declaration was punctuated by the sound of her slapping his ministrations away.

There was a sharp gasp—he must have ignored her assertions and pressed against a wound. And then a low curse came from Grey as she retaliated.

We came through the trees to find Anvil sitting on a stump, laughing while a grim-faced Steed attempted to hold Ruby still.

"Touch me one more time," she warned the both of them, "and you will pay."

Grey held out a finger as if considering, and she narrowed her gaze on him. Steed's mouth screwed up as he waited, clearly reassessing his position.

"Ruby," I cut in, "are you well?"

She shrugged Steed's hands free. "Yes. Quite."

I felt my chest ease a bit, though she still looked a little pale. I glanced at Grey, who seemed annoyed but no longer fearful.

"Great," I said. "Clean yourself up. We've got a ceremony to attend."

She smirked at Steed before turning an eyebrow up at Grey as if daring him to challenge her.

Anvil laughed again.

~

THE CEREMONY WAS COMPLETED as the sun fell beneath the horizon. We stood in full dress as the flames licked the air and trailed smoke into the twilight sky. The others would see it—the families of the council members would know we had lost people as well. But there would be nothing left but ash.

As I watched the fire dance, I could not help but think of my mother. She had burned with no honor, but at least I could finally lay her to rest. When the blaze subsided, I would be able to let it go. The battle was over. The fire that had haunted me for so long would be gone.

I closed my eyes and breathed deeply, letting the sharp scent of night flowers on the wind cut through the last of the acrid smoke. But it was only the briefest reprieve because when I opened them again, I saw a warning flickering among the trees.

I felt my jaw tighten but held fast. It would wait. We would see the ceremony through.

As the final ember darkened, I looked to my guard. They were still, somber, and had apparently not noticed our audience.

I waited until the first shifting boot sounded before directing Steed to ready the horses. He moved to do so without reservation, but I saw the question on the others' faces.

"We will not ride back to Camber," I answered. I glanced to the trees, searching for sign of any remaining fey. "There isn't time."

The townspeople were preparing for their own return, but I was certain they would make it to Camber safely. It had only been a scout, a mere warning.

"Are you sure?" Ruby asked, inspecting them skeptically as they packed their weapons and armor.

I wasn't sure.

"They are loyal," Rhys said. "With this, you have won their trust."

Anvil shifted, still favoring his injured shoulder. "Aye. You have them."

I nodded, watching a limping Bayrd climb onto his horse. I could only hope they were right, but it didn't matter. "We have no other choice."

"Where do we ride, then?" Anvil asked.

I sighed heavily before answering, "Junnie."

There was no doubt they were concerned by my words, but the set of my shoulders and the way my eyes scanned the trees must have made it clear that it was not the time to discuss it.

"I will inform the others," Chevelle said, heading toward Emeline and her husband.

"Shall we gather the scrolls?" Ruby asked.

"No, leave those for the villagers," I said. "They are of no use to anyone now." I forced a smile. "You fought well, Ruby."

She was clearly caught off guard by my compliment. Her expression fell blank. "Did I?"

I nodded then cuffed her on the back. "Next time, try to take no more than your share."

From the corner of my eye, I saw Anvil's mouth tweak up in amusement.

Steed rode up, mounted on a fine black stallion, and tilted his head toward the waiting group of horses. "They are fresh and ready for whatever you've got planned."

I resisted the urge to sigh again. "Thank you," I said, glancing over my shoulder for Chevelle.

"Here," he said from beside me, a large satchel over his shoulder. He must have seen me looking. "The townspeople wish you well and have sent provisions so that we may travel speedily."

My eyes narrowed on him, and I wondered how they'd know what we needed.

He only shrugged.

Steed called the horses to us, and as I swung onto my own, several of the townspeople bowed their respect. Among them, one form stood out.

Cold, dark eyes met mine before a gloved hand rose in a gesture that vowed success. It was Camren's son.

I tried not to dwell on that gaze as we rode, but images of the battle were all I could seem to replace it with. The cool night turned to day, but even the sun didn't warm us. Camren had fallen avenging her husband, the boy's father. Wind had saved us from the wall of water, I reminded myself, and had saved the boy as well. Camren's lifeless body had lain among the rest as the fires set them to rights.

Anvil took another hit as I relived the fight, and Steed's face twisted as pain cut through him. And then Ruby stared blankly up at me, the blood and mud surrounding her so darkly against her pale skin. I shook myself, glancing again at her to confirm that she was fine, her cheeks flushed, her emerald eyes clear and bright.

Looking ahead once more, I saw Rhys and Rider leading and remembered their fearless efforts. It was as if I could see the power move between them, seamlessly shifting where it was needed.

"Freya." Ruby's voice cut my contemplation.

I was startled to realize how deeply I'd fallen from the others. I blinked, and she smiled. I was pretty sure she was laughing at me. The sky was overcast, hiding what I estimated to be a noon sun. "Yes, Ruby?"

"Are you going to tell us where we're going?" she whispered.

"We have to find Junnie."

She waited. She already knew that.

I couldn't stop myself from glancing around before answering. "We may have a slight problem," I said.

Ruby's brows shifted in a what's-new motion.

I watched Chevelle as I continued, and it dawned on me that he didn't seem anxious or surprised by my revelation. I guessed he'd seen the visitor as well. "There was a scout at the ceremony. A fire sprite, I think."

Ruby's nose crinkled. "Are you sure? Maybe it was just drawn to the action."

I shook my head. "No. It was a warning."

"But I thought you sent a message to Veil," she said.

"I did." I met her gaze evenly. "That's why we have to find Junnie."

Her brows drew together as she opened her mouth as if for another question, but a sudden call stopped her short.

It was the wolves.

23

Suddenly, the rhythmic thump of our horses' hooves turned into the hammering of drums as they pounded the dirt in a full run. The wind caught my cloak to whip behind me, and I held fast, closing my eyes to find the wolves. My mind brushed theirs before reaching a falcon tucked within the cover of a tall pine near them.

The wolves were running.

I swung widely, searching for their prey then behind for an attacker. When I realized they weren't being pursued but coming for us, the falcon swooped down in front of them so they would know I'd found them. Instead of stopping to wait for us, they turned to run in the opposite direction. I opened my eyes.

"West," I called, and the others adjusted their course without slowing. We ran through the forest, dodging brush and low limbs, into another clearing before we began to catch up with them.

"What is it?" Chevelle yelled.

I shook my head. "I don't know. They are alone."

And then I saw smoke.

"There!" Rider shouted as his horse narrowly avoided a thin oak.

We broke into a short clearing in time to see Finn and Keaton rushing through the trees ahead. At the next clearing, we saw the reason for the smoke.

A large circle of ash covered the ground before us. Smoldering stumps and scattered embers were all that remained. It was as if a dragon had raged through the copse, but there were no dragons nearby. The remnants smelled of maple trees. The fire had obviously burned fiercely, gone barely before we'd seen the smoke. The section of trees had been destroyed cleanly. Nothing around it was disturbed, but another copse was already burning.

I scanned the scene as we ran, kicking up gray dust that still held heat, and saw that two more patches of ash lay to the north. Understanding was slow to come, but I knew that someone was burning the forest in some systematic way. Just south of us, two more pillars of smoke rose, but Finn and Keaton took us north of the older fires.

The underbrush became dense, and the horses struggled through briars and thickets. They'd been fresh when we'd left the temple, but they were nearly finished by then, drawing deep, purring breaths as sweat drenched their overworked bodies. Thunder rumbled in the distance, and I glanced up at the darkening sky.

A break in the brush revealed an area of smooth rock where the wolves waited for us. They stood, their chests heaving and their tongues lolling to the side, and I was suddenly struck with their utter transformation—I'd never before seen them so wholly animal. I wondered how long they had been running.

The eight of us swung from our horses, landing on the flat stones of a dry spring and moving to stand before their silvery-gray forms. Finn nodded toward Rhys, and the two were off, running swiftly and silently through the trees beside us, heading for the fires. After some signal from Keaton, Steed sent the horses farther north, away from the blazes. The echo of cracking limbs and falling timbers muffled their escape, but the wind picked up, and even the sounds of destruction were overcome by the rustling leaves surrounding us. I suddenly wished it was a dragon we were about to face.

Chevelle moved beside me, as uneasy as the rest of us, and we watched Keaton together. The wolf stood still, his eyes closed in some strange meditation, and I wondered if he was in the mind of his brother. I closed my own eyes, searching the forests, but the birds were gone, having fled from the danger. A light brush of something else distracted me, but my eyes shot open at the sound of a snapping branch nearby.

Finn burst back into the opening with Rhys steps behind.

"Rowan," Rhys said. "They've found Rowan and he's hunting Junnie, trying to burn her out."

"What? Why?" I stammered.

Rhys shook his head. "I don't know, but he's cursing her to the flames. He's vowed to kill her."

Chevelle stiffened. "Is he alone?"

"No," Rhys answered. "We couldn't get close enough to see without being spotted, but he's definitely got at least one ally with him. He was shouting orders."

Keaton growled.

I glanced briefly at the wolf as my next question came. "Why isn't she fighting? Or running?"

Anvil stepped forward. "If she were pinned down, that filthy son of an imp wouldn't be burning these groves."

"So he doesn't know where she is," Rider said. "But why is she hiding?"

Finn pawed the ground at my feet with an insistence that made me pause. I cursed.

The others focused on me, plainly unsure what to make of it. "The baby," I explained. "Junnie's protecting the human."

"Why would Rowan care about the baby?" Steed asked.

My brows pulled together, but before I could answer, an explosion of flame erupted less than a hundred yards south of us.

A furry shoulder nudged my leg, and I glanced down at Finn. He was trying to tell me something, but the brush of a being against my mind, even though the feeling was drowned in distress, prickled my skin.

"We have to get Junnie," I said, ignoring the worry snaking its way through my gut. Before the others had a chance to respond, I was running toward the flames.

I could hear them behind me, following as I bore down on that connection. It was different, less lucid and harder to grasp, but I could pin down its location—*her* location.

Keaton bounced in front of me as we ran, but I didn't slow. There was a sudden urgency, a strong sense of pain and fear coming through the link. I had to get to them. Flames erupted beside us, and I heard the voice. Rowan called to Junnie, taunting her with death and suffering. He couldn't be more than a hundred yards from us, and Junnie was hiding somewhere in between us and her attacker.

It surprised me that Rowan hadn't found her already, but from the sound of his tirade, he'd clearly been driven to madness. He must have been pushed—something must have caused him to break. I thought of the wolves and their recent absence just as they leapt to a stop in front of me, their muzzles pulled back in a snarl.

I stopped, crouched, and turned my face away as the blaze exploded before us. "There," I whispered, staring back into the flames. "Junnie is in there."

Without a word, Ruby vaulted over the brush and into the mass of trees. Junnie had formed them perfectly, a natural barrier of oak and pine so solid they would have had to be destroyed to reach her. They were being destroyed.

Heat burned my face as the smoke and flame rose. Rowan's voice echoed through what was left of the forest, promising Junnie's death to the inferno. I wanted to shut him up permanently.

Two more heartbeats, and the flames began to waver. I took a breath, knowing Ruby had her, had them. Chevelle's hand grasped my arm, but I couldn't look away. I had to be sure.

The instant Ruby pushed through the trees, the rest of us turned to run. The blaze had parted for her, obeying her talent like water on a current, and she broke through with Junnie in tow. The bundle in Junnie's arms was safe, though mildly singed, and my relief at knowing Junnie was alive was only surpassed by the relief of finally knowing she wasn't the one. Junnie had not been a part of the attacks on me—all doubt over the responsible party was gone, and my bargain with Veil had been a good one.

I wasn't certain where we were running, where Rhys and Rider were leading us, but as we crossed a low ridge, two massive silver wolves crashed into me, knocking me solidly off my feet. We were not airborne for long, as my back slammed into a bank of dirt with eighty pounds of Keaton's furry body landing on top of me. He chuffed, I gasped, and we both rolled to the side to cough air back into our lungs.

A kind of roar escaped someone on the ridge, and I forced my head up to find Chevelle. He stood before a barrier of flame, which I assumed was more of Rowan's doing until I saw Ruby. Her body was rigid as she poured all of her power into the wall, though I couldn't bring my mind to comprehend her motives. A soft whine came from the wolf beside me, and I followed his gaze to find Finn lying still among the ground ivy.

I crawled to him, relieved to see his chest heaving with breath, and ran my hand over his side, searching for broken bones. Finn's head rose, the silver-blue of his eyes meeting mine with more emotion than any ordinary beast could have held, and I understood. He'd taken a strike.

His nose twitched and pointed toward his shoulder. I brushed the fur aside, searching for the wound. There was a clean, small puncture directly beside the bone. I stared back into his eyes, knowing the pain I would cause when I turned him over, and lifted his legs to roll the other shoulder free. I glanced over my own shoulder, finding Keaton's back to me as he stood guard. Anvil and Grey remained on the ridge by Ruby. Rhys and Chevelle ran toward us.

As I looked down once more, my hand crossed the point of something sharp in Finn's side. I pulled my hand back, pressing the finger I'd pricked, and a drop of blood formed on my fingertip over the ash from Finn's coat. I looked up at Chevelle as his boots landed beside me, and he bent down to slide a hand around the base of my arm, but he wasn't looking at the blood. He was looking at Rhys, who held the weapon that had pierced Finn's shoulder. The bitter tang of poison reached me through the shock, and my stomach turned as I stared at the spear of steeled ice.

24

The hand gripping my arm pulled me to standing, and Chevelle pressed my finger to his mouth. He turned his head, spat, then nodded once, apparently satisfied that it had not tasted of poison.

He glanced over my shoulder at Rhys. "Move him to the pines. We will free Ruby."

My mind whirled, attempting to catch up, and I realized why Ruby had created a wall of fire. My feet were moving without thought. *Finn will need her. We would face the ice.*

"Ruby!" I shouted over the noise. Wind whipped the top of the ridge and was pulled into the inferno to strengthen the flame. The overcast sky had gone dark grey, bruised with purple and blue. Light flickered through the clouds, and I glanced over Ruby's shoulder at Anvil as the exposed skin of my arms prickled.

"Frey," she whispered, not looking away from her barrier.

Her outstretched arms trembled, and I placed a hand on the one nearest me. "Let it go, Ruby. Finn needs you."

She swallowed, nodded, and dropped her arms. The fire remained as she glanced at me, but then it fell to nothing when she turned away.

Anvil, Grey, Steed, and Rider stood alongside Chevelle and me atop the ridge. The barrier gone, we could see Rowan calling to the skies. I dared not look for Junnie, who I knew lay at the base of the bank behind us, protecting the child. The wind was cutting without the heat of the flame. Though thunder rolled across the clouds, Rowan's words still reached my ears.

"Kill them. Asher's throne will be yours."

For a moment, I couldn't understand, but I soon realized that the flicker of light above had not been lightning, but a fey.

"Down!" I yelled, rolling from the edge of the ridge onto its slant.

Several shards of solid, toxic ice pierced the earth where we'd been standing, driving through both soil and stone. I glanced up as the attacker dove past and saw dark wings adorned with flecks the yellow-orange of a monarch butterfly. Suddenly, a burst of power struck, and I spun away as rock and dirt exploded beside me. I got to my feet to see Rowan cursing and spitting.

Chevelle and Steed remained on the slope near me. The others had spread across the top of the ridge and the opposite side. I hoped Junnie was no longer alone.

Chevelle flung a strike at Rowan, but he moved too swiftly and remained unharmed.

Steed eyed the air above us. "So that's the ice boy, eh?"

"Not for long," I answered, narrowing my gaze on the tiny bit of orange visible against the dark clouds.

Before I released a blow, the slim black wings opened, and the fairy was diving toward me once more. I hadn't planned on killing him, merely stunning him to the ground to capture and explaining Rowan's folly and Asher's madness, so I only allowed a small measure of power into the assault.

When it reached the winged beast, he froze midflight, twisting, writhing, then jerking against my energy. I believed him to be strug-gling to overcome the blast, but Rowan laughed from his vantage point across the charred field, and I realized what was happening. I frantically pulled back, trying to draw the energy in, but it was too late. I hadn't thought it possible, hadn't believed that half-blood fey was strong enough, but he was stealing my power.

"Take cover!" I screamed, severing the tie, and the dark-fey beast shrieked with a hideous cry.

Steed threw himself against me, and Chevelle leapt in front of us both, blocking debris from the barely missed blast. I gritted my teeth at being knocked once more from the path of destruction so violently and found my feet again. Rowan used the opportunity to take another shot at me, which infuriated me so severely that I sent an excess of power his way. Somehow, it missed, and a crater appeared in the dirt.

"He's like a snake," I seethed.

Emboldened by his victory, the dark fey floated closer. "She is not so formidable, Rowan." His head tilted to the side as he examined me from the air, keeping out of reach. "If not for Father's strength, she would be nothing."

"Stop wasting time, Scian!" Rowan yelled from his position of safety. "Kill her."

The fey smiled then, and his face changed. He was not a boy, but a man. He was slight and thin, but signs of age lined his face. His long, black hair was fine and dull, and his papery wings were tattered and fraying.

"Scian," I whispered, wondering if Chevelle knew the meaning of the name.

His palm brushed my back, and I knew he did. *The second.*

Asher had planned it all along, I suddenly knew. Vita, a unique and powerful light elf who had borne Aunt Fannie, had been the first, but he hadn't stopped there. When she'd been a disappointment, he'd moved on to the fey. My mother must have been born after those attempts. And maybe he'd even given up on others for a while when she'd shown promise.

But what was happening was Asher's second attempt, blatantly named as such.

I could see him there, in the fey's eyes, and the resemblance made my stomach turn.

"It doesn't have to end this way," I offered. "You have been misled."

Scian's mouth bent into a smirk. "She is afraid, Rowan. She knows she will die."

Anvil chose that moment to step over the ridge. When Rowan commanded, "End it," the skies came alive with light.

"No!" I screamed. But it didn't come in time.

My skin pricked, and my chest tightened an instant before a deafening crack tore from the sky. Anvil must have thrown everything into the attack, and the lightning gathered among the clouds for one long second before threading into several strands that tracked straight for the fey. A blinding flash lit the air around us, followed by an instant of dead silence before an explosion.

Scian had fallen from the sky, but he was far from lifeless. His body thrashed and shook, and his chest heaved in a few wicked coughs. Then the screeching sounded again, and that time it pierced our ears, strangled at first but quickly stronger, louder, and more chilling.

Steed cursed.

I'd no more than began to process what had happened when a large, wet raindrop splatted against my cheek. My head tilted back automatically, and several more landed on my face and chest. I drew in a breath, but Chevelle was already calling out a command: "Run!"

Suddenly, the air was vacant as Scian drew in the moisture from around us. My feet scrambled for purchase on the slope, which was littered with dips and rubble from the conflict, and I looked for the ridge above. The eerie hollowness of the air was intensified by silence, the sudden lack of thunder and wind, and I knew we didn't have long.

Anvil grabbed my arm, pulling me over the ridge, and I caught sight of the trees ahead, lifeless as their leaves had abruptly stilled. I felt the power build and release behind us but could do nothing to stop it.

Anvil had clearly felt it too, and we were spinning, turning to face the coming onslaught. The others were behind us, and I met Chevelle's eyes for one brief moment before he turned to shield me.

Steel rained down upon us. The ice didn't carry the tang of poison, but it was death. Blades of hardened water shone like glass, flying toward us in an endless assault. We could do nothing to Scian, could not give him more power to use against us. We could only watch as he laughed and cackled.

We crouched, huddled together on the edge of the ridge. Steed and Chevelle were in front of me, with Anvil and Rider at my sides. Grey had disappeared. We blocked every shard we could, but they were razors, cutting the air with no more than a whisper of sound until they pierced the earth around us. Steed flinched as one caught his arm, and another connected with Rider. Blood dampened my cheek an instant before I felt a blade-thin shard brush against it.

Scian raised his arms to the sky, and the ice turned to daggers, great crystal spikes in the form of a hailstorm. Anvil was knocked back as a spear took him in the shoulder, and Steed faltered as one planted deep into his leg. Chevelle cursed, trying to pick up the momentary lapse in our shield.

A solid thump rang through my bones before my ears caught the *zshk* of a too-close shard, and I looked down to find a spear of ice lodged in the side of my chest.

A squeal of delight erupted from the dark-fey elf, and I glanced up in time to see him dancing in triumph. Numbly, I watched as he spun to a stop and smiled back at me. The ice had stopped too, and the others fell slightly away as they turned to see what had his attention.

Chevelle had gone white. He reached up as if to touch the blade but stopped, instead staring into my eyes. I became very aware of our surroundings and the sudden silence amplifying the chaos. The ridge was destroyed. My guard lay bleeding around me.

I knew that Scian would overtake us. Any strike against him would not only be useless—it would be returned tenfold.

We were hurt, hopeless.

Finn and Keaton howled from somewhere among the pines.

And then I saw, in Chevelle's sapphire eyes, that he hadn't given up.

Suddenly, a jolt ran through me. Chevelle hadn't left the blade in my chest because there was no chance. He had left it because I was still breathing. The ice hadn't pierced my lung but was embedded in the muscle between my chest and shoulder. My leather would hold it there, keeping me from further damage, and it wasn't poisoned.

It was, however, the only thing keeping Scian from continuing the attack.

I kept my face slack, letting Scian think I was in shock as I took in the scene. I knew it would be a brief reprieve, regardless, but there had to be some way, some *thing* we could do to fight him.

There was the barest sound from the base of the ridge behind us, some small shifting of stone, and then abruptly, a large grey wolf stood beside us. Keaton had bounded onto the demolished earth of the ridge, his paws clattering the sharpened ice against stone. He growled at Scian.

His muzzle was still pulled back in a snarl when he turned to us, but his eyes shone brightly. The wolf looked first at Rider, and then to me. When he was clearly certain he had my attention, he moved his gaze slowly to Chevelle.

I couldn't say how long it took for the message to sink in, but when Keaton finally got through, I nodded. I reached forward to clasp Chevelle's hand.

"The power," I whispered. "Hold it for me."

His eyes never left my face as I directed the energy to release. I could feel the line as it stretched within me, as it fell to Chevelle, and as it ran free to its target.

The impact threw Scian off his feet to land soundly in the ash behind him. A puff of dust rose from the destroyed trees then settled around him as he writhed and moaned. He struggled to control his power, but as he wrapped himself fully around it, the energy would not work free. He let out a high-pitched keen, and then his neck snapped up to look at us.

There was no way he could tell, no possibility he would understand, but Scian knew something had changed. He fought to his knees, twitching and jerking, and tried to center his focus.

He pulled harder against it, struggling to wrench the energy free, but it only stretched thinner. Through our connection, I could feel Chevelle as he anchored the power. I'd had no control over Asher's power alone, but it was steadily fastened within our bond, similar to the way Rhys and Rider had shared it. And our target was growing weaker.

My mouth pulled up in a smile as Scian realized he was no longer assured victory. His face fell, and his eyes moved along the ridge. I followed his stare to find Junnie, her bow raised and drawn in readiness. There was a sharp screech, the call of a bird, and she loosed the arrow.

Junnie didn't wait for it to hit the mark but jerked her head toward the clearing.

Rowan stood opposite us, watching with horror as the events unfolded. He didn't see the figure slip up behind him, nor the too-quick blade that sliced his throat. Rowan's hand came up automatically, his blood flooding through the shield of useless fingers.

When he fell, Grey stood behind him.

25

I stared blankly at Grey's lithe form, watching as he drew the dagger across his leg to clean the blade.

"Freya," Chevelle whispered, sliding his hand up to cradle my face, my neck.

My eyes met his, and his hand continued to my shoulder, where he squeezed, and I suddenly realized he was bracing me. A choking gasp escaped my throat when Steed pulled the shard free, and then Junnie was there, stitching up the wound.

I blinked, staring up at her, and she smiled in greeting. "Freya."

A long breath fell from me, and I sagged as the tension dissipated. We had done it. "Are we all alive?" I asked, watching Chevelle hold Steed's leg while Anvil removed the hardened ice.

Junnie glared across the field at Rowan's prone form. "The important ones, yes."

Grey was making his way up the slope of the ridge but detoured to check on Scian's body. Junnie's arrow had pierced the dark fey's heart.

"There," Junnie said as she patted my shoulder. "The wounds are clean. The blades were thin and sharp, so the cuts fall right together, and once sealed"—she glanced at Steed's leg—"they will heal well in time."

Grey kicked a shard of ice as he approached, appearing completely unscathed. Rowan had been slippery, but he'd met his match. He smiled as Ruby came to join us.

"How is Finn?" Rider asked as he took his turn at Junnie's hand.

Ruby smirked. "He's the best patient I've ever had." She eyed the lot of us, bruised and bloody, and all mirth dropped from her expression. "He's had it the worst," she explained, "because of the poison." She shrugged. "But lucky for us, Frey was attacked weeks ago, and I've had some time to study the toxin."

"Yeah," I muttered. "Lucky."

She smiled down at me. "He'll be fine."

Anvil passed me a canteen, and I drank from it deeply. I'd thought I was done with water for a while, but I couldn't seem to get enough of it. Eventually, the others gathered in the pines with Rhys and Finn as we prepared to return to the castle. I remained on the ridge with Junnie, where she cradled a small, half-human child.

"Junnie," I began, sliding the pendant from my belt, "what do you know of this?"

Her eyes narrowed on Veil's gift, and I explained his visit and our theory in more detail.

She nodded. "That's four. The ice and silver, you know." Her gaze came up to mine. "And bone," she said. "Freya, that's you."

"What?" I argued. "Why would I be a danger to myself?"

Junnie shook her head. "It wasn't a warning for you, Freya. It was the four who could claim the throne."

"But Asher had more," I contended. "There were so many."

"Yes," she agreed. "But not all of them were capable of ascending the throne."

I sighed. "Then who is the fourth?"

Her eyes stayed on me for a long moment—too long—and then we both looked at the child in her arms.

"No," I moaned.

"Blood," Junnie answered levelly. "She is of the blood, Frey. Half human and Asher's own child."

Half human, *like me.*

Rowan had burned the woods to find Asher's baby. Junnie had risked her own life to save her.

Junnie's bright-blue eyes peered into mine—beseeching me or daring me, I didn't know. But I could feel the child, the slightest brush of her mind, and I knew she would live.

When she saw the change in me, Junnie's posture relaxed, and it was only then that I realized she hadn't wanted to fight either. She hadn't wanted it to be me any more than I'd wanted it to be her.

"Ah, Junnie," I sighed. "There's more."

ONCE I'D EXPLAINED my bargain with Veil, Junnie and I said goodbye to go our separate ways. She and the child would set the new Council into power and restructure the South. And I, with my guard, would rule the North.

"Are you well?" Chevelle asked as he helped me onto my horse.

My brows furrowed. "Yes, I guess I am."

He shook his head at my answer before climbing onto his own mount, and we kicked them up to where the others waited.

It was a long ride home beneath the graying skies. Finn had been secured atop a horse with Keaton running beside them. Anvil's previously injured shoulder had been sliced through and patched up so that he tilted in the saddle. Ruby looked tired but refused to give in, and Chevelle had received more cuts than he'd let on.

I had too much time to think.

When we finally made it home, it was late the following afternoon. The eight of us slid, stiff and wobbly, off the horses, staggering numbly through the stable-side entry. There were a few reports, a couple of called-out orders, and one angry mountain lion before I at last found a bath. I soaked for an endless hour, possibly dozing off once or twice, then slid into a clean, fresh dressing gown.

After tying a loose robe over me, I stretched my arms to test the movement. Junnie had been right. It was tender, but there didn't seem to be any real damage done.

When I opened my door, I glanced out to be certain the corridor was empty.

My bare feet slapped lightly against the cool stone as I ran, heading to my favorite perch. I passed two doorways then turned, suddenly abandoning my plan—it was not where I wanted to be.

I walked steadily in the direction I'd come, past my own door and turning down the corridor that led deeper into the castle. The sconces lining the walls were spaced unevenly, their flickering light throwing shadow against dark stone. I did not need a single torch. I had known the way for as long as I could remember.

I stood before Chevelle's door for a long moment, staring at the wooded planks. When I finally pushed it open, I saw his silhouette against the filigreed window. Sliding the door shut behind me, I walked slowly across the room. My arms wrapped around his chest, and I pressed my cheek firmly against his back as he stared out the window.

He took a deep breath and rested his hand over mine.

As we stood together, my eye caught the glint of a chipped basin on the corner table, and I smiled.

At first, his room appeared sparse, as if he'd never intended to stay, but I realized that everything had a memory attached to it: the basin I'd broken as a child, the blanket he'd hidden when I'd accidentally caught my room on fire and scorched it, the sword his mother had given him when we'd snuck out to meet her.

"What is it?" Chevelle asked as he turned to hold me in his arms.

"I was just thinking," I lied, "that we should move into the main suites. Now that we are bound." My head tilted briefly to the side. "If you can give up this view, that is."

He stared down at me, forgetting the window, and the corner of his mouth pulled up in a slow smile. "I quite prefer another view."

I laid my hand on his chest over the beat of his heart, and he leaned down. His lips brushed softly over mine.

The kiss was sweet and slow. It said we had time.

It said we had forever.

THE NEXT DAY, I sat kneeling in front of my bureau. It had been my first real night with Chevelle, and I'd woken refreshed, my dreams no longer haunted by flame. My issues had been laid to rest, if temporarily.

The fey had been watching us for a long time, maybe guiding things to their own advantage. But for the time being, I felt safe. We had the North, and Junnie's new council occupied the South. We had balanced the power, so there was no need for war. And if Veil were pushed, if the fey struck, we could overcome them together.

"You have almost nothing of interest in here," Ruby complained from the wardrobe behind me.

"Well," I answered, not looking away from my task, "then it should be easy to move."

Ruby laughed, but I did, in truth, have plenty of interest there. I thought of the box, hidden beneath the stone floor below the bed.

It was time to start a new life with new memories. The others would stay buried within the box, as they should be.

"I still have some things to work out," Ruby murmured. "But at least I know where the wolves were all that time."

I slid the bureau drawer shut and stacked the filled box with the others.

"Like these," Ruby continued, walking over to hand me a small slip of paper.

I turned, taking one last, long look out my window before reading. *Fellon Strago Dreg*, it said.

Even Chevelle had not known the meaning when he'd used that message so long ago. He'd simply seen the opportunity and taken it.

"What's it mean?" Ruby asked.

I glanced down at the message written in my mother's hand.

The warning had followed me and questioned my every move.

And it was still there, even in the midst of so much rightness. But I had accepted my place under the weight of the throne.

I couldn't help the sardonic smile that crossed my lips before I answered her question.

"Nothing as it seems, Ruby. Nothing as it seems."

Please look for book four in the Frey Saga: *Venom and Steel*

ALSO BY MELISSA WRIGHT

THE FREY SAGA

Frey

Pieces of Eight

Molly (a short story)

Rise of the Seven

Venom and Steel

Shadow and Stone

Feather and Bone

DESCENDANTS SERIES

Bound by Prophecy

Shifting Fate

Reign of Shadows

SHATTERED REALMS

King of Ash and Bone

Queen of Iron and Blood

HAVENWOOD FALLS

Toil and Trouble

BAD MEDICINE

Blood & Brute & Ginger Root

Visit the author on the web at

www.melissa-wright.com